HIGHLAND
WARRIOR

HIGHLAND WARRIOR

SONS OF SINCLAIR

HEATHER McCOLLUM

Entangled Publishing, LLC
10940 S Parker Road
Suite 327
Parker, CO 80134
Visit our website at www.entangledpublishing.com.

Amara is an imprint of Entangled Publishing, LLC.

Edited by Alethea Spiridon
Cover design by
LJ Anderson, Mayhem Cover Creations
Cover art by Photographer: VJ Dunraven/Period Images
and martinm303/Depositphotos
Interior design by Toni Kerr

MMP ISBN 978-1-68281-570-0
ebook ISBN 978-1-68281-592-2

Manufactured in the United States of America

First Edition May 2021

AMARA

ALSO BY HEATHER McCOLLUM

SONS OF SINCLAIR SERIES

Highland Conquest

THE CAMPBELLS SERIES

The Scottish Rogue
The Savage Highlander
The Wicked Viscount
The Highland Outlaw

HIGHLAND ISLES SERIES

The Beast of Aros Castle
The Rogue of Islay Isle
The Wolf of Kisimul Castle
The Devil of Dunakin Castle

HIGHLAND HEARTS SERIES

Captured Heart
Tangled Hearts
Untamed Hearts
Crimson Heart
Highland Heart

To those who work to grow peace in our world…
Thank you

SCOTS GAELIC AND OLD ENGLISH WORDS USED IN *HIGHLAND WARRIOR*

aàlainn — lovely

bacraut — asshole (Old Norse)

blaigeard — bastard

blide-maet — joy-food (Old Norse-Norn), served to those visiting a newly born baby

broch — halo around the moon (Old Norse — name of Kára's horse)

cac — shite

daingead — damn it

dróttning — chief, queen (Old Norse)

fuil — blood (name of Joshua's horse)

konungr — king (Old Norse)

magairlean — ballocks

sgian dubh — black-handled dagger

targe — shield, usually made of wood and lined with steel

tolla-thon — arsehole

Whitna whalp — What a devil (Old Norse)

BOOK OF REVELATIONS

1   I watched as the Lamb opened the first of the seven seals. Then I heard one of the four living creatures say in a voice like thunder, "Come!"

2   I looked, and there before me was a white horse! Its rider held a bow, and he was given a crown, and he rode out as a conqueror bent on conquest.

3   When the Lamb opened the second seal, I heard the second living creature say, "Come!"

4   Then another horse came out, a fiery red one. Its rider was given power to take peace from the earth and to make people kill one another. To him was given a large sword.

5   When the Lamb opened the third seal, I heard the third living creature say, "Come!" I looked, and there before me was a black horse! Its rider was holding a pair of scales in his hand.

6   Then I heard what sounded like a voice among the four living creatures, saying, "Two pounds of wheat for a day's wages, and six pounds of barley for a day's wages, and do not damage the oil and the wine!"

7   When the Lamb opened the fourth seal, I heard the voice of the fourth living creature say, "Come!"

8   I looked, and there before me was a pale horse! Its rider was named Death…

CHAPTER ONE

"A wise warrior avoids the battle."
Sun Tzu – The Art of War

"Retreating, Sinclair?" John Dishington, the sheriff for Lord Robert Stuart, smirked from his place by the table in the receiving hall of the Earl's Palace. Cocky, scarred, and always looking for a fight, Dishington was one warrior Joshua Sinclair certainly would not miss when he left Orkney Isle.

"I will retreat only if God calls his Horsemen back to Heaven," Joshua said, using the legend around him being the Horseman of War. It was a familiar role and usually shut the mouths of fools. "I am journeying back home to the mainland of Scotland for Samhain, not retreating."

Dishington laughed, pushing away from the table. "A pardon for the confusion. You retreated from the field at South Ronaldsay." Dishington, who called himself The Brute of Orkney, had more thirst for fighting than wish to stay alive.

Joshua inhaled deeply, his nostrils opening to feed his blood with warrior energy as he turned, the promise of death cutting into the lines of his face. "Lies will see your tongue cut from your screaming mouth," he said, his tone low. The two warriors assigned to watch the arrow slits in the interior wall backed up near the hearth as if wishing to stay out of an inevitable battle.

Dishington picked up his tankard, using it to salute Joshua. "Och now, Sinclair. I know you count the battle as a win for your side, but when that lad fell, you carried him from the field. It looked like a retreat to me."

Adam. The boy's face, still and pale as the blood from his wound soaked his tunic. The vision haunted Joshua like a specter stalking him everywhere. His hands fisted as if he could change the outcome of that horrible day. "The battle was over," he said. "And despite both sides taking too many casualties, we were the victors."

Dishington saluted him again with his tankard and took a drink. "As you say," he said, wiping his mouth, which twisted into a wry grin.

"I should have lopped your head off at South Ronaldsay," Joshua said, turning away to nod at the two men he had trained for the last three months. "Stay strong, Tuck, Alec." They nodded back, and he strode out to the broad double doors of the castle that Lord Robert Stuart, the first Earl of Orkney, called a palace. A bloody palace with arrow and gun slits built into all the lower walls right alongside glazed windows and murals of biblical scenes. When Joshua had agreed to train Lord Robert's men, the earl had even promised to commission a fresco of the Four Horsemen from Revelations, with Joshua as the Horseman of War in the front.

"If you had lopped off my head," Dishington called, following him, "we would not have shared these three months working alongside each other to shape these men into warriors for Lord Robert. Think of all the mirthful sport you would have missed."

Sport? Mirthful? "*Cac*," Joshua cursed under his breath as he traipsed outside into the autumn chill that seemed worse than at his home in Caithness even though it was not too much farther south.

Ignoring Dishington, Joshua strode straight for Lord Robert and his son who were in the middle of the interior courtyard by the central well. Patrick was his second eldest son and wore a sword and a frown. Like his brothers, Patrick had become the perfect copy of his sire, with an even worse temperament, especially with regard to the local Orkney inhabitants.

"I will be off, Lord Robert," Joshua said, bowing his head to his employer without even a twitch of respect toward his son.

"You are a damn mercenary, Joshua Sinclair," Lord Robert said with a half frown. "And yet gold does not sway you to remain at my palace."

Joshua looked toward his saddled bay, Fuil, who stood waiting beside Angus Gunn, a friend Joshua had made at the palace. Angus held a handful of oats under his horse's nose, and Fuil lipped it up.

"I am the Horseman of War," Joshua said, his breath puffing white in the snowflakes whipping down from the heavy clouds. "Winter will freeze your enemies, bringing peace until spring, which is too dull for me."

The truth was that Joshua did not wish to fight Robert's battles anymore. In fact, Joshua did not want to fight *any* battles anymore, a secret he shared only with God. When he realized that Robert Stuart's clashes with the people of Orkney would never end, the realization had made Joshua itch to move on. That and the oncoming winter.

"Damn snow. Bloody damn wind," he murmured, glancing up at the snowflakes swirling down to pock his bare arms. His feet were like ice in his boots. Yet he walked forward with only a sash from the end of his kilt over his bare chest so Robert's people could see and remember the tattoos around his muscular arms and across his back. The dark swirls on his arm in the shape of a horse, along with the massive sword strapped across his back, reminded them that Joshua was War incarnate, the second Horseman of the Apocalypse, sent from God, to rage and win against his foes. At least that was what his father had told him every day of his life. Maintaining an outward appearance that promised death, to intimidate Sinclair enemies, was an act that Joshua had honed until it became who he truly was.

He nodded to a small group of the earl's warriors whom he'd been training, some of them good men. They nodded back, a few raising an arm in response. He stopped before his handsome, muscular warhorse. Fuil's bay coat shined red, which was why Joshua had named him the Gaelic word for blood. His black tail swooshed with a need to be off on whatever adventure was next.

"Angus," he said, his brow rising. "Watch your woman well." He let his gaze slide to Mathias Campbell, the unscarred lad who'd been attracting all the lasses living in the village north of the castle where the soldiers resided when off duty. He was a rogue with honor, which made him a very poor scoundrel.

"What is that?" Angus asked, frowning at Mathias. "What about my woman?"

"Bloody hell, Joshua," Mathias yelled, his smile broad. "Even leaving ye cause trouble."

Joshua laughed. "To keep ye all alert!"

Angus grumbled a curse but grinned. "Stay alive, Horseman of War."

Joshua nodded to him. "I always do." Several of the men he'd been training laughed.

It was a shame the Scotsmen hired by Robert to live and work for him could not easily leave Orkney. But Joshua was a free man, and he'd had enough of Robert's elitist ways. Nay, it was time to head home to Caithness and Girnigoe Castle on the mainland of Scotland, in time for the Samhain festival.

Liam, another warrior, gave him a wry grin through his thick beard where he stood by the gate of the half-finished outer wall, another of Joshua's recommended improvements. "I am surprised that Jean unleashed you from her bed," he said, keeping his voice low. Jean Stuart, Robert's second eldest daughter, was voluptuous and territorial, not to mention spoiled. The lass was as prickly as her brothers but had enjoyed sparring with Joshua. And tumbling in her luxurious bed.

"Ah, sweet Jean," Joshua said, sliding his hand down Fuil's neck. "She has likely already lured in another for sport." Throwing a boot up, he mounted easily from the ground and turned Fuil in a tight circle toward the open gate where two other young warriors worked at moving bags of grain. Joshua drew a pebble, which he'd picked up before mounting, from the fold in his kilt. With a flick of his wrist, he shot one at Hamish Kincaid, hitting him in the back of his head. Hamish whipped around to glare at his friend, Randall, who worked next to him.

"Why'd ye do that?" Hamish asked, rubbing his head.

"What?" Randall asked. "Lift a bag of oats?"

"Hit me in the head," Hamish yelled, making Joshua grin. Aye, he would miss tricking these men.

Randall caught Joshua's smile and hit Hamish's arm, gesturing to him. "Are ye making mischief even as ye leave?" Hamish asked, hands on his hips.

Joshua smiled, showing his teeth. "Never assume ye know who the true enemy is, Hamish."

The man shook his head but grinned. "We will *not* miss ye, Highlander."

"Och, but I think ye will," Joshua parried back. He continued out the gate, his bare arm, encircled by tattoos, high in the air to bid them farewell. He was far enough away that they would not see the chill bumps on his skin.

As he exited, a young lad jumped out of his path. "Pardon, sir," he said. He was about twelve years old and stood with a younger lad, the two of them with wooden swords. "We are training like ye did with Lord Robert's warriors so we can fight." He grinned, his face tilted up at him. "Hamish Kincaid is our da."

He nodded to the boy who had a few freckles. "My da says you are the wisest warrior he has ever known," the boy said, and they both looked at him expectantly.

Joshua's stomach clenched hard as the first lad's

face seemed to change to one with a broad smattering of freckles and a serious frown. He nodded to the boys. "The wisest decision a warrior can make is whether or not he *should* fight."

Both boys lost their smiles and nodded as if taking in his wisdom, even though they would probably forget his words before he was out of sight over the rolling hills.

Shouts made him pull his horse to the side near the boys. Several of Robert's soldiers marched down the hill toward the fortress on the sea. In the center of them walked a man, a completely naked man. Henry Sinclair, Robert's eldest son, led the man by a rope encircling his neck, a cruel grin on his face. Henry nodded to Joshua as he walked past him on his way into the bailey.

The prisoner had scars across his bare chest and a slash on his side that had dried into a dark line of blood. Despite the frigid weather, he held his head even, staring out as he walked at sword point into the bailey. Just the sight of his bare skin made a shiver run through Joshua. *Fok. Too cold for that.* The brutal torture warred against Joshua's determination to put this frozen isle behind him, and he watched Lord Robert turn a vicious smile on the prisoner as he halted by the central well.

"Ah," Robert said, his words carrying to Joshua on the wind that never ceased to blow across treeless Orkney. "King Erik Flett, naked and near frozen." Lord Robert and Patrick had already forgotten about Joshua leaving as they grinned at their prize, who was stripped of absolutely everything. Robert nearly strutted as he followed the prisoner into the castle with his sons and hired brute.

Joshua narrowed his eyes at the man who had employed him to make his men clever, strong, and fast. *I should have killed him and his sons.* The isle would be better for it. But Robert Stuart was the recognized son of the dead King James V of Scotland. Killing him and his family would surely bring royal armies to his clan, the Sinclairs of Caithness, on the mainland.

At least the prisoner was no longer out of doors. *God, grant the man a quick and honorable death.* Joshua turned back to face the land that sloped upward away from the castle perched before the frigid Birsay Bay, which led to the open sea.

His horse slid easily into a canter with a touch of Joshua's heels. As soon as they reached the top of the rise, he pulled him to a halt. There wasn't a single tree on Orkney to stand behind, but he was far enough away that no one would see him reveal himself as fully human. He reached into his leather satchel and yanked out a thick tunic, a fur to throw over his shoulders, and a wool blanket to wrap across his lap and Fuil's back.

He patted his horse. "I will keep us both warm." Fuil's ears turned, listening.

Joshua had earned enough gold training Robert's men that he could go anywhere. But he missed the soaring oaks and birches and pines of Caithness. Had his brother, Cain Sinclair, the new chief of their clan, managed to keep the peace with the surrounding clans? Or had he showed enough weakness that strife continued? Never having left Girnigoe Castle for any length of time before,

Joshua had not lived under anyone other than his father and then his brother. Observing the leadership at the Earl's Palace of Birsay with the likes of Robert Stuart made Joshua realize how intelligent and fair his brother actually was. Cain had married a Sutherland lass right when Joshua left. Was his bride, Ella, already with child? And what of his other brothers and sister? Was Aunt Merida still making cures and predicting peoples' deaths?

He watched a flock of birds skimming the moorland. They rose high into the sky as they came upon the Earl's Palace and all the men surrounding it. The sight made his shoulders ache with tension. "Aye, 'tis time to go home," he murmured. If he left now, he could be setting the celebratory fires at Girnigoe Castle in time for Samhain to honor those who had died. Maybe he would stay through Hogmanay and set out again when it warmed. *South this time.* Surely there were warriors he could train in the south, too. Armies he could build up enough to intimidate the English from advancing farther into their country.

Leaning forward in the saddle, Joshua and Fuil shot ahead, flying over the brown-green landscape. Tall grasses lay combed flat, waves of frigid air blowing through the weeds as if a green sea rolled inland across the low hills, the colors being slowly muted with the falling snow. Ahead was the bay south of Birsay, where he could find transport to the mainland of Scotland.

The sun began its descent toward the line between sea and sky as he rode into the small village situated on a bluff above the rocky coast. A row of thatch-roofed cottages faced away from the ocean as if the people had seen enough of it and wished to keep it at their backs. Several dwellings had been burned badly. In fact, the town looked rather abandoned. If he couldn't find the captain of the cargo boat anchored in the harbor below the cliffs, he'd have to ride farther south to the Bay of Skaill.

Joshua dismounted in front of the squat, two-story tavern, looping Fuil's reins loosely around a rusty iron spike stuck into the stone wall running the building's length. He slid a hand down his horse's nose. "I will find ye a treat inside." He left the blanket draped over the horse and took his satchel. Two men walked on the far side of the road, eyeing him cautiously. Joshua cast a frown at them that would keep them moving on.

The blast of warmth from the hearth fire inside the tavern was a balm against the cold beating at Joshua's body. Hopefully, the tavern keeper had a bed to rent for the night and a snug barn for Fuil.

The low-ceilinged room was nearly empty. An old man with deep creases in his face stood behind a stone bar, his bulbous nose perched above a tankard as he took a drink. With no trees about, most of the locals' furniture and houses were made of the plentiful gray stone that held Orkney up out of the angry sea.

A woman leaned toward him over the bar, her trousers-clad arse nicely rounded and generous and leading to long legs. She wore a short cape and a pair of boots that were laced over fur pelts, a fashion he'd adopted from the islanders to stay warm. Her pale gold hair was woven into an intricate braid that slid down her back, the end tied and tapered as if pointing an arrow toward the crux of her legs.

"Even if Erik is gone, you should still accept Torben," the old man said before raising his eyes to Joshua. His tankard plunked down on the bar top.

She slapped her palm down. "To appease Fiona?" She shook her head, making her braid swing gently in contrast to the snapping hardness in her voice. "I will not tie myself to a man again."

So the lass was free of any restraints, like marriage. Joshua's brow rose.

The old man nodded toward Joshua, and she snapped around, surprise lighting her distinct features. High cheekbones sat in an angular face with a straight nose. Wisps of hair had broken free of her braid to lie in waves along her tan skin. Long eyelashes framed wide-set eyes, but he could not tell their color in the low light given off by the hearth and several oil lamps. Anger narrowed them. What would they look like under a bright sun?

The silence stretched with the wind whistling beyond the walls. Och but Orkney even *sounded* cold.

"I would like to rent a bed and a stall for my horse for the night," Joshua said.

"No beds are open," the old man said.

Joshua glanced pointedly around the empty room. Did the man know Joshua had helped Lord Robert's men become more efficient to deter the local islanders from raiding his building materials and hunting on his land?

"Then a barn for my horse," Joshua said and

pulled out several coins, letting them clink on the bar top.

"No barn, either."

Joshua pointed over his shoulder. "Like the one across the road?"

"All the stalls are full."

Joshua crossed his arms over his broad chest. "Then my horse and I will stay the night in here."

The old man snorted. "You haven't enough of Lord Robert's gold to pay for that."

Joshua turned his face to the lass. "Will Lord Robert's gold pay for a drink for the lady and me and a turnip for my horse?"

The tavern keeper looked at the woman as if asking her permission.

"Honey mead," she said, putting the man in motion. He poured one for her and one for Joshua, sliding the carved tankard to him across the polished stone.

"Turnip is in the cellar," the elderly man mumbled and shuffled through a closed door behind him.

Joshua studied the lass's strong profile. She was beautiful with a sharp edge to her, and from her shape, he could tell she was not a girl but a woman. "I am Joshua Sinclair." He took a drink of the sweet, fermented brew.

"I know who you are," she said.

He raised an eyebrow. "Who are ye then?"

"No one you need to trifle with." She slid a glance toward him and then back to her cup. She was as icy as the rest of the isle.

He leaned his back against the bar and propped his elbows on it. "I'm looking to pay for passage to the mainland of Scotland."

She set her cup down with a *clunk*. "You are leaving Orkney?"

"Aye."

"Then you do not war for Lord Robert anymore?"

"I war for no man," he answered and took a swallow of the refreshing mead.

"How about a woman? Could you war for a woman, be loyal to her?" Her gaze traveled down his form, and Joshua felt rather like she was stripping him bare. He'd had women look at him often as if they imagined him naked, but this woman seemed to be judging him.

He straightened, standing to his full height. "I am loyal only to my own clan back on the mainland." He tipped his head to the door. "Do ye know the captain of the cargo ship in the bay?"

"Aye. He will be around in the morn." Her brows furrowed slightly as she continued to inspect him.

Joshua braced his legs in a battle stance, arms crossing again. Hell, if she wanted to strip him naked with a look, or with her hands, he certainly would not mind. Would *she*?

His gaze traveled along her bare neck to the slope of her breasts that he could see in the open part of her cape. Her waist tapered inward only to flare out over full hips. He'd declared to his brother once that all lasses should wear trousers, and this woman added merit to the opinion. Och but he wanted to run his hands down those slopes. She looked warm and supple, her mouth lush.

"Here," said the old man, pushing through the back door to drop the turnip on the counter.

Thudding, it rolled to the edge. He picked up the pennies Joshua had left and tucked them in his tunic.

"Any of these cottages in town open to travelers?" Joshua asked the woman. If not, he would have to find shelter for Fuil and then come back and buy tankards of mead until the old man fell asleep so he could spend the night on a cold stone bench.

"There might be a place for you to stay," the woman answered. "I will…ask."

"I am obliged." Joshua let his mouth bend up in a half smile that usually softened the lasses back home. He let the appreciation for her form show in his gaze. Not too much, or he'd been known to look predatory, which frightened off the majority of lasses. Nay, just mild interest showed instead of the thrumming rush he felt inside.

Her lips parted slightly as if she needed to draw in more breath, and she pushed away from the bar. Stopping next to him, her hand rose with awkward hesitation to touch his arm. "I will return once I know." It curled into a fist but then flattened out to slide down the length of his bicep. "You will wait?"

Her touch momentarily robbed him of thought. She had asked a question. "Will I wait?" he repeated slowly. "For ye?" Recovering, he let charm grow in his smile. "An army of horses could not drag me from here." Behind him, he heard the barkeeper snort.

She strode away, taking the heat in her touch with her. The door slammed shut as she pushed out into the cold, and Joshua turned to the frowning man, still standing behind the bar. "What is her name?"

The man pursed his lips tightly and shook his head. "I call her *dróttning*."

Joshua's gaze slid to the door and back to the man. Three months on the isle, and he still had not picked up much of the local language. It was as if they guarded it against those speaking English or Gaelic. "What does it mean?"

"'Tis from old Norse," he said. "And it means you best treat her well."

"I have every intention of treating her very well," Joshua said and snatched up the turnip, tossing it into the air to catch easily as it fell back to earth. He pushed out through the door into the twilight. And stopped. "Bloody hell," he yelled, the turnip dropping from his hand to roll away. Fuil was gone!

CHAPTER TWO

*"The whole secret lies in confusing the enemy, so
that he cannot fathom our real intent."*
Sun Tzu – The Art of War

Joshua whipped around, his fingers going to his
mouth where he blew two short whistles. A neigh,
from behind one of the buildings, tore through the
growing twilight. Yells followed.

Bandits. *Fools!* Fuil was a warhorse and listened
to no one but him. The only thing that would have
made him move was a treat dangled before him.
Damn horse thieves! Maybe Robert's rant about the
native people eating horseflesh was true. Had he
starved his people enough to turn them into barbar-
ians?

Joshua ran around the side of the thatched
cottage, skidding to a halt before three men trying to
control his raging steed. Their eyes were wide as
they raised hands to the snorting beast, the whites of
Fuil's eyes showing and his ears laid back. The horse
could kill them on his own, but the thieves might
injure his friend. Fury roared in Joshua's ears, and
energy shot through his blood at the thought that
they would steal him. *And eat him!*

Barely noting that the woman from the tavern
stood nearby, he drew his sword from the scabbard
strapped to his back, stalking forward. Sucking in
large swaths of air through his nostrils, he prepared

to win this contest by intimidation alone.

One of the fiends turned to see him advancing, his panicked eyes growing even wider. He had no sword and raised his fists before him, the snorting horse behind him. *Damn*. The thief was young, probably only recently growing into his pitiful beard.

The second man was dressed in ragged clothing, insufficient against the cold. He held a dagger and a wild glare. The third bastard surged toward Joshua, sword held by his two hands, striking downward. Joshua met the attack, the two blades clanging together. Desperate or foolish? Joshua wasn't sure, but the man seemed immune to intimidation.

Joshua easily parried the man's lunge, spinning to bring his elbow down at the base of the man's skull, knocking him flat, his face in the dirt. Pivoting to the man holding his puny dagger, he yelled, "I will jam your own blade into your foolish skull."

The man's lips curled back as he spit. "There are worse things." It was the look of desperation that made Joshua drop his sword to the turf. Even a horse thief could lose hope. That did not mean he deserved to be skewered.

In two strides, Joshua knocked the dagger from the man's hand and threw a punch into his nose, dropping him to the ground without any effort.

"Foking monster!" the barely-a-man yelled. He charged, his fists still raised. Joshua held up his own fists, but instead of swinging at the lad, he swiped his leg across as he sidestepped, tripping the thief, who fell hard. Three steps back, Joshua swooped up his sword and spun back to Fuil.

"Stop!" came a voice from the road.

Fire ripped across the outside of Joshua's upper arm. He looked down to see a slice in his tunic where a dagger had cut through as it grazed him, the weapon skidding across the pebbled ground beyond. He'd been merciful with the thieves and yet they sought to kill him. Rage added even more strength to his sword arm. Lifting it high, he spun and charged toward the foe who had drawn his blood.

"No!" screamed the woman from the shadows, but Joshua didn't slow. A part of him realized she ran toward them, but he focused on his enemy. The thrower's size broke through Joshua's fury. Round eyes. Thin frame. Pale, shocked face. It was a boy, a young boy. Just like…

At the last second, Joshua diverted the thrust of his sword, swinging it down along the lad's side, and skidded to a halt. Breathing hard, he loomed over the boy. The promise of death surfaced on his face, one that would hopefully stick in the lad's nightmares so he wouldn't fight someone three times his size again. "Ye bloodied me."

"Stop!" yelled the woman, grabbing Joshua's injured arm.

Before the frightened lad could respond, the young thief, who Joshua had tripped, yanked the boy around, yelling at him in their local dialect. The two of them ran off into the growing darkness, their arms pumping. The woman dropped her hold on him and clenched her hands together. Her chest rose and fell. The other two men remained unconscious where they had fallen, and Fuil stepped over their prone bodies as he came up to Joshua. The horse nosed him as if asking where his treat had ended up.

"Fuil," he mumbled, letting the chill in the wind calm his anger. "Your blasted stomach gets us into such bloody trouble."

Joshua watched the worry mix with anger on the woman's fine features, and she finally turned away from the lads who faded into the shadows. She murmured something in her ancient language and grabbed his arm to inspect the wound.

"Do ye know them?" he asked.

"This needs to be cleaned, but no stitches are warranted." She squatted to catch together a small pile of fresh snow, standing to wipe the blood from the cut.

He caught her chin to bring her gaze up to his, her eyes growing round for a split second before narrowing. Questions pressed within him. *Who are you? Were you helping them? Why were you standing back watching?* But answers to those questions might lead her to walk away from him, for which he was definitely not ready. He leaned in, tethering her gaze completely. "Were they going to eat my horse?"

Her lips rose into a grin, and she jerked back, breaking free of his hold. "No, Highlander. Despite Lord Robert's lies, we do not eat horseflesh. Although, if the choice between eating you or eating your horse arose…" She squeezed his arm as if testing the meat on his bones. "No, even then your horse would be safe." She shook her head. "I would choose to eat you."

His frown relaxed, and for a moment they stared at each other. Her mouth softened with the faintest hint of humor. The wind calmed, the snow falling straight down to catch in her pale hair. "It is good to know my faithful steed is secure."

"Do you not worry for yourself?" Her gaze traveled down his form. "Because ye look…delicious."

Lightning coursed through his body at her words, making his jack awaken below the layers of his woolen plaid. Although, he was fairly certain it had been paying attention since he'd seen her standing in the tavern, all curves and long legs. "I can take care of myself," he said.

Her brow rose, and Joshua watched as the tip of her tongue came out to touch the edge of her bottom lip. Heat began to roll through him. Was he reading her signals correctly? A woman like this did not seem like the type to tease. She seemed more like someone who knew what she wanted and almost always got it. And if she wanted him right now, he, bloody hell, wouldn't refuse her.

"Did ye find a place for my horse and me to stay for the night?" he asked, keeping his gaze locked to hers. Snowflakes swirled about, hitting his cheeks. The intensity in the woman's almond-shaped eyes made the rest of the world disappear, even the bite in the sea breeze.

"Aye," she said, sliding a finger up to tuck the wisps of her hair behind her ear. "You can stay with me. That is, if you can find me."

His heart beat faster at her words, and his grin grew. "Ye are right here, so I have already won."

Without warning, she spun, jogging inland away from the village. Was the woman insane? Where would she go? There were no trees in which to hide, and the landscape of rolling hills was free of most dwellings. "I will find ye easily. I have a horse, lass," he called, noticing the twilight was deepening quickly.

She turned to jog backward. "And I have cunning, Highlander," she called and raced off.

He watched her run, the sway of her braid like an entrancing pendulum. She glanced several times over her shoulder as if making sure he would follow, but her form was quickly fading into the darkening landscape. He strode to Fuil to mount but yelled over his shoulder, "I can easily run ye down and catch ye."

Her laughter floated back to him on the twilight wind.

. . .

Kára pumped her arms as she ran, her boots easily finding purchase on the familiar moor. *He will follow.* A man like the infamous Joshua Sinclair, Horseman of War, would not turn away from a challenge.

When he'd walked into the tavern, she had known instantly who he was. Very few were as large as the Highland warrior and no one as darkly handsome. The first things one noticed about Joshua Sinclair were his broad shoulders and towering height, which displayed his muscular frame so perfectly that he resembled the pictures her brother drew of the warrior Danes from long ago. He wore the belted wool wrappings of his homeland around his narrow hips and fur leg wraps above his boots. His hands were large and calloused from holding the massive sword strapped across his back. When he'd stared into her eyes, his full mouth curving into a seductive smile over white teeth, heat had slid down through Kára, like honey warmed in the sun. Now *that* was a reaction to capture a woman's notice, but her plan was still ridiculous. What the hell was she thinking, baiting him to chase after her?

Her grandmother's words rang in her ears. *We need to find a warrior to lead us to victory against Robert Stuart.*

Joshua Sinclair was the largest, deadliest warrior on Orkney, and probably all of Scotland. A shudder that had nothing to do with the cold ran between Kára's shoulder blades at the memory of the Highlander's downward strike that fell next to her nine-year-old son, Geir. Why had her brother, Osk, brought him to the village? Joshua could have easily killed him, killed them both. And foolish Langdon and Lamont were left in the dirt. No doubt they would wake with aching heads. Better than dead.

Her legs churned as she focused on her goal in the gloaming, the small barn that marked the entrance to her den, an earthen house under the thick peat field. The Highlander might find the barn, but he would need help finding her den.

Slow down so he can catch you. The whisper in her head teased the ache between her legs that had roared to life as his gaze traveled down her body in the tavern. Before Geir had run into the fray, Kára had marveled at the effortless way the Highlander had felled the three would-be horse thieves, even as she gave thanks that he wasn't using his sword. She'd told the fools to leave his horse alone, but her brother had little self-restraint since their father had been killed last spring.

Her heart hammered with the run, but also with her hastily drawn plan. *Seduction.* What did she know of it? *Very little.* She'd already employed all the advice her friend, Brenna, had given her on attracting a man. Touching his arm, gazing down his body as if he were a honey tart she wished to lick, and touching her tongue to her lip the tiniest bit. And Brenna insisted that men liked to chase.

Kára breathed in and out through her parted lips as she leaped over the meandering berm that cut through the moorland on its way to the sea. A glance behind her showed that Brenna had been right. Even though he was way back at the village, Kára could see that Joshua Sinclair was following. Brenna would smile her knowing smile when Kára told her later.

Brenna had pushed Kára to find another man ever since Kára had become a widow nine years ago. And Torben Spence had done everything his foolish mind could come up with to get her to accept his proposal to wed. Even old Asmund was now trying to sway her to accept him. No one seemed to understand that she never would. She'd married once, and it had ended before she could lose herself in love. And yet, she'd mourned. In this uncertain world, she'd be a fool to chance it again.

Bed the Highlander. Would showing Torben that she wasn't the type of woman who could be faithful convince him to stop trying to woo her? Perhaps. But that was not why she was going to seduce Joshua Sinclair. Nay, she was going to persuade him to lead her people to victory. *And his arms are like warm, thick steel.*

Instead of leaping down into the stone-lined hole that looked like an abandoned well, Kára dodged into the barn. She didn't have a horse now, but it housed her few sheep and Ninny, her goat, who welcomed her with a long bleat.

"You had food two hours ago," she whispered as the sets of expectant eyes turned her way. She ran to the back to leap onto a broken wagon that held a bag of oats and a shock of hay. Grabbing the rope that hung from the loft, she climbed by wrapping her feet in it and pulling herself up and onto the platform above.

The sound of rapid hoofbeats made her drop into a crouch to spy over the edge. She had jumped down from the loft many times, landing near the door; if she decided to escape instead of… What exactly? Now that her plan was succeeding, she wasn't quite sure she could go through with seducing a stranger, even if he was the brawniest man she'd ever seen. Even though the look that the Highlander had given her had awakened a yearning she'd long since forgotten. Anxious energy made her hands tremble.

The door of the barn swung inward. "*Dróttning*, are ye in here?"

Dróttning? Old Asmund was calling her a queen because Erik had been taken by Robert's forces that morn.

Lord. Poor Erik. He'd made them swear never to risk themselves to save him but to carry on. Maybe Joshua Sinclair could help them rescue him before he could be killed by Robert Stuart.

Her thoughts twisted into a single focus as the Highlander walked through the barn door. She peered down onto his head, his hair long and wavy, although it was almost impossible to see in the darkness of the barn. It had looked clean in the tavern, and his teeth had been white, indicating that he took care of his body. What did he look like under the furs and wool?

He stalked around the barn, glancing at her animals, and his eyes stopped on the rope where it swayed from her climb. "'Tis a cozy home ye have," he said, and she almost snorted. He thought she lived with her animals. When she didn't answer, he went back to the door and brought his horse inside. Perhaps he thought merely to shelter them both for the night, but the intensity of his eyes as he slid his gaze down her form earlier had spoken that he was game to much more than warmth and sleep.

Do not be too easily won. Smile as if you know things, but then walk away. They always follow if there is a chase involved. Brenna's continual prompting surfaced in Kára's mind. She had ignored her friend's advice, because there had been absolutely no one about whom she'd want to encourage. That had changed with one casual grin and request to buy her a drink. And the knowledge that she could truly help save her people.

The Highlander moved about the barn with methodical focus, taking his horse's saddle off and leading him to the water trough. He gave the majestic creature a couple handfuls of oats from the bag on the wagon and walked back outside. Kára leaned farther over the edge, her ears straining to hear above the whistle of wind through the small holes in the daubed walls. The sound of splashing water made her smile. He'd found the real well. Had he first gone to her doorway realizing there was only stone and earth below?

The door whipped open as the wind caught it, and the Highlander strode in with his furs in his hands, shutting the door behind him. "Your tracks stop here, lass," he called. He dropped the furs with his sheathed sword and ran hands down his face as if ridding it of water. His tunic was open, showing he had washed quickly despite the cold. She sucked in a silent breath as he drew it over his head. "I have caught ye," he said. "That was your challenge."

Kára's gaze traveled along his form, barely visible in the darkness of the barn. Lord help her, she wanted to see him completely bare.

"Shall I come above?" he asked, batting at the rope to make it swing.

Bang. Twang. "Fok," he cursed low as he knocked her pitchfork over, making it hit the stone stool that sat in the corner. "If sleep is all ye have in mind this eve, I will sleep below. I will not hurt ye, lass. I do not rape."

Good to know. Kára untied her outer cloak in the darkness, watching his predatory pacing around the corners of the bottom floor. He did not attack women, but he most certainly tupped. His body looked to be made for it. He had probably bedded many women, beguiling, beautiful women. Should she tease and then stop him? Lure him back to her village to finish her seduction?

Seduction? She almost laughed. She had no idea what to do with him, her half-made plan forming as she went. But one thing was certain—she couldn't let him leave Orkney now that he wasn't working for Robert. If there was a chance of wooing him to her side of this war, she must try. And if her bringing him to Hillside as her lover deterred Torben from pursuing her, so much the better.

She moved silently back to the rope, holding to the top where she could slide down. He stood below in the darkness. There was only enough light from the cracks in the wooden door for her to see his broad bare shoulders directly below her. *I will slide down. Then kiss him, coyly tease him, and invite him back to Hillside Village.*

Using the rope, she swung over the edge and down the length, her legs raised to settle over his shoulders. Her heels caught against his chest so she could clench his head with her thighs. "Fortunately for you, Highlander, I do not rape, either," she said, squeezing.

Before she could do anything else, he grabbed her hips, the strength in his grip slightly biting as he yanked her around. Her heels slid to his upper back, bringing the crux of her legs right before his face. She heard him inhale deeply as if smelling her heat. "Mmmmm," he murmured, and his hands dug into the back of her arse, pushing her hips forward against his mouth.

He exhaled from the back of his throat, forcing hot breath out. The heat penetrated her trousers, straight to the ache between her legs, making her breath catch as a pulse of lustful fire flared up from it. Without thinking, she rocked into him, her legs clenching around his head, and he repeated the fiery exhale.

Stunned at her immediate response, she loosened her hold to slide her legs down the slope of his back, settling her crossed feet on his arse, her legs wrapped around his thick body. Coming level with his mouth, she kissed him. A carnal, overwhelming heat surged within Kára as his warm lips slid against hers. *Holy hell.*

He tugged the end of her braid to free its binding and raked upward through her loosening hair. His fingers slid to her nape and up along her scalp as they pressed bodies and mouths together in the dark. Hunger swelled inside Kára, hunger like she'd never felt before, not even with her husband when they were married. She felt ravenous for this man, as if she were starving, her body breaking and shedding the ice in which she'd encased herself over these lonely years. Her plan to lure him with teasing burned to ash under the pressure of his body against hers.

Despite the savage way they clung to each other, his kisses did not bruise. She swept her tongue inside his mouth. He growled low, holding her under her arse and letting her slide farther down until her crux met the thickness of his cod through the wrapping over his hips. He tasted of honey mead and smelled of wild wind, raw strength, and clean man. Kára felt hot and lost. Without thought, she ground her pelvis against the largeness of him. It had become instinct, a deep need.

His lips slid a path along her jaw to her ear. "Ye smell of lust, *dróttning*."

"Kára," she rasped. "My name is Kára. It means wild."

He chuckled softly. "Kára," he whispered near her ear, the word coming slow as if he savored her name on his tongue, tasting it as if tasting her. She shuddered.

"Kára, lass, I am going to lick every sweet, hidden part of ye." He pulled back slightly, and she heard his breath coming hard like hers. "That is, if ye wish it."

She shivered, pulling his face back down, his lips hovering less than an inch over her own. "I wish it," she said, and the foolish plan to lure him back to Hillside faded like the mist. She pressed against his evident arousal. "Stay with me."

"Aye, lass," he said in her ear, pressing her to him. "I will most certainly."

CHAPTER THREE

"Thus the expert in battle moves the enemy,
and is not moved by him."
Sun Tzu – The Art of War

Kára's heart hammered, her breathing hard, and she melted back into him with wild abandon, which he met with equal force. She let out a hum at the back of her throat between kisses as his hands stroked up her tunic to the binding around her chest where he yanked it down, releasing her breasts. Her nipples were already hard and sensitive, and she sucked in as his hand came around to cup one globe, pinching the peak and palming the fullness.

Unhooking her ankles, she dropped down his length until her boots hit the earthen floor. With two steps, he backed her up against the cold wall of the barn, holding her there and yanking her tunic up and over her head. The mountainous outline of the warrior was the only thing she could see in the darkness, but she could definitely feel.

His large hands stroked over her skin. "Ye are so bloody soft and ripe with curves."

Sliding her palms over the muscles of his chest, her fingers scraped down through the fine hair that led toward the edge of the wool wrapped around his hips. What was her plan again? Her hands spanned his mass of masculine strength, unable to think, only to feel. She let her instincts take over.

Kára bent her face forward, her hot breath branding his skin. He shuddered as she planted wet kisses up his chest, licking over his taut nipple. The fact that she could affect this formidable man made her even more bold.

When she reached his neck by standing on the toes of her boots, she pushed a hand against his shoulder, shoving him around and back so that he leaned against the wall, trading places with her. His chuckle turned into a low growl as his hand stroked up under her heavy hair to cup her head, pulling her forward to stand between his straddled legs.

Joshua Sinclair wasn't some easily bruised lad. He was built large and hard. Was the rest of him the same? Kára slid her hand up his thigh and under his kilt to the raging erection there. Wrapping her fingers around him, she stroked up and down, her mouth going back to his. "Such power," she said against his lips, slanting to kiss him thoroughly. Her stroke pulled a groan from deep down within his chest, the vibration teasing more sensation through Kára until she trembled with lust. Nothing else mattered but this man in her hands, his strength and heat, and her need for him.

With a growl, the Highlander spun her around so her back was once again pressed against the wall, the roughness of the layers of flat stone cold on her naked back. His mouth dove down to her breast, covering her nipple as he loved first one and then the other, lapping and palming her breasts until they felt like they were swelling, yearning for the touch of his tongue. A line of heat tightened within her aching body from her nipples down to her core, fanning the fire already burning there. Resting her head back, she let her moan fill the barn. Ninny answered with a bleat, making the Highlander raise his head.

Kára grabbed his arm. "This is not where I sleep." Leaving her tunic and his clothes, she led him to the door.

"Ye will freeze," he said, stopping her.

"'Tis not far." She pushed out into the night, her hand still clasping his. Four steps brought them up to the abandoned well that wasn't a well but an opening into her cozy den. She'd discovered it years ago, cut down inside the hillside, a dwelling from ancient times. When her son, Geir, had begun to sleep at her brother's home, leaving her because he felt he was starting to grow into a man, she'd made the hollowed-out earth home into a comfortable nest. Here she was hidden away from the world and the pressures of helping her uncle save her people.

"Slide down the rope," she said, letting go of his hand to grab the old well rope. For a moment, she stopped to stare at him in the slight moonlight. His chest and shoulders bare, she saw scrollwork tattooed around his biceps. Toned muscles and absolute strength made her mouth go dry. Could he hear the rapid thud of her heart? What the bloody hell was she doing? *Seducing the only man powerful enough to conquer Robert Stuart.*

When his gaze traveled to her breasts propped up by the lowered bindings, she swallowed hard. She couldn't deny her want of him, but the intensity she felt made him dangerous. Even the cold wind couldn't squash the flames raging inside her. Her plans had burned up with his touch, so she would have to continue completely on instinct. And her instincts told her that Joshua Sinclair needed to fall in lust with her in order for him to stay on Orkney.

Taking a deep breath, Kára smiled with what she hoped was a seductive grin. "Come down into my hole, Highlander," she said, and grabbed the rope to kick her legs over the well's edge.

• • •

Joshua Sinclair watched the woman lower gracefully down the rope into the dried-up well he'd seen before outside the barn. He never would have guessed that it led anywhere. *Maybe she's a selkie and leading me to a watery death.* If he got a chance to taste her further, he didn't care.

Grabbing the gently swaying rope, he climbed over the ring of rocks marking the well. Immediately, he felt warmth radiating upward and lowered toward it. Glancing below he saw red cinders. It was a chimney to a hearth. Lined with stones in a broad rectangular form, the tunnel dropped a good twelve feet before opening into a dug-out space. Releasing the rope, he landed with his legs wide, straddling the remains of a fire, the heat funneling right up his kilt. He hopped off to the side, his hand instinctively reaching back for his sword that wasn't there. *Fool.* He'd left it above, his lust making him careless. He looked up the well at a rectangular space of night sky.

"I am here," the woman called, and he turned to see her lighting an oil lamp. His breath caught at the sight of her, bare breasts perched on the bindings around her ribs, her hair skimming past her shoulders and along her full breasts, where it hung like pale silk that he already knew was soft and fragrant. She unwound the bindings, dropping them so that she was naked down to the edge of her trousers. Hips swaying with natural grace, she walked toward him as she unlaced the front ties of her trousers. Keeping her gaze centered on his face, she stepped around him, teasing him by skimming close without touching him. She crouched before the embers to blow them back to life and added two bricks of peat from a pile that was stacked in a small tower nearby.

When the peat caught, she stood tall and straight, turning to him, and he fisted his hands to keep from reaching immediately for her. "Welcome to my den," she said, a half grin turning up one corner of her lush mouth.

"Are ye Calisto, the woman turned into a bear and living in the stars?" he asked. He inhaled as her gaze dropped to his obvious arousal pushing against his kilt.

She tipped her head as she met his gaze. "Have no fear. I will not maul you…too much." Her fingers slid down her stomach into the *V* made by her open trousers, touching herself.

The sight, mixed with her playful words, shot another jolt of want through him. "Bloody hell," he murmured. He felt like he could rip apart anything that stood between them, his need to mate stronger than his need to breathe. His breath came ragged as his gaze roamed the contours of her strong, beautifully unique face.

Joshua tugged his belt open, and the folds of woven wool dropped to his boots, leaving him bare and hard as the rocks around them. Her eyes widened, but she met his watchful gaze with a small smile. In two strides, he stood before her. As he was about to reel her in, she turned away, bending over. Her shapely arse, still clad in the trousers, lifted into the air, and she untied the fur wrappings and her boots. Och, but he wanted to take her from behind, but then also in a way he could stare into her face as she shattered in bliss. He would tease every little tingle of pleasure out of her.

Joshua nearly tripped over the pooling of his clothes, cursed, and bent to untie his own furs and boots, shucking them before she could turn around. She straightened, her blond hair pulled to one side, exposing the slim muscles of her back and the seductive spot at the base of her skull. He came up behind her, his naked body pressed against her still-covered arse, his jack hard and lifted between them. His hands were icy, so he pressed them against the outsides of his thighs, hoping his body heat would warm them.

Leaning in, his hot mouth trailed across the space between her shoulder and neck. Her hair spilled backward as her face tipped up to the low ceiling of rock, giving him access to her throat. His mouth settled against her thrumming pulse. She smelled more delicious than any sweet he'd ever tasted, a mix of warm spice and womanly lust. Everything about her called him: the softness of her skin, the heat from her body, her scent and bravery to bring him into her secluded home.

Reaching around, he cupped her breasts, lifting them as she pressed her back against him, moving her arse in a wanton circle. His groan rumbled up from his chest on a long exhale. Stretching her arms upward, she turned, and he watched the graceful length in them and her fingers. Her long limbs lay down over his shoulders where she pulled his mouth back to hers, slanting immediately into a hot, open kiss. Their mutual touching was well underway, and Joshua couldn't think of a better prize for finding her.

She rubbed against his jack, and he slid his hands down her sides, following the slopes inward and over to the front of her open trousers. Down in the center, his fingers dove, drawn to the wet heat of her. She pushed into his hand and moaned as he entered her.

"Och, but ye are soaked and so hot inside, Kára lass," he said, his voice rough. She moaned as he worked her flesh. Lips parted, her hands plucked at her trousers, sliding them down to her feet to kick aside. Her beautiful body was completely bare. Full breasts and flared hips, she was no virginal girl. Nay, Kára was all exquisitely ripe woman.

"Stay with me, Highlander," she whispered at his ear, kissing along his jawline and neck as she rubbed the crux of her legs against him.

With a little hop, she lifted her legs up around his hips again, kissing his mouth with wild abandon. He caught her arse in his two hands, backing them up toward a large area of furs and quilts. His legs took them there without conscious thought. Their breaths mingled, and he lowered them, until she was flat upon the furs.

The firelight cast her skin in gold and shadows as she plumped her own breasts. Her legs slid out wide, the core of her beckoning him with an invitation he would never refuse.

"I want to taste ye, lass," he said, bending his head between her knees. Kára's breath sucked in as his mouth covered her, savoring the proof of her desire. He played her expertly, bringing her higher and higher. For long minutes she thrashed above him, her fingers curling into the quilts.

"Joshua Sinclair," she gasped. He loved to hear his name on her tongue and continued loving her until she yelled, filling the underground space with the sound of her ultimate satisfaction.

Rising above her, he moved up her body, taking in the flushed glow of her skin in the firelight and her wide eyes. Her wry grin had been replaced by astonishment. Had no one ever pleasured her like that before? He smiled at the thought. "I promised to lick every bit of ye."

Her breathing was labored. "I ache still." She let her knees fall back out, and he grabbed around her hips, tilting her pelvis upward to meet him.

"Kára?" He fought for control, waiting for her answer. Aye or nay, although nay might strike him dead right there. "Kára? May I?"

"Aye," she said, staring up into his face. With a guttural cry, Joshua thrust inside, and his eyes tipped upward as if he had found Heaven and wished to worship. Hot and wet, Kára totally engulfed him, and he rocked into her open body.

Gasping upon his first thrust, she drew shallow

breaths and hooked her ankles across his back as if she wished to lock him up inside her. He would give his soul to be her prisoner.

They quickly created a rhythm, giving and taking with equal force. Her kisses were as open as her body and just as wild. Fingers raked through his hair and scratched his back, and he balled his fist into her long tresses as the tempo increased. When he felt upon the edge, he tried to pull out of her body, but she held him to her, continuing to thrust upward.

"I would not burden ye with a bastard, lass," he managed to say, but she didn't release him. "Kára—"

"Fill me full, Highlander."

Her words tore through him. It was as if he could not physically leave her body as the two of them teetered on the edge with each thrust without restraint. Rising up higher on her body, he angled himself so the base of his jack rubbed against her most sensitive spot between them. Her eyes widened; her lips parted. Sweat beaded on Joshua's forehead as their bodies strained together. He couldn't look away, couldn't shift his gaze from her beautiful eyes.

"My holy stars," she screamed, and he felt her body clench.

Joshua roared as his release rolled through his body, and he swore she ripped a part of his soul from inside him. His teeth clapped together as they continued to ride out the waves of ecstasy, staring into each other's eyes, firelight splashing gold against their skin.

Long, exquisite minutes later, they slowed. "Bloody holy stars" was right. He tried to move to the side, but she kept him there. He smiled. "Are ye keeping me prisoner then?"

Stretching her arms up over her head, he felt himself already start to harden at the rise of her breasts and feel of her body under him. "I would if I could," she said and finally released her legs, so he could pull her to his side. He hugged her close, inhaling the mix of their scents.

The fire warmed the den that he hadn't had time or desire to investigate before. Surrounded by interlocking stone, the walls of the medium-sized room rose up about eight feet in a rectangle. The floor was stone and scattered with woven rugs. The hearth sat in the center of the room where the smoke rose through the hole they had descended. A table and several shelves were made of stone and held baskets of food and bladders, hopefully of ale or fresh water.

Kára pulled a sewn quilt, painted with colorful flowers, over them, and he realized they lay in a nest of furs, pillows, and blankets on a thick tick on the stone floor. But what drew his eyes were the paintings on the walls. Bright renditions of birds and seascapes, of wind blowing wildflowers, and beautiful horses covered the stone all around them. When he looked back to her face, he realized she was watching him closely.

"What do you think of my den?" she asked.

"Surprising, beautiful, mysterious, and warm," he said, leaning in to kiss her. "Like ye, Calisto."

She smiled widely and rolled out of their nest to pad across the room, and grabbed a bladder from a shelf. Totally naked and comfortable with it, she uncorked the bladder and drank. He watched the slender column of her throat as she swallowed, her lovely body laid bare to his gaze. It made him even thirstier. Her hips swayed naturally as she walked back, handing it to him.

Clear, fresh ale slid down his throat. When he lowered it, she was watching him, a tilt to her head and brows bent, studying him as if he were a riddle she must solve.

"What are ye thinking?" he asked, and she shook her head.

Kára lifted the quilt and climbed back under with him. She rolled onto her side, presenting her arse, and shifted until she pressed her entire backside into the curve of his body. His arm came over to stroke her stomach, marveling at the softness there.

"Let us sleep for a bit," she said.

He laid his head back on the pillows, looking at the waves in her thick, golden hair. "Only for a bit?"

Her hand slid behind, her fingernail trailing along the muscles of his hip and thigh. "Until you're ready for me to make you roar again," she said, leaning back to smile up into his face, her earlier questioning look wiped away.

He returned her grin. "Then ye better fall asleep quickly, because I will be ready in less than five minutes."

CHAPTER FOUR

"There are roads which must not be followed, armies which must not be attacked, towns which must not be besieged, positions which must not be contested, commands of the sovereign which must not be obeyed."
Sun Tzu – The Art of War

Kára poured the warmed rabbit stew into two pottery bowls. She wore a soft woolen smock and slippers and padded over to the table where Joshua sat polishing the three daggers that she'd shown him. One was her father's, one was her dead husband's, and one was her own. She set the bowls down and moved to sit across from him, noticing he'd put a plump pillow on the seat of her stool.

Without looking up he said, "I thought ye might be a bit sore down there." He glanced at the juncture of her legs, a roguish grin on his handsome face. "At last count we came together four times."

"You count?" she asked, watching his strong fingers work the dry cloth over the steel until it shone in the firelight.

"Bloody hell, aye," he said. "A man has got to have something about which to boast."

She laughed. "Remind me not to introduce you to my amma then," she said, speaking about her grandmother. It was easy jesting with Joshua, and after what they had shared over the last night and morning, she felt completely open to him. Except, of course, about her family and her desperate need to get him to stay on Orkney and lead them in war against Robert Stuart.

"Amma means grandmother?"

She nodded, and he smiled.

"Does she live near?"

Did she trust him enough to tell him where their village hid under the hills on the coast? If he was going to train them to fight and lead them, he would have to meet her people. "Aye, we call our small village Hillside. It sits on the coast north of here."

"I have seen no village along the coast, except the one with the tavern along the bay."

She watched him closely. "It is mostly hidden. I can take you there today."

His smile faded. "I was planning to find the captain of that ship in the bay today to secure a passage to the mainland."

Alarm shot through Kára, but she kept her words even. "You knocked the captain flat on his face last night outside the tavern. Doubtful he will take you onboard."

"Bloody hell," he murmured. "I will have to ride south to another port."

"Why are you so anxious to return to Scotia?" she asked, using the ancient word for Scotland. Did he miss someone there? The thought tightened inside her. "You can stay with us for the winter. With me. Right here." She moved her arm out to the side to indicate her cozy home.

"My three brothers, sister, and aunt are there," he said, setting down the daggers to lift his spoon.

She watched him take several bites, swallowing appreciatively. "I should see how they fare. And I miss my horses."

"You have more than the one horse in the barn above?"

"Aye." He chuckled. "I have over one hundred bays."

She blinked. "One hundred horses?" He was wealthy? On top of being the most renowned warrior in the land and such a generous lover that she would remember him all the way to the grave?

"My brothers each have a hundred also. We have a large army of mounted warriors." He pointed his spoon at the walls. "Perhaps ye should come to Girnigoe Castle with me. Ye seem to like horses."

She inhaled fully and nodded, giving him a small smile. "And not to eat."

He grinned, shoveling more of the stew into his mouth, a mouth that had done such wanton and wonderful things to various parts of her body. She swallowed hard against the memory.

"Ye paint well," he said, turning his gaze to the images across her walls. Flowers, horses, ocean scenes decorated most of the flat surfaces in her den.

"My amma is an artist. She can paint anything to look just like the real object. She taught me some of her ways, but I do not have her talent." She shrugged. "I spend much time down here when the winter blows in for months. So I surround myself with spring."

He studied the herds she'd painted from his seat. "Ye capture the free spirit of horses well." She could see him slowly working his way across her scenes, stopping at the larger painting of her horse, Broch.

"Would your brothers and sister come to Orkney with their armies of horses if you asked?" she asked softly.

He turned back to her, his brows lowered. "Getting the horses across the firth would be difficult," he said, meeting her eyes. There were questions in his stare. "Multiple ships would be required to sail them the six hours over to Birsay. Once on Orkney, there'd be nowhere to house our horses or men."

Was his sister also a warrior? Were Joshua's brothers as large as he? Would they fight with him to conquer Robert and his cruel sons?

"Did ye have a horse at one time?" he asked when she didn't respond.

She nodded, her lips twitching into a smile past the ache of sadness in her eyes. "My family owned several, but I loved Broch the most. She was frisky and ran as fast as the wind along the cliffs." She blinked.

"Broch? Does it mean something in your language?"

"The halo that encircles the full moon is called a *broch*. She was born with a white circle around one eye." She nodded to the painting on the wall.

He glanced that way and then back to her, a frown tightening his face. "How did she die?"

Kára put down her spoon, losing her appetite. "I do not know. She was taken from me."

He studied the painting. "I think I have seen that horse," he said. "Alive."

Her lovely mare was still alive? Kára's face fell as her chest clenched. She leaned forward, her fist tightening. "Was she being treated well?" she whispered. Torture through terror was worse than death, something she knew too well.

He leaned forward, too, his hand sliding across to squeeze hers on the table. "From what I could see, aye. Did Lord Robert take her from ye?"

Kára nodded. "She is not… He does not beat her then?"

"His daughter, Jean, rides her. The mare's spirit seems high. I saw no signs of abuse."

Tears came to Kára's eyes, and she sniffed them back. When Broch had been taken, she had mourned her as if she'd died.

Joshua nodded to emphasize his words. "Lord Robert may treat his workers terribly, but his horses are kept fed and groomed. And his daughter is kinder than he."

Kára knew of Jean Stuart, Lord Robert's second eldest daughter. She was a well-known beauty who was said to keep many lovers. Had Joshua been one? A tightening twisted in her middle like a worm.

"Which is why I was leaving his service," Joshua continued.

Kára looked at him. "Because of Jean?"

"Nay, because Robert is a bloody tyrant," he said. "And I refused to raise my sword against the Orkney inhabitants."

"And yet you left him and his henchmen alive to threaten, steal, and torture us himself," she said and stood, pacing to the bed. "Us, the Orkney inhabitants." She couldn't quite keep the sneer out of her voice.

Joshua turned on his stool, his gaze following her.

"I am not of this land, Kára," he said, his brows low. "I do not wish to become involved with the politics."

"You became involved as soon as you started training his men to become more efficient at subduing or killing us," she said.

He stood, going to her. Clasping her upper arms, he bent to meet her eyes. "I trained his men to protect themselves when set upon. It was easy to see that the inhabitants here are not a true threat, so I did not train them offensively."

She held his stare without blinking. "We *could* be a true threat if we had someone strong to lead us, someone who knows how to win a war against a tyrant."

Joshua exhaled, dropping his arms to cross them over his chest. "Lord Robert is the uncle of James, the king of Scotland. If I kill him, I could bring war to my clan in Scotland."

"Robert is an illegitimate uncle," she countered.

"Legitimate enough for the king's father to have given Robert the earldom of Orkney before he died." He stared into her eyes, his face turning to stone. "Has Robert done something to ye, Kára, something other than take your horse? Because if he has…" Joshua's lips curled back, showing his teeth in a near snarl. "I will rip his ballocks off and choke him with them before cutting him from neck to navel for his guts to roll out."

Her eyes widened at the detailed threat. What could she say? Robert had not raped her, if that was what he asked. But he had harmed her, nonetheless. And then there were his sons.

"Or…" Kára said slowly, "he and his eldest son,

Henry, could disappear in the sea. Without any witnesses, King James would have no reason to suspect you."

"Did either of them do something to ye?" he asked, rooted to the spot, his barely held anger ready to explode into violence. She could lie and incite him to race off to kill Robert and perhaps even Henry and Patrick, maybe even the sheriff that called himself The Brute of Orkney. But without his armies or help from her people, the Stuart soldiers and the bloody Brute would surely kill her last hope for vengeance. One man against a hundred armed soldiers could not win, no matter how well trained he was.

She shook her head, the lie falling easily from her lips. "No."

His frown relaxed, and he slid the bend of his finger along her cheek. "We have been wrapped up together for a night and a day, and I know nothing about ye. And I want to."

"Stay then," she said, pressing closer. "Do not go back to your Scotia."

"It is my home, lass. I have plans to be there for Samhain to honor my father's spirit."

She huffed, and her lips pressed tightly. "Come to my home first. Meet my family," she said. "Someone in Hillside may know how to get you across the firth if Lamont will not take you." She needed more time to convince him to help her. Getting him to stay on Orkney was the first step toward persuading him to fight for them. She interlaced her fingers with his, tugging him toward the bed. "This evening, come to Hillside. Right now, though, are you up for number five?"

He growled low, making her gasp as he caught her around her hips to lift her in the air. He nuzzled against her breasts. She wrapped her hand around his arm over the dark lines that made up the tattooed design of his ancestors on his bicep, the head of a horse and encircling design of the ancient Gaels.

On his back was the symbol for war, a fiery horseshoe with a sword across it. She had memorized every scar and mark on his beautifully chiseled body. He'd held nothing back from her, giving her access to every part of his physical form. Now if she could also seduce his mind and heart to stay. She must. *For my people.*

• • •

Snow spit down from heavy clouds in small squalls as Joshua held Kára before him on Fuil. They had slept and tupped through the night and morning. Kára was certainly not some shy virgin. With little prompting, she had told him exactly what she liked, and he was more than eager to give it to her.

They'd emerged from her den in the late afternoon to ride to her village. Hopefully, he would be able to find a captain willing to shuttle him across the firth, although the thought of sailing away from the intriguing Kára Flett made a sourness creep into his stomach. He'd bedded his share of wild women before, but none had held his attention for more than one night. Kára intrigued him. She was courageous and willing to give boldly. When he looked into her eyes, he saw there was much going on in her mind even if she was unwilling to share it. A woman with secrets? He smiled to himself at the challenge of uncovering every single one. Could he do it in the time before he sailed? Perhaps he would visit Orkney again despite the cold.

Joshua steered them toward one of the many rises that rolled across the treeless isle. Kára had added her flowered quilt to his wool blanket to wrap around them, and their combined body heat underneath the layers made it a cozy nest.

He inhaled along her ear, where the warmth radiated with her spicy floral scent. "I could stay wrapped up with ye through a freezing blizzard and be content."

Under the blanket, her hand slid along his thigh. "I would like that."

As they climbed the incline, three squat stone cottages sat along the coast. Smoke snaked up from center chimney holes through their thatched roofs. "Welcome to Hillside," she said, sitting up straighter so that she didn't lean into him. The distance brought a little chill with it, and he resisted the urge to pull her back. Bloody hell, he'd never wanted a woman so much. Even after sating his lust for her numerous times, he only wanted more. He would have to come back in the spring.

Ahead, several men emerged from the houses, crude pikes and swords and pitchforks in their hands. Kára worked her arm out of the blankets and raised it straight in the air, her hand fisted. Weapons lowered, and more people emerged. How many lived in three medium-sized cottages?

Several dogs ran out of the house, barking wildly. Luckily, Fuil did not shy from dogs. "I see why ye have a den for privacy," he said near her ear and pulled Fuil to a stop. His gaze scanned the frowning people, most of them men with a few women. Several children stood back in the doorways. Their clothes were worn but cared for, and furs wrapped their legs.

"Joshua," she said, turning her face partway toward him so that she would not be heard by the people. "There's a man here who thinks I will wed with him even though I have refused him. There may be a bit of hostility from those who support his suit."

Bloody hell. "Explain."

"*Dróttning* Kára," one older man said, while two other men shooed the barking dogs away. He bowed his head, and the others followed.

"Just Kára, Corey," she called, ignoring Joshua's order.

The old man shook his head. "Erik is presumed dead, and you are the next in line to lead us." His gaze moved past her to Joshua. "Osk told us you would be away for a day, but we did not believe him."

Who was Osk, and how would he know that Kára would be away? But that question was overshadowed by many others. Erik? Was he the man she mentioned? The one who wanted to wed her even though she'd said no?

A woman of mid-age, handsome in face, stepped out of the cottage. Her gaze locked onto him as she strode forward, frowning. "Who is this, and why is he up against your person?" The vehemence in her voice cut sharper than the wind.

Kára kept her voice soft, as she turned her head toward Joshua. "And he has a mother." Her tone held a frustration that was beginning to sprout inside Joshua as well. Hostile was quite accurate. Despite her regal bearing, the woman looked like she might throw a *sgian dubh* at his heart. He'd obviously dealt with aggression in the past. Before coming to Orkney, he'd thrived upon it. But he'd never had to draw on his battle experience to protect himself from a woman nearly two score in years older than him.

I should be halfway to Caithness by now.

Kára let the blankets fall from her body, and the cold immediately dispersed the heat around them, the wind carrying it away. *Bloody damn cold.* Now he remembered. Kára's heat had managed to convince him not to continue his journey home.

"This is Joshua Sinclair, Horseman of War from Scotia," she called out.

"Have you come to kill us?" one man asked.

"Or steal our young women?" the angry mother of the rejected swain called.

"He has come to meet those who call Hillside and Orkney their home," Kára answered.

"Meet? Helping would be better," another woman called from the doorway where a child hid in her skirts.

One of the men spit on the ground, drawing Kára's immediate stare. "And he will be treated as a guest," she said.

"A guest would not lure a bride away from her groom," the first woman said.

"Fiona," Kára said, keeping her voice even but full of authority. "I have told Torben that I am not marrying him. I am a free woman and intend to stay as such."

Fiona rattled something off in their Norn language and traipsed down the hill behind the three cottages. The remaining people all stared at him, judging and frowning. It was exceedingly apparent these people thought he was a seducer of women and a killer. They did not seem the type to lose their minds and attack him outright, bringing them early deaths, but a little intimidation would help remind them not to be foolish.

His familiar scowl formed in the contours of his face: hard, narrowed eyes, full inhales, the edge of his teeth bared through his scowl. Joshua let the rest of the blankets fall off him because it was virtually impossible to frighten someone while wearing a flower-painted quilt. The cold mattered not, as he leaped down from Fuil, his sword strapped to his back. His height and build should deter any attack. He did not want to kill any of Kára's people. *How about the man who will not take no for an answer?*

He turned to help her down, but she'd already dismounted. "This way," she said and caught his arm.

"My horse."

She summoned two lads in her native language, and they ran forward. "They used to handle our horses before they were stolen and have some turnips to lure him to the barn." Kára smiled wryly. "I also reminded the boys not to eat him."

Joshua snorted and patted his gallant bay. He wished he could say that Fuil would not fall for another trick of turnips to get him to move, but his always hungry warhorse would prove him a liar immediately. When they returned home to Girnigoe, resisting temptation and remaining focused were lessons Joshua would be emphasizing with his young bay. Maybe with himself as well.

He followed Kára up the hillside, watching her hips sway naturally. "Your people seem to hate me," he said.

"You do not seem the type to worry over what people think of you," she said, glancing at him before turning to trudge on down the hill behind the cottages. "Once they believe that you do not work for Lord Robert anymore, they will not hate you."

"Ye could have mentioned this suitor before we arrived," he said.

"It did not seem important," she threw over her shoulder, and he took two faster strides to come even with her.

"Aye, it is important," he said, stopping her by clasping her wrist.

She turned to look at him, her eyes narrowing as she studied his face. "Why?"

Because he wanted to tear apart any man that might lay a claim on the wild beauty standing before him, but he bloody hell couldn't say that. "A warrior must always know when he could be seen as the enemy, so he can be on guard against attack."

One side of her lush mouth lifted into a half smile. "I did not think the Horseman of War would worry over a group of women and old men or a simple man whom I had sent off with a refusal."

She was using shame as her weapon. Joshua

knew the tactic of irritating an opponent so that they walked away from what could be an argument. He'd employed it often back home, along with poking at vulnerabilities and plucking at anything a person found uncomfortable. *Mo chreach*. It was a wonder his brothers hadn't locked him up or exiled him for his crimes against their peace.

Joshua met her challenging gaze with narrowed eyes. "Do not keep anything else from me, Kára Flett," he said and watched her smile slip away. A strike of warning shot through him, but she turned away and trudged on before he could pry out any truths. They walked in silence next to each other.

Over the crest, the hill fell away where a series of doors sat cut into the back side. He counted five crude doors. With the size of the hill, there could possibly be ten rooms hidden under the windblown sod. Smoke snaked up from various holes in the hillside, but the wind scattered it so fast that the holes were hardly noticeable unless one inadvertently stepped into one.

Kára waited for him by an open door, tipping her head to get him to follow her inside. Joshua ducked to enter the stone passageway. As in Kára's den, the rocks were fitted tightly together to make walls, held in place by the thick earth packed against them. His head brushed the stone ceiling, and he bent to move quickly down the tunnel. It opened into a good-sized room with a central fire pit that was lit and radiating heat throughout, along with a haze of trapped smoke. Furs sat along a wall beside a stack of pallets. A long table held bowls and baskets in the middle.

"Follow me." Her voice, alluring as the first time

he'd met her, came from an open doorway on the interior wall.

She could be a siren and this a trap, but her bloody spell had already been cast back in her barn the moment she'd lowered her legs onto his shoulders and he'd inhaled her scent. Mind made, he walked directly into what looked to be a bedchamber, half the size of the first earthbound room. Kára stood beside a bonny lass who was quite obviously with child and the lad with the sparse beard from the village. An elderly woman, with her white hair braided and coiled around her head, sat on the bed.

"Horse thief," Joshua said, nodding at the wide-eyed young man, who did not strike him as a suitor for as capable a lass as Kára.

"You brought him *here*?" the lad said to Kára. She answered in their own language, making Joshua frown. Those who spoke purposefully in another language were hiding something. But then he'd already guessed she had secrets.

"Where is Geir?" Kára asked in English.

"Learning with Corey," the man said.

"Corey met us on the hill. Geir was not there."

"He probably stayed inside when you two rode up."

Who was Geir? Not knowing the players in all this…whatever *this* was, put him at a disadvantage. Joshua's instincts prickled. Why exactly had Kára brought him there?

Joshua turned to the elderly woman, bowing his head. "I am Joshua Sinclair from Caithness in the north of mainland Scotland. Thank ye for welcoming me into your home."

The woman's firmly set mouth turned up at the corners, her brow rising. "Robert's Horseman of War has manners."

"I am God's Horseman of War," he corrected.

She stared at his eyes for a long moment and then nodded. "I am Harriett Flett, Kára's grandmother." She pointed to the horse thief. "And Oskar's. He is her brother." *Brother?* Had Kára been helping her brother steal Fuil the other night?

"I am Brenna Muir," the pregnant woman said, slowly lowering into the one chair in the room. "Kára's closest friend." She rested her hands on her stomach and blew upward at a piece of hair that had fallen over her nose. The whole time she stared between Kára and him, her eyes wide with questions.

"Brenna?" a man called from the front room. "The Horseman of—" He stopped when he ran into the room that was now quite tight with all the bodies. "Stay away from her," he said, going over to help the woman out of her seat even though she'd just sat down. He ran a hand over her large middle with obvious familiarity, and she didn't swat his hand away. At least Joshua knew he was not the man who wanted to wed Kára.

"Are you well?" the man asked, passing only a quick glance to her to catch her nod, before continuing to keep Joshua before him. He held a dagger in his other hand.

"I do not slaughter unarmed women, especially those heavy with child," Joshua said, annoyed. They held as many untruths about him as he did about them eating horseflesh. Although he was responsible for their mistrust by encouraging the wild rumors of his warring feats and brutality for the last three months. His intimidation had been honed to perfection over his score and seven years.

Brenna frowned and looked behind her. "There are no women heavy with child here. Just us maidens."

"Maidens?" Joshua looked to Kára who was very much not a shy, innocent virgin and then to Brenna. "Ye are ripe enough for us to worry that a bairn will drop out from your skirts any moment."

She gasped, and Joshua heard Kára's brother snort.

"Maybe your husband should explain this to ye," Joshua said, indicating her protruding belly while meeting the man's gaze.

"Calder is not my husband," Brenna said.

"God may disagree," Harriett Flett said.

Brenna blushed. "It is not God who needs convincing."

Calder tried to hold her hand, but Brenna yanked it away. "I have not been wed, asked to wed, or barely wooed," she said. The woman's face had turned red as she snapped angry eyes toward the slack-jawed man. "Not a peep about wedding me. So I am a free, foolish woman who acted without a care because I drank too much mead." She turned in her seat as much as her middle allowed to point at Joshua. "I could drink some fine whisky and bed him next."

"No," Kára said.

"No," the bairn's obvious father said at the same time.

Joshua looked between Kára and Brenna.

Brenna's brows raised high as she stared back at him, her lips pressed tightly together. She nodded, tipping her chin up and down slowly.

Joshua blinked, turning his gaze to take in the people surrounding him in the room. Even though his instincts bellowed that this was some type of trap, he was not about to draw his sword against an old woman and a pregnant lass who could possibly be mad. His gaze stopped on Kára. "What exactly am I doing here?"

CHAPTER FIVE

*"Victory comes from finding
opportunities in problems."*
Sun Tzu – The Art of War

A blast of cold air funneled past the bedroom door
flap seconds before a man threw it aside to enter.
Tall and broad, he looked like someone who could
be trained into an effective warrior. Light-colored
hair was tied at the back of his head, making him
look as if he could be another of Kára's brothers.

"Kára," the man said, pinning her with a frown
that quickly moved to Joshua. He then rattled off a
question in their Norn language.

"'Tis none of your concern," Kára answered,
crossing her arms over her chest.

"Whitna whalp!" the man yelled, turning his
glare on Joshua before rattling off more in Norn. He
had the obvious look of a wooer who'd been
scorned. This was Torben.

"The lass said it was none of your concern,"
Joshua said, his voice low in warning.

The man met his stare with a sneer. "You are the
enemy."

Osk rubbed his chin, looking between the man
and Joshua. "Perhaps that is something my sister
already knows, Torben." He tipped his head, brows
raised high in a comical frown at the man.

Silent communication seemed to ping about the

cramped room. It was obvious Kára had a mission of her own, one that involved more than carnal bliss. His chest tightened. *I care not.*

The pregnant woman, Brenna, whispered something into her mate's ear. He took two steps to stand in front of Torben. "Come away, friend," he said, clasping the jilted suitor's upper arm to pull him back out the door.

"Leave off!" Torben yanked away to dodge around Calder, going straight toward Joshua.

Brenna squealed and climbed awkwardly onto the bed. The spry elderly woman followed her, throwing out her arms to shield Brenna.

"Torben," Calder yelled, and Osk leaped forward to stand next to Kára. But Torben was going for Joshua. The fool. Joshua kept his stance ready. The man probably had a blade on him, and the space was too small for Joshua to pull his own sword, but he, too, had blades about his body.

Torben came within a foot of him, staring hard into Joshua's face. Although he looked strong, he had no scars that Joshua could see. *Inexperienced young fool.*

"Your services are not needed here, Highlander or Horseman or whatever you bloody call yourself," Torben said, his words seething. *Services?*

Joshua took in all the details of the man, letting his gaze move back up to meet his. Joshua tipped his head slightly to the side, his eyes narrowed. "If my services are to expertly coax moans and screams of pure carnal bliss from that bonny lass over there, I believe I am the only one on Orkney who could do that."

Brenna gasped from the bed, balancing there with both hands over her mouth. Kára made some sort of noise, her hands going to her cheeks.

"You son of a whore!" Torben yelled and lunged, grabbing Joshua's tunic at the neck. With his hands full of linen, it was easy enough for Joshua to send his fist upward into the man's jaw. The surprise made him stumble back, hands going to his face. Joshua took aim and punched him in the nose, sending him sprawling backward where Calder had to jump away to miss being hit by Torben's large body.

Joshua reached down, dragging the man up as he tried to stop the blood pouring from his nose. "The first punch was for my mother, who was a saint," Joshua said, lifting Torben and throwing him out through the door flap to land in the main room. "The second was for Kára, whom ye hunt even though she has refused ye. Find your dignity and move on."

Calder followed Torben out into the main room, helping him up to move toward the door. Joshua turned back to the onlookers. His gaze found Kára where she stood by Osk, hands still on her cheeks. He narrowed his eyes. "Why exactly am I here?"

Did the people in the small room know what was in the lass's mind? "Kára?" he asked. His hands fisted, his muscles contracting as if he knew deep down that the beautiful woman, who had taken him to bed and likely spoiled all other women for him for the rest of his life, had her own mission. And he was part of it. "I become quite dangerous when I feel I have been tricked," he said.

Kára lowered her hands and met Joshua's gaze, her eyes dark in the dim light of several sconces.

Even though it was a small space, the distance in her eyes and stance made her feel much farther away.

He stopped himself from stepping closer, using his control and natural stubbornness to root him to the stone under his boots. "Have I been tricked?" he asked, a fierce warning in the tone of his words.

"No one is holding you here," she answered. "So do not get yourself in a lather." Her hands moved around her as she spoke, but she would not meet his gaze. The old woman and Brenna held onto each other's arms on the bed, and Osk stood like a sentry next to his sister.

"Kára," Joshua said and waited until her eyes settled back on him. "Why did ye ask me to come to Hillside?"

Her hands clenched where they lay against her thighs. "Joshua Sinclair…" Her chin tipped higher, and she stared him directly in his eyes as she inhaled fully. "My people need you. That is why you are here."

His chest clenched. What had last night and this morning been about? Their constant tupping? Laughing together? Clinging together? Learning each other's taste and smell and exploring every inch of each other's bodies?

Kára walked closer and took another large inhale. "Joshua, Horseman of War, I need you to lead my people in war against a tyrant."

Betrayal snaked its way through him, changing the hurt, at finding out Kára's actions had been about using him, into anger. Growing up, hurt always flipped immediately to anger within him. Even as an adult, the change happened in the space of a heartbeat.

He took a step forward, too, meeting her in the middle of the room to look down into her beautiful face that was tight with conviction. He did not touch her. "Kára Flett, *Dróttning*, chief of your people." His eyes narrowed, his face reflecting the twisting of pain that his anger could not suppress. "No."

• • •

Kára stood staring up into the face of fury, a death mask that changed slowly into something worse— indifference.

Without thought, she grabbed his arms, holding him there as if he would turn his back on them and sail home to Scotia that very moment. "You helped Robert's warriors learn how to kill us with ease," she said. "And now you prepare to leave us like lambs to be slaughtered by his band of wolves." Her fingers clamped tighter as if to shake him, which would prove only futile. Who could shake a mountain except God? *God?*

She swallowed. "You call yourself a Horseman of God and yet you will not fight for those who pray continually for His holy help," she said. Her eyes squinted as she held his unblinking stare. "God put you in my path at the tavern, a last chance to take back our isle. How can you say no?"

"God did not seduce me into staying here," he answered. "That was all ye."

She felt the flush, that had flared hot at Joshua's words to Torben, reignite. What would Amma say when they were alone? Would Osk tell her son that she'd slept with Joshua to keep him on Orkney?

As if unable to hold himself apart anymore, Joshua's hand went around Kára's back. She let go of his arms, and he thrust her up against him as if they were once again coming together in wild passion. It knocked the breath from her, her head tipping back to meet his gaze.

He leaned in, looming until they were inches apart, and began to speak. "Ye know very little about me, lass, but I will reveal this to ye. I do not respond well to deception," he said, his words succinct with venom.

Her mouth opened to deny her tricking him. Unfortunately, that was exactly how it had begun, a desperate plan to seduce him into staying, and perhaps to once and for all end Torben's insistence that they wed. And they had recently found out that Erik Flett, Kára's uncle and the chief of the Orkney inhabitants on mainland Orkney, had been captured by Robert's son. If the leadership of the Hillside people fell to her, she'd do anything for a chance to save them. *Even give a stranger your body?* The voice in her head made her cheeks flame hot, but she silenced it with resolute will.

She met his gaze without wavering. "You would have left this morning. Before I could bring you to meet those who will die without you leading them," she whispered, hoping at least Brenna could not hear her. Why hadn't Calder come back for her? Instead, they all stood listening. Damn close quarters. There were no secrets at Hillside.

Her lips pulled back slightly as if she snarled. "Be our teeth to bite back at the wolves. They have taken our people and spilled our blood. Lead us against them. With you, we will finally find victory against the Stuarts."

Kára couldn't read whether her words affected the statue of strength before her. If she didn't feel the heat of his body against hers, she would think he was truly made of rock. Hard, without regret, unmoved by her words. *What will move him?* Her mind whirled. Tears? Doubtful. Threats? Laughable. Passion? She'd tried that, but she hadn't been enough. She almost looked away with her apparent failure, but with a steadying breath, she kept his stare.

"Lead us, Joshua Sinclair," she whispered.

Without any softening, he dropped his arms. "I leave at dawn." He turned, striding past the bed where Brenna and Amma had witnessed the ridiculousness of her attempt to capture such a beast.

Her stomach hollowed in shame, bringing the usual pang of desperation. The familiar nightmare surfaced in her mind like it was yesterday instead of months ago, reminding her of her failure. Pale faces, as if they lay sleeping, among their few possessions in the fur-lined grave. Her mother, father, and older sister.

She looked at Brenna who had lowered down off the bed with the help of her amma. Fear lurked in her friend's eyes. How cruel Kára had been, bringing Joshua to Hillside. His presence had given her people the hope that the Horseman of War might fight for them, and tomorrow they would watch him ride away from them, from her.

"He will not help us," Brenna whispered.

"As if you could trust him," Osk said, a sneer on his face. "He is a selfish bastard."

Anger pushed past the shame Kára felt, and she rounded on him. "He could have easily slaughtered you last night, all of you." She threw her arms wide. "Even Geir, but he showed you fools mercy. There is kindness in him." And generosity. After being wrapped up with Joshua Sinclair, she knew there was much more to him than bloodlust and anger.

Kára looked to Brenna and Amma. Did they condemn her as sinful for trying to lure Joshua with…hell, the best experience she'd ever had in her life? Would Torben tell everyone in Hillside that she'd abandoned her people for a day of lust with the Highlander? Would their disapproval all be for naught if the Horseman of War rode away? "If I can get him to stay, he could give us the edge to stop Robert and his brutal sons."

I leave at dawn. His words mocked her in the silence of the room, as if the people there were repeating them in their own minds, knowing she would fail as their new chief. Kára's hands fisted tightly against her legs as she exhaled slowly, feeling her hope try to leave her on the breath.

With the numbers of her people falling, Robert's power growing, and winter setting in, failure seemed ensured. She took a full breath, meeting the strong gaze of her amma. The wise woman gave Kára a slow nod, the strength behind years of survival in the harsh conditions on Orkney making her as stubborn as the rocks around them.

"There is nothing you can do to stop him, Kára," Brenna said, holding her protruding belly as if she might hide the babe she would not acknowledge aloud.

Bloody hell. Kára reached up, sliding hands over her face to cup the back of her skull. Luring Joshua back to her den had been a risky plan, one of which she had quickly lost control. But… *I got him here*. The Horseman of War had done what she'd asked. If she were going to fail, Kára would do so after trying everything in her power to save her people.

"He is going to leave," Brenna said.

"Not if I have anything to do with it," she said, turning to her grandmother. "Amma, do you have any of the sleeping draught I give Geir when he cannot stop tossing from worry?"

"Aye." Amma rose from her spot on the bed. She smiled. "The lemon flavor goes nicely in honey mead."

"What are you going to do?" Brenna asked, her eyes wide.

"I am keeping him here until I can convince him to kill Robert and his spawn."

. . .

"Bloody foking hell," Joshua roared as he stalked naked around the small stone barn. Opening the door to let in a swirl of snow, he spied the sun through the heavy clouds.

Even though the Orkney sun did not rise high this time of year, he could still see it was near the apex of its climb. He had fallen asleep after eating and drinking what Kára had sent to him the night before. She hadn't brought it herself, making him almost seek her out, but fury still ate at him. Fury at himself for falling for her tricks and at her for being so damn clever and beautiful.

A shiver tore through him, and he slammed the heavy door against the icy breeze and patches of snow tucked into the tall grasses. "'Tis the middle of the bloody day," he said. He had never slept so long before. It wasn't natural. "She poisoned me and took my clothes." He turned in a tight circle. "My furs, my sword, my woolen wrap…and my boots!" he yelled, looking down at his bare feet, toes curling up from the cold ground. He was certain that he'd fallen asleep with them on last night, his tunic as well.

"She *must* have poisoned me," he said low through gritted teeth. The only scrap he had, besides the strip around his arm wound, was the flower-painted quilt she had sent, along with peat and a torch to light a fire inside the barn. He grabbed the blanket off the wool tick that he had slept on next to Fuil and folded it around his waist into a mockery of a pleated wrap. It looked ridiculous, the brightly stitched flowers against his large form.

He had never been deceived by a woman before, or a man, for that matter. His brothers and he had played pranks on one another growing up, but he hadn't anticipated a trick by the lass. He had not anticipated her asking him to lead her people to their deaths in a futile fight, either. *Why the hell else would she have led you to her tupping den?* Was it all a farce to get him to stay on Orkney? Joshua's fist hit a hanging pail, the metallic *twang* loud in the quiet barn. Cracked, it fell to the earth with the force. Was there no limit to Chief Kára

Flett's boldness?

He looked to Fuil who had tossed his head at the explosive sound. "And *ye* let her strip me naked." The bay horse raised his hoof to scrape the stall door. "Damn woman," he said from between clenched teeth.

He pushed through the barn door, and the icy wind of the desolate landscape stole his breath. Why the hell wasn't he back at Girnigoe Castle right now? *Because you let a bonny lass trick you, you arse.*

Stalking, completely naked under the blanket, his damn ballocks pulled up higher than when he had to swim in a frost-edged loch, Joshua strode across toward the hill. The bottoms of his feet burned with cold as he crunched through the thin layer of snow and frost, his fury the only thing heating him. Aunt Merida would scold him for risking illness. He knew that God did not protect him more than other men. 'Twas a legend made by his da, but he would not die from something as piddling as cold, even if he seemed more sensitive to it. Besides, the fire of his anger beat away the attacking wind.

Down the other side of the slope he saw a lad who looked like the one who had grazed him with the thrown dagger outside the tavern. The boy ran into the door of the underground cottage where he'd left Kára standing with her family last night. *She better be in there.* Along with his clothes and Sinclair sword.

He jogged down the slope and stepped through the door. The heat from the central fire washed over him, but what stopped him from moving farther inside was the crowd, the very…short…crowd. All of them sitting across the floor, perfectly quiet and still, except for a few who wiggled in place.

"Joshua Sinclair…" Kára's voice shot toward him from the doorway of the bedchamber. "Meet the children of Hillside."

CHAPTER SIX

"It is the rule in war, if ten times the enemy's strength, surround them; if five times, attack them; if double, be able to divide them; if equal, engage them; if fewer, defend against them; if weaker, be able to avoid them."
Sun Tzu – The Art of War

Joshua swallowed down the curse on his tongue, glaring at Kára. She met his gaze unabashedly and then nodded to one little lass who stared back at her. The child looked to be about five years old. Curls framing her round face, the wee one came forward holding a jar.

"Jam from my *móðir*, my mum," she said, tilting her chin high. He stood still, unsure what to do. With a determined frown, the child shook the jar before him. Joshua forced his fist to relax enough to unfurl his fingers and take the jar. The little girl flashed him a smile and turned, sitting back down among the throng. There must have been twenty children in there, perhaps more.

A lad stood next, serious in face, with a wooden sword strapped to his side. "For your mighty horse," he said, handing Joshua a turnip. "I heard he is fond of them." Joshua nodded and then focused on balancing the vegetable on the top of the jar.

Next stood an older lass with a knitted woolen scarf. She walked toward him, her arms extended. "I made it," she said, giving him a shy smile.

One by one, they rose, each one of them handing something to him in some sort of tribute until a pile of wool, dried flowers, food, and painted stones balanced against his bare chest. He would have lowered them to the ground but was afraid they'd topple and the loosely tied blanket covering his loins would fall.

When the last child sat, Kára crossed her arms over her chest, her feet braced in a battle stance. "I thought you might want to meet the children who will be forced to work on Lord Robert's new palace this spring. Without pay. Without food. Without the ability to say no."

He held all the little gifts in silence. Kára clapped her hands together once, and the children stood as if they'd rehearsed this attack on his conscience. They formed a line to leave, each one stopping before him to curtsy or bow. "Please stay," the little girl who brought the jam said.

"I can help you with your horse," the turnip-gifting lad said.

"I can knit you another plaid in wool," the older girl said, giving a curtsy.

"I think you are the strongest person alive," said a little lass with wide eyes.

"We need you on our side."

"Take us to victory," said a boy who was just shy of being called a man. "I will fight with you." The smattering of freckles over the bridge of his nose brought a hollow twisting to Joshua's stomach.

The boy had no idea of the ghosts he conjured within him. All the children plucked at Joshua's resolve. He looked up at Kára, knowing it had been *her* plan. He frowned, his gaze rising to where she maintained her stance in the bedroom doorway. Her brother, Osk, peeked by her shoulder along with the younger lad who had been waiting outside, apparently on guard to alert them of his coming. Kára did not look smug nor victorious. She looked damned determined.

She whispered into the boy's ear. Who was he, the lad who had kept watch for him and had not tried to sway him with jam and turnips? The boy frowned but strode forward, around the line, and headed back out into the cold.

As the last child exited, Joshua stood there, arms full, meeting Kára's gaze. "Ye use children to sway me." His words were tight, his anger reined in.

She exhaled. "You need to understand what I am fighting for."

It was because of children and the weak, the ones hurt the most by the misery of war, that Joshua had sworn to stop fighting ongoing, constant battles that only wore down each side until one was weaker and surrendered. A war with no winners was brutal and cruel, one he would not fight. And dammit! Kára was asking him to do it again.

"Kára," he said, walking closer, swaying slightly to keep the gifts from tumbling to the stone floor. "We must talk."

"I told you it would not work," her brother, Osk, said, a sneer on his face. "He is too selfish to help even children."

"How is leading children into battle against a royal-backed army helping them?"

"Coward," Osk murmured.

At the same time that Osk chose to risk his life by taunting him, Joshua noticed his stolen boots were on the man's feet. The combination lit the inferno that had been subdued long enough to allow the children's words. Taking the time to crouch low, setting his pile carefully on the floor of the main room, Joshua straightened. Without warning, he plowed forward, grabbing Osk off the floor before he could yelp. Joshua threw him through the doorway into the bedroom and onto the bed, grabbing his foot in one hand as he yanked the laces on the boot.

"What the hell, you *bacraut*!" Osk yelled, his other foot trying to kick Joshua with awkward thrashing that he easily dodged.

"Ye stole my bloody boots," he gritted out. With a yank, the boot came off, obviously too big for the boy. Joshua dropped Osk's stockinged foot and grabbed the other boot, yanking it off. Scooping them up, he strode to the other side of the room to jam his numb toes into his fur-lined boots. The lad had already warmed them up, and Joshua grunted at the relief, quickly donning the second one.

Joshua turned in a circle. "Where is my kilt?"

The pregnant woman, Brenna, stood in the doorway to the room, holding his familiar wrap. "She slept with it last night." She tipped her head toward Kára.

"Brenna," Kára said, the name a snap of rebuke.

Brenna shrugged. "Well, you did," she answered, her eyes wide with feigned innocence.

He looked back at Kára, ignoring her brother

rooting around under the bed, probably for another pair of boots.

"Ye slept with my kilt?"

She didn't answer, turning away, but he held it to his nose where the fragrance of her on the wool confirmed her friend's comment. It shouldn't matter, but somehow it did, and the fact melted some of his anger.

"And my tunic," he demanded, looking at Osk.

Osk held his hands up and then plucked at his shirt. "This is mine."

Brenna shook out his shirt. "Your furs and wool blanket are back in my dwelling where Kára slept." She tossed it to him.

Joshua looked back at Kára. "Ye poisoned me, stripped me naked, and stole my clothes and sword."

Kára met his gaze with strength and conviction. "You said you were leaving at dawn." She shook her head. "I could not let you walk away."

"So ye poisoned me?" he asked, trying to keep his voice lower than a roar.

"It was a sleeping draught that we use here," she answered. "Not poison. A mix of herbs that go well in honey mead."

"A sleeping draught powerful enough to prevent me from waking, as ye pulled my clothes and boots off, is a poison." He jabbed a finger at her. "Never do that to me again."

"Pull your clothes and boots off?" she asked, baiting him, and her brother made a gagging noise from the bed.

With a tug, the flowered quilt unraveled from Joshua's body. He heard Brenna's intake of breath but didn't bother to react. Let her leave if she found his nakedness unnerving. She had obviously seen a naked man before, no matter that she lied about being a maid.

"What the bloody hell?" Her…whatever he was, Calder, yelled from the doorway, but Joshua ignored him, too, as he threw his tunic on over his head.

Torben was close on his heels and followed Calder inside the cramped room. "'Tis not civilized to walk around naked before ladies." His words had a nasal quality, his nose being stuffed with wool. Black circles colored the skin under his eyes, showing that Joshua had broken his nose the day before. "You bloody Scot," he said.

"Those offended should leave," Joshua said, his words low. Was the fool willing to risk more pain? Did he love Kára that much? "And last I checked," Joshua said, "Orkney Isle was part of Scotland." His gaze pierced Torben. "Ye bloody Scot." Hopefully, the idiot heard the warning in his growl, because he had only so much restraint. Joshua let out the long piece of plaid wool, pleating it quickly as he stood to wrap it around his waist, belting it in place.

"Joshua," Kára said, stepping before him, "we have lost our chief, my uncle, Erik Flett, which leaves me in charge of our dwindling numbers. We are persecuted here on Orkney, our home. Anyone with strength is forced to build Robert's palaces. His newest project is at Kirkwall for his son, Henry."

Joshua had known Robert was building another castle, but not that the Orkney people were being forced to work on it. "Without pay?" he asked.

"Of course without pay," Osk said. "And he runs us off lands that we used to hunt on. His soldiers harass our women and capture our men to work, children too. Our healer is still held captive in his damn palace to tend only him, his children, and grandchildren."

"He uses our people and then throws them away," Torben said.

Joshua had never seen a healer or nursemaid at Robert's fortress, but that did not mean she wasn't held above in the nursery down the hall from Jean's bedchamber.

"And we need her back *very* soon," Calder said, his gaze falling pointedly to Brenna, who stood with him in the doorway.

She slapped his arm and frowned. "There are no babes here for you to be glancing at," Brenna said. She crossed her arms to rest on top of her disputed middle. "We hide from Robert's men," she said, "but even when his men do not take our people, cold, poor nutrition, and then disease take many." Her hands slid over her belly.

"The Horseman of War does not care," Torben said. Would the man die if Joshua ripped out his tongue? Would Kára frown upon that or be relieved?

Osk stood with his hands fisted. "Our mother and father and—"

Kára held up her hand, cutting him off. "We have all suffered loss at the hands of Robert Stuart, his sons, and the men who work in his employ." She caught Joshua's arm. "With you leading us, we could break through his tyranny."

"Kill him then?" he asked, trying to comprehend her vision for her people. Joshua understood blind vengeance, had fallen prey to it before, and this request held the stench of it.

"Aye, and free our people from his rule," she said.

He leaned closer. "He is an acknowledged uncle of the king of Scotland, bastard or not. Whoever kills him will be marked as a traitor to the crown."

"It can be done without witnesses," she said in a false whisper that was easy for everyone to hear.

"Aye, but then his son will be in power. Have ye met Henry Stuart?"

Her lips pursed tightly together. "Aye." The one word was filled with bitterness. Joshua knew Robert's eldest son. Strong, entitled, and confident, he acted much like his father. The glint in her eyes spurred more questions, questions he knew she wouldn't answer before everyone.

He crossed his arms over his chest. "Then we quietly kill Henry, and then Robert's second son, Patrick, takes over." He shook his head. "They are all very much like their father. Once word gets to Edinburgh that all the Stuarts are mysteriously disappearing, James will send his army to quell the hostilities he will judge to be here. And King James is not one to side with the common man."

Kára crossed her arms, too. In the blue woolen dress, her long hair partly pulled up on top of her head, she looked like a simple country lass. But the strength in her face, the conviction there, made her a warrior, a warrior who would surrender to nothing except death. The realization that she would rather die than surrender to Robert tightened his gut. "I would speak to Chief Flett without so many ears about," he said.

Kára glanced past him to the door and tipped her head in a silent order. Her brother, still barefoot, came to stand next to her as if he were her guard. "You too, Osk," she said. "And you, Torben. Out."

The Torben arse blocked Joshua and rounded on Kára, grabbing her shoulders to look down into her face. *I'll cut his hands off along with his tongue,* Joshua thought, his teeth clenched.

"Kára, I will not leave you alone—"

"Go," she ordered and stepped out from under his grasp. Torben cut Joshua a glare as he walked around him. Either Joshua was losing his intimidating look, or the idiot had more courage than intelligence.

Kára and Joshua stared at each other as the sounds of others' footsteps on the stone floor of the main room faded, the outer door closing. They stood in heavy silence.

He waited. She was the one asking for his help, arranging this whole trickery to win his agreement, so she should be the one to start. As it was, he didn't know what to say. Arms crossing again under her full breasts, she looked like she was readying for battle. He would rather kiss her, but to tell her that might get him stabbed. And he was angry at her. *Aye, furious.* Why was it so hard to hold on to that? Back home he was known for his bad temper and had been compared to his warring father.

Her lips opened, and for a moment nothing came out. She dropped her arms. "What do I say?" She shook her head. "You know firsthand of what

Robert and his sons, The Brute, and all their men are capable. You trained them."

Remorse made Joshua's jaw ache, but he kept his silence. He'd already explained that he taught them only defensive measures and common-sense strategies to fortify their palace. Although there was often a fine line between defense and offense.

"My people have been here on Orkney since it was ruled by Norway," she said. "In fact, we are more of that country than of your Scotia, Highlander."

"Ye are not the first people to be subdued by conquerors," he said. She needed to understand truths without the affliction of emotion. "Being persecuted and run off one's land has been happening since the beginning of time, Kára. History is full of unfair and murderous conquest." Damn him. He'd certainly participated and won many of those back home. Sinclairs were slowly taking over the northern territory of Scotland.

She took a step closer. "You have never been on the side of the conquered, have you?"

He breathed in through his nose. Had she heard of the disaster on South Ronaldsay down at the southern tip of Orkney? Heard how the Horseman of War had led common people to a slaughter?

"I have, and I have no intention of repeating it." It was why he had begun reading his small translation of *The Art of War* again. It gave clear instructions on when *not* to fight. Instructions he had been too arrogant to follow, and those who had trusted him had paid the price.

"Have you witnessed the horrors of watching

your family thrown from their home, falling onto the frozen ground, or your horses stolen before your eyes by smiling bandits who say that they are more worthy of your mount than you?" Her eyes narrowed. "Mighty Horseman of War…have you been told you cannot find food to stay alive because it has hopped onto someone else's land? That you must starve and hope the animal comes back to your little square of turf?"

How could he make her understand? "In my experience, of which I have much—"

"Which, I am thinking, does not include living in the aftermath of losing a war," she said.

"In my *vast* experience in war," he continued, "I have learned that to fight endlessly against a bigger army leads only to more and more death and misery for the smaller. Surrender is the best option for the masses when the alternative is complete extinction. Either learning to work within the new system, or moving to a new location to start anew, saves lives and can bring a sense of peace back to your people." He reached forward, resting his hands on her straight shoulders. He dropped them when he realized he was reenacting what Torben had done, but he remained close, looking down into her face.

"Be the chief of your people, Kára," he said, his voice low. "Lead them to a better life away from this misery. Your family can come join ours on the mainland. Become part of the Sinclair clan." The thought had been growing in his mind, ever since that first tug inside at the thought of sailing away from Kára.

"And leave Orkney behind?"

A slight smile relaxed across his mouth. "We have trees."

But she did not smile back or soften. "The truth," she said, "is that you do not wish to help us, because you may lose."

His eyes closed for a moment as frustration burned inside him. Joshua inhaled, meeting Kára's steely gaze. "If we fight Robert, we *will* lose, your people will lose, and you will lead them to their deaths."

"Is dying for something that is right and just better than living under tyranny?"

"That is a question for each person to decide on their own," he said. "And again, ye can come to northern Scotland, to Caithness. Your people could blend in with ours. Ye could have many horses." He knew his brother, Cain, who was the chief of the Sinclairs and conquered Mackays, would take her people in.

She turned away. "Bribery does not sway me."

Joshua's hands fisted at his sides. "How about common sense? Does common sense sway ye at all, or are ye as blind as priests standing before the doors of their churches when soldiers come to burn them down, praying God will deliver them and strike down their foes?"

She turned back to him. "You are the foking Horseman of War from God, are you not? If you fight for us, train us, lead us, we may win."

"If God refuses to interfere even with his priests praying for earthly salvation, He is not going to send lightning bolts down to strike Robert Stuart, his sheriff, and his sons."

She jabbed him in the chest over his heart. "You are the lightning bolt, Joshua. You strike them down, and my people will handle the rest."

Joshua's hands went to his face, sliding down. "Kára…" Her name trailed off, because honestly he did not know what to say. She was so determined that she wasn't letting his words or logic sink in. "Have ye ever read *The Art of War*? 'Tis a book from China, translated into French."

Her brows drew together in angry confusion, as if he'd just asked her if she would like to go on holiday to visit the queen of England. Her mouth opened and then snapped shut.

The front door of the underground cottage opened, and Calder barreled into the back room, out of breath. Kára's hand went to the six-inch dagger she had at her side as if she were used to having to draw it. She'd grown up in war, but then so had he. But she'd grown up on the weaker side. He had never really known those on the weaker side until he'd come to Orkney.

"'Tis Brenna," Calder said. "Her waters… She is soaked. She needs a healer. Now."

"I told ye she was about to drop a bairn from between her—"

"I will be right there," Kára said. "Get her into bed and send my amma to be with her."

He nodded and shot back out. Kára ran for a set of shelves to grab some linens. "I must go help," she said.

"Aye. Her bairn is—"

"We do not mention it," Kára said. "'Tis superstition, but with death hunting our people, we do nothing to bring the wrath of the fae or trolls or whatever Brenna might believe in."

"So ye cannot mention the bairn?"

She shook her head. "Not until it is born and healthy, and then it is guarded for days before anyone can see it." She grabbed up two smocks, shoving them into a bag with some jars.

"There is food in the main room," she said. He pulled back the question about it being tainted with more sleeping poison.

She stopped her frantic packing, meeting his gaze. "Will you leave then? Now that you have your clothing?"

"Ye still have my sword."

"Aye, I do," she said. "Although, I am sure ye have more in your castle with hundreds of horses about," she said, slanting her northern accent more toward his own.

"We are not done talking," he said, frowning over her notion of how he lived. "And it is my favorite sword." He also wasn't ready to abandon her yet. Maybe he could still talk some sense into her and her people.

"I may be gone for days if things are difficult," she said. She shifted, and the jars knocked softly in the satchel when she lifted it over her shoulder.

He caught her chin, letting her see the truth in his eyes. "I will be here," he said, giving up the idea of making it home in time for Samhain. "I have decided that I want ye to live."

Her brows rose with hope, and he shook his head. "By making ye see reason why ye cannot attack Robert Stuart."

She huffed, gave him one last piercing gaze, and dodged around him. Joshua turned in time to see her disappear, the flap of the animal skin door slapping back into place.

CHAPTER SEVEN

"Rapidity is the essence of war: take advantage of the enemy's unreadiness, make your way by unexpected routes, and attack unguarded spots."
Sun Tzu – The Art of War

The sun had dropped below the horizon by the time Joshua stepped out of the underground house. As winter came, the sun would sit lower and lower in the sky until it was up for only five hours a day.

A breeze lifted his kilt. *What the bloody hell am I doing here?* He knew the answer even if he did not want to admit it. Kára was like no other woman he'd ever met. She was fiercely determined to succeed. In different circumstances, and with a larger army, she could be another Boudica trying to take back Britain from the Roman Empire. But she didn't have a powerful army or even enough Orkney inhabitants to raise one. If she stayed on the isle, she would likely die, if not by a soldier's hand in battle, then by the noose after she was declared a traitor to Scotland. The thought twisted inside his gut. Even though her quarrel was justified, she couldn't win this game against the royal uncle of the king.

Walking up the hillside that acted as a hiding place and roof for however many dwellings were underneath, Joshua stopped to watch the islanders. Two men stood near Fuil while a small group of children fed his mount handfuls of wild grasses and stroked his face. Fuil, for all his war training and viciousness on the battlefield, stood patiently, lowering his head for them to scratch behind his ears.

Two women and Torben's frowning mother hurried past him to disappear inside the hill, probably to help with the birth that no one could talk about. Kára's brother, Osk, and a second man patted Calder on his back, talking to him. Joshua was glad to see Torben had vanished. The man was foolish and brazen enough to get himself pummeled, and Joshua did not need to gain more censure from these people.

A small pack of deerhounds rolled around, and several men walked up from the shoreline carrying gutted sea trout on lines. These were peaceful people, not the raiders and vicious thieves that Lord Robert described them to be. They had no wealth, and barely enough on which to survive.

A boy stalked up to Fuil and the other children, waving his hands, and the children backed off from the horse. It was the boy he'd spared in the village who had stood silently beside Kára as she used the children of Hillside to sway him. Fuil had been defending himself then, so the lad knew how dangerous his warhorse could be. Joshua pulled one of his daggers out from where he'd replaced it in his boot and strode down the hill toward him.

The boy turned around, his eyes going wide. Either he was brave or he didn't want to act the coward before his people, which were both appropriate reasons for not running away. "My horse will not harm them," Joshua said.

"Does his name not mean blood in Gaelic?" the boy asked, tipping up his chin defiantly. The children stared wide-eyed between him and the horse.

"Aye, but he was named so for his red coat, lad."

"I am almost a man, not a lad," the boy said, making Joshua grin. Despite the poor throw, the boy reminded him of himself when he was young. He also reminded Joshua of another boy, one that haunted his nightmares, and his smile faded.

Joshua waved the boy closer, and the other children went back to Fuil. Joshua lowered his voice. "If ye are a man, then ye must learn to throw like a man," he said. To stand with any type of chance at not being slaughtered by Robert's men, the boy needed to know how to throw accurately. Joshua flipped his dagger in the air to land handle outward.

The boy frowned. "My concentration was off from all that was going on. Your wild horse and you knocking everyone to the ground."

"That is when your aim must be at its best," Joshua said. "When the world is crashing down around ye." He stepped closer to him, trying not to notice the few freckles that lay across his nose like young Adam from South Ronaldsay.

Joshua glanced upward, watching a small flock of birds stretching out in flight over the water. "When I was a lad, my da would yell and throw his arms up, jumping like a jester all around me while I threw daggers at a target. It taught me how to focus."

The boy crossed his arms over his chest, tipping his head to study Joshua. "I thought you were the Horseman of War, sent from God, already a man."

Joshua chuckled. "I like my enemies to think

that, but nay, I was born a wee bairn and grew," he said, indicating his size, "with lots of training and hard work." He thrust the handle of the dagger toward him. "Do ye want to learn my technique for throwing?"

The boy shrugged, but his gaze latched onto Joshua's *sgian dubh*, and he took it.

"Show me where we can throw that we will not skewer anyone," Joshua said. "But first I should tie my horse away."

The boy shrugged as he studied the dagger. "You have the pick of the best stalls in the barn, since Robert the Bastard stole all of ours."

Joshua was raised to respect and love horses more than people. Giants of spirit, as well as strength, horses represented the Sinclair Clan well. Anger simmered within him at the thought of someone stealing Fuil, the anger that nearly cost this lad his life the other night.

Joshua clicked to his faithful mount and rubbed a hand down his neck before leading him next to the boy. The children called their goodbyes to his beast and ran off to the cottages, the two men following them as if eager to leave Joshua behind. The barn was empty like that morning, and Joshua returned Fuil to the large stall that they had shared overnight. Joshua made certain there were oats and fresh hay, as well as unfettered water, in the stall. "I am Joshua," he said. "What is your name?"

"Geir Flett, son of Geir Spence of Birsay and Hillside, grandson of King Zaire."

"King? The king I know is James. Are ye related to King Frederick or King Christian of Norway?"

The king of Norway had recently died, and his eldest son, Christian, had taken over, even though he was only a lad of eleven. Since Kára's family had been occupying Orkney for generations, they could not be of Norwegian royal blood unless it was from long ago, with the line having been abandoned to Scotland.

Geir narrowed his eyes. "You know a lot about Norway."

"I know a lot about a lot of things," he answered. Even though his father had spent most of his waking hours training his sons in war, leadership, and conquest, he had hired a tutor for his children. An ignorant man was as weak as a child.

"Like war and battle?" Geir asked, looking at him sideways with one eye squinted.

"Aye," Joshua answered. "Among other things."

Geir held his palm up to Fuil, who sniffed it. If there was a chance of another treat, his mighty warhorse was willing to forgive Geir's involvement the other night.

Joshua studied the lad. He would be taller than most when he aged. He had the slender look of several of the Hillside men on the hill. His hair was a light brown, shorn short, and his nose was straight, his jaw well formed. "So are ye all related to some long-ago king of Norway?" Joshua asked.

They walked out of the barn together. "I do not know. The elders say so." He shrugged. "Since we are ruled by Scotia, my grandfather was only our chief, but we called him *konungr* or king, like my mother is now *dróttning*, the queen. But she wants only to be called chief like Chief Erik."

Joshua's steps stilled, the boy taking several forward before stopping to look back at him. There was a resemblance. Angular features and large eyes, although his coloring was darker. "Kára Flett is your mother?" Joshua said.

"Aye."

"Where is your father?" He held his inhale.

"Dead when I was not yet born. Struck down by Henry Stuart."

Joshua exhaled. Was that the source of the edge to Kára when he'd asked if she knew Robert's son? Had she loved her husband? The boy looked to be about nine or ten years old, so it had been some time. But did the loss still pain her? Make her seek revenge even at the cost of her people? His own father had taken the pain of losing his wife out on every enemy until he was killed.

"'Tis why I will kill him some day," Geir said, his face deadly serious.

Joshua's hand wiped over his mouth to rub his chin. *Lord help them.* Vengeance lay thick in Hillside from years of loss and abuse. Joshua began to walk with Geir again toward a roll of hay in a field. He dropped his arms. "Well then, son of the *dróttning* or chief," Joshua said, "I will teach ye how to throw a *sgian dubh* so that next time ye throw, ye do more than graze your opponent."

• • •

"I cannot," Brenna wailed, sinking back as the contraction ebbed.

"Aye. You. Can." Kára wiped a damp cloth over

Brenna's sweaty forehead, her stomach twisting with worry. The babe was not coming as it should.

Brenna rolled her head side to side on the pillows that propped her into a sitting position, her knees bent with a sheet over them. Amma lifted her face from where she'd checked her progress to meet Kára's questioning gaze. The worry in the wise woman's eyes cut like the sharpest of knives through Kára. Her breath stopped until Brenna began to pant again like she had for the last day. Wave after wave of pain had been robbing her of strength, and still the babe had not come.

Kára called Fiona over to hold Brenna through the pain while she beckoned Amma to the corner with her. "What is wrong?"

Amma shook her head. "The babe may be coming feet first. I am not as talented with birthing as Hilda." Kára's great-aunt, her amma's sister, was a renowned healer and midwife on Orkney. Because of that, Lord Robert had taken her to tend his own wife, mistresses, and children, nine legitimate and numerous bastards. Instead of hiring Hilda and sending for her when needed, he stole her away from her family to keep her at his palace. She'd been a prisoner there since spring when Robert and Henry had burned the small village on the bay, killing those Kára loved.

The worry gnawing inside Kára would turn her useless. It wouldn't abate, not with prayers or tears. The restlessness beat within her, this absolute need to help her best friend survive.

"I will bring Hilda," Kára said.

Amma caught her arm before she could turn

away. "No good will come of you being captured by Robert. And his son—"

"Will feel my blade between his ribs if he tries to touch me again." Kára shook her head. "Nothing will stop me from finding help for Brenna." She looked over at her straining friend. "We know there is a back way in and out of the palace," Kára said. "I will find it if it is my only way in." Although that might require a swim in the icy sea to reach the side facing it.

"Erik said it was too dangerous to go anywhere near the palace," Amma said.

"Erik's capture proves it is too dangerous everywhere, but I cannot sit here," she lowered her voice, "and watch her die." Behind Amma, Brenna panted. "I will bring Hilda," Kára said. Torben's mother, Fiona, and the two other helpers turned wide eyes toward her.

"'Tis foolish," Fiona said, her words coming like a hiss. "You would leave Osk in charge of our people? If you had wed Torben, he could lead us."

Kára ignored her and ran to Brenna, forcing a reassuring smile on her face. "We will make sure this little one knows how hard you worked to bring him into the world."

Desperation and exhaustion pinched her friend's face. It was the fear she saw in her beautiful wide eyes that caught at Kára's breath. "I will bring Hilda," Kára said. "She will coax that little one out." She nodded, and Brenna followed her example. "You rest and listen to Amma while I run out to fetch her."

Brenna clasped her hand, staring up at her with

trusting eyes. "Kára. Thank you."

Kára smiled again, kissing her forehead. She turned and strode out of the buried bedchamber. Calder sat in the main room and leaped up when she strode by. "Brenna?" he asked.

The worried tightness of Kára's face drained the color from his. "I am going to get Hilda from the palace," Kára said.

"I will go with you."

She shook her head. "You need to be here with Brenna. If… If Amma calls you, go hold her through whatever comes."

He swallowed hard, as if his throat was too tight to allow it, and nodded. Kára ran out the door, her legs slapping against her heavy skirts. She must change into her hunting clothes for sneaking into and out of Robert's palace. She ducked into her home, the banked fire low with the lateness of the evening. Her brother and son were certainly sleeping in one of the back rooms, and she held her breath as she entered the bedchamber she had been using. *Has he left?*

The darkness made her blind, and she ran back into the front room to light a torch, sliding it into a sconce carved from the stone lining her old chamber. She turned toward the bed where a mountain of blankets and furs moved. She released her breath. Joshua's head shot up from what looked like every blanket and fur that they had in the house. Hair askew, he leaped out of bed, raising a short sword, completely naked. The blade looked too small for his mountainous form.

"Kára?"

"Go back to sleep," she said, yanking her tight-fitting trousers and wool tunic from a chest at the end of the bed.

He lowered his sword. "Is the bairn born?"

"No."

"What are ye doing?"

"I need to get the healer to help Brenna or she will die."

"*Cac*," he whispered. "Where is the healer? I will take ye."

"No. She is my aunt, and she is a prisoner at the Earl's Palace."

"Fok, Kára," he said. "I am absolutely taking ye."

She turned, indicating his brawny, naked body. "First of all, you are not dressed."

He mimicked her gesture. "And ye are quickly becoming undressed." He grabbed his own tunic, throwing it over his head as Kára wrapped her breasts and yanked on her trousers.

"Two," she said, snapping her tunic out before her to throw on over her head, "Brenna is my best friend. I am the one who must go to find someone to save her."

"The fact that ye are emotional about this makes it even more important for me to come." He caught his pleated kilt with his belt and shoved his feet into his boots at the same time Kára did. They worked nearly in unison across from each other in the dim light, shoving and yanking clothing into place.

She threw her hood up over her head, grabbed the torch, and turned to run back out the door. Of course, he followed.

"Thirdly," he said behind her, "I have a horse to

get us there swiftly. Fourthly, I know the guards and could get us inside easier."

"I know of a back passageway," she threw over her shoulder, but she found herself running toward the barn where the only horse they had was standing, Joshua's warhorse.

"The back passage is locked and guarded by the ocean if the tide is high."

Shite. Is it high tide?

He caught her free arm, pulling her around. "And fifthly," he said, stepping in to her, "I am not letting ye sacrifice yourself for Brenna."

She stared into his hard face, as hard as the stones that held Orkney out of the sea. "She is one of my people," she said. "A leader makes sacrifices for her people."

"Not before I teach ye how to battle first."

Her eyes opened the slightest amount. "Are you agreeing to—?"

"To keep you alive tonight," he said, still without committing to help them in a full war on Robert Stuart. Face hard, he stared into her eyes. "I am not ready to see ye dead."

• • •

"She is likely housed with the children," Joshua said as they squatted below the hill line that led down to the south side of the Earl's Palace, his horse farther back. "They are housed on the east side of the castle."

"I agree, from what our source has said," Kára answered. "But Robert's room is three doors down."

He could tell without looking that her beautiful features were tight with a mix of worry and determination. "We could use the back passageway. I think the tide is going out."

"If Robert followed my advice, a guard will be there when the tide recedes." As an advisor on safety, Joshua had implemented a rigid guard routine to better protect the palace from local bandits. Guilt tugged at him. *Mo chreach.*

The enemy had always been so clear back at Girnigoe—anyone who threatened the Sinclairs. His father had taught him that the more powerful must always be in control, the conqueror, to bring peace to everyone and protect them from others.

"Ye stay here," Joshua said. "I will bring her out."

She frowned at him. "You will just ride up there, hop off, stride in and walk out with her to ride away?" She shrugged. "With no issue?"

"I have spent the last three months training these men. They know me, and I set their routines." He looked back toward the dark castle behind the half-built wall he had suggested for better defense. "There are two men awake through the night inside the fortress where they spy through the small musket holes for any movement in the bailey. Since they do not think of ye as much of a threat right now, there will be only two guards walking the half-built outer wall, on the inside, glancing through built-in holes." He pointed toward the guard house. "Two men will be sitting up there with muskets, but they'll know me when I ride up."

She grabbed his arm. "Ride with me hidden behind you with a drape over me. I will press up close against you, and they will see only a blanket draped."

He frowned. "Ye are not going to stay here, are ye?"

"No."

If he left her there, she would probably sneak around the shoreline, encountering frigid water and an armed guard. If he brought her with him into the palace, he could have her stand guard over Fuil in the stable outside the keep.

"Ye may come if ye listen to me," he said, his voice gruff.

In the diffused light from the cloud-covered moon, he saw her smirk. "I will listen to you because you have knowledge that will help me free Hilda as quickly as possible, not so I can gain permission to go with you."

He sighed heavily and looked back over the top of the hillside where tall grass hid them. "Ye are armed?"

"Three blades on me."

"I will have to make do with two, since my sword was stolen earlier," he grumbled.

She didn't say anything as they strode back to Fuil. He mounted first and then helped lift her to sit behind him. Would Robert's men think it odd he had a blanket around his shoulders when he usually rode shirtless despite the cold?

Sliding her arms around his middle, Kára flattened her body against his back. Even her legs pressed along the backs of his thighs and calves. Body heat penetrated his tunic immediately, her enticing scent burrowing into him with each inhale.

Memories of their naked bodies sliding against each other made his blood surge. *Find the healer. In and out of the palace. Quick, silent, relaxed. Focus!*

Twisting, he threw his heavy wool cloak around his back to cover them both. Kára's fingers grazed his neck as she lifted it over her head to tuck it there. Her grip around his middle was strong as she drew as close as possible, her legs spread wide around his hips. He almost groaned with the feel of her straddling him, the crux of her heat pressed against his arse.

With a slight tap, Fuil started off across the moor leading to the palace gate. Arriving, he raised one arm up, fist tight, into the air, the signal that he was a friend and not to shoot. He recognized the man holding a torch up high. "Tuck," Joshua called. "I am coming in."

"Joshua Sinclair? What are ye bloody doing back here? I thought ye were on your way back to true Scotland."

"I killed the boat captain when he tried to steal my horse. 'Tis very inconvenient." Joshua felt Kára stiffen at his callousness. Hopefully, she knew he was putting on an act. *Like I have my whole life.* The dangerous thought thinned and disappeared as Joshua squashed it down inside with the other things that made him weak. Things like remorse and the faces of those he'd failed.

"'Tis not there another ship?" Tuck asked.

"Aye, on the morrow, but I tire of sleeping with my horse in the village. Is Jean within?"

Tuck grinned down at him. "Aye, she is likely abed. I cannot say if she is alone or not."

"She will kick another out of her bed if she knows I am here." Conceit was an easy role to play. Kára didn't move behind him, but it felt like she might be pressing harder forward along his legs.

Tuck laughed, drawing the attention of the second man in the tower. Joshua nodded to Liam. "Come along inside then," Tuck said. There was a portcullis, but since the wall was not completed, there was no need to close it for the night. Joshua kept as close to the shadows as he could and rode under the pointy maw into the bailey where the earl's barn of horses sat off to the left next to hay and peat stacks, some under eaves, but most out in the open. Several men would be sleeping inside the barn, warriors who would rouse for their turn in the night watch. "Stay silent," he whispered over his shoulder.

Fuil clopped into the barn. One man jumped up. "Who is it?" he called out.

"Stand down, Alec," Joshua said. "I am bringing Fuil in for a bit while I retrieve something I forgot here."

"Something important enough to come all the way back?" he asked, sleep in his voice. Joshua could see him wiping a hand down his face.

"My sword."

"It was sitting straight down your back when ye rode out," Alec said, suspicion lacing his words. Och, but Joshua didn't want to kill the man. They hadn't spent time together, since Alec devoted most of his free time finding lasses to bed in the village north of the palace where the families of Robert's men lived.

"My short sword. I left it with Jean. I will be gone

by morning, less than an hour if she is entertaining someone else."

Alec rubbed his chin. "There is a stall open next to Lady Jean's horse."

Jean's horse? Joshua willed Kára to remain still as he pressed Fuil to walk down the long aisle. He couldn't dismount in the light of Alec's torch or he would see Kára. Coming to the end, he halted Fuil in the corner full of shadows and twisted, grabbing Kára around the waist. His eyes remained on Alec while Joshua dismounted, holding Kára against him. Alec settled back into a clump of hay near the sliding doors. Two other men tossed and snored across from him. Kára kept behind Joshua under the cape as he walked Fuil into the stall, looping the reins on a hook so he would be ready to ride as soon as he came back out, hopefully with her aunt, Hilda. Kára crouched, sliding out from the cape.

A small noise escaped her. She stood in the back corner where a low wall, which needed mending, showed the stall next to them, the stall with Jean's horse, which wasn't her horse at all. Broch, the bay horse with the white spot around one of her eyes, turned to look at Kára, moving her bulk toward her. The unique mare tossed her head, her nose sniffing in the darkness. Joshua had never seen a horse with such a marking, and he'd seen hundreds of horses.

Without a sound, Kára slid her arms around the horse's neck as Broch rested her head seemingly over her shoulder, the two of them comforting each other in silent communication. Bloody hell, he was going to be rescuing a healer and a horse that night. How was he to do so without raising Robert's army to chase them back to the Flett homestead?

For the first time since coming to Orkney, Joshua wished his older brother, Cain, was there. Horseman of Conquest, Cain had been raised to build effective plans in a very short amount of time. His guidance here would guarantee success. At least tonight. Success in conquering a battalion of trained warriors with a group of locals was not possible even if Kára couldn't surrender her need for revenge.

Joshua walked over to Kára, her horse raising its head to peer at him. His mouth moved close to Kára's ear. "Saddle your horse as quietly as ye can while I am inside the fortress. If anyone sees ye, ride her to town for your tavern friend to keep, and I will meet ye in our den."

Round eyes met his, and she nodded, but lifted on tiptoe to whisper at his ear. "Do not leave here without Hilda." He nodded, and reluctantly pulled away from her to walk down the aisle.

CHAPTER EIGHT

*"To know your Enemy, you must
become your Enemy."*
Sun Tzu – The Art of War

"All well?" Alec asked from his pallet in the corner near the door.

"I may be making a quick trip back out if Jean will not take me in."

"Ye can sleep in the great hall if she won't have ye. There are extra pallets stacked in the corner."

Joshua strode to the fortress Robert had named the Earl's Palace. It was an odd name considering the walls looking out at the bailey on the first floor had musket holes cut into the walls instead of proper windows. Palace? Despite its lavash furnishings and frescos, it was a bloody fortress. The bedchambers and great hall sat on the second floor with proper windows paned with glass. The whole structure, made of local stone, was situated around a square courtyard and freshwater well in the middle. Towers soared upward from three of the four corners where more people could be housed, mostly Robert's many children who still lived with him. Henry, who would move into his own palace on the east coast of Mainland Orkney, also lived there. Dishington, or The Brute as he called himself, had been given quarters, like Joshua, in one of the towers.

Stepping into the dark entryway, he nodded to two guards who did not question his presence. He had worked with them for three months, gaining their loyalty on the training field as well as off. Killing them would be a burden after befriending many. Did they know the fate of the bandits from whom they stole? Did they know Robert had taken land, horses, and the strongest of Kára's men to build his palaces under cruel conditions? Did the men care? He had trained the strongest to be stronger so they could subdue any threat with minimal casualties. But if he had known Kára then, known she would never be subdued, would he have continued to train them? Nay. He did not need the coin. He would have moved on. But if he had, Kára's people would have little chance to survive against Robert.

Several men, sleeping around the perimeter of the lower level garrison, snored. One of them moved from musket hole to musket hole, watching. The guard, Connor, nodded to him, obviously having seen him questioned and allowed to enter the gate. Would he question Joshua when he led the healer out?

Joshua climbed the stairs quietly, with the casual air of a rogue seeking a willing woman. Her father did not really care, as long as she didn't become pregnant, something Joshua had guarded against. As he walked past Robert's door, he heard the headboard ramming against the wall. Robert was obviously tupping, mistress or wife. The next door was Jean's, but he slipped past it. Two more doors down, he stopped to listen. The faint sound of a fussing bairn came through the door. *The nursery.*

"Joshua?" Jean's stunned whisper made him pivot. She stood outside her door, wrapped in a white cloak. "You came back?" She lowered the hood, her brows furrowing. "Why are you at the nursery door?"

A story grew in his mind, even as his lips began to move. He smiled. "I thought I heard ye behind this door, but it must have been one of your wee sisters."

She wrinkled her nose. "One of them is always whining about some pain or ache in the head."

He walked to her. Even in the dimness of the hallway, he could see her lips were red with rouge, and he smelled the heavy perfume scent she favored. "Ye are on your way out?" he said, his fingers touching the edge of the royal-looking cape. It would be the perfect garment to hide Hilda under. He met her gaze. "To meet a lover."

Her bottom lip stuck out. "Because you left. You did not expect me to pine away for you, did you?" She came closer to him, sliding one flattened hand up his chest to curve over his shoulder. "But, since you are here…"

The artificial scent itched his nose and made him want to put distance between them, but he remained, letting her pet him. Kára did not wear the cloying scents that Jean and her sisters wore. Nay. Kára smelled of wild, fresh wind and the slightest bit of flowers and spice from her soap.

Jean leaned up on her toes, pressing her unstayed breasts against him, and drew his mouth down to hers. "Who are ye meeting?" he asked before she could kiss him. He clasped her hands behind his head, pulling them around to rest between them.

"That is none of your concern," she said tartly.

He caught her forearms as she pulled away. "Jean, lass, ye should guard well your person. Not every lad is as honorable as I, or as kind."

She yanked her arm away. "Kind enough to leave me? You are not one to talk of honor and kindness."

"I told ye I had to return to my brothers."

"And yet you are back here? Why?" Her hands settled on the slender set of hips he had known quite well during his stay at the palace.

He could lie and tell her he came for one more kiss from her, that he couldn't get her out of his mind, that he craved to bed her again. All lies. "I came to retrieve something."

"Something you forgot?"

He didn't answer her. "Jean, do not fall for the lies of rough men. Ye should guard yourself for someone who cares for your heart and mind, not just your body."

With a wicked grin, she pulled the ribbon tied at her throat, letting the cape drop to the floor outside her room. She was naked underneath, except for tiny slippers. *Fok.* All he needed was for her father to step out into the hall and see this. Pulling her close, Joshua pushed her backward into her room, shutting them inside.

Her arms went immediately around his neck again, her painted lips sliding against his, and her hand slipped under his kilt to grab his jack. Was she shocked he wasn't hard? Had she ever felt him so? Nay. But nothing about Jean Stuart enticed him now.

"Jean," he said against her mouth, and she trailed her lips down his neck as she stroked him, his jack blindly coming half to life.

His hand caught hers, pulling her out from under his kilt. "I cannot relax thinking some other man might come up here looking for ye," he said as an excuse. "And…" He pulled her back from him to look into her heavily lidded eyes. "Jean, lass, I am leaving Orkney. I just came back to retrieve something."

"Stay the night," she whispered, giving him a saucy grin.

He exhaled, running a hand down the stubble on his jawline. "I know your father has ignored ye for much of your life, lass, but ye do not need to use your body to lure men to ye." He touched her cheek. "Ye are clever and a good person when ye want to be. Find a clever, good man to love."

Her face pinched tight as her round eyes squinted into a glare. "Says the man who spent night after night happily making love to this body."

Ballocks. He certainly didn't need to make her mad enough to wake the castle, not when the mission to extract Hilda must succeed to save Brenna and her bairn. He forced a casual smile and leaned in to kiss her gently. "Ye are very right, lass. Ye are clever, kind, and luscious."

His words brought the smile back to her lips, and she tugged him toward her large bed. But he had no intention of falling into it. Not only had his desire for Robert's daughter died, but he also felt sad for her and wouldn't lead her into thinking he cared for her by tupping her again, even if he didn't have a mission and a pale-haired angel of a lass waiting for him in the barn. He'd always been straightforward with the lasses he bedded. They knew he had never been loyal to only one woman before.

He broke the kiss as she tumbled back onto her velvet coverlet. "Lass, I need to find what I forgot, and I would send the man ye were to meet away."

She pouted, pulling the blanket over her loins. "Very well. Send John away and come back up for the night. You can leave before my father wakes and tries to entice you to stay."

"John Dishington?" The Brute?

She twirled a finger around her nipple. "He is as energetic as you."

"Jean, he is dangerous."

"So are you, my Horseman of War."

Damn. The woman had no proper upbringing, not that he had, either. But there was no time to spend trying to convince her to be more selective in her choices. He had to find the healer.

"Stay here," he said, and she stretched out like a cat in the sun. He exited into the hallway, grabbed up her abandoned cloak, and went directly to the nursery door. Stepping inside, he closed it behind him as silently as possible. An old woman rose into a sitting position on her small bed. Joshua laid his finger over his lips and came closer to her, his gaze drifting over the three sleeping children.

He leaned in to her and whispered near her ear, "Brenna's bairn will not be born. Kára has sent me to take ye there to assist."

Clinking broke the hush as Hilda lifted a chain that locked around her middle. It was short, the end tied through the center of an eight-inch rock. It would keep her from going anywhere out of the room without notice, but it was not linked to the wall. Trying to break her free of it would be loud and could split the edge of his short sword.

Carefully lifting the rock to carry so as not to yank the elderly woman, Joshua beckoned her to follow him and handed her the cloak to put on over her dirty gown. Had she been imprisoned here without means to wash? The smell of curdled milk and urine mixed with the potent perfume coming from Jean's cloak as she threw it around her shoulders. The poor woman had been locked up here while he bedded Jean two doors away. Self-loathing poured through him. To how much had he been blind?

Out in the hallway, she followed right behind him without a word. Not only was Hilda Flett wise, she was also brave. If Robert came out, Joshua would have to stop him. Killing him would bring the wrath of his nephew, King James. And if Jean came out to look for him, she'd wake the whole palace with her shrieking.

They moved swiftly to the steps and down the dim circular tower, Joshua bracing himself in case the woman was to lose her footing and fall into him. "I have a horse in the stable," he whispered to her as they reached the bottom. He paused in the archway, his gaze sweeping the ten sleeping men within the great hall. Relief funneled through him when he saw that Angus had replaced Connor in his circuit around the perimeter. Joshua's gaze dropped to Hilda. "I will carry ye. Keep your face tucked into me."

She gave a quick nod, pulling the cloak over her gray hair. He handed her the heavy stone she could hold only with two hands. Lifting under her knees, he picked her up. The rock and chain nestled into her lap, which she covered with the cloak. Joshua walked with light feet into the great hall.

Angus turned toward him immediately, his mouth opening to yell. But he froze, his eyes going wide. Joshua slowly shook his head, and Angus shut his mouth.

Halfway across, one of the sleeping men sat up, blinking at him. "What goes on here?" Connor, who had not completely given in to sleep yet, also sat up.

"Back to sleep, William," Joshua said, authority in his voice, and he nodded to Connor. "The Lady Jean and I are taking things outside."

"Lusty bastard," William murmured and lay back down. Connor glanced at Angus, and then, fortunately for him, decided his shift was over and returned to his pallet.

Joshua nodded again to Angus and strode through the hall to enter the dark bailey, passing another watchman as he made his rounds. Apparently, the Horseman of War had not been gone long enough for him to look out of place on the palace grounds, especially carrying a woman wrapped up in Jean's cloak. He entered the barn, expecting to see the three sleeping guards from before, but they were gone.

"Come find me, love." John Dishington's rough voice came from the far end of the stables where Fuil was tethered and Kára was hiding. Bloody hell. There was no way around him to get out without being noticed.

Joshua set Hilda's feet on the packed dirt floor and lowered the rock and chain. "Wait here in the shadows," he whispered. "Keep draped."

She nodded, and he moved quietly along the stalls lining the aisle toward the back where John apparently waited for Jean. As the silence continued, the hairs on the back of Joshua's neck rose. His fists clenched, one of them wrapped around the hilt of his short sword. If John was still breathing with Kára back here, fully armed and vengeful, was she dead?

"John Dishington," Joshua called out, barely keeping the promise of death out of his voice. "Show yourself."

John kicked open the stall where Kára's horse stood, pushing out into the aisle with Kára before him, a dagger at her throat. "I had planned on tupping Jean out here, but after I kill you, I will sample your woman instead."

• • •

The Brute clutched Kára up against him, and she could feel his jack pressed against her backside. Brutality apparently heightened his lust. One of his meaty arms encircled her waist while the other bruised her chest with the pressure of the *mattucashlass* he held against her throat. She would die before she let him rape her, and she had no intention of dying that night, not when Brenna depended on her.

"Drop the sword, Sinclair," The Brute said. "Or I will lay her neck wide open."

Kára stared at Joshua where he stood motionless, his largeness and strength obvious even in the shadows and slices of torchlight. Was he alone? Had he not found Hilda?

Thump. Joshua's short sword hit the dirt floor, and he stood there, his arms open wide. Death painted his face almost like a mask, and she understood how others could believe he was the biblical Horseman of War sent to herald the end of times.

"Let her go. Now," Joshua said, the rough warning in his tone sending a shiver between Kára's shoulder blades. Blood would surely wet the earth beneath them.

"You did not leave Orkney? Are you working with the native rabble now?" The Brute asked. "I thought you had learned your lesson down in South Ronaldsay. Did not you swear never to help the helpless again?"

His words pricked along Kára's spine. There was history between them. South Ronaldsay? Had Joshua been involved in the slaughter there?

Joshua's gaze never wavered from The Brute's. "Let her go."

The Brute pulled her in tighter, his crooked nose inhaling deeply along the skin of her neck. The brush of him against her made the small meal she'd had earlier wash around inside her middle like a whirlpool.

"I agree there is merit to knowing this bit of rabble," he said. The bastard sucked in through his teeth. "Have you not educated her on the consequences when you become a spoil of war?" He paused a moment to let Joshua answer. When Joshua did not reply, The Brute shrugged, making the blade slide against the surface of her neck, and she felt its sting. "I am certain Henry will not mind sharing her."

By the devil! She would never let Henry touch her again. She would throw herself onto a blade before she let him take another thing from her.

Not a single muscle in Joshua's face twitched. He slowly crossed his arms over his chest, his legs braced as if he stood on the deck of a ship. "I came to retrieve something. That is all. The lass but rode with me. If ye do not release her unharmed, ye will die tonight. 'Tis your choice, Dishington."

"The new chief of the weak islanders happened to ride with you here in the dead of night because you left something behind. If you think that is a believable tale, then you are a fool."

"Then let us battle," Joshua said. "The two of us, honorably. As we did in South Ronaldsay. Or are ye afraid I will beat ye again?"

"There was no true winner," The Brute said, his deep voice snapping out the words. Joshua said nothing, and the bastard continued. "These islanders are a weak people, Sinclair. We are the strong, the mighty, and Lord Robert and the Stuarts will rule this isle. These fools," he said, yanking Kára up higher against his body, "will die trying to win back their isle."

She could smell his foul breath as his lips moved near her head. "Bunch of inbred bastards. There is no honor in you if you mix with them or help them. 'Twill lead only to their complete extinction."

Rage flamed up inside Kára. John Dishington, The bloody Brute, knew nothing of the hardships her people suffered. Cold, hungry, forced to work on Robert's palaces and fortress walls. Their numbers were dwindling from cruelty and sickness while this bloodthirsty man raped and tortured without justice.

Kára stretched her fingers along her leg to line up with the dagger sheathed in her tall boot, but she couldn't reach it. The Brute slid his bristled jaw along her cheek, the stubble scratching her.

Joshua's arms uncrossed to hang ready by his sides. "I said…release her."

With the blade against her throat, she could barely swallow without drawing blood. Switching up her plan, Kára lifted her hands at the same time she said the devil's name. "John Dishington, I have a secret for you."

The Brute snorted. "Oh I am sure you have some secret places upon you I will uncover shortly."

Staring directly into Joshua's eyes, Kára slowly drew in breath, fueling her muscles. If she was to die, she wanted to see the strength in Joshua's face as she left this world.

Pulling one more breath in, Kára curled her tongue to let out a high-pitched whistle. Surprise lit Joshua's eyes, and his own lips came together as if her action reminded him that he was still armed. He whistled two short bursts of sound, too.

Kára's mare, Broch, charged through the stall door that was ajar, and Kára shoved against The Brute's arm. The surprise gave her a heartbeat to react. She dropped and yanked her dagger from her boot, to leap upright, her arm coming around to slash at the bastard's face.

The Brute grunted as her blade sliced open the skin of his cheek, and he jumped back, his eyes going beyond her to where Joshua no doubt charged. But before he could reach them, Joshua's horse kicked his stall door, splintering it. Pieces of wood shot everywhere, and deadly hooves flew out of the stall like an avenging angel sent straight from Heaven. The horse's nostrils flared, ears back, like when Kára's brother stupidly tried to steal him from the village. The horse barreled into The Brute, knocking him down, his powerful legs trampling over him.

Joshua grabbed Kára, pulling her out of the way of the two horses. The Brute lay flat on the ground, eyes closed, mouth open, his face bleeding freely.

"Is he dead?" she said, her breath heavy as they faced him.

"What goes on in here?" a voice called from the entrance.

"Bring your horse," Joshua said and clicked to his own mount before running toward the door on foot, his sword out. He was going to cut their way through whatever waited for them there.

Ignoring the trembling in her hand, Kára grabbed the horn of the saddle that she'd placed on Broch before The Brute found her, climbing up to follow behind Joshua and his horse, who trotted after him. When she reached the torchlight circle near the doors, Robert's warrior was on the ground unconscious. A woman in a white cloak stood there, a chain attaching her to a large rock that sat next to the bloody man.

"Courage runs in your clan," Joshua said, lifting the rock and leading the woman over to Kára. "Ye are a clever lot."

"Hilda?" Kára whispered.

Her aunt glanced at the unconscious warrior. "I was not going to let him ruin things after you got past The Brute."

"Drape the cloak around the two of ye," Joshua said and handed the rock chained to her aunt up to Kára. He lifted Hilda behind her. The woman quickly draped the wide cloak around Kára for her to clasp in the front.

Joshua stared up at Kára as Hilda tucked the long cape around their legs. "Ye are Jean," he said, "going out for a midnight ride with me." He waited for Kára to nod her understanding.

She studied him in the sharp glow of the flame, and her chest tightened. "Is that lip paint on your face?" Her gaze dropped as her brows rose, anger shooting through her. "And down your neck?" Had he been kissing Jean Stuart, or even tupping her, while Kára hid and then got pawed by The Brute? Could there have been time for that?

"Walk slow until we reach the hill," Joshua answered, ignoring her questions. It wasn't the time to ask, but his non-answer was answer enough.

Unable to stop herself, Kára murmured, "Her perfume stink clings to this cloak."

"If Robert's men give chase, ye ride on to your den to hide with Hilda while I lead them off."

"I need to get her to Brenna," she countered.

He grabbed her hand where it fisted around her

reins. "Ye will not be taken. Is that clear? If they are following ye, get somewhere safe. I will bring Brenna to ye."

"After you kill all of them? By yourself?"

His answer was to turn on his heels to stride to his horse, throwing a leg up to pull himself easily into the saddle of his tall mount. Hilda wrapped her arms around Kára under the cloak, pulling her body close against her. Kára had the irrational desire to fling Jean's rich cape off, but it was the only way to get them both out of this palace prison.

Joshua waited for her to come up behind him to throw the torch in a trough of water near the door, dousing it. "Stay close," he said. "Keep your hair covered."

Of course, she would keep her hair covered. Jean's tresses were dark while her hair was pale. Anger boiled inside her, threatening to bubble out across her tongue, but she kept her lips pinched. Red lips had slid all over Joshua's neck and face. Had he even tried to stop her? Would any man?

They rode forward to the raised portcullis. "I thought ye were staying the night," the gatekeeper called down.

Joshua grinned up at the man and reached over to take Kára's hand fondly. "'Tis hard to keep quiet with her father sleeping next door. Do not give us away."

The man laughed low and gave him a salute. "Come, love," Joshua said.

Love? With evidence of Jean's lips all over him? She almost snatched her hand back but made herself withdraw it slowly to take up her reins. They rode side by side out into the darkness.

"A bit faster now," Joshua said softly, and she followed him into a trot and finally a full run. The moon kept hidden as they flew across the moor toward Brenna and her unborn bairn.

CHAPTER NINE

"A leader leads by example, not by force."
Sun Tzu – The Art of War

Kára was angry.

Joshua knew enough about women that he spotted jealousy quickly, and he knew better than to smile over it. The lass didn't like the idea of him tangling with Robert's loose daughter. He would clear up her worries, whatever they were, but for the moment there wasn't time, and the idea that Kára did not want to share him with another woman lightened his mood considerably.

Robert's men did not give chase as he'd worried. Was John Dishington dead or merely asleep? Damn, Joshua wished he'd had the chance to knock the stupid grin off his ugly face. After the disaster of South Ronaldsay, where they'd been on opposite sides of the dispute, they had both traveled up to Birsay. Dishington was a mercenary, fighting for whomever had the most gold to give him. Even though Joshua didn't need the coin, he needed a purpose, and training warriors had seemed like a good one—until he realized whom he was training them to conquer.

They halted the two horses before the three cottages and barn at Hillside. Geir ran out to grab her horse's reins. "Broch!" he called. "You saved her," he said, looking to Joshua as he dismounted.

"Your mother saved her," Joshua answered. If Kára had allowed Dishington to sound the alarm, they would not have gotten past fifty armed men without him having to kill many. "Do ye have an ax nearby?" He dismounted Fuil to help the elderly healer down.

"An ax? Aye," Geir said and bolted into the empty barn to bring back a short-handled ax.

"Stand here against this boulder," Joshua said to Hilda as he set the length of chain encircling her waist over the granite.

"You cannot just chop it off her," Kára said.

"I know," Joshua answered.

Kára grabbed his arm, halting him. "If you—"

"I think he has a plan, Kára," Hilda said, "that does not involve chopping me in half."

Joshua wedged the blade of his *sgian dubh* through a thick link and lay it onto the top of the rock. He looked to Kára. "Hold it steady while I hit it."

She held the blade handle so it wouldn't slide away with the impact. Joshua aimed the ax and slammed the back of it down onto the dull side of the one-sided dagger. *Clang.* With one strike, the blade cleaved through the iron link where it had been soldered. The chain slid away from Hilda's waist, and he heard her inhale fully as if she were also shaking off the mental chains of captivity.

"Where is Brenna?" Hilda asked and started walking in the direction Kára pointed. "Tell me what has been done so far."

Joshua followed them below the hill, into an underground cottage, which was set up in the same way as Kára's. No one stopped him from continuing into the bedchamber in the back. He should explain that nothing happened between Jean and him.

"Kára," he said, but the word was lost under the exhausted keening sound of a woman being tortured. The sound shot the hairs up on the back of his neck, and he froze as if encased in ice there in the doorway. Pungent herbs and heat filled the space. Brenna lay on the bed, her face covered with sweat and contorted by pain. Eyes shut, she lay there panting, hands grasping the twisted sheets as agony gripped her. He'd never seen anything so horrible. It was as if she were being ripped apart from the inside out.

"Brenna," Kára called, hurrying up to the bed. "Hilda is here. She will help you."

Brenna opened her eyes, tears coming from them. It seemed she couldn't focus. "Calder?"

Kára looked to Joshua. He retreated from the room, glad for the crisp air of outdoors. He ran up the hill and ducked into the first upside cottage where several men stood near a table in the center.

"Brenna is asking for Calder," he said.

"He is not here," one of the older men said. "Gone south to fetch a minister."

The grim faces told Joshua nothing more. Did Calder think Brenna would die and needed a cleric to bless her as she breathed her last? Kára thought she could die, but that was without the help of the healer. And from the look of the pain-bludgeoned woman, Joshua agreed, although he had never seen a woman give birth before. What man had?

"Tell him to come below as soon as he returns,"

Joshua said and turned back to tell Kára. He dodged Osk, who was walking in as he ran back out into the dawning light. The woman had been laboring for two days at this point. How much more could she endure?

He noticed Geir had gone to the edge of the bank that led to the sea below. The lad was practicing throwing *sgian dubhs* the way Joshua had shown him. Kára's son had good aim, and he would grow in muscle. *As long as Robert Stuart and his sons do not work him to death.*

In through the door, Joshua strode directly to the bedroom where Kára held a panting Brenna around the shoulders. Kára met his gaze, and she closed her eyes briefly when he shook his head.

"She must be raised up," Hilda called, pointing to a thick rope that had been looped through a hook above for bed curtains.

Hilda pointed at him. "You. Lift Brenna up into the ropes and help support her there."

"Me?" he asked, his muscles tightening as if readying for battle. Wasn't he supposed to vanish from the birthing chamber like every other male so that they did not show their weakness or see things they should not?

"You are the strongest here, and we need her up," Hilda said. "The babe is coming finally, but it will be easier on them both that way." She beckoned quickly to him, and he found himself walking over, inhaling fully to gain strength. But the heat and smells did not help him. *'Tis like birthing a foal*, he told himself, which he had done many times before.

He stepped up onto the bed, his boots planting

behind the heavily burdened woman.

"Do not let her slip," Kára said, letting him grasp Brenna under her arms. He had no choice but to hold her under her ample bosom.

Just like a mare in trouble. Like a horse. That is all. Done this dozens of times before. If Brenna could only neigh, he would have little problem with this. He opened his mouth to ask but decided against it. No woman he had ever met responded well to being asked to neigh.

Joshua lifted and Brenna groaned, a sound torn from her straining body. Kára leaped up to loop her friend's arms through the rope.

"She is too weak to hold on," Kára said, looking at him. "Hold her there."

"Hold her here?" he asked, his voice rising, but she had already jumped down to the floor, leaving him. "Through the entire foaling…birthing?"

"I see a wee foot," Hilda called from under Brenna's wet and bloody smock.

Joshua kept his gaze focused on the door, the place he longed to go. Nothing would make him look down at all the blood and fluids pouring from the woman. He'd rather watch entrails fall out of a man. Or maybe even his own arm cut clean off. The loss of his own blood would not make him feel more unsteady than he did at that moment.

"Brenna!" Calder yelled from the front room. He pushed the cloth separating the room aside and strode in with another man behind him, a man Joshua knew.

"Pastor John?" Joshua called from his position on the bed. The cleric's wide-eyed gaze snapped up to meet his. "What are ye doing on Orkney?" The last he saw the young holy man, Pastor John was performing the wedding ceremony between Joshua's brother, Cain, and Ella Sutherland back in Caithness.

He swallowed, his gaze dropping to Brenna and then back up to Joshua. "Chief Sinclair knew I was headed this way and…" He had to raise his voice to be heard over Brenna's keening. "And uh… uh… Cain wanted me to see if you were well." His gaze dropped again to Brenna, one hand going to his own forehead before he looked back up with wide eyes. "Are…are you well?"

Kára's grandmother threw her arms out to stop him from answering, which was good because Joshua had no idea if he was well or not. "This is women's work," Harriett Flett called loudly.

"He is no woman!" Calder shouted, pointing at Joshua.

"Calder?" Brenna asked, and Joshua felt a bit of strength return to her body.

"What the hell is going on?" Calder asked.

But Joshua did not have time to answer as the lass yelled again, her body tensing with another wave of pain.

"Dearest Lord, we call upon your blessings. Bring peace and strength," Pastor John said, closing his eyes and laying one hand on his Bible.

"He is a minister," Calder said.

"What?" Brenna yelled, the word full of sudden strength. "I am not dying! I need no holy man." Anger seemed to give her more strength, helping her heels push into the bed under her.

"She is not dying," Kára added, fury pinching the beautiful determination in her face.

"Not for last rites," Calder called, dodging around Kára's grandmother to tip his face up to Brenna's. "Will you wed with me, Brenna Muir? Right now, before our child enters this world?"

Another contraction pulled her strength, and Joshua braced himself as her muscles contracted. A deep groan issued from her as her entire body tensed.

"Two feet now," Hilda called. "We must work the shoulders out."

"Aye, aye," Brenna panted, her eyes once more opening to focus on the soon-to-be father. Calder waved Pastor John over. Poor fellow looked pale and shocked by the violent scene. Joshua did not blame him. Men were meant to take life from the world and were not meant for the horrors of bringing life into the world.

Calder glanced at the stains on the bed and Brenna's smock, his face also going pale as his lips opened.

"'Tis like a horse birth," Joshua called down to them both. "Think of it that way. But do not ask her to neigh."

Everyone in the room, except Brenna, looked at Joshua as if he'd lost his mind. "It will keep ye standing to think of it that way," he said.

"I...I have not seen a horse birth," Calder said.

"Well, damn," Joshua said. "Deep breaths then, I guess."

A tortured groan came from Brenna, and Pastor John closed his eyes, his lips moving in silent prayer.

"Pastor," Joshua called down. "Ye best start if your blessing is to come before the bairn."

His eyes snapped open, and he nodded quickly like a nervous bird. "Do you, Calder Flett, take Brenna Muir to be your wife before God and these witnesses, in sickness and in health, forsaking all others, until death do you part?"

"Aye, aye," Calder breathed.

"And do you, Brenna—"

"Aye," she screamed. "I take him until death do us part. Aye, forsaking all others…" The last word was drawn out with her wail.

Pastor John drew the sign of the cross in the air. "You two are wed. May God bless you and your child." Without another word, he fled the room, likely to find some whisky, because that was exactly what Joshua was going to do when he managed to escape.

"Good girl," Hilda said through another of Brenna's low cries. "The shoulders…"

Brenna grunted, and her breath flew from her with the sound of… Whatever it was, it sounded wet. *Holy bloody hell.* Joshua drew in a deep breath to keep his feet beneath him while he held her.

"I have it," Hilda yelled, pulling out from under Brenna's smock. She held a bloody, slippery bairn, a thick cord over its shoulders. Kára moved forward, catching the child roughly in a towel, rubbing it.

Harriett cut through the fleshy cord with a sharp dagger. "Lower Brenna slowly," Hilda instructed. *Thank the good Lord*, Joshua prayed and bent slowly forward with Brenna.

Thump. Calder was no longer standing.

"I caught his head," Amma said as she lowered

Calder to the stone floor, his eyes closed in unconsciousness.

Kára's head was bent over the bairn, working frantically as Joshua lowered Brenna to the bed. "Come on, little boy," Kára whispered in the suddenly quiet room. Joshua held his breath as she worked.

"Clear his mouth," Hilda said. A weak cry came from the bairn, and Joshua released his breath. A small sob made Brenna shake, and tears washed down her cheeks, but she smiled weakly at the noise that proved her bairn had made it out of her body alive.

"There is too much blood," Hilda said. "Kára, knead her abdomen. Harriett, come look at this tear. Do we need to stitch it?"

Tear? Bloody hell! Joshua's eyes went wide as Kára stepped over Calder, carrying the bairn that she'd wrapped in a fresh blanket. "Hold him."

"What?" he asked.

She shoved the tiny bundle into his arms and hurried back to the bed. "Like a baby horse," she said, a slight grin on her face as her hands went out to massage the new mother's round abdomen.

He looked down at the blinking little eyes of the bairn. "I will scare it," he said, but no one paid him any attention except Brenna.

"Smile at him," she ordered.

He tried but it likely came out like a grimace. The bairn had a spit of dark hair on his head, which was wet with… He did not want to think about it. The lad's blinks were slow, as if he had drunk too much ale.

"I feel like I need to push again," Brenna said.

"'Tis the afterbirth needing to come out." Hilda patted her arm.

"*Magairlean*," he murmured, turning his back on the process behind him. He looked down at the wee bairn. His little hand lay across the blanket, his long fingers extended. Were they supposed to be long like that? He looked closer. "Och, but he has wee fingernails," he said, pushing his thumb under the miniature hand. The bairn's fingers curled around his thumb, and his breath caught. He chuckled. "Ye have a strong grip."

Joshua glanced down at Calder, who moved a hand to his face, his eyes blinking. "What happened?"

"Ye no doubt got your strength from your mother," Joshua said to the bairn. In the background, the women helped Brenna, or at least her lower half while she continued to watch him hold her son.

"What will ye name him?" he asked.

"I…I do not know," she said, exhaustion and joy on her face with brief pinches of pain. "I tried hard not to think of the babe while I carried him so as not to draw death to him."

He studied the wee face. "I am not your father, little one. He is still on the floor. Perhaps I should not show ye that," he said and turned away from where Calder struggled to sit up.

"What names are in your family?" Brenna asked him.

The wee one still held strongly to his finger. "My brothers are Cain, Gideon, and Bàs."

"Bass? Is that short for anything?" she asked.

"It means death in Gaelic. He was born to execute our enemies," he said, smiling down, his chest full as he studied the bairn's puckered lips.

"Death?" Brenna screeched. "Give me my babe now," she yelled.

"Ho now," Joshua said, turning to her. "'Tis an appropriate name. He is the Horseman of Death."

"Give him to me!"

He dodged Calder, who stood but still propped his hands on his knees. Joshua laid the bundle in Brenna's arms. She frowned up at him. "What type of mother would name her babe Death?"

He opened his mouth to explain that, since his mother died birthing him, she was Bàs's first execution, and his father had named him Death. But Joshua had enough common sense to shut his mouth.

"Brenna? You are well?" Calder asked, straightening to his full height. He came around to look down on his fresh new son, and Joshua stepped backward toward the doorway.

Kára had stopped massaging Brenna and straightened. Joshua couldn't help but glance at Kára's middle. Had he planted his bairn within her? Would she have to battle to birth it? Would it have tiny fingernails and a grip worthy of a warrior like Brenna's babe?

As if feeling his stare, Kára met his gaze. Pieces of hair had worked their way out of her braid to frame her flushed face with her pale blond locks. They all must look exhausted from the night of adventure and danger. But the grin on her face, when she looked up from Brenna holding her newborn bairn, lit the darkness under her eyes. Kára Flett was beautiful, and something tightened in Joshua's chest, something like a cord being tied into a taut knot. Or a noose, depending on how one looked at it.

She met him at the doorway, pulling him into the main room. Even with the heat from the fire, the main room was not nearly as stuffy as the bedchamber. Kára dropped his hand. "Thank you for getting Hilda and for holding Brenna up there."

"We were fortunate your healer was easy to locate, and we could escape on horseback without too much trouble." Was John Dishington dead or merely knocked out? Would Robert know instantly, from having learned that Joshua was in his palace, that he was responsible?

"Without too much trouble," she murmured. Was she worried Robert would retaliate today? She frowned, her gaze moving from his eyes to his lips. Turning, she yanked a rag off a shelf and rubbed hard there and on his cheek. "Jean's lip rouge." And continued down his neck as if she wished to scrape his skin off along with the red stain.

Joshua caught her hand to stop it. "I did not initiate—"

"Not on a mission, I know. You have more honor than that," she said and tipped her chin up. "But it still looks ugly on you."

He agreed. If he were to wear red, he'd prefer blood of a victorious battle to the smear of red lip rouge of a deceptive tryst.

She lowered her hand but didn't move away. "I should go back to help. It is tradition that we guard the babe for a few days and nights, taking turns rocking the cradle while Brenna sleeps."

He frowned. "Who would steal it?" The thought that someone might come during the night to take a bairn made Joshua's muscles clench. He would cleave anyone trying to take the wee lad who had blinked up at him and held his thumb tightly.

"The same fae folk or trolls who would have harmed him while Brenna was pregnant. We will have the christening in another day to help protect the babe, too, especially since Calder brought the minister." She smiled. "And we will have a wedding feast along with the *blide-maet*." She shook her head. "There is much to do and with Lord Robert possibly attacking after we took Hilda…"

Joshua could not stop himself. He pulled her to him with a hand around her back, sliding it along the gentle arc above her hips. "I will stay to make sure no one harms Brenna or her son."

Hope spread across Kára's face, and he realized what he had said. He cleared his throat. "I will stay through Samhain and show your warriors how to protect themselves if attacked."

The hope faded as she stared up into his eyes. She gave a little nod, lowering her gaze to his chest. "Not if attacked. When attacked," she said softly and tipped her head back again to meet his eyes. "Because it is coming. Retaliation is something of which Lord Robert is quite fond."

She shut her eyes then. "I need to go back to Brenna," she said, and he slowly released her. Without looking at him again, Kára turned and strode back into the bedchamber.

He almost went after her, pulling her to him and not letting go until she understood what he had seen before. Did she know what could be worse than them hiding under the earth or leaving their home? Truly know? The wailing of those remaining as they fell over their slaughtered loved ones?

In South Ronaldsay no one but John Dishington talked about who had won and who had lost. Even if the numbers tallied in Joshua's favor, they had all lost. Aye, he had won, but Joshua had truly learned what it meant to lose that day and night that saw not only men die, but lads as well. He shook his head. "I will not lead them to death."

CHAPTER TEN

*"Treat your men as you would your own
beloved sons. And they will follow
you into the deepest valley."*
Sun Tzu – The Art of War

Joshua walked out into the dawning light, the black
of the night sky turning into a deep blue. A figure
pushed off the side of the hill next to another
partially hidden door.

"Joshua," Pastor John said. "The bairn and
mother?"

"Are well."

"Praise the good Lord," he murmured. "You did
a mighty fine job helping. I have seen a few horse
births, but that down in there... It was much more...
well, everything." He inhaled as if to fortify himself
against a memory that would haunt him. "Life is a
messy business."

Joshua stretched his arms overhead, trying to rid
himself of some stiffness. "Did Cain send ye to
Orkney to see what mischief I was making?"

Pastor John grinned. "He said as much, but I
think he worries about you."

"Ye can tell him I am whole and sound and will
return soon." He crossed his arms. "How goes life at
Girnigoe? Has Cain kept control of Varrich Castle
and the MacKay Clan? Are the Sutherlands still our
allies with young Jamie and his regent in control of

Dunrobin Castle?"

Pastor John nodded. "There is peace, the first I have ever seen there. The Sutherlands are practicing with Sinclair warriors with your youngest brother, Bàs, leading the training sessions. Gideon has plans to move into Varrich Castle to keep the MacKay Clan in line. So far, the MacKays seem to be happy the wicked steward and foolish young chief are no more. Oh, and Lady Ella is with child."

Joshua dropped his arms, a smile relaxing his face. "Cain is to be a father?"

"As of when I left three weeks ago. Your Aunt Merida and sister are taking good care of Lady Sinclair."

Cain was going to be a father, like Calder was now, except Cain would not fall on the floor if he were forced to witness the birthing. "I will be an uncle," Joshua said and chuckled, thinking of all the mischief he could help his nephew or niece get into. Would Ella let him hold the bairn or snatch it away like Brenna? Perhaps he should have his own son or daughter, a bairn that no one could whisk away. The thought tightened his stomach, and he glanced back at the door that hid Kára.

"Three weeks," Joshua said and looked back to the clergyman who had done so much to help his clan back home. "Did ye have a hard time finding a way across the firth?"

"Nay," John said. "'Twas a quick trip, but I stayed in southern Orkney for a fortnight, trying to help the poor people there." The man's gaze met Joshua's with questions in it. "You were in South Ronaldsay. They said the Horseman of War was there, that he fought with them."

They stared at each other for a long moment before Joshua looked past him. "Aye," he said, his brows bending downward. "I tried to help them, but 'twas wrong to encourage the war when the price of winning would be too high."

"They speak of you giving them hope," Pastor John said, bringing Joshua's gaze back to his. "They are rebuilding, and the new leaders are in discussions for a lasting truce after seeing what such slaughter did to hurt them."

"Perhaps the old leaders should have been killed, instead of over half their people with them," Joshua said, his voice low, Adam's face surfacing in his mind like a spirit from the grave.

"And who are the leaders in the war up here?" Pastor John asked.

"Robert Stuart, Earl of Orkney." He nodded toward the north where the palace lay. "And currently, Chief Kára Flett." He indicated the door.

"Stuart? Related to King James?"

"Aye, his bastard uncle. Robert's sons are also a problem, forcing the people here to work for them without pay or choice, not letting them hunt to supply food for their families, stealing their horses and anything of worth. The list of abuses is long."

"And you wish to help these people against him?" Pastor John took in a full breath, letting it out slowly as if Joshua had already answered. "King James will not like his representatives here slaughtered by a powerful Sinclair, especially people of his blood."

Joshua rubbed the back of his neck. "It would be

better if I could convince Kára and her clan to move to Caithness on the mainland."

The cleric nodded his head quickly. "Aye. Keep the Sinclairs free of this squabble and still not abandon these poor souls."

Joshua exhaled long. "Aye," he said, glancing toward the hidden village of Hillside. If only he could reason with the poor souls.

• • •

"Calder wants to name our babe after Joshua," Brenna said, holding her son against her breast where he nursed. "He says your Highlander saved us both by getting Hilda. I mean, you helped in that as well." She shrugged the opposite shoulder slightly. "And then the whole Joshua holding me up during the birth. Lord help me. I do not think I can look at him again without flushing red."

"Hilda kept you covered below."

"To think his brother is named Death," Brenna said, whispering the last word as if it might summon the affliction.

Kára lay on the bed next to her friend, pillows holding them both up. "Not a name in any language for a child."

Brenna looked down on the tiny head against her. "But Joshua is a nice name. I like the sound of it." She looked up at Kára. "He is still here?"

It had been four days since the birth. Brenna had come through the difficult battle for life as well as she could. She had some stitches, but they were healing, and so far, Hilda's brews had kept her free of fever. Once her milk came in, everyone breathed a sigh of relief. Kára had been teaching her ways to hold her babe while feeding him, the memories coming back of when Geir was born.

Kára nodded but felt her frown grow. "He is training our warriors in defense so when Robert finds us, we can better fend him off."

"Is that not what you wanted?" Brenna asked.

Kára exhaled. She hadn't spent any time alone with Joshua since they'd spoken outside the birthing room. Each day she had woken, expecting to hear he had left. *I will stay until Samhain.* The holiday to honor the dead and bless the harvest in preparation for the dark winter ahead started at sundown the next day.

"He is still here," Kára said, "but he has not agreed to lead us against Robert and his sons, and The Brute." John Dishington had not died and was now angrier than ever, giving Joshua and Kára a warning through Asmund at the tavern. Henry Stuart and Dishington had ridden into the deserted town on the bay and had thrown Asmund to the ground when he feigned ignorance of their location. Asmund would rather die than tell Stuarts about Hillside.

A small group of Robert's men had come up to the three cottages yesterday, but Kára's people had a routine they would play out when strangers came near. Three small families would show themselves above. The rest of the Hillside families would stand on guard quietly in the underground dwellings with shocks of barley laid against the doors to hide them. They had hidden this way for as long as Kára could remember, using the dwellings of the ancient Orkney inhabitants. Children huddled together. Mothers desperately keeping their babes hushed. Fathers and sons holding what weapons they had.

When Joshua had emerged after Robert's men rode away, he stood watching them all come out looking like frightened rabbits, silent and spying about for danger. He'd started working with her warriors that day, including Geir. Even Osk had begrudgingly decided that what Joshua had to say was worth his time.

He has a book on war, Osk had told her, a look of admiration in his eyes. *'Tis in French, but he can read it.* Hopefully, some of the information in it would make them strong enough to stand against Robert, his sons, and the whole bloody crown of Scotland. "Dammit," she murmured.

If they kept growing in size, however, they would need to dig out more underground homes or split into groups, living apart. Her uncle, Erik Flett, had brought the issue up at the last council meeting where the elders gathered to discuss the ongoing threats to their people.

The pressure of grief grew behind her eyes. She wished they could go into Robert's palace and free Erik as easily as they had Hilda. He was a good leader, even if he was stubborn. But he would be guarded there, if he was still alive. And like every leader of their group, Erik had made them swear not to endanger themselves to save him. All efforts were to save the family as a whole. The group would not try to rescue her if she were taken, either. Direct confrontation with Robert had led only to their deaths, which was why she needed Joshua. If anyone could change the balance of power in their favor, it was the Highlander who was built to win wars.

"If Joshua will not lead us in a battle against him, at least he is teaching us to defend ourselves," Brenna said, stroking her babe's swaddled back. "We will go on hiding and surviving." She smiled reassuringly. "It is what we do."

Kára pushed up off the pillows, pulling in a fast breath through her nose. "I want more for us." She looked at Brenna. "I want us to stand together out in the open without worrying someone will see us and attack. I want your lad to laugh loudly and roll down the grassy hills with the other children without having to constantly look over his shoulder for Robert's patrols." She ran a hand down her face. "I want our people to hunt and raise livestock without fear of them being stolen by men who have riches and luxuries." She exhaled long. *I would die to keep my people safe and living with their dignity*, she thought.

Kára squeezed Brenna's leg through her smock and robe as she lay on the bed. "I will convince Joshua to lead us against Robert. I must. If we do not act now, as Robert's children grow—"

"Like that pig, Henry."

"Aye." Kára sighed. "There will be no freedom for us if they continue to live and rule this isle." As Brenna tipped the sleeping babe from her breast and covered herself, Kára touched the wee babe's head gently, marveling in the little movements of his lips as he slumbered. "I do not want to live always in shadows," she whispered. "And I do not want you to live in them, either."

"If we must, we must," Brenna whispered, meeting Kára's gaze. "And there are plenty of shadows on Orkney."

The outer door opened and closed, and heavy footfalls came to the bedchamber door. Calder poked his head in, saw his sleeping son, and smiled broadly. "Full and sleepy?"

"Aye," Brenna said and smiled. Since Calder had married her, Brenna had been smiling nearly all the time. Thank God, the man had finally committed. Was it the fear of losing her that had brought him around?

Calder walked into the room with a wooden cradle. Brenna crossed her arms over her son's back so that he lay completely against her. "I am not putting him in that to sleep. He will always sleep right here on me."

"As long as you want," Calder said, setting it down. He lifted a dagger and Bible out of it. "To protect wee Joshua?" The name was a question, and he waited.

Brenna nodded, glancing at Kára before going back to Calder. "Aye, wee Joshua."

Calder grinned and nodded. "I have left the dagger and Bible in the cradle since he was born, and we will lay them underneath it to protect him when you are ready to set him inside."

"Not until he is christened," Brenna said.

"Tomorrow morn, and we've already wet his head and given him a nip of whisky for luck," Calder said.

Kára rolled out the side of the bed. "I am going

to wash and see if Amma needs help preparing the *blide-maet* meal for those coming to meet little Joshua."

Calder looked at her, his smile fading. "I forgot to say, Torben is looking to talk with you as soon as you emerge from Brenna's nest."

Kára puffed her cheeks out with her exhale, bracing herself for another of his long explanations of why she must marry him. With Joshua at Hillside, the man seemed even more determined to win her for himself despite her refusals.

Kára walked out the door into the muted sun of late morning. Orkney was headed into the dark season of winter. Usually, that meant less aggression from Robert, but now Kára wasn't sure of anything after rescuing Hilda and Broch.

She spotted a group of men standing on the up-side of the hill and walked toward them. The clergyman from Scotia stood, watching the gathering. She had seen him talking quietly with Joshua after the birth. Was he trying to convince Joshua to return with him?

Her heart pounded a little harder when she saw Joshua standing in the middle of the group, opposite Osk. Where her brother was still thin in muscle, Joshua was a mountain of strength, twice his size.

Before she could get close enough to hear, Torben walked out of one of the three up-ground cottages. "Kára," he called, striding toward her.

She kept her eyes turned toward the group. "Torben," she said. At one time she had considered marrying him, especially with Brenna pressing her to find another husband so they could have their babes together. But when her friend became pregnant without a wedding, she hadn't pressed so hard.

"You are allowed out from Brenna?" he asked.

"Calder is with her and Joshua."

"Joshua?" The word came out like a curse. "What is he doing with them?"

She glanced at Torben. He was handsome, with light-colored hair and strong features, his strength built up with the strain of daily living and farming off their rocky land. He used to laugh often but not recently. "Brenna named the babe Joshua."

Torben rolled his eyes. "The Sinclair is not our savior. He is selfish, cocky, and will not help us."

She stared out toward the group and captured a strand of hair that continued to blow across her eyes, tucking it behind one ear. "To Brenna, Joshua Sinclair is her savior for bringing Hilda and holding her up during a difficult birth. And…" She gestured down the hill. "He seems to be helping us."

Torben looked out and crossed his arms. "But he will not lead us to lay siege to the Earl's Palace and Robert. Nor to kill Henry or Patrick or The Brute. He fears King James's reaction."

It was hard to imagine Joshua Sinclair afraid of anything. "Not fear but prudence guides him, Torben. There is a difference." She held up her hand when he tried to argue. "And I have not yet given up swaying him."

"That is part of the bloody problem," he mumbled. "I do not like you around him. He is dangerous."

She squeezed his arm. The two of them had grown up together, and even though she had never become very fond of him because of his caustic remarks and judgmental slander, he was a part of their extended family. "Thank you for your worry, but we want him dangerous. It rather goes along with him being the Horseman of War."

"Horseman of War?" He snorted. "I do not see him connected to God in any way. The devil more like it."

She sighed, crossing her arms. "Torben, we will never marry," she said, switching topics to the likely underlying cause of his disdain.

He captured her arms, leaning in. "We could be so happy together. I could help you lead our people. My mother would be so joyful." His look was intense, but she saw no love in them.

Kára narrowed her eyes. "Your mother would be joyful?"

"Aye," he said, looking past her as if looking for the sour woman. "She talks of nothing except our people seeking revenge against the Stuarts for all they have done to us. If we were to wed, she would have something happy to focus upon."

Kára sighed. "Do not wed to bring your mother happiness." She shook her head. "It should be for *your* happiness."

His eyes widened. "I would be happy, too, of course."

She would not be happy, but that did not seem to matter to him. Kára glanced toward the men working with Joshua. "I wish to hear what they are saying," she said and pulled away to traipse down the hill. Torben cursed, turning to go back into the house.

The wind whipped tall grasses around her boots

as she strode closer until she could hear the deep rumble of Joshua's voice. "Ye need to use your opponent's attack against them," Joshua said. "So, if I come at Osk…" He took two steps forward, a wooden training sword in hand. "What should he do?"

"Run," one of Osk's friends yelled, which made the younger men laugh and the older ones smile. But Osk did not let down his guard. He kept his gaze on Joshua, his feet braced apart and his training sword ready.

"I anticipate which way you will strike and watch for signs in your body as you near," Osk said over the rabble.

"Aye." Joshua took another step forward. He turned his hips slightly and moved as if time had slowed. "I am swinging which way?"

Osk nodded to his right hip. "You will swing with strength from that side."

"And what will ye do?"

The young warrior wet his lips as if nervous but then pursed them. "Strike in the middle when you pull back to strike."

"Go ahead," Joshua said.

He slid his sword forward as Joshua brought his sword upward to slice down and across. Joshua turned his hips more so that Osk's sword missed his middle and Joshua could bring his own weapon down across her brother's shoulders, back, or neck.

Kára's throat tightened at seeing how vulnerable her brother was. Were all of Robert's warriors trained so well? Of course they were. Joshua had trained them himself.

Joshua backed away from her brother, and Osk turned red in the face.

"That is a move most men would make," Joshua said. "And it *could* work if your enemy does not anticipate the forward attack and turns so your strike brushes by them."

Joshua nodded to Osk. "Again." Osk took up his stance. "Instead of going for my middle, knowing my body weight will be swinging this way…" He slowly showed his sword swiping across again. "Turn your body so my weight throws me off-balance." The two came together, but this time Osk twisted out of the way as Joshua brought his sword over to slice him. "Keep going," Joshua called.

Osk turned where he could bring his sword down on Joshua's unprotected back.

"Good," Joshua said and then looked at the men before him. "Instead of always going in for the attack, use the enemy's own weight and speed against them. Get out of the way. Let them fall off-balance and then strike." Many of the men nodded, their faces grim but focused.

Corey called out, "Form two lines across from one another. We will pair off and practice."

Joshua's gaze stopped on Kára where she stood at the base of the hill. He handed the wooden sword to Geir and strode toward her. He had removed his furs and cloak and still looked big, his broad shoulders supporting all the muscle that he'd built upon his frame. He walked the distance effortlessly, his power propelling him to her. Lord! She should have washed and brushed her hair before coming up.

"All is well?" he asked, stopping before her, close, so very close.

"Yes," she said. "I was going to wash and change. Calder is with Brenna."

He nodded. "And the wee bairn?"

"Still strong and nursing like a hungry lad."

The side of Joshua's lush mouth turned upward in a grin, showing the edge of his white teeth. In the daylight, she could see the darker flecks of blue in the lightness of his eyes. They were different than any she'd seen before and seemed to pull her into their depths like pale blue whirlpools. With her own eyes being a grayish blue, would their children have blue eyes?

Kára looked past him toward the gray ocean, heavy clouds seeming to reach down to the surface. "They have named the babe Joshua," she said and looked back to him.

His grin faded, his brows bending inward.

"Because of your efforts to bring him safely into this world," she added.

"I was but one helper," he said, and she could not tell from his tone if he were angered or stunned by the gesture.

She shrugged, tucking a wildly dancing strand of hair behind her ear. "I am sure if the babe were a girl, they would have named her Kára or Hilda or Harriett. Not many men are strong enough to keep on their feet in a birthing chamber." Calder surely had not.

Joshua rubbed his fingers through his loose, shoulder-length hair, scratching his head. "I had always thought women were strong, but after witnessing what Brenna endured, I know it firsthand now. I have rarely seen such endurance and courage in men." He looked toward where Geir practiced against Osk. "Was your birthing as difficult?"

"No," she said. "Geir came early, so he was small and came properly headfirst."

He looked at her. "Early?"

She nodded, watching her son, the tightness of worry digging its claws into the old familiar wounds from nine years ago. She swallowed, keeping her gaze away from Joshua. "He came a month early, and we worried he would not live. But look at him now." She smiled against the sadness that pressed on her.

"What makes a bairn come early?" Joshua asked, turning to stand next to her and watching Geir, both their gazes outward.

"It could be poor nutrition, something wrong with the babe, an illness in the mother. Or…a fright to the mother can bring on labor early."

"What type of fright?" Joshua asked, his voice low.

Images moved behind Kára's eyes. Unbidden, the memories welled up as if needing to be released or threaten to cut her in an effort to escape the tight hold she kept on them. "Seeing one's unarmed husband slaughtered." She turned to meet his gaze. The sight of Joshua, so strong and invincible, pushed the nightmarish memories back, breaking up the pictures until they were just words again. "And being stolen away by the murderer while the father of your child bleeds out on the ground."

"Kára," Joshua murmured, his gentle grip on her

arm pulling her around to face him. "Who did this?"

"Henry Stuart," she answered. "By the time he wrestled me off his horse back at the Earl's Palace, my water had broken." It was the mess that had kept the monster from raping her.

She took a deep breath. "Lord Robert scolded him and made him turn me out of the gate to walk home. Geir was born later that night." There was a long pause.

"What was your husband's name?" he asked, his voice soft.

Even though she faced him, Kára looked straight ahead at Joshua's muscular chest, her gaze resting on the exposed tanned skin where the tunic tied. "I named Geir after his father." She glanced up to meet his pale eyes that held strength and anger instead of pity. They were easier to look at without pity in them. "So there would be a Geir on Orkney, and I swore to bring him up to be strong and able to protect those he loves."

"I am sorry, Kára," Joshua said. "I am glad your son has grown strong."

"Train him to use a blade well." She tipped her head upward to stare into his beautiful eyes. "Please." She let her desperation fill the word, releasing a bit of the emotion she kept locked inside. The memories had weakened her, and Kára turned away before Joshua could make her crumble with another denial.

CHAPTER ELEVEN

"Bravery without forethought causes a man to fight blindly and desperately like a mad bull."
Sun Tzu – The Art of War

"Protected under the name of God," Pastor John said, pouring the water onto wee Joshua's head as Brenna held him. Calder quickly dried it, the two parents smiling broadly as the young pastor announced that the bairn was now christened and under God's protection from evil.

Joshua stood across from Kára in the crowded room under the earth. *Please.* Kára's simple entreaty shot over and over through Joshua's mind as his gaze traveled over the villagers of Hillside who had gathered. They were good people. Honest, helpful to one another, and hard workers. They deserved respect and a good life, a life away from Robert Stuart.

But Kára ignored any suggestion that her people move away from Orkney. Joshua could understand her resistance. He missed his home at Girnigoe Castle on the northern part of Scotland in Caithness and would die defending it and his family. He would be there with them now except that remorse for equipping Robert's men with deadly skills kept him on Orkney. Remorse and…Kára Flett.

His gaze rested on her where she stood, straight and proud, her long, pale tresses cascading in curls down her back. Someone had tied ribbons in her hair, a simple decoration that held part of the silky mass, plaited and encircled on her head like a crown. She wore a straight blue wool gown, the bottom embroidered with flowers and birds. It reminded him of the costumes of the ancient Norse who had inhabited the isle, straight and simple. Two brooches sat over her shoulders, wrought in looped designs in silver. Even without a crown of gold, she resembled a queen.

He longed to know more about her. She had opened up a small amount on the hill yesterday but had retreated before he could ask... What would he ask? Joshua's aunt, Merida, had always advised him not to ask questions to which he did not really want to know the answers. But without answers, the questions swam in his head like fish in a barrel.

Had Kára loved her husband? Joshua wanted the answer to be no. She must have married very young to have a son of nine. Had Henry Stuart forced himself on her? That question he *did* want to know the answer. If it was aye, Robert's son would die before Joshua left Orkney, regardless of his blood link to King James.

A song began, the voices of the people rising to fill the crowded room, spilling out the open door for those outside to join. It was in their ancient Norn language, the power of it intense with hope and determination so that knowledge of the words was not needed to lift the spirit. Pastor John smiled, his face lit with awe and joy at the show of unity. No doubt the resonating voices raised chill bumps along his skin as they did on Joshua.

His gaze drifted over the warriors of Hillside, counting them, ranking them in skill. So far, he had taught them defensive tactics, maneuvers to keep them alive if attacked, giving them the opportunity to retreat with their lives.

Even though the skills were similar, he had not talked with them about attacking first. Should he begin to teach them offensive tactics and strategies for a siege against Robert? Lead them through exercises, physically and mentally, to transform them into ruthless hunters of human life to kill without mercy?

Joshua thought of some of the men who had become friends to him while he was living at the palace at Birsay. Angus and Mathias, Liam, even Tuck, who talked too much. They had either been assigned to apprentice with Robert or had been hired to guard his lands. They each had their own families back on the mainland, some following them to Orkney and living in the village beyond the palace. A full-out war would see most of them dead or in misery, their families grieving.

It was true that the odds would not be in favor of the Hillside men, but Joshua's experience could hone them into deadly weapons. They would either kill and conquer or Kára's people would die out trying. Either way, death would lie heavy on the shoulders of Orkney.

The song ended and people began to file out of the room, smiles and laughter in contrast to his dark thoughts. Joshua felt a brush against his arm and glanced down. Kára's amma, Harriett, stared up at him. She was draped in a gown similar to the one

Kára wore but had a shawl of embroidered lace over her white hair. "You are thinking hard about something, Highlander."

He turned back to watch Kára lift the bairn from Brenna's arms, kissing his little forehead and looking down into his face with a joyous smile. "War changes people," he said. Kára turned gently in a tight circle as if dancing with the bairn.

"We have always been at war," Harriett answered.

In truth, hadn't Joshua? From the time he could lift a wooden sword, his father had told him he must grow strong to battle. When his mother died and his father lost his mind in grief, expecting that it was truly the biblical end of days, George Sinclair had officially declared Joshua Horseman of War. From that day on, it was all he was supposed to care about. War and winning war. Even though the numbers showed he had won in South Ronaldsay when he'd tried to help a small group defend their home from a neighboring family, he counted the battle as his first loss. Death and misery had piled up on both sides. He swore never again to lead people where he thought they would die.

"To have a chance at winning against Robert," he continued, "I would have to make them into brutal, uncaring warriors. Even then they will likely die."

Kára showed the bairn to her own son, Geir. The lad smiled down at the newborn, gently touching its cheek with the back of his finger.

"The training changes people," Joshua said. "Brutality twists their souls."

They stood quietly for a long moment. "How

twisted is your soul, Highlander?" Harriett asked, making him look down into her dark blue-gray eyes, the same color as Kára's.

The piercing gaze seemed to slice into him, searching his multitude of sins. How many battles had he fought, ignoring the fear and pleading in men's eyes before he killed them? He looked back to the happy smiles of the people still in the room and connected with Kára. She still held the bairn. Her look was curious. Did she wonder what her grandmother was saying to him? Did she hope her wise words would sway him to their side of this unwinnable battle?

"War changes people on both sides, and not for the better," Joshua answered, avoiding her direct question. He tore his gaze from Kára and met the eyes of the old woman. "Which is why I do not recommend it for your family."

"You would have us abandon our isle," she said, her tone giving no hint of her feelings regarding the suggestion.

He had mentioned it only once to Kára. Had she told her grandmother? "Aye," he said.

"You do not seem the type of man who has ever retreated," she said.

The very idea made his fists clench, and he crossed his arms over his chest, sliding easily into a familiar battle stance. "I have not." Even in the battle in South Ronaldsay, with John Dishington fighting him, he had not stopped until both families were decimated.

"I do not think my granddaughter is in favor of retreat, either," she said.

Across the room, Kára, bairn still on her shoulder, began to make her way over to him. "But my clan is large and the most powerful in Scotland."

"Powerful enough to overthrow Robert's rule here?" Harriett asked.

Certainly, but then King James would outlaw the Sinclair Clan and try to take their lands and castle. Civil war would rage across northern Scotland, and they would need to take the crown from King James to win. The lives of the common people would be misery, and death would rule the land for years before things settled, leaving the borders vulnerable to English and French invaders. The thought left bitterness in Joshua's mouth, making him want to spit.

"Such frowns over here," Kára said, stopping before them, her gaze going from her grandmother to Joshua. "What are you two talking about?"

"War and twisted souls," Harriett said.

"'Tis not something to talk about at a celebration of life," Joshua murmured, his gaze going to the wee lad wrapped in bright blue swaddling.

Kára brought him off her shoulder so he could see that the lad was awake, his blue eyes taking in whatever he could see. Osk came up to stand at Joshua's shoulder. "He looks lusty and full of health after such a difficult time being born," Osk said.

"You can hold him," Kára said to Joshua. "He is named after you." She lifted the bairn away from her, settling him into his arms.

The bundle felt awkward, so light and fragile, nothing like the bulk of a newborn foal. "He is smiling at me," Joshua said, balancing the bundle in the crook of one arm. He reached into the bunting to pull out one of the lad's little hands.

"He is too young to smile," Harriett said.

Joshua looked at her. "Too young to smile or too young to know not to smile at a Horseman of War?"

"Both," she said and walked toward the door to join her sister, Hilda.

Joshua looked back down at the miniature face that started to scrunch up. "He is going to fuss," he said.

"He nursed before the ceremony," Kára said. "There is probably a bubble trapped inside. Pat his back."

Joshua shifted to clasp him in two hands, and the bairn's face relaxed into a smile. "See, he smiles at me." He lifted him into the air and looked upward at him.

Kára tipped her head back to look up at the bairn near the ceiling. "I would not—"

Like a river of foamy white, the bairn's puke shot out from his wee lips. Years of training his reflexes to save him, Joshua twisted to the side, and the spit-up flew over his shoulder.

"Aak," Osk yelled as the bairn's puke hit him in the face.

Joshua lowered the bairn to rest over his shoulder, his large hand spanning him to pat his back.

Osk sputtered, wiping his face. "What the bloody hell!"

"If we ever take bairns into battle, we should make sure to feed them well first," Joshua said and grinned. Kára held a hand over her mouth to keep her laughter from erupting.

"Give me my bairn," Brenna said, suddenly next to him, her fingers reaching and her frown fierce. "No one is taking him into battle."

Joshua looked to Kára. "She is always snatching him away from me."

"Have your own babe," Brenna said. "Then you can flip him up into the rafters and make him empty his breakfast." She huffed. "Now I have to feed him again."

"He is perfectly healthy and happy," Joshua said, pointing to the little face. "See, he does smile at me."

"If he is already smiling, it is at me," Brenna said and whisked the baby away.

Kára's grin spread wide, and a soft chuckle came out. "New mothers are a protective lot. Do not mess with her or Brenna might slice your throat."

Joshua's hand went to his neck, rubbing it absently. "Hmmm...I was going to gift wee Joshua with one of my *sgian dubhs*, but perhaps that is not the best, given his mother's bloodthirstiness."

Kára laughed. "What else would you give him then?"

Joshua tilted his head in the direction of Kára's underground cottage where the stack of tributes from the children still sat. "I have a pile of painted rocks, jams, and woolen scarves. Perhaps one of those."

Kára's eyes widened in mock disbelief. "And make a child cry that you gave their gift away?"

"Gifts? More like bribes," he said, meeting her smile.

She flipped her hand this way and that. "But they were bribes given from the heart."

"Well, then, I suppose I will gift him my *sgian dubh* and stay well away from his mother."

"You are wise, Joshua Sinclair," Kára said, smiling as she stared up into his eyes. Open and happy, as if the world were a safe and wondrous place. He had never seen anything so…freeing, as if his whole life he had not been able to take a full breath until that very moment.

He reached forward to capture her chin in his fingers and leaned in to her. His gaze traveled the softness of her cheeks, the freckles over her straight nose, the long lashes bordering her eyes, and ended on the perfect curves of her lush mouth. "How can I keep this happiness on your face?" he asked, his brows furrowing.

Her exuberant, teasing smile faded, and it was as if a shadow of darkness had fallen over her, bringing a chill to the room. "Happiness in my world is fleeting. It is impossible to keep."

Sensing her withdrawal, he dropped his hand. "Perhaps we should find a new world, then?"

After a pause, Kára looked toward the door. "I should go to town to help set up for the Fire Festival to celebrate Samhain this eve."

Joshua cleared his throat and crossed his arms. Behind him, Geir made gagging noises and laughed as Osk continued to wipe away the bairn's puke. "'Tis clever not to light the fires here at Hillside to draw attention," Joshua said.

"We still must be on guard for Robert's retaliation in town."

"I will set up a perimeter with a rotation for guarding the festival," Joshua said. The chill that

Kára's frown had brought clung to him. *Damn cold.* Would he never feel warm again?

Harriett, Kára's grandmother, stood near the door with her sister. They spoke and then both looked at him. *How twisted is your soul, Highlander?*

The faces that appeared in his nightmares, damning eyes staring lifelessly at him, tried to push their way forward as if summoned by the old woman's question. He walked through the room toward the cold outdoors. If Kára could see the dead stalking after him, the people who had fallen to his sword or his poor judgment, would she curse her own people with the same nightmares he battled?

• • •

Damn, Kára thought as she caught the toe of her slipper in the hem of her straight gown.

She should have changed into her trousers and tunic before the festival. Her face flushed as she glanced across the fire where Joshua spoke with a group of men he'd been training. She had remained in the dress because it was pretty with the embroidery on the hem and neckline. The traditional blue wool costume had been her mother's. Amma had insisted Kára not bury her in it, but to keep it to wear and honor her memory. So Kára's mother had been buried in an older frock, along with her scant pieces of silver jewelry and her favorite mixing bowl.

Samhain was the night when spirits could walk the earth once more, visiting those they left behind. A long table for the dead had been set up behind Asmund's tavern, and she walked over to where Osk stood, wearing a clean tunic. He arranged the four plates and cups that represented their loss. "Da would want whisky. I have wine for Ma and Eydis," he said and glanced at her. "What would Geir want to drink?"

What did it matter? Her husband wouldn't come back, even on Samhain. None of them would. But the laying out of food for the dead was not for the deceased. It was for those who remained behind, surviving without them. "Ale, Geir liked ale over whisky," she said, patting her brother's shoulder. He had been just a lad when her husband was killed, the same age her son was now.

The pastor who had come over from Scotia spoke with some of the villagers nearby, learning of their losses. She glanced over the three plates they added this year. Last Samhain, they had only one to put out for her husband. Her parents and sister had been with her to celebrate the harvest and take the blessings of walking between the fires. *Some good that did them.* There had been no blessings when the village was attacked by Robert and his sons and her mother and sister were caught inside a burning building. Or when she and her father went after Robert to avenge them. Her father had been skewered by Henry Stuart, and both of their horses had been taken. Kára had been forced to hide in the tall grasses to survive, failing them all.

She felt pressure gather in her eyes, and she blinked, denying the tears that would show her to be weak when her people needed her to be strong. But they would not stay inside her. Kára took a fortifying breath and walked toward the bank where the sea beat at the rocks and seaweed spread out in the foamy water below.

Staring out at the waves turned orange with the setting sun, she let her tears slide down her cheeks unchecked. She would grieve for them here, bleed it out of her so she could stand strong tonight and try to enjoy the festival. She had not cried much for her slain husband, her world consumed with a newborn son. With her family around her, she did not have to raise him alone. But now…she must guide Osk and Geir with only her amma's help and wisdom. Loneliness pressed inside her, filling her chest cavity until it felt difficult to inhale. Aye, she must bleed some of the sorrow away.

With the wind blowing, she did not hear anyone approach, and started as Joshua halted next to her. He looked out at the waves, too. She stopped herself from wiping her wet cheeks, giving her tears away, and breathed deeply to keep herself from sniffing. The wind dried trails of salt-sticky tears on her cheeks.

"Ye grieve for your husband," Joshua said, his words even. "I am sorry, Kára, that ye lost him to live on alone without the comfort and help he could give in raising Geir."

She didn't say anything even though she opened her mouth and closed it.

Joshua stood with his hands clasped behind his back, the wind pushing against their faces as if it tried to keep them from plunging off the edge. "Ye married him young then? Ye must have loved him very much."

She swallowed, clearing her throat. "We were

young, both of us. Thrown together, really, by our parents, who wished us to have a chance to live our lives before anything could happen. I cared for him, even if we were together less than a year."

"Ye kept his son alive," Joshua said, his words caught by the wind, making it hard for her to hear. She moved a step closer to him. "Geir is a tribute to him," Joshua continued.

She watched two seabirds dive down on the wind currents and wrapped her arms around herself. "I poured all my anger into keeping my babe thriving, even as he struggled at the beginning, since he was small," she said, the words tumbling out.

Joshua stepped closer until she could feel his arm press up against hers. The warmth of his touch made more tears leak from her eyes. "It is my parents and sister…" she started and sniffed.

He glanced back toward the table. "I saw Osk setting out four plates."

She nodded, not trusting herself to speak at first. "The loss of them is still fresh and raw within me. I would not have my people see me so weak."

His arm moved around her shoulders, and he pulled her gently into his side. "There is no shame in grief. Tears let the poison of sadness out. Otherwise, it will fester inside, making ye act unwise."

She turned her eyes up to him. Strength and hurt warred in the lines of his face. "Do you let your tears out, Joshua, Horseman of War?"

Joshua inhaled. "My emotion bleeds out of me in rage more often, but if my brothers or sister were taken away, struck down by illness or a blade, I would surely weep. To refuse to do so would harm me even more." He nodded, glancing behind them. "But I understand. I, too, hide my rage and sorrow if possible." He pulled her into him, both arms circling her. She settled her face against his chest and let him hold her. "Ye need to let them out, Kára. I will carry your tears to my grave."

Joshua Sinclair was strength and acceptance. He asked nothing of her but stood there letting her grieve without judgment. She relaxed into him and felt the hotness of her tears flow freely out against him. He did not stroke her but held her as if he were a boulder for her to cling to while a river flowed viciously around her, wanting to sweep her away in the current. Her arms dropped to wrap around his waist, the faces of her mother, father, and sister rising up behind her squeezed eyes, pushing the tears out.

He stood there without comment. He did not try to fix the unfixable or soothe when he knew the sorrow must come out. Joshua Sinclair was safe, apart from her world, someone who did not look on her as an example. He was not someone who needed her to be strong. For long moments, she wept, letting the venom flow out from her until the tension in her shoulders and arms ebbed.

When she opened her eyes against his soaked tunic, the sun was down. How long had he held her? She stepped back, and he kept his hands on her upper arms as she wiped her damp cheeks. Perhaps he worried she would step backward off the cliff or that the wind would carry her away. Sometimes she felt like it would if she did not always fight to remain rooted to the land.

"We should go to the fires," she said with a big inhale. The music had started in the background, a merry tune to lift the spirits of the living as they remembered the spirits of the dead.

She gazed up into his face. It was as strong as ever, the fire casting splashes of light against it with the shadows. "I think we could both use a nip of whisky," he said, his brows raising in question.

She smiled. "Aye." She glanced away from him toward the dark blue sky over the sea. "Thank you," she whispered.

He nodded and took her hand, threading his fingers through hers. Melding them together. She looked at it for a moment. It was intimate. In some ways more so than when they'd rolled around in her den tupping.

She almost pulled her hand away but then stopped. Instead, she slid her hand farther into place and curled her fingers inward, so their palms were warm against each other. They walked together toward the fires.

CHAPTER TWELVE

*"A kingdom that has once been destroyed can never
come again into being; nor can the
dead ever be brought back to life."*
Sun Tzu – The Art of War

Normally, Samhain was a raucous festival, but with
the recent abduction of their leader, Erik, and the
many deaths over the past year, the smiles were
subdued. No one danced, although many swayed
and drank from tankards. But their eyes turned
often to the night falling across the landscape
outside the circle of the three bonfires, as if to see
wolves sneaking up on them, wolves in the uniforms
of men, riding for the Stuarts.

They moved to the fires where one of the elders,
Corey Muir, organized the line of children to walk
between for their blessing. "First the babes with
their mothers," he called. "Then the children. Hold
hands," he said, pointing to the line of lads and
lasses. "Aye, like that," he said, smiling encouragingly.
"Follow the one in front of you."

Joshua watched the lines weave around the three
fires, Pastor John praying nearby. Next came the
young lasses. "I better go through," Kára said,
stepping away from him. He watched her pale gold
hair as it lay in waves over her back like moonlit
water on a windblown loch. She caught up with
some other women, about ten in all, as they walked

through. Overall, he counted about twenty women and about thirty-five men. Even if the women fought, leaving the mothers of bairns and elderly at home, they would still be slaughtered by Robert's men if he led them to attack.

I could teach them how to break through the defenses I taught the Stuarts. Joshua ran both hands down his face. *Bloody hell.* He'd trained one group and now he was considering how to train another to get around the first. He truly was an apocalyptic Horseman of foking War.

I should have stayed in Caithness. He could be helping his brother, Cain, rule the three clans under Sinclair in peace. *Leave Orkney.* He could travel back with Pastor John, ensuring his safety.

It had been his plan all along, to adventure in other places, using his talents and knowledge of war to help people. But so far all he had done was create more misery in the world. He should leave now. In the morning. But Kára… She'd trusted him enough to let him see her tears. Could he abandon her?

He exhaled long. "Fok," he murmured.

"Not as jolly as your Samhain back home?" Calder asked from behind.

Joshua glanced back at him. "Ye have good reason to keep things solemn and quieter."

"'Tis our turn through," Calder said, nodding toward the fires. "And then you can lead your horse through with Kára leading Broch and then her animals."

Joshua walked with him. They rounded the first fire in silence. The heat from the flames slowed Joshua's steps to remain in the glow of the warmth for as long as he could.

"Thank you," Calder said. "I do not think I said that before, about you fetching Hilda and holding Brenna up when I was…"

Joshua nodded. "Ye have a bonny family. 'Tis a good start." Which would end in death if they went against Robert, even with his training. How many places would be set at next year's Samhain? Would Brenna and her bairn weep over Calder's?

They rounded the first fire. "Have you trained your whole life at winning battles?" Calder asked.

Winning battles? The field at South Ronaldsay surfaced in his mind. Scavenger birds circling as people carried away their family members. A mother crying over the boy covered in mud. Her wiping his face with her skirts until his freckles showed through on his pale skin.

Joshua forced himself past the memories that would never leave him. "Aye. I was raised to war," he said, his words solemn.

"Have you been taught by masters of war?" Calder was attentive, eager to learn. A year ago, Joshua would have smiled at his enthusiasm.

"Aye, from my father and… I have a book. Have ye heard of *The Art of War*?"

"No." Calder shook his head.

"It was written over a millennium ago by a great warrior from a secluded country named China. Although the country is closed off to most travelers, spice traders and spiritual seekers have taken sea routes to reach it."

They rounded another fire, the flames bending toward them with a gust of breeze. "And you have this book of wisdom? And can read it?"

"A Jesuit priest translated the teachings into French. My father, hearing of the book, went to great lengths to track a rare copy down in Edinburgh. After all, his second son was War." Joshua's hands gripped into tight fists, the remorse for not studying it more pressing heavily on him. "I spent the next year learning French to decipher it."

"What great teachings did you learn?" Calder asked, his brows lower.

"Many," Joshua said. "I have my copy with me and can read ye some." He stretched his arms behind him, his gaze scanning ahead of them out into the darkness that the Hillside warriors were watching. "Intimidation works to deter attack."

"You are very intimidating," Calder said with a chuckle.

"If intimidation is not enough to deter the enemy, a swift, brutal strike can end a war quickly and ultimately save many more lives."

He slowed, and Calder matched his pace, watching him as if he meant to commit each of Joshua's words to memory. "And there are more times that it is wise not to attack than to act offensively." Like when a lad pleaded with him to help his family attack an oppressor, and he did not properly scout the area or get to know the enemy first.

They made it back around in time to see Geir walking Fuil through the fires himself. Kára's boy had obviously learned not to fear his warhorse. Kára had her own horse, Broch, walking beside him.

Pastor John meandered over with two more

Hillside men, joining him and Calder where they stood in the glow of the fire. "Tell us about Scotia," one said. "About your festivals where there are five hundred horses and hundreds of people and sheep and livestock needing to weave through the fires."

The other one handed him an ale. Joshua took a drink, swallowing down his self-loathing with it. He cleared his throat. "It is much louder and rather unruly. We usually have a horse or two charge off into the night to be rounded up by the lads."

Pastor John shook his head, smiling. "'Tis right muddled with all the people and horses and lots of drink."

They followed Calder to some boulders acting as benches and sat with the men Joshua had been working with over the last week. "And we have tournaments. Throwing daggers, stones, and cabers."

"Cabers are trees?" Calder asked.

"Aye," Pastor John said, stretching his arms out wide. "About one hundred fifty pounds and twenty feet long."

"I have never seen a tree that size," one man said. "Why do you throw it?" He shook his head, laughing.

"'Tis useful," Joshua said, taking a quick sip and relaxing into the easy talk. "A way to ford a river if some bastards are chasing ye."

"But first you would have to cut it down," Osk said from where he stood off to the side. He walked closer into the circle that had formed. "By then the bastards would be upon you."

Joshua pointed at him, his brow rising. "Aye, unless we have carried one with us into battle," he said, half jesting.

"You carry trees about?" the first man said, and they all waited for his nod before breaking into loud laughter.

"No wonder you are as strong as three men," another said.

"If we had trees," Osk said, "I would carry one about." He nodded seriously and drank deeply off his tankard.

Joshua grinned at them, but then his chest tightened with the thought of them battling trained warriors, being struck down under Robert Stuart's orders, the whole lot wiped out in one heated battle. On South Ronaldsay, both sides lost, but against Robert, the Hillside people would surely falter. It was a matter of numbers and experience.

He looked down and then up to meet Calder's gaze. "If ye came to my home in mainland Scotland, there'd be whole forests for ye to carry about."

The men laughed, but Calder stared at him. "Enough wood to build cottages and furniture?"

Joshua nodded. "And a clan of hundreds to protect yer families. Free lands to hunt upon. Horses to ride."

The laughter subsided. Did they hear his invitation? Did they hate him for it? The scowl that had taken over Osk's face said "aye." Pastor John did not say anything, being wise enough to read the sudden stillness.

Joshua shrugged and raised his tankard, knowing at least he had planted the seed of a new plan forming in his mind. "To home. Wherever that may be."

The others raised their cups. "To Orkney," Osk said.

"To our fallen," said Calder.

"Aye," came from the rest of them as they drank heartily.

"May God bless us all," Pastor John said, lifting his own tankard that he'd set on the ground.

Joshua heard footsteps, and he glanced over his shoulder to see Kára walking up to them, her previous sadness dulled by talking with the ladies. She still wore the gown from the earlier christening. It slid along her full curves, her stays accenting her narrow waist and her lifted breasts. Coming from the shadows with the bright fire before her, she looked like a princess of old, gliding forward with strength, grace, and authority. The men sitting stood as she approached.

"To our queen, Kára Flett," Calder said, raising his tankard. The others followed, even Osk.

"There is no queen without a throne," Kára said, a casual smile on her face. "But you may call me chief."

"To our chief, Kára Flett," one of the men said, and the rest called it out in unison. Either this was their version of a swearing of loyalty ceremony, or they merely liked to have excuses to raise their cups and drink.

Kára looked to Corey Spence. "We should meet tomorrow to make plans for the upcoming winter."

Corey nodded, an encouraging smile on his weathered face. "I will inform the council members."

Calder returned from where he'd fetched a tankard for Kára, handing it to her. Torben walked with him, his usual frown in place when he spotted Joshua. "We were listening to Joshua's tales of life on Scotia," Calder said, tipping his head to Joshua. "At his home in Caithness, there is open land and trees and horses."

Kára's smile faltered, and her gaze shifted to Joshua. Did she suspect him of trying to win her people away from Orkney? Wasn't that exactly what he was trying to do? Although, they did start by asking him about his life back there.

"It is quite different there," she said, staring directly at him. "Rainbows arching over green grasses and bonny buttercups. Trees that are easy to fell and stack on their own into huge houses for all the people. No illness or famine. No wars." She tilted her head. "Why ever did you even come to Orkney then?"

Osk snorted and Torben laughed outright. "Do you hunt unicorns there in your forests?" he asked, and the other men turned to study Joshua as if suspicious of the picture he'd painted for them. A few chuckled.

"There is certainly illness and war at times," Pastor John said, his brows lowering. "But there is vast land to grow crops, and the woodlands are full of deer."

Joshua cleared his throat. "I came to Orkney because I wanted to be of use in helping warriors grow strong to defend themselves and their people. 'Tis my occupation in life."

Torben crossed his arms, mutiny on his face. "To train people to kill one another?"

Joshua's gaze slid across the group of men who

had gathered. "I was raised around war. I have studied it and know it firsthand. I have seen the misery it causes if it stretches out for a long time. The common people suffer the most as warriors and leaders fight. Famine and disease feed fear and desperation. It is better to make a swift victory and treat the defeated with respect, bringing them into one's clan."

Now more than ever before, Joshua understood what his older brother, Cain, was trying to do with the Sutherland and the MacKay Clans back home. Joshua had thought Cain was too lenient on their foes, because he assumed they would rise back up and the war would continue. If he were chief, he would have conquered the rulers of the clans soundly, leaving the people unharmed but too frightened to retaliate. But looking into the determined faces of the defeated here on Orkney, Joshua realized defeating people did not always frighten them into accepting one's rule over them. Although, Cain Sinclair was nothing like Robert Stuart.

"And if they are not treated with respect?" Calder asked. From his face, he was the only one possibly admitting they were the defeated.

Joshua breathed deeply. "Then they rise up to battle until the last blood of their clan soaks into the soil, or…" Joshua let his gaze move from Calder to Kára. "They move on to new territory."

"Bloody hell," Osk murmured and spit.

"You ask us to abandon our land, our home?" Torben asked, his eyes wide with incredulity.

"It is the way of war, the way of the human

condition," Joshua said. "Since the beginning of time, whether ye like it or not. Either the defeated put up with their terrible treatment, or they war against their foe until they die, or they move on to find peace elsewhere. They need to figure out what they want to do as a people." He slid his gaze from Kára over the others gathered, meeting Corey's eyes. He was one of the council members. Perhaps he could bring up Joshua's invitation at the meeting.

"And where would our ancestors roam to try to find us if we were not on Orkney?" Osk asked, his arm flinging out toward the long table that they had set for those who were being remembered.

Calder frowned at him, his arms crossed. "Why don't you sit with them tonight and ask their opinion?"

"You mock our customs," Torben accused.

Joshua met his gaze directly. "I mock those who think the dead need a map and compass to find those they love here on earth."

Kára's voice was soft. "I see no plate and cup set for your father and mother here on Orkney." Her eyes met his, but there was no challenge in them. Silence stretched among them all as the fire snapped in the breeze before them, casting gold splashes of light.

"We will discuss ideas at the council meeting on the morrow," Corey said.

Kára looked away toward the gathering that had grown, listening in as the tensions grew. "Aye, tonight is to honor and celebrate."

One of the men raised his cup. "And drink!" Several yelled their agreement.

Osk walked off toward the table, Torben with him. Joshua stood. "As long as those watching the perimeter stay alert." He stared out into the falling night. Their fires would stand out like beacons across the windswept hills.

Kára turned to Corey. "Let us finish the blessings, and you can head back to Hillside."

Her tone did not reveal anything about how she was feeling about the discussion. She turned away and walked to her goat and sheep to lead them through.

"Blessings are my specialty," Pastor John said, smiling. "I can help." He walked next to Corey toward the fires.

Joshua stood, walking alone to the fires. He stared into one as it rose up, sending sparks flying in the air. The heat from it chased the cold from his bones. Back at home, people had thought him obsessed with fire, ready to light a bonfire whenever there was the slightest reason. But the truth was he sought to chase off the cold that settled through the Highlands as the sun dipped.

When one side felt roasted, he turned to look out at the night, letting the flames warm his backside. Too bad there was not a Horseman of Fire, because Joshua would volunteer for the job. Not only did it strike fear in many an enemy, it kept him warm.

Small groups walked away from the fires and village out into the Orkney night toward Hillside. The children stopped at the table, touching the plates before hurrying after their parents. They seemed to spread out, as if their smaller groupings could hide easier if Robert's men came.

Geir traipsed over to him. "I need to set these out," he said, holding up four little figures braided from the tall grasses that grew all over the isle. Crude renditions of two women with long woven hair and two men. He and Joshua walked to the long table where the woven figures of people and animals lay upon the plates, left by the children. There were also hearts and crosses, some plates heaped full of several creations. Geir placed one of his figures on each of the four plates Osk had set for Kára's husband and her family.

Lord. There were so many plates, so many deaths. "Is there a spare plate for me to put out?"

Geir nodded and ran over to a small stack near the far end, coming back to place it next to their four. "Who is it for?"

"A boy. A bit older than ye. His name was Adam, and he liked to shoot arrows and tease his sister." Joshua touched the clay disk, letting the memory of the young lad surface. It came easily, always ready to haunt him with eyes filled with trust. *Lead us to victory*, he'd said. And Joshua had been too prideful to say no.

Hissss. Joshua turned to see plumes of steam rise over the fires as seawater was dumped on them. The men kicked dirt over the damp coals and trudged away.

"I will take Broch and Fuil back to Hillside," Geir said. He smiled. "I have two turnips."

"Thank ye," Joshua said, nodding to him. The lad had made great progress with winning Fuil over this week.

Kára stood at the fires, watching the drenched

dark spots on the wind-whipped grasses. He walked over slowly to stand next to her, and the mostly deadened fires still gave off a bit of heat. She didn't look up.

"My first Samhain as chief," she said. "And it is the worst ever. The world is a dark place, and I do not know if it will ever be light again."

Joshua did not speak, only touched her hand. Slowly their fingers intertwined, and she tipped her face up to his, her eyes searching. "We will go back to my den," she said. It was a statement, but the inflection made it into a question. She was vulnerable. Sadness and regret and mourning made terrible bedfellows.

"Kára—"

"That is right," she said, cutting him off. "Just Kára for the night. No chief or queen or mother or sister or daughter of dead parents. Just Kára." She stepped into him so the wind could hardly find a passage between their bodies. "I have thought of death too much today, and sorrow has taken my strength. Tonight, I wish to be a woman first, and you only a man. Not the Horseman of War or someone who tries to persuade us to leave our isle."

He opened his mouth to refute her statement, but she reached up, brushing a kiss against his lips. She pulled back. "Tomorrow will bring very hard choices and…" She looked up at him in the glow of the lantern she'd left at her feet. "I feel life will not be the same." She searched his eyes as if trying to peer into his soul. "Love me tonight, Highlander."

His free hand rose to slide along her cheek, pushing her hair back from where it danced there in the chilled night air. "Aye, Kára lass."

She exhaled as if she'd held her breath. Could she possibly think he'd deny her? He pulled her up against him, his lips settling against hers. Lush and warm, her touch shot through him, igniting the simmering fire like a torch catching light on an arrow soaked in black pitch. She pulled away, her mouth open on a shallow breath.

Without a word, she tugged him, and he followed her into the night.

CHAPTER THIRTEEN

"Opportunities multiply as they are seized."
Sun Tzu – The Art of War

Kára listened, her heart thumping harder, as Joshua stalked across her underground earthen den toward her.

Even without much illumination, his shadow in the muted light from the well opening was imposing. Her heart beat faster, her lips still damp from his savage kiss at the top of the well before they parted to slide down the rope. Neither of them said anything.

She heard him inhale. Was he finding her by the smell of woodsmoke that had settled into her hair and clothes from the bonfires? She stood still, lips open so her breath moved in and out silently. The large mass that was Joshua Sinclair pushed the stone stool out of the way as he walked forward.

Breath in. Breath out. She could not hear his advance, his feet setting down with predatory silence and the wind whistling over the opening above her cave. But she knew he was close, her senses attuned to him. If she put her hands forward, they would probably touch him. She shut her eyes, for there was no sense in trying to see through the dense shadows. Instead, she inhaled and took a step closer to where she knew he must be. Her eyes opened but it was as if they were closed, the darkness so thick. She

inhaled again and caught the slightest scent of
woodsmoke, wool, leather, and fresh air. He was
right before her.

Standing there, listening to him breathe, inhaling
his scent, Kára's blood thrummed through her with
anticipation. Who would touch first? What part of
her would feel the warmth he gave off? Her nipples
pulled taut as she waited there in the dark.

A brushing against her breasts. Then pressure as
Joshua's chest met her own, and she tilted her face
up toward the darkness above her where his face
would be. Did he wait for permission? The thought
lit a wildness through her. Here was a man, a man
who could bring all sorts of pain to foes, who could
no doubt kill with his bare hands, and he was
honorable and kind and waiting for her to direct
him.

A small hum came from the back of her throat,
her hands coming up in the darkness. Palms flat, she
set them on his chest, which was already bare. She
slid them up over the contours of his muscles. "Aye,"
she whispered. "Aye, Joshua."

A rumble of a growl answered her in the deep
darkness. Hands, large and restrained, grabbed her
upper arms, sliding up to cup her face. Powerful,
wild, and fervent, Joshua's mouth came down to
meet her lips.

Like the driest kindling shot by lightning, throwing up a shower of sparks, the flame of anticipation
exploded within Kára. Heat surged from within, and
she slanted her mouth against his, her fingers scrap-
ing through his hair, wrapping it in her fists so he
could not pull away. Hands stroked down over her

shoulders and the boned stays under her wool dress. She pulled the thin lace at the top of her stays, letting it open enough to release her breasts. She shrugged her shoulders, letting her gown slip lower to expose her. It felt deliciously wicked to feel the chill on her skin, her breasts perched there, even if he could not see them. Finding one of his hands at her waist, she slid it up until he could feel the swell of her above the neckline.

"Och, lass," he murmured, his voice thick with appreciation and want. The rumble of it seemed to vibrate in her blood, making it rush faster so that the ache between her legs grew.

Kára tugged on his belt until she felt it give. *Thud*. His wrappings dropped to the floor.

He groaned as she pressed into him, rubbing her abdomen against the huge erection she could feel rising between them. His hands slid down her back to lift under her arse, raising her up to rub the juncture of her legs against him through her gown.

Kisses. A tasting, a giving. They turned wild. They grew open and savage until Kára felt like she could lose herself within Joshua Sinclair. And tonight, that was exactly what she wanted, what she needed.

Unpinning the brooches at her shoulders, Kára's gown slid the rest of the way down. She pushed him slightly back so she could step out of it, leaving her in her unlaced stays over a white smock. His hands rucked up the back, his fingers deftly exploring the contours of her bare arse. Shallow breaths, the distant whistle of wind, the scratch of cotton against skin, the thudding of her heart, and the brush of skin against skin were the only sounds in Kára's world.

Joshua added a soft kiss sound as he trailed his lips from her mouth to her jaw and down her neck, sending tantalizing chills along Kára's limbs. She untied the rest of the laces of her stays and shrugged her shoulders until her smock floated down around her hips to fall into a ghostly puddle around her feet.

She heard him work at the lacings on his boots and shove one off, the weight of it thumping on the floor. Everything about Joshua was heavy and hard, except his skin. She bent to untie her own boots, and he seemed to give her space to do it.

While down, she inhaled, thinking of how he'd pleasured her while they were in her den before. Never had she thought to use her mouth for something other than kissing. They were next to the bed, and she grabbed one of the furs that lay strewn across it, shoving it under her knees where she knelt on the floor before him.

She reached for him, knowing he must be right before her. His gasp added to the music of near silence around them. Without the sense of sight, touch and smell seemed heightened. Wrapping her hand around his length, she marveled at the softness of the skin stretched over something so hard and powerful. Tentatively, she leaned into him, opening her mouth.

"Sweet bloody hell." His whisper came in a rush of breath as she took him into her wet, warm mouth. Massive and powerful, like the rest of her Highlander. She felt his hands fist in her hair, but he did not direct her.

Sliding back and forth, listening to his intake of breath and the low groans of pleasure, Kára felt powerful, even as she kneeled before him. The trust he had for her made her bold, and his noises of pleasure made heat spread down through her body. She felt his hips thrust against her, gently at first, but the motion grew more forceful until Joshua lifted under her arms, pulling her up to standing.

The room was cold, but the heat within her warred against it. She shivered from the contrast. Joshua's mouth fell on her own, kissing her with wild want. Pushing backward, they fell across her bed, the furs tickling against her skin. Without breaking their kisses, they slid up the bed. His fingers moved between her legs, searching her out.

She gasped as he entered, touching where only one other ever had before. The ache grew heavy there, and she thrust upward against his hand. His mouth drew her nipple inside, the hot, wet suction pulling a moan from her. In the quiet, the sound of her wetness as he worked her flesh spiraled another coil of desperate want through Kára. She panted above his bowed head as he sucked on one and then the other of her breasts.

Without words to break the spell, Kára opened her legs far across the bed, her knees coming up to clamp around Joshua's hips. Her hands slid along his taut arse, pushing him toward her. Eyes wide, but too dark to see anything, Kára felt his presence hover over her, and she let her knees fall open. He sought her below, and she held on to his broad, muscle-encased shoulders. And then he surged straight into her.

Kára gasped, passion's fire exploding within her at the immense pressure filling her. His lips came back down to hers, and she clung to them, her heels digging into the bed to meet his thrusts with her own. Her hands strained to pull him down on her.

Suddenly, he pulled out of her, but she did not have time to voice anything before he rolled her to her stomach, his hands lifting her hips up. His hot jack slid down her arse, poised from behind. She pushed up onto her hands, arching her back, her full breasts hanging.

Joshua's stomach, hot and hard, lay along her back, and he thrust back inside her.

"Oh God," she breathed.

His hands wrapped around to the front, one holding her stomach so that she couldn't fall flat, the other finding her most sensitive spot down below. Agile and strong, his fingers strummed against her, and she moaned as he kept their rhythm going, her legs wide, her body completely open and presented to him. The sound of his body slapping against her backside added to the hunger consuming Kára.

Joshua's hand moved to capture her weighty breast, squeezing and rolling her hard nipple between his fingers. The sensation shot down through her to join the incredible heat at the juncture of her legs and the pressure building inside.

Aye. The word throbbed through Kára's head as she met each thrust. *Aye.* The sensations building together within her. *Aye.* His fingers moved against her so expertly, so firmly that the waves of pleasure shattered, and she yelled out, "Oh God, aye!"

His arms wrapped around her, holding her to him. His roar filled the vastness of the den as his body filled her, continuing the rhythm to wring out every little bit of pleasure. Kára's head dropped to hang between her shoulders. Joshua's hands stroked along her form, still embedded within her. He pulled her to their sides, yanking the blankets up and over them. Arms around her, he held her as their breathing slowed over many minutes.

Kára listened to his inhales and exhales, feeling the whisper of his breath against her nape and the thud of his heart against her back. Slowly, she turned within the circle of his arms to face him. They still couldn't see each other. She reached up cautiously, catching his whiskered cheeks to kiss him softly. He kissed her back, then tucked her head under his chin. She felt his lips press against her forehead, and then she nuzzled her face into his neck.

Never before had she felt so… What did she feel? Safe, warm, satiated. Aye, but even more, Kára felt cherished, for who she was, not who she was supposed to be. A queen, a chief, a woman warrior. With Joshua, she was only Kára, and that was all he seemed to want.

Tucked away from responsibility, bloodshed, and sorrow, she wished she could stay there forever. Her hand slid lower over her abdomen. It was too soon to wonder, and yet she hoped.

Naked, their combined scent and heat wrapping around them, Kára nuzzled closer into Joshua almost as if she could hide away inside his large body. He held her there, seeming to know what she wanted, what she needed at that moment. Joshua was all around her. She breathed evenly, her thoughts beginning to float on the flow of her breath. For the first time she could remember, she let herself fall completely into the depths of sleep without worry.

• • •

"We will head back to Hillside?" Joshua asked as he belted his wool plaid around his waist without taking his gaze from the beautiful sight of Kára dressing.

The white smock floated down around her curvaceous form, her breasts swelling high as she tightened the front ties of her stays. It was a shame to cover all that beauty. His urge to tumble her back into the bed was strong and insistent.

He had never disliked the sunrise as much as he had that morning. The darkness had cloaked them in warmth, keeping them together all night long as they each gave and took pleasure from the other. But daylight brought the world back, all the hard decisions, remorse, and war.

"You head back," she said, throwing her wool dress over her smock and stays. "I need to stop in the village first."

"I will go with ye."

She shook her head, righting the dress around her. "'Tis still Samhain. I must visit my parents' and sister's graves. Better that I am alone. I have things to say to them." A smile grew across her face, and she stepped in to him. "I will not be long." She lifted her arms, kissing him before he could insist he escort her.

The kiss was leisurely until Kára sighed and

pulled away. She picked up her two brooches, fastening one and then the other at her shoulders. "Are your brooches from your family, handed down?" he asked, nodding to them.

"Aye, handed down for hundreds of years, actually," she said, sliding her finger along the polished silver circle. "They were brought by the first of my kinsmen to come to Orkney from Norway. Legend has it we were related to the aristocracy there, and rivals for the crown sought to kill us off."

He pulled her back into him, looking down at her beautiful face. "So ye *are* a queen."

She smiled broadly. "I think you should call me that all the time."

His brow rose as a wicked grin spread across his mouth. "After what ye did to me last night, ye are definitely my queen."

In the light filtering down the well, he saw a slight blush come to her cheeks, but she kept her smile, and it reached her eyes. "I have never done that before to a man," she said. "You seemed to like it."

Surprise blended quickly with selfish happiness that she had not given such pleasure to her husband. "I more than liked it," he said, pulling her into him so she could feel that just the thought had rendered him hard again.

For a long moment, she gave in to their kiss, until it seemed like it would grow wild. Her hands slid up his chest, pressing lightly. "The council is probably waiting for me," she said through the kiss.

He rested his forehead against hers. "Very well." Letting her go, he watched her gather her cloak. "What are ye going to tell them?"

"Honestly…I am not sure." She sat to pull on her boots, looking at him from the bent position. "If we were to travel to Scotia, we would be welcome on your land?"

His heart jumped as the muscles in his chest clenched. "Ye are considering it?"

"I need to know the facts. If those of my people wanted to escape Robert instead of fighting him or staying on Orkney, hiding from him, would they be welcome? Would there be places where they could make their homes? We have about one hundred in total across the mainland of Orkney, but I am certain not all would choose to leave our isle."

Would her brother? Would the annoying Torben? Calder seemed interested in carrying his new family to safety.

Joshua forced himself to take a breath to calm the excitement that tried to bubble up inside him. "Aye, they would be welcome. My clan is allied with the clan to our south and has taken leadership of the clan to the west. There are miles and miles between us where your people could spread out or stay closer to our castle Girnigoe, where my brother lives."

She finished the other boot and stood. He came up before her, his hands finding her shoulders. "Kára," he said and waited for her eyes to meet his. "Would ye be one of them to come over?" He held his breath, watching her closely.

"I am now the leader of my people. If most wish to leave Orkney, then I must lead them—"

Joshua grabbed Kára up before she could finish, wrapping his arms around her to lift her off the ground. She laughed as he spun her around and kissed her on the lips before setting her back down. *She might still stay.* The warning fell to a whisper under the weight of his hope. *She might come!*

"I need to speak with the council, Joshua," she said, echoing his internal warning. But he was too happy with the chance to save her people without marching them toward certain death and incurring the wrath of King James that he couldn't squelch his hope. As if reading his mind, she said, "Do not become too hopeful yet."

"There are trees and horses and friendly people," he said. "And food. Do not forget to tell the council about the deer we have in abundance. And the Sinclairs will teach them how to make homes of wood and grow crops. And Christmastide and Hogmanay are coming up. My sister decorates the castle with holly, and the tarts are delicious."

"Or," she continued, shaking her head, "you can completely lose your mind and assume we are packing up tonight to leave at dawn."

They climbed out the back stairway that led to a trapdoor under the old wagon in Kára's barn. Joshua had to slide along the dirt and hay on his stomach and rose up, swatting it all off his tunic.

They stepped out into the cold, brisk morning. Even though the sun was not high, it was midmorning from the placement of it. They walked together back toward the village, his boots kicking through the spindly winter grasses. Instead of their hands being intertwined like last night, their arms swayed next to them, staying apart. Was it the light of day that forged a wedge between them? Or was it the vast decisions that must be made? He did not talk, letting her mind churn over her thoughts.

Joshua wanted nothing more than to pull Kára into him, chaining her to his side so he could whisk her back to his home in Caithness on the northern coast of mainland Scotland. Glancing beside him, he watched the wind play among the curls in her long blond hair. She had left it free of her usual braid, and it danced around her straight shoulders, a pale drape over her blue gown. She truly looked like a queen of Norway from long ago, stepped through from history to lead her people.

Och, but what if leading her people meant she would stay on Orkney to fight? He had never felt such helplessness before.

Pushing the dour thought away, Joshua whistled lightly as they walked. It was a happy tune he remembered his father whistling before their mother died long ago when Joshua was eight years old. They reached the edge of town, and Kára halted.

"Go on back to Hillside," she said. "I will meet you there."

Up ahead was the small chapel sitting on a rise above the one-street town. "I would see ye safely to their graves."

She frowned but didn't stop him from following her. The streets were barren, adding a haunted feeling to the place, and Joshua could see the scorch marks of the three fires up on the hillside. No one seemed to be about. Except for Asmund, he had not seen anyone living there, as if it were a false village to trick Robert into thinking Kára's people lived there.

The wind blew fresh off the sea below the village.

Approaching the weathered gate, Kára stopped and turned to him. "I wish to talk to them alone, Joshua." She looked down, shaking her head. "Not that I think they are there. Only their graves." Her blue eyes turned back up to meet his gaze. "There are hard decisions to be made. It helps me to talk it out."

Joshua nodded, his mouth relaxing. He certainly understood the need to think alone. "I can wait for ye in the tavern."

"I may be awhile."

"Asmund will keep me entertained."

A smile spread across her lips, and she laughed lightly. "I am fairly sure Asmund has not entertained anyone in two decades."

"I will help him count his turnips," he said, making her smile broaden.

The gate squeaked on its rusted hinges as she pushed into the graveyard. He watched her walk along the path of tall grasses that partially hid the older monuments to the Orkney dead. Her hair floated in a swirling gust of wind, and she pulled it to one side, trying to tame it. The blue gown caught on some of the twiggy grasses, making the back of the skirt straighten out behind her as if it were the train trailing a queen at court.

His chest tightened. Aye, if he did not convince her to leave Orkney, she would die here, not of old age but from some violence brought down upon her by Robert Stuart, his son, or his mercenary. She disappeared behind the corner of the chapel. Joshua cupped the back of his head, stretching the muscles of his chest, and glanced about. Without trees, there was no worry that a battalion waited in the forest to emerge with deadly force. He turned and walked back down the hill toward the village.

Maybe if he found out more information about Kára's people, he would discover a way to ensure they left Orkney Isle. He glanced over his shoulder, but the chapel still hid her, the queen of Orkney, the one he realized he could not leave behind.

· · ·

"What do you think, Papa?" Kára whispered, her eyes tracing the chiseled letters in the stone over her father's grave. What would Zaire Flett do? Stay and fight or take his people to a new land, a new life with so much potential that she would be a fool not to consider it?

"He says we would be welcome. That there is plentiful food and trees to build houses. No wars right now and the protection of hundreds of trained warriors." The wind rustled the tall grasses growing all around her. "What should I do?"

She leaned forward, setting the few wildflowers she'd found still growing in the sun onto her mother's and sister's graves next to her father. "I would not leave you, but…Brenna just had her first babe. I know Calder wants to take her somewhere safe."

Her hand went to her abdomen. "And Geir should have a better chance to grow strong, he and any other children I may have." Could she be pregnant after three nights with Joshua? They had come together at least seven times, and it'd been the middle of her month. And now her flux was late. "I cannot fight when huge with child," she whispered. But she could not regret any life that may have taken root. Life meant hope, something she was feeling for the first time in nine years.

She sat, letting the ocean breeze wash over her, listening to the rustle of grasses and the caw of seabirds. Placing her hand on the cold stone of her father's grave, she closed her eyes, hoping she could hear his answers. *What do I do, Papa?*

"A flower among the weeds," a voice called, making her eyes fly open, her head snapping around to the side of the chapel.

Stomach tightening along with her fists, Kára's gaze landed on the tall form of Henry Stuart, his unmarked, smooth face smiling wickedly.

CHAPTER FOURTEEN

"Move swift as the Wind and closely formed as the Wood. Attack like the Fire and be still as the Mountain."
Sun Tzu – The Art of War

Henry Stuart bowed his head in a mock display of respect, but his leer showed the monster that lived beneath his smooth features.

It was the face of her nightmares, the man who had killed her husband and nearly her son growing within her as he dragged her back to his father's palace, touching her intimately while he trapped her against his body on horseback. Since then, the sinewy-strong man had stalked her whenever he could. The fact that his father planned to wed him to some highborn lady made no difference to Henry. His father had several mistresses and a handful of bastards, like he had been a bastard of the old Scottish king.

Kára slowly stood, a blade in one of her boots. A short sword against her hip. That was the sum of her weapons—the blades and her seething hatred of the man. Two of his men, large and bearded, emerged from the front of the chapel behind Henry. She swallowed past the thickness of panic wedged in her throat. Of course, he did not come alone. But she was. And to think she had called her uncle, Erik, a fool for being caught alone by Robert's scouts only to find herself falling into the same trap. She should have let Joshua stay.

"This is a place to revere the dead," she said. "Leave here before they rise up and strike you down."

He laughed, walking closer. His hand ran along one of the stone markers as he tilted his head. The wind ruffled his short-cropped hair. "Even though it is still Samhain, and the veil between the real world and the spirit world is thin, I do not see any spirits coming to your aid." The larger of his two men looked nervous, but the other smiled wickedly. Was he hoping Henry would share her with him? The pig. Because she knew that was what Henry ultimately wanted—her body and her helplessness. Years ago, riding back to the palace, her body ripe with child, the man had rammed his dirty hand up her skirts. She still remembered the pain and humiliation of his touch. How she'd prayed he would not kill her unborn child.

Kára breathed deeply, a plan forming in her head. Thank God her father had included her when he'd taught strategy to Osk. She'd been an apt student when her brother usually ended up rolling in the grass with the dogs.

All three men walked into the churchyard, the gate slamming shut behind them. Kára wove around the headstones as she hurried to the side of the chapel. A quick glance showed a deserted lane through the town. *Joshua.* Was he truly inside the tavern counting turnips?

She tugged at her dress as it stuck on the thistle and tall grasses, wishing again that she'd worn trousers. Harder to be raped and easier to fight. Glancing over her shoulder, her heart squeezed as Henry and his men made their way after her in a triangular formation, Henry walking forward in the center. She must take at least one of them out of the attack before they reached her.

"Stay back," she said, her voice strong with warning.

Henry smiled, his condescending grin making nausea roll through her stomach. "I do not want to stay back. In fact, I would like to be very close to ye, Kára Flett. Especially now that ye are not warped with a huge belly. And, since ye stole my father's healer and my sister's horse right from under his nose, he will not make me release ye this time. In fact, I think he will let me…punish ye however I want." His hand went to his cod with obvious intent.

"Broch is *my* horse, not your sister's, and Hilda is a person who does not deserve to be locked up for your bastard father's personal use," she said. Her right arm was most accurate at throwing. She could grab her *mattucashlass* and throw it directly into one of Henry's men. *I should kill Henry.* Should she? Would it bring the wrath of his father down on her and her people?

"My father is in charge of Orkney," Henry said, "no matter what you peasants think. We are of royal blood and have the power and might of King James. My father is practically king of Orkney. Ye should bow down to him."

She'd rather lose her head than bow it to any of the Stuarts. Kára gritted her teeth, breathing through her nose. The grinning guard would be her target.

The other was more occupied with looking at all the graves as if ghosts lurked there.

"Go away now, Henry," she said. "Before I kill you with my bare hands for your crimes against me and my people." Let him think her unarmed.

He motioned to his guards to advance on her.

"You have been warned," she said. Her hand grasped the blade in her right boot. With a practiced twist, she released it directly at the leering guard. *Thwack.* It struck with force, point first directly into his forehead, and he dropped into the tall grass.

"Fok," the second guard yelled, bending down to see his friend releasing his final breath.

"You will twist in the flames of Hell with him today if you come any closer," she yelled.

Henry frowned. "Ye will pay for that life. For every life under the protection of the Stuarts that ye take, we will take a life of your dwindling group." Teeth together, the man seethed, showing the truth behind his previous smile. "Get her," he yelled, and the second man jumped forward to grab her. He was nearly six feet tall and broad with muscled arms.

Kára yanked her short sword from her scabbard, brandishing it before her. "You will die if you come closer," she said, but his eyes narrowed. Even if he was wary of spirits, he apparently did not worry about a woman wielding a sword.

He drew his own sword and brought it around toward her.

"Do not maim her," Henry yelled. "I want her whole."

Maybe she *would* kill Henry. But first she must get past this beast. The guard moved slower than she, either because of his bulk, his laziness, or his belief that she would be easy to seize. He came at her, and she spun out of his way, slicing down as she moved. He grunted as she caught his arm. A red line appeared where her sharp blade sliced his tunic.

"Bloody hell," he cursed, coming back around at her with more force.

Clang. Their blades met, but his strength was superior to hers. Her sword flew from her grip, clanging against a grave marker to drop into the grass. He lunged for her. Forgetting his sword, he wrapped his arms around her, lifting her off the ground.

"Let go!" She struggled in his rough hold, kicking out with her booted feet, but he did not budge. He smelled of sweat and ale and held her up against his frame, her face over his meaty shoulder.

"Halt your squirming, lass," he said, tightening his hold around her until she could hardly breathe in. His strength overpowered any strategy or expertise she might have honed. His lips came to her ear as he whispered, "Just let him up your skirts, and ye will suffer less."

Like hell! Kicking against the man's firm hold, her mind raced over the weapons at hand. There were rocks about, but they were as useless to her as her sword lying with them below in the grass.

She threw her hand up, scratching the side of his face.

"Ye bitch," he yelled, throwing her arm away.

One of her brooches ripped off her shoulder, falling below. *My brooch.* With her still-free hand, she yanked the remaining silver circle off her other shoulder, the long spike sticking out.

"Let go!" she yelled as she slammed the pin against the guard's head. The sharp steel spike pierced his skin easily, cutting through flesh into his skull.

He screamed, releasing her as he dropped to his knees, the brooch stuck into the soft skin of his temple. Grabbing his head, he fell forward, but Kára didn't wait to see if he moved as she spun toward Henry.

The murderer of her husband stared at his two fallen men. Kára stood rigid, her hand and nails out before her. Her muscles felt weak after her struggles against the two hulking men. Without the brooches holding her straps together, her wool gown fell, revealing her trussed form, her stays making her heaving bosom rise over the edge of her smock.

Henry's gaze focused on them, and he feasted on her as if she were naked. Kára leaped out of the woolen folds tangled around her feet. *Go for his eyes*, she thought, readying her fingers. The wind cut right through the thin fabric, but the chill she felt in her bones came from the promise of lustful violence in Henry's eyes.

"Leave here, or you will die, too," she said, letting all her hatred seethe in her tone.

"Ye have brought doom to your people, Kára, for killing my men," Henry said, taking one step closer. "My father will retaliate against your whole family unless ye come with me to confess and take your punishment. I think we will start by having ye walk naked into the bailey like a common, stripped prisoner."

He took another step toward her. If she could make it around the chapel, perhaps Joshua would see her. She moved to the side as he stalked forward, several gravestones between them. "They attacked me," she said. "And they were warned, like I am warning you. Stay away from me."

For every step back she took, he took a step forward, like a cat cornering a mouse. Could she outrun him? Jump the stonewall in her smock before he could catch her? Damn. If there was no wall, she might be able to run down into the village. The closeness of it had given her a false sense that she was safe here.

The wind blew, molding the white linen against her bare legs. Henry shook his head. "But ye see, I cannot stay away from ye, especially when ye look so damn tempting, lass. It really is your own fault, whatever happens. If ye had stayed with me when I took ye first, I would be tired of ye by now. I may even have let your child live." He shrugged. "If ye had asked me nicely. But ye are all frowns and gnashing of teeth," he said, curling his fingers up like he had claws in an imitation of her ready stance. Another few steps and she could slide along the side of the chapel.

Joshua. Joshua, be outside. See me. Her pleading turned into a type of prayer. Her body trembled with waiting energy, but would it be enough to hold Henry Stuart off without a weapon? Even her other brooch was lost in the grass far from her.

"Ask you nicely?" She let him see the hate and ridicule in her gaze. "You had just murdered my husband, the father of my child, for no other reason

except that he demanded you leave us alone."
Another step back. She was around the side facing
the village but didn't dare take her gaze off Henry.
He moved quickly over to stand between two
gravestones. He had a straight line to her, the stone
wall at his back. Maybe if she could keep him
talking, Joshua would spot them. "Geir did not
threaten you. He tried to protect me when you
decided that I was something you wanted. You
deserve only contempt and—"

Henry rushed her, covering the space before she
could gasp. He threw his body forward in an all-out
run and plowed into her, sending her careening back
against the chapel. Her head snapped back, hitting
the stone, making everything in her sight shake, and
small sparks danced in her vision. Another rock
stuck into her back as he shoved her against the
chapel wall, one hand on her breast, the other one
grabbing her hair in his fist. He used his pelvis to pin
her lower half, his erection obvious as he ground it
into her. His face came inches before her face. "I
deserve ye, Kára. Ye are beneath me in society, and
ye are going to be beneath me..." He shoved his cod
against her brutally. "Aye, beneath me whenever I
wish it, starting right now."

"Get off me!" Pulling the last of the moisture in
her mouth, she spit in his face.

Releasing her hair, he wiped it away, his pelvis
still holding her with his weight against the chapel.
His leer had changed into a face of fury, and his free
hand landed on her throat, bruising it so that she
could not draw breath. Twisting, she tried to kick out
at him, but he was strong and heavy. With him

blocking her air, she couldn't even curse him.

His other hand reached down to ruck up her smock, and the wind bit into the skin of her bare legs. Stars started to flash in her eyes as she struggled to draw breath. Did he mean to kill her then? Right there? Raping her still-warm body? She blinked, looking away from the smug victory in Henry's face. Movement outside the stone wall held her gaze, and she dropped her hands, going limp with relief.

Joshua.

• • •

The four-foot stone wall was no obstacle. Joshua would have punched his way through the rocks to get to Kára, but all he had to do was launch himself over the barrier encircling the churchyard.

Warrior's blood pumped through him as if he were in the deadliest battle he'd ever seen. It shot energy into his muscles, helping him focus past the horror of seeing horses grazing outside the chapel wall. Condensing his churning dark thoughts, he pulled them into a single goal—to kill whoever was harming Kára. It didn't matter if it were King James himself; the fool shoving Kára against the chapel wall and now holding her by the neck would die.

Without breaking his stride, Joshua leaped over the wall. The bastard holding her had barely turned to see him coming when Joshua yanked him away from Kára. In the back of his mind, Joshua recognized him as Henry Stuart, Robert's eldest son, but it changed nothing. Before Henry could utter a word, Joshua shoved his sword into his chest, the blade going halfway through so he could then rip it downward through bone, muscle, and sinew.

Henry's gurgled curse came from his stretched lips as Joshua split him open with his tempered blade from chest to abdomen. Only the man's belt stopped him from sawing through his foking jack. "The Horseman of War sends ye to Hell," Joshua said and yanked his sword free. "For your crimes against this woman and her people."

Henry Stuart crumpled into the trampled grass, his entrails rolling out with his blood. Joshua threw his bloodstained sword down and stopped before Kára where she leaned gasping against the chapel wall, hands at her bruised throat. His arms raised before him, but his palms hovered over her, not touching for fear it would hurt her.

"Kára. Kára. Kára." Her name rolled from his lips like a prayer as he drew in large drafts of air after his frantic run. "Can I…?" His hands cupped the back of his head, his chest rising and falling fast as if he were still running. "Where can I touch ye? Are ye bleeding? Oh God, I will follow him to Hell and kill him again."

She held up one hand as if she could not talk but wanted him to stop. Tears ran down her face. "I…I will recover," she said, the words coming slow and pained on a hoarse whisper.

His hands reached for her slowly. His cloak having dropped away somewhere on the hill as he'd raced up it, he had nothing but himself with which to cover her. He didn't want to startle her, but he must hold her, feel her warm and breathing in his arms. Touching her stiff shoulders, he slid his hands around her back, gently pulling her into his chest. She went willingly, her weight heavy in his arms as if she surrendered all of her strength, letting him hold her body up. He gladly took it.

"Kára, och but I should have stayed here," he whispered. "I should have gotten here faster. I did not see the horses until I stepped out the tavern door."

His gaze scanned the gravestones. "There were *three* horses."

"I killed the other two," she said, her hand flipping weakly from her side to gesture toward the other end of the graveyard.

He held her tighter, trying to fight against his need to squeeze her into him, and kissed the top of her head, her face buried in his chest. "Ye are truly a warrior queen, Kára Flett, and as brave as any lass I have known."

"Robert will come after my people."

His hand pulled away from where he'd touched her head, blood smeared on it. "Ye are bleeding," he said. "Your head."

"And probably my back."

She remained tucked into him as his fingers probed gently through her hair, finding the cut. "I need to look at it."

She pulled slightly back, and he turned her around to lean up against the chapel wall. The back of her smock was sliced from the rock, a thick line of red blood stark against the white of the material. He parted the fabric to see the skin. "The cut on your back is superficial and will heal easily if washed and bandaged."

His gaze moved up to her head, and his inhale stopped. Blood, red and seeping, colored her pale locks. He exhaled slowly, parting her hair to look closer at the cut. "Your scalp is bleeding more, but that is the nature of head wounds," he said, forcing the worry out of his voice. He yanked a rag from his belt and pressed it to her head, holding it there as he gently turned her around. "I do not think ye need stitches, but it might be damaged inside." He met her eyes. "Are ye hurt anywhere else?"

Had Henry managed to penetrate her body with anything, a finger, his jack, anything? Joshua would make certain to cut off whatever it was and throw it to the dogs.

She shook her head, his hand keeping the cloth pressed to her red-tinged locks, and cleared her throat. He felt her wince. "My throat. He was set to rape me, too. I think he was torn between that and killing me."

Foking bastard would have done both. The urge to kick the lump of a man in the grass churned up through Joshua like sour burps, but he would not let go of Kára for anything in the world, not even revenge.

Kára pulled away slightly and looked up into his face. Her tears had stopped but worry threatened to bring them back. She trembled, making him fear she was in shock. What did one do if someone was in shock? *Keep them warm. Give them a sip of whisky.* Damn, he wished his sister, Hannah, was there to help. "We should get ye to Hilda," he said. "She will heal ye."

"They will hunt me down at Hillside," she said,

and he watched her work at swallowing. "I cannot return there. Even gone, Robert might still ransack anywhere he thinks I could be. Henry said he hunts me for taking Hilda and Broch. But killing his son…"

Joshua caught her chin in his fingers. "Kára, ye had no choice but to defend yourself. And ye did not kill Robert's son. I did."

He pulled her back into his arms, willing his comfort and strength into her. "And Robert will not know, anyway. I will dispose of the bodies," he said, looking toward the sea and then down over the rolling hills toward Birsay. Damn, treeless expanse. He'd have to work fast before the three were noticed missing.

"Come," he said. "I will take ye to your den. No one will find ye there."

"My brooches, sword, and *mattucashlass* are over there," she said, pointing. They walked through the swaying grasses, Joshua continually scanning the terrain for more of Robert's men or the earl himself.

He left her holding the rag to her head beside the chapel as he went to claim her items. The brooch was lodged in the temple of one warrior Joshua had known, a decent fellow when training, but easily swayed to evil, apparently. Joshua yanked the brooch out. After some time in the sea, no one would even be able to tell that he'd been pierced, if they even surfaced.

Joshua grabbed her short sword and then wiped the *mattucashlass* free of blood after yanking it from the other brute's forehead. Kára was a damn good shot. Thank God, or she would likely be dead right now. The thought made his skin itch and his heart thump wildly, his untamed warrior fury threatening to take over his reasoning.

Nay, he could not storm into Robert's palace and slaughter everyone. There would always be another Stuart, another stronger warlord to kick and suppress Kára's people. He must convince her to leave Orkney. But first…

He went to her, shaking out her woolen gown and cloak. "Let us get ye warm," he said, wrapping her in the cloak and pulling her into him again, using the chapel wall to block the wind. "But we need to leave before anyone finds us with them here."

She nodded, her forehead brushing his chest, and raised her face to his. He hated the numbness he saw there, the trembling. Glancing up, she blinked. "I will help you clean up."

"Nay. If someone comes upon this, 'tis better if they find only me. Nothing should tie ye to this."

"Robert knows you are helping us after The Brute and Jean saw us at the palace."

He leveled his gaze with hers, his brows raised. "I want ye safe and sound and warm, away from this. I can carry ye to your den."

He saw the shine of unbidden tears in her eyes. It tore into him, and he had to guard against his grip tightening on her arms with his fury. It was all he could do not to run back over to Henry and slice him to bits.

Kára inhaled a shaky breath. Thank the Lord she couldn't peer into his mind to see the bloody retribution he imagined. She nodded. "I can walk."

Looking out across the empty moor hills, Joshua

kept her tucked against him as they walked to the village below where Asmund was standing out before the tavern. Several other men from the village stood with him. They watched them approach, Asmund wringing his hands. "*Dróttning*," he said.

"She needs to rest tucked away," Joshua said.

Kára stood straighter before the men. "I am well."

Joshua recognized one of the men who had tried to take Fuil the night he first saw Kára. "Ye have the ship in the harbor?"

"Aye."

Joshua glanced back toward the chapel on the hill. "I have a job for ye."

CHAPTER FIFTEEN

"He who wishes to fight must first count the cost."
Sun Tzu – The Art of War

"Do not look cross at me," Kára said, staring Joshua down where he stood in the path leading back into the village. "I told you I was not going to nap the day away."

Joshua had left her in her den to help the ship's captain load the bodies onto his boat to carry out and dump in the sea. She'd waited a full hour, warming herself, rubbing some liniment on her neck bruises, and putting a sticky poultice on her head wound, before walking the short distance back toward Asmund's tavern.

She walked past Joshua, deciding that a cup of Asmund's mead would bolster her even more.

Joshua's boots crunched the pebbles behind her. "If ye wobble with dizziness or grow pale, I will lift ye and carry ye back there. I have seen men hit their heads and die days later or go about puking and dizzy for weeks before the world righted itself in their heads."

"I feel completely well." A lie. Her throat ached, her voice still hoarse, and her scalp burned where the poultice worked. "I will not hide away when there is work to be done to help my family." She glanced past him toward the chapel. "Did you send the horses away?"

"I rode one, leading the other two, about two miles past the chapel. If I have a chance, I will lead them farther once I retrieve Fuil."

She pushed through Asmund's door, Joshua right on her heels. Her friend stood behind the bar. Relief washed over his familiar grumpy face, and he came around. He bowed his head before wrapping her in a quick hug. "I went to help the Highlander clean up on the hill and saw what ye had to do to defend yourself," he whispered and nodded. "Your father is proud in Heaven, a clever and courageous daughter."

She would argue against both for having gone up there alone in the first place and then trembling like a blade of grass in a tempest. But she smiled softly instead. "Thank you for helping…clean up."

"Langdon is about to pull anchor. Lamont is helping him dump the bastards far out." Asmund leaned in. "Robert will never find a trace of them. I even hauled up a bucket of water to wash the grass free of blood."

She squeezed his hands tightly. "I am grateful."

Joshua stood at the open door, half in and half out. It was still Samhain. Didn't he know it was dangerous to stand in thresholds? She walked over, but he stopped her from exiting, a hand holding her shoulder. "Someone approaches," he said, barely moving his lips as he stared out. He moved them back inside, shutting the door. "Hide until we know who it is."

"*Dróttning*," Asmund said, beckoning her toward the back of the room where steps led above. "Stay tucked up there."

She ran up the steps and perched at the top in the shadows where she could still hear. Pulling her knees up under her dress, she rested her chin, barely breathing as the door opened. Several sets of boots thudded on the wooden floor.

"Joshua Sinclair."

"Lord Patrick," Joshua responded, a bored tone to his voice. "What brings ye out from behind your father's walls?" Patrick was Robert's second eldest legitimate son. She knew little about him, except that he was not as cruel but still condescending and privileged.

"Ye have blood on ye," Patrick said. Kára could hear the suspicion in his voice.

"I am the Horseman of War," Joshua answered. "I always have blood on me."

Kára heard someone slide chairs on the floor as if to sit. How many guards did he have with him? She pulled her *mattucashlass* from her boot and held it, her fingers curling tightly around the handle. The trembling had come back to her hands, and she breathed deeply, trying to dispel it. But all the breathing did was hurt her throat and make stars spark in her vision. She'd be little use to Joshua like this.

"Ye said ye were leaving Orkney, but then ye show up to steal away my father's healer and my sister's horse. Ye are helping the thieves now." Patrick *tsk*ed. "He has given us free license to kill ye for it."

Kára's heart hammered, beating at the inside of her chest. *Holy Lord.* She did not want to kill anyone else this day. She pushed herself up against the wall as if trying to shrink into the wood boards framing the stairs.

"The healer," Joshua said, "is not Robert's. He does not employ her, giving her a wage for her services. Instead, he chained her to a rock, an old woman, inside his palace, enslaving her, leaving her in filth. I merely freed her."

"We will retrieve her," Patrick said, and Kára could imagine him waving his hand, dismissing all his father's sins as if he were the Pope. "And Jean's horse."

"The horse was also imprisoned from its true owner. Ye can add horse thievery to your father's sins. 'Tis a hangable crime where I come from."

"Is that why ye are working for the enemy now, Sinclair?" Patrick asked. "Whatever money they pay ye is likely ours. They have won your loyalty with stolen gold."

"I am loyal to God and no one else," Joshua said. Kára could hear the warning in his voice. She longed to see the expressions of those below but didn't dare move. Even a pebble kicked from the steps would alert them that she hid there.

"How about the King of Scotland, my cousin?" Patrick asked. Would Joshua admit his disloyalty to the crown before Patrick and his men, marking him as a traitor?

"Questioning loyalty?" Joshua asked, a grin in his voice. "With an inscription that calls Robert the king of Scotland carved in stone over his door?" It was a much-refuted engraving on the entry arch of the Earl's Palace: *Lord Robert Stuart, King of the Scots, son of James V, erected this building.*

"'Tis a grammatical error in the Latin," Patrick said.

"An error that has never been corrected." Could Patrick hear the underlying warning in Joshua's tone? "Let King James come to Orkney to see how Robert treats his subjects and what he calls himself, King of Scotland, written in stone."

The sound of someone drinking was followed by the *tap* of a tankard on the stone bar. "Like ye said, my cousin does not care what goes on here far from Edinburgh."

The sound of men rising, their scabbards jostling against stone tables and the bar, made Kára suck in a full inhale, her empty hand going to her sore throat at the ache it caused.

"Then let us not worry over royal backing. Tell your father, Patrick, to leave the people of Orkney unmolested. Pay them fairly to work and give them access to hunt on their lands."

Patrick's scoff made a chill prickle Kára's arms. Perhaps he was as bad as his brother. "Or what, Sinclair?"

Joshua's tone, even and low, held the promise of death. "Or suffer the wrath of the Horseman of War."

"Foking cocky," Patrick said. "One warrior against a crew that he trained. Save yourself and leave the isle." Kára heard the door open.

"Barkeep," Patrick called. "Have ye seen my brother, Henry, ride this way today?"

"Nay," Asmund said. "Been minding my bar inside."

Patrick muttered something she couldn't hear,

and the door shut. Silence held for several seconds while Kára listened to the men calling for Henry outdoors, but there would be no reply.

After a long, silent pause, Joshua's face appeared at the bottom of the staircase. "They are leaving the village."

Her breath came in a huff as she tried to shake off the heaviness of dread that threatened to crumple her. She couldn't act with bravery when she still quaked. Stepping lightly, she met him at the bottom of the stairs. Asmund stared out the window. "They are riding toward the chapel." He shook his head. "Bloody plague on this isle," he said, not looking away.

"Perhaps it is time to live somewhere else," Joshua said, his gaze fastened to hers. "Somewhere fresh and bountiful."

"You make Scotia sound like Eden," Kára whispered.

Joshua shrugged, the fury cut into the lines of his face softening. "'Tis close, but colder. And no one runs around naked."

"I heard reports that you practically did," she said, noting his previous lack of tunic when he left Robert's, his tattoos shown off to all who laid eyes on him.

"We should get ye to Hilda," Joshua said, not commenting.

She looked to Asmund. "After a cup of mead. I am in need of your sweet brew, and I would give Patrick time to ride off." She pushed onto a stool. Joshua came over, sitting next to her.

She touched his tunic where blood lay across it.

"Ye are stained by Henry's death," she whispered.

He leaned toward her, not seeming to care that Asmund stood across from them pouring mead into tankards. Joshua brushed her hair back from her cheek and softly pressed his lips to hers. "'Tis your blood, lass, from the wound on your bonny head." His gaze lifted as if to see it, and she touched the back where the unbound poultice was hardly noticeable, forgotten with Patrick's visit.

"It will be well," she said. He leaned down, inspecting her throat. "So will that," she said and glanced toward Asmund. Her old friend had walked back to the window, to peer out to watch for Stuarts or give them privacy, she wasn't sure.

Kára held her hand out over the bar where it still shook. "It is this that needs to go away as fast as possible," she said, balling her hand into a fist and pulling it back to her lap.

Joshua's warm hand found it there and encased it, squeezing gently. "'Tis warrior energy that feeds the muscles, Kára. Not fear. Fear would have made ye crumple in the churchyard, not fight. 'Tis nothing to worry over."

She looked into his eyes, marveling once again at the calm wisdom she saw. There were so many sides to Joshua Sinclair. Earlier, his face had contorted with the promise of death. When he'd jumped across the wall, his sword poised to inflict not only death but immense pain on Henry, he had looked like an avenging angel truly sent from a wrathful God. And now he exuded encouragement and light.

Wetting her lips, she exhaled, ignoring the pain in her throat. "Worry, I fear, will never be over," she whispered. "For my people, my son." She shook her head. "'Tis something that nags my soul. The only time I am free of it"—she touched the side of his face, running her finger across his lips—"is when you fly me away from it on passion."

He kissed her fingers, keeping her gaze. "I would fly ye away every day, but to save your people and your son, I need to take ye away from this isle."

Kára released her breath, letting her gaze drop to the stone floor. She nodded and raised her eyes back to Joshua's patient gaze. "Let us talk to the council."

Stepping into the late afternoon, the familiar wash of wind filled Kára's inhale. Down in the bay, Lamont and Langston worked to get their sails raised. They would sail out to sea until Orkney was barely visible and dump Henry and his two guards who had attacked her. It was a shame for the guards' families not to know what had become of them, but perhaps it was better they did not know the black hearts within them.

Joshua walked beside her, the two of them scanning the surrounding hills for more of Robert's men. "If John Dishington rides up, he will try to kill us," Joshua said, glancing at her.

"Patrick said his father wants you dead for taking Hilda and Broch."

Joshua snorted. "Freeing them." He exhaled. "Dishington wants me dead even without Robert's order because I knocked him unconscious."

"I have my *mattucashlass* and short sword and brooches," she said, patting her shoulders. With Joshua beside her, courage prevailed over the fear, making her stride more direct. But she still felt exposed on the landscape of grasses. She'd hidden in them before, but Joshua's bulk would be hard to hide. What would it be like to be surrounded by thick trees with branches to climb and trunks behind which to hide?

"What do you miss about Scotia?" she asked, their walk turning brisk.

They continued across the rocky ground and onto a length of spongy peat until she thought he might not answer. Surely he must miss something. She looked sideways and saw him inhale fully.

"I could say the trees and plentiful food, the loud laughter at the festivals that comes from not hiding, since we are the strongest clan in Scotland." He glanced at her before looking back out before him. "But 'tis the people that I miss most." He cursed softly. "Being away from my older brother for these months makes me think that he might actually know a thing or two about leading our clan. And peace with our neighbors might be better than crushing them so they cannot war back."

"Would you have crushed us?" she asked.

His brows lowered. "Nay, not unless ye tried to kill my clan, the people or horses. It is those in power who are the problem in most instances. The local people just want to keep food in their bellies and grow their children without fear."

"We have neither here on Orkney."

He said nothing, but she knew he agreed. It was why he wanted them to return to Scotia with him. "You live on the sea, there in Caithness?"

"Aye, with wicked wind like here. But if ye travel inland a bit, the bite of the wind fades, stills."

She pushed her hair out of her eyes. What would that be like? To have no wind trying to shove her every time she stepped outside?

"I would still rule my people," Kára said, watching him closely, their arms swinging easily by their sides.

"Aye, but ye would need to swear fealty to my brother, Cain Sinclair, to benefit from the protection of his armies."

"And yours?"

He clasped her hand where it swung next to her leg, stopping her. She looked up into his face, breathing rapidly past the pain in her throat.

"Ye have my army, Kára Flett," he said. "Ye have me and my army." His words had the timbre of an oath, and it sent a thrill through her.

"You can promise that without talking to your brother?" she asked.

He shrugged. "If ye decide ye want my army of bay horses to attack Girnigoe and kill the horses and people, then I will have to rethink my words. Otherwise, Cain will not care if I aid the Fletts of Orkney."

She smiled, but then a thought wormed its way inside. "What if King James decides the Fletts are enemies?"

She watched his jawline harden as he looked out to the distance where the three cottages marked the hidden village of Hillside. "It would not be the first time the Sinclairs have disagreed with the crown," he said. "But I will send word to Cain. My younger brother, Gideon, the Horseman of Justice, will be certain to keep the Sinclairs free of my actions, but there should be no reason to blame your people for anything."

As long as no one tied them to Henry Stuart's death.

They walked up to the cottages, and Amma rushed out. "What has happened?" she asked, staring directly at the bruising on her neck. Her fingers lifted to Kára's throat, her face pinching in anger. "This is the work of Stuarts."

"It is taken care of," Joshua said, his voice hard.

The fewer people knowing about the conflict, the better. "I will tell you about it later, Amma. Right now, we need to find my trousers and clean clothes for Joshua. I would stand as a warrior before the council."

CHAPTER SIXTEEN

"The art of war is of vital importance to the State.
It is a matter of life and death, a road
either to safety or to ruin."
Sun Tzu – The Art of War

Joshua felt the stretch of the seams on the borrowed tunic as he walked up the hill next to Kára. Calder was fairly large, but his tunic was still tighter than was comfortable. Joshua hoped he wouldn't rip it, but he did not need questions about the blood that had smeared and splattered against his own, a mix of Kára's head wound and Henry's all-over wound.

From the vileness of the man, Joshua would have guessed his blood to be black. But that was one of the mysteries of life, how blood flowed the same, regardless of evil intent or righteousness. God gifted every newborn bairn with the same potential for good or bad. If only decisions were as simple as cutting oneself and seeing the color to know if one's intentions were sound or self-righteous.

He glanced at Kára, her features full of strength, as if she felt the weight of a crown pressing down on her and she was determined to hold it up. For her people, she had become the *dróttning*, the queen. And he had convinced her to lead them away from their isle. Were his intentions for their benefit or his own? Life was much simpler at home.

He shook his head, clearing away the press of

guilt. Taking the Hillside people to Caithness would help them, protect them from the warriors he had honed into brutal fighting soldiers for Robert.

Kára stopped before the closed door of the cottage on top of the hill. He watched her shoulders rise, stretching them, letting them sink down her back as she straightened the scarf around her bruised neck. Head high, all signs of fear replaced by calm fortitude. She glanced at him. "I will not mention Henry."

"'Tis best not to."

Kára pushed into the cottage and stopped. The room was filled. Chairs were arranged in a half circle toward the back, filled with elderly people, the middle chair left open. But the rest of the room was packed shoulder to shoulder with Hillside people, women and men, no children, not even Geir. Torben stood with his arms crossed, a pout on his face. His mother stood next to him, casting evil glances Joshua's way.

Was Kára's son with Osk? Nay. Osk stood inside the door and made motions for people to move so Kára could walk to the chair. She sat in it as regally as if it were a throne. Her grandmother, Harriett, perched next to her. Hilda and Corey sat there, too, representing the remaining elders of the group, along with two other men. Joshua entered, shutting the door behind him to lean against.

"I call this council meeting of Hillside Village open," Kára said as if she'd been leading these people her whole life. The slight murmur at her entrance quieted to silence.

"Since Chief Erik has not returned, I will serve in

his place if the council agrees," Kára said.

Corey stood and bowed his head to her. "You have our loyalty, Kára Flett, eldest living child of Zaire Flett."

"Aye." The room erupted with the single word.

Kára nodded, and Corey took his seat. She looked out at the gathered. "We have winter coming quickly, and I would like to know what we have stored."

Calder stepped into the little space before the council. "We farmed barley and black oats this summer, which did well. As you know, however, Robert Stuart took half the yield in the midsummer raid, leaving us with limited supply for the rest of the winter into spring." A man at the end of the row of elders wrote in a bound book.

Damn, Robert. Joshua remembered the bags of oats the man had brought in, saying it was taxes from those on the isle, since they could not pay in gold. Would he have taken so much if he had known how many people resided at Hillside? Joshua sighed softly. It probably would not have mattered to the man.

"Our meat supplies? And dairy?" Kára asked.

Another man stepped forward as Calder retreated. "The limited hunting grounds have made it difficult to catch rabbits, but we have sufficient fish dried to keep families going if we ration well and continue to bring in fresh catches through the winter. We could also resort to digging up voles. My wife says they make a reasonable pie."

"Each family must understand their ration of food until more food can grow," Harriett said, looking at Kára. "Unless our chief has a different plan for us."

All eyes turned to Kára. Silence filled every nook and cranny of the cottage. She took her time letting her gaze move from person to person. "Lord Robert has begun a new fortress near Kirkwall for…his son, Henry Stuart. At the first sign of spring, he will once again force our people to labor without pay, giving false promises of easing up on hunting restrictions. But his taxes of grain and crops will continue, and his tyranny will not end."

"We should end his reign here," Osk said, and several of the warriors Joshua had been working with for the last week nodded, including Torben.

Kára looked directly at her brother. "I want Lord Robert dead as much as you do, brother." She let her gaze move to the others. "But who comes after him?"

"Henry," someone said.

"He is missing," another said. "His brother, Patrick, has been riding the isle looking for him."

Kára held up her hands. "After Henry comes Patrick, and then John, James, the youngest Robert. The number of children and grandchildren continues to grow between his wife and mistresses, and they are all raised to be tyrants to replace him. 'Tis like a wretched disease spreading across Orkney."

"We kill them all," Osk said, crossing his arms over his not-yet-filled-out chest. "Wipe out the disease completely. Like burning a corrupted barley field."

Kára gripped the arms of the chair. "Before, when Erik led our people, I would have said that, too. But charging into Birsay to battle and kill, to seek the satisfaction of revenge… It is good for the individual. Even if I were to die, I would feel good in the sacrifice."

Kára stood slowly out of her seat. "But as the one responsible for our families, the one who must consider the repercussions of bringing the Scottish crown to Orkney if we kill Robert and his family, repercussions for not just me but for all of you… I must not give in to the desire to see our dead revenged, which could very well send us to the grave with them. I must think of the future of our people."

Her gaze slid to Joshua, their eyes seeming linked. "A future where we can survive in peace. Where we will have food and homes. Where our children can sing and play without constantly watching for riders who could steal, molest, or kill them. Where we are not looked down upon as if we are less than."

"You would have us abandon our isle, our home?" Fiona, Torben's mother, called out, her arms crossed over her bosom.

Kára looked straight at her. "Aye."

A murmur rose in the room, but she continued to talk, her voice strong and overriding. "I would have us abandon Robert's tyranny and disrespect of our ways. I would have us abandon the worry each autumn that we will not have enough to survive the winter." Her voice grew in strength to easily override the murmurs. "I pray for us to abandon a land that cannot protect our children and wise ones dying of cold and disease because we haven't the resources to keep warm and fed." She held the woman's stare. "Aye, Fiona, I would have us abandon Orkney."

"Where will we go?" Hilda asked, her voice strong as if she already knew the answer and wanted Kára to tell them all about Joshua's home.

"Scotia," Kára said. "The mainland of Scotland, over the sea to the south. There are trees, deer, fish, good land for crops, and protection." She looked to Joshua.

"Aye," he said, nodding. "I pledge to help the people of Orkney settle on Sinclair land. My brother is the chief, and we are at peace with the two surrounding clans. The land is stable, and life will be better for ye if ye make it so. That, of course, is up to ye."

"And we will have to work for your brother and the Sinclairs?" Osk asked, bitterness showing that he had already judged his clan. Joshua likely would have, too, if their circumstances were switched.

"We have over five hundred horses and warriors who take care of and train them. Ye would be welcome to join our armies, swear fealty to Cain Sinclair, and benefit from the protection our clan has to offer ye and your families. But there is no forced labor within my clan. Wages are provided, as well as food, friendship, and respect." Joshua shrugged. "But if ye wish to journey on from our lands, ye are free to go. Or to come back to Orkney in the spring if ye find the mainland inhospitable. No one will stop ye."

"I do not trust you," Osk said, and several of the men looked like they agreed.

"Then trust your *dróttning*," he said. "Do what she said. Decide on your own. If half your people decide to leave Orkney, those who remain will have more food for the winter. If Robert does not let up on his pressure against ye, follow us to the mainland of Scotland in the spring."

"Our ancestors are here," a woman said from the corner.

"Their bones are here," Joshua countered. "Their spirit goes with whomever remembers them."

The woman gave a little nod, her gaze turning to meet the eyes of the man next to her, her husband perhaps.

Kára turned to take in the gathered people in a slow rotation. "Everyone, speak with your families. We will reconvene here tomorrow. If you wish to go to Scotia and would like to help plan the journey, see me after tomorrow's meeting." She returned to her chair. "For those with specific questions, Joshua Sinclair and I will remain here now to hear them."

Her prompting was obvious, and Joshua started to move forward. Osk caught his arm. Joshua looked down into his frown. "You will wed her then, my sister?"

Wed Kára? Did she want that? Joshua looked to where she spoke with her grandmother, Harriett, a small line of villagers forming before her. She could be with his child already, and he would never abandon a child.

"If she follows you all the way to your home and then you leave her aside for some other woman…" Osk gritted his teeth, his hand fisted. "If she does not kill you, I will."

"Your loyalty to your sister is honorable, Osk Flett, but ye will leave this matter to Kára and me."

Before Osk could say anything foolish that would endanger himself or push Joshua's patience, Joshua walked away.

Kára spoke with the woman from the corner. "I am sure there are many strong men who could wed your daughter there, but since she is only twelve right now, you can wait to worry about that, Alyce."

Alyce looked at her husband. "Here, everyone seems related so closely by blood. She could meet a Sinclair there, a strong warrior with horses."

"Maybe that's what worries me," the husband grumbled.

"When I left," Joshua said, "there was talk of starting a school to teach writing, reading, and cipher. Both for lads and lasses."

The woman smacked the man's arm. "She could be educated, too."

The man nodded thoughtfully. "My angel is very clever."

Alyce looked back to Kára. "We will go with you, the three of us." She yanked her husband's arm, and they walked toward the door where several small groups still spoke.

Hilda sat beside Kára. "Will Robert call on his nephew, the king, to harass the Sinclairs for giving us a place to live?"

"I do not intend to tell him where we are going," Kára said. "He may not even realize that our numbers have declined until spring when he comes to round us up to work on his new fortress in Kirkwall."

"But when he discovers that we have gone with Joshua," Harriett said, glancing his way, "if he puts in a complaint to the king, James could ride against the Sinclairs."

Before the death of his father, Joshua had heard his sire's plans to take over all of Scotland, dethroning King James. He had kept such treasonous ideas only among his four sons and himself. Since his death, Gideon tried to plant the seed of treason in his eldest brother's ear. Of all the Sinclair brothers, the third eldest was the one with far-reaching plans for success. But Cain had seemed to care little for taking the throne of Scotland, despite him being raised as the Horseman of Conquest.

Joshua met Hilda's wise eyes. "King James would be a fool to waste his resources battling the combined strength of the Sinclair, Sutherland, and Mackay clans for a mere one hundred people. If Robert petitions for intervention, my brothers and I will see that nothing comes of it." Surely, Gideon could convince the king that turning the Sinclairs and their allies against him would not be in the best interest of the Scottish realm.

"And will you wed my granddaughter?" Harriett Flett asked.

Kára coughed into her hand. "Amma, I have no plans to marry again," she said, passing a glance his way before turning her gaze back to her grandmother.

Harriett looked directly at Joshua, assessing him, and he saw the resemblance to Osk in her fiery stare. Turning back to Kára, she crossed her arms over her chest. "You should make plans to, then," she said.

Kára did not want to marry again? Would she turn him away if he asked Kára right then and

there? His heart beat a little faster at the thought.
Of what? Of him tying himself to one woman in a
union before God or her saying no to the idea? His
jaw clenched, and he made himself release the
crushing press of his upper and lower teeth.

"Amma—" Kára started.

The woman held up a hand. "Aye, this journey
would be to help your people, but you are a young
woman who should remarry. A husband is helpful in
many ways, especially if children come from your
carnal adventures."

Kára dropped her forehead into her cupped
hands.

Carnal adventures? Joshua looked between Kára
and her grandmother, ignoring her elderly Aunt
Hilda whose gaze made him think she would ask
him to strip for her medical assessment of his manly
virtues. No one said anything for a long moment,
and he cleared his throat. "Ye are wise to worry
about your granddaughter," he said. "I will not
abandon her or any who decide to journey to the
mainland."

Harriett pointed at him. "You should marry her."

He'd never had a grandmother, or any family
member, want him to wed a lass from their family.
The Horseman of War had never been serious
enough to attract a woman who might want marriage. They certainly wanted his jack and strength,
but not his heart.

No plans to marry. He frowned. Was Kára Flett
another lass who wanted him only for the pleasure
he could bring her? Before, that would not have
mattered in the least. Before what? Before he'd

committed to helping move her people to safety? Or before he couldn't go an hour without thinking of the taste of her lips, the warmth of her touch, and the sound of her laughter and moans?

The room was slowly emptying. "I must check on Fuil," he said, walking out of the tense room. The constant wind whipped around the eaves of the three aboveground houses, the cold hitting him like an icy slap. Aye, he needed to go back to Caithness before he lost bits of himself to frost, likes toes and the tip of his nose. He raised and lowered his shoulders to conceal his shiver and stomped forward toward the barn. Bloody hell, everything on Orkney was cold. Except Kára. She was warm. A fire to his ice. With her beside him, he could withstand the worst strike of cold.

He walked into the barn. With only two horses in it, the air was still icy, but the wind was blocked. Joshua ran a hand down his horse's neck. "We will be back to Girnigoe Castle before the winter is fully here. I promise."

Fuil tossed his head as if he understood, making Joshua smile. The door opened behind him, and his hand grabbed the hilt of the Sinclair sword that had been returned to him. He released it as Kára's light tread moved over the dirt floor. She stopped to greet her horse, Broch, who lowered her head over the stall door for her to scratch.

"I think most of them will go," she said. "And Amma will make sure Osk comes with us."

He turned, leaning against the stall door. Kára stroked her horse, her strong, nimble hands following the pits and bony rises of her horse's uniquely colored face. "Ye will not wed again?" he asked.

Her hand stayed for a moment but then continued. She did not look at him. "I married when I was seventeen. My heart was young and unguarded. When my husband was killed…the emotions of giving birth early, of worrying I would lose my babe as well…" She shook her head, not willing to look his way. "The more connections one makes, the more that can be lost, and the losses make me weak."

"The thoughts of a warrior," he said, crossing his arms.

"I am a warrior," she said, giving him a small frown with a glance.

"Aye." He heartily agreed with that. "Your heart can be armored, standing alone as a leader and warrior. But is it enough?"

Kára dropped her hands to rest on top of the stall door and turned her body toward him. "Enough for what?"

He shrugged. "Enough for being happy. 'Tis a long life if ye are lucky. But will it be years of bitter loneliness with your heart so guarded?"

She narrowed her eyes, a wry grin growing on those luscious lips. "You speak to me about matters of the heart, Horseman of War?"

"I know very little about the subject," he conceded. "Although it seems lasses need more than…" He flipped his hand in the air, searching for the right words, words he did not know.

"More than what?"

"More than just leading and protecting," he said, but the inflection made it sound like a question. The squinting of her eyes triggered his warrior instincts. "I thought lasses wanted more." He shrugged.

"Wanting and needing are very different things," she said, tipping her head to the side as she studied him. She stepped a little closer. "Like right now I want to touch you."

His jack twitched in answer. Joshua raised an eyebrow as she stood right up against him, her breasts pressed into him slightly. "Ye do not jest?"

She shook her head, and he pulled her into him. The clever woman had ended their conversation about her not wanting to wed, but at the moment he did not care. His lips hovered directly over hers to where he could feel her shallow exhale as she waited for him to act.

"Ye *want* to touch me…" He inhaled the fragrance of her skin, sliding over to her ear. "But I will make ye *need* my touch, Kára lass," he whispered there, his lips trailing over her warm neck. He felt her shiver, and his arms wrapped completely around her, pulling her up against his hard body.

Looking down into her face, flushed with want that he would turn to need, she was an angel with the desire for sin. She was the perfect match of heavenly beauty and delicious wickedness, and he felt his own desire turn to need.

Joshua watched her eyes close as he descended, and then he was lost in the feel of her open lips against his. Her fingers crept over his shoulders to tangle in his hair, pulling him to round down over her, engulfing her and surrounding her at the same time. He felt her leg hitch up over his hip, grinding the crux of her against his already raging jack.

"Kára!" Osk's voice broke through the fire surging through Joshua.

He lifted his face from Kára's, her lashes splayed under her closed eyes.

"Kára! Erik! 'Tis Chief Erik," Osk yelled, and Kára's body stiffened, pulling out of the circle Joshua had created with his arms.

"Erik?" Kára asked, her breath coming fast like Joshua's.

"Aye," Osk said, casting a glance between the two of them, but his gaze landed on his sister. "He has returned." He shook his head, anger tightening his face. "But he is…" Osk shook his head, "altered."

CHAPTER SEVENTEEN

*"The quality of decision is like the well-trained
swoop of a falcon which enables it to
strike and destroy its victim."*
Sun Tzu – The Art of War

Osk ran out, and Kára glanced back at Joshua where
he fought against his hard jack, adjusting it under his
kilt. Thank heavens she did not have to deal with
such obvious proof of her ardor, since every time she
came in contact with the Highlander, fire licked up
inside to melt away any mundane intentions.

"I need to go," she said, pressing cool palms
against her heated cheeks.

He nodded. "We will finish later."

She let a grin settle on her lips and shrugged.
"Because I *want* to."

A roguish smile spread across his perfect lips,
obviously seeing through her baiting. "Want or need.
As long as I am buried between your thighs," he
whispered, and the edges of his white teeth came
together. The words and the promise-filled gesture
made her lower body clench in… It bloody hell felt
like need, and she rubbed her hand over the crux of
her legs to push the ache away, very much as if she
had her own unruly jack with which to deal.

He grinned but only stepped forward to grasp
her other hand, and the two of them walked out of
the barn. It seemed all of Hillside was gathered

around the cottage where the council meeting had finished. Asmund walked over to her, sweat upon his face. "A couple of Robert's men dumped him in the middle of the village."

Asmund's words froze the heat in Kára's blood faster than the icy wind in her face. Was her uncle dead?

Her people turned to her in silence as she walked forward, frowns on every face and a few women dabbing their eyes. A path opened so she could enter the cottage. *Not dead.* Erik sat on the center chair that Kára had vacated not long ago. Hilda sat beside him, unwrapping…

"Bloody hell," Joshua murmured beside her, and Kára rushed forward.

"Uncle," she said, kneeling down before him to see the bloody stump, his right forearm cut clean away. The pain he must have endured… "Robert cut off your arm," she whispered.

"My sword arm," Erik said, his voice rough, as if he had barely survived without proper water. "So I could never raise it against him again. Strangely, I do not remember lifting a sword to any of his men."

Amma brought him a cup of something, holding it to his lips, but he took it with his left hand. The proud man was dressed in tatters as if his clothing had been rent before being stomped in dirt and given back to him. Joshua said he'd seen him marched into the palace naked.

As if remembering him from the day of his capture, Erik's pained face filled with hatred as he looked over her shoulder to where Joshua stood. "You are the Horseman of Death to our people. The one training Robert's warriors to slaughter us." His face snapped around to Kára. "You have brought the devil to Hillside?"

Kára's gaze moved between the two proud men. "He is not allied with Robert."

"I am the Horseman of War," Joshua said, his face hardened to resemble someone who could bloody well bring the end of the world. "My loyalty is to God and Clan Sinclair, not to Robert Stuart."

Erik's dirty, unshaven face still pinched with unleashed fury. "Yet you trained them to kill us."

"I trained them to defend themselves from raiders, but I tired of Robert's tyranny and left."

Erik glanced at Kára. "And are you teaching my people to defend themselves, too? So we can tear each other apart like baited animals?"

"No," Kára said, shaking her head. "Joshua did not know our plight before coming here. He was on his way back to Scotia but has agreed to help us."

"I do not want war for your people," Joshua said. "War will bring only further misery and death."

"Is not that what you feed on, Horseman?" Erik said.

"King Erik!" Torben called as he strode into the cottage. He cast a dark glance toward Joshua before coming to kneel before her uncle. "A word from you, and my men and I will attack the palace."

"And all will die," Kára said. "And incite Robert to order a full attack on our people."

"When he finds out his son, Henry, is dead by our hand, he will attack anyway," Erik said, making Kára's gaze snap to him. "Asmund told me," he said.

"I killed the foking bastard, not Kára," Joshua

said. "And Robert Stuart or his other son, or his mercenary, The Brute, are welcome to attack me."

"His hundred men against you?" Torben said with a bitter laugh. "Cocky arse, go right ahead. You deserve to be slaughtered for killing his son. If he finds that we were involved in any way—"

"If Henry's death remains a mystery, Robert will have no need to attack," Kára said, her voice riding over Torben's tantrum. Her gaze connected with each of the five people in the room, landing on Erik. She had thought Asmund wise enough to keep his mouth shut, although having found their chief, the man would have felt obligated to inform him about what had transpired. Hopefully, Asmund was not now whispering what he knew to all the people of Hillside.

Hilda finished slathering a thick salve over the raw end of Erik's stump and took clean linens from Amma, wrapping them deftly around it. The only sign that Erik was in pain was his silence and closing of his eyes, the muscles in his jaws twitching as he clenched his teeth. They all waited for him to open his eyes.

Erik let out a weary exhale, looking to Torben. "Ready the men for war. We march tonight against Robert and those who stand with him."

"Ye will lead your people to death," Joshua said, his arms crossed.

"You are not expected to come," Erik said.

Kára stood straight, legs braced. "There is a better way. We are welcome in Scotia. Joshua will lead us to the mainland of Scotland where we can build a safe and—"

Erik held his palm out to stop her and pushed slowly out of the chair. He took a step toward her, a slight limp that made Hilda look down at his leg. "We attack tonight," Erik repeated. "With or without the Horseman of War."

Joshua stared straight at him, not backing down an inch. "Then have your women stay behind and dig your graves."

Erik continued to stare in Kára's eyes, his brows pinching sharply inward. "Better my grave than a boy's."

Boy? Kára couldn't speak, the world suspended in that moment, waiting to see if the weight would fall off her shoulders or crush her.

"What boy?" Joshua asked, coming up next to her.

Erik did not break the tether of their gazes as he answered. "They have Geir."

• • •

"Kára, wait," Joshua called as he raced after her toward the small stable where they had just kissed. How bloody much could change in a matter of minutes. He caught her at the barn door and wrapped his hand around her wrist. She twisted toward him, the wind whipping her hair before her eyes. "Ye cannot get on Broch and ride to Robert by yourself, demanding Geir's return."

Her face was a mix of agony and determined fury. Teeth gritted and eyes narrowed, she yanked her arm from him. "The hell I can't."

He followed her into the barn, stopping her at

her horse's stall by pinning her arms against the door. "Let go of me," she ordered.

"I will when ye have moved past blind hatred, which will only see ye dead, into rational thought." He leaned forward so they stood face-to-face.

He stared into her eyes until her rapid breathing slowed. She blinked. "They will kill him," she whispered, and he could see the fury give way to despair as the sheen of unshed tears washed across her gray-blue eyes. "Or worse. Torture." She shook her head and swallowed. "He is only nine." Her eyes squeezed shut. "Right now…he is so frightened. I know he is."

Joshua slid his hold on her wrists to her hands, intertwining their fingers. "Geir has the bravery of both his mother and father, Kára. It will keep him strong until we can free him."

"I must free him," she said. "I gladly give myself for him."

He pulled her into his arms even though she was stiff. "I know. Let us do so with a plan instead of running headlong into Robert's clutches." He tipped her chin up to meet his eyes. "Trust me. Can ye? To do everything I can to help ye get him back whole?"

Several heartbeats thudded through him before she nodded. "Aye," she whispered. "I trust you."

He pulled in a full breath with her words. "Let us go inside and form a plan."

She gave a small nod and pulled away, but her hand found his on the way to the door. Her fingers tangled with his, and the returned gesture made his chest squeeze with something he had not felt before. It made him want to wrap Kára up so nothing could hurt her. The fact that he could not made the feeling painful. He breathed out, forcing his muscles to relax.

Erik Flett stood in fresh clothing before a group of Hillside men at the top of the hill. Their faces grim, they turned to look at Joshua as he came up. "Have you come to help us fight or continue to talk about my people abandoning their home?" Erik asked.

Joshua wished he'd been born with his other brothers' patience. As the trickster who was never told to pull back when angry, since he was the Horseman of War, the act of staying calm was almost too hard. His jaw ached with the control he exerted on himself. He allowed his familiar mask of brutality to surface across his face as he stared at Erik. "And what are ye going to do to help, weakened from torture and healing?"

Erik raised his chin. "I will command them in their attack and throw down my life to help." Several men nodded around them.

Joshua let go of Kára, his hands fisted at his sides to stop him from scrubbing them down his face in frustration. "So," he said, "ye plan to throw yourself on Robert or trip his men with your dead body in the middle of it."

No one said anything. Let them be shocked at his candor. He had no talent or time to walk carefully around their tempers. Joshua let his gaze meet those of the men he had been working with over the week. "Will ye do the same then? Run in there to be shot down, adding to Erik's barricade?"

Joshua scratched his chin. "I know Robert is a

fool, but his men know enough to march around your bodies. The still-warm corpses will hardly slow them down as they proceed on to Hillside to imprison or slaughter your women and children in retaliation."

"What do you want us to do then?" Osk yelled from the back. "Abandon Geir along with our isle?"

Joshua didn't care what Kára's brother thought, but what did she think? He looked to her, and she lifted her gaze to the men. "Joshua will not leave Geir behind, but when we retrieve him, I will be taking him to Scotia, and I advise you all to follow us."

Erik's face was still hard as granite. "And what if Geir cannot be saved? Will you leave the isle where he is buried?"

She looked straight at him. "No, because I will then be buried with him."

The thought tore through Joshua. He had seen death, lots of death in battle. He remembered his mother's death three days after she gave birth to Bàs, his youngest brother. How his father had cursed the sky and God and the world around him. How he'd turned his sorrow into rage, going on to name his sons the Four Horsemen of the Apocalypse as if the end of days were near. Would he go insane, too, if he saw Kára cold and lifeless, her blank eyes staring up at the gray sky?

"I will prepare your warriors," Joshua said. "Prepare them to fight and lead them into battle against Robert Stuart." The promise tumbled from his mouth despite the warnings shooting through his head.

His hand curved over the tops of her shoulders as he stared into her eyes, hoping she would see the resolve in his gaze, in his soul. "I will save Geir and take ye both to my home where a Stuart can never touch ye or anyone ye love again." Could she hear the oath in his words? For he felt them as if he held his fist over his heart and his sword in his hand.

Pastor John stood with the men, his eyes wide, but he said nothing. Did he realize Joshua was endangering the Sinclair clan by going up against the royal house of Stuart?

Joshua looked away. He would not let Kára die, so there was no question of him reconsidering. He looked to Calder who stood next to Torben. "We need pitch from the bogs. Your men must soak their wooden shields in water. I want arrow tips wrapped in wool and long ropes in case they ride at us on horses."

His gaze rose to the forty men before him. "All your swords and daggers must be sharp. And each man must find a sack and fill it with dry grass until it is the size of his head." He looked to Calder. "We need whatever spears, brooms, or staffs can be found. Or anything that can be made to look like a weapon."

Calder began to yell orders to the men who ran off in various directions. Joshua's eyes sought Kára's, and he saw the flush in her cheeks. "Thank you," she said.

He nodded. "Have those who stay behind prepare to flee to mainland Scotland or hide underground. The doors below the hill should be better hidden with scruff and boulders. And we need to have Asmund set up passage with your ship captain as soon as he returns from his task at sea."

She nodded, striding across to the tavern keeper. Joshua watched her walk away, the growing distance almost like a physical ache. So much could happen to her when she was far from him. The wind blew, and he wrapped his cloak tighter around his arms.

"And what am I to do, Horseman?" Erik asked.

Joshua tore his gaze from Kára to take in the battered chief. Making him stay behind to heal would lead only to his revolt and senseless death. "We will need a protected source of fire to take with us."

"You will send in a volley of lit arrows?"

"I know where inside the bailey they keep their hay piles and peat stacks." He stared hard at Erik. "But ye know that not even a surging bonfire will stop a hundred trained warriors bent on blood."

Erik's face was grim. "We need to distract them enough to find one person." But his look did not say that the one person was Geir.

"Ye intend to kill Robert no matter what," Joshua said.

"He took my arm, and I will take his head," Erik said.

There would be no sense in arguing with the chief. If someone had taken Joshua's sword arm, he would feel the same conviction. "Do not get in my way and do not order the men whom I command, or I will take *your* head," Joshua said. They stared at each other a long moment until Erik nodded and turned to walk back into the house on the hill.

Pastor John came over. "Joshua," he said, the

wind whipping his robes about. "An attack against a Stuart…" He left the statement unfinished, knowing Joshua must see the possible consequences against the Sinclairs.

Joshua fished out the small sheaf of parchment from his sash. He had composed the short letter after killing Henry Stuart at the chapel.

"I must get word to Cain. Please…" He held the letter out to the pastor.

Pastor John took it, unfolding the stiff sheet.

First Day of November 1589
Chief Sinclair and Brother,

I break my oath to you and the Sinclair clan. My actions are my own and go against your orders to support the royal Stuart family. I know that if I am found guilty in my actions, you will execute me like a traitor, and that you and Clan Sinclair remain loyal to King James and the house of Stuart. Consider me dead and lost to you.

Your unfaithful brother,
Joshua Sinclair

"Joshua," John murmured, his head shaking the slightest as if he mourned what Joshua must do to protect his clan.

"Ye must leave within the hour." Joshua's gaze caught and held the young clergyman's stare. "On my horse, Fuil." Just like the warriors back in Caithness, Pastor John helped keep horses for Clan Sinclair. He knew how to care for them and ride.

"On your horse?"

"Aye. Ride him back to South Ronaldsay and

find passage for ye and my horse back to Girnigoe Castle as quickly as possible. Ye must deliver my message to Cain. I am a rebel and working alone against the Stuart Clan here on Orkney." A wry grin tipped up the corner of his mouth. "I am the Horseman of War, after all. 'Tis what I do and how I will die."

"But Joshua—"

"If I live, I am no longer part of the Sinclair clan. I break my oath to Chief Cain Sinclair and find myself as enemy to his people. Do ye understand, Pastor?"

Pastor John nodded, sorrow and understanding heavy in the lines of his face. "I will go."

Joshua clasped his arm. "Take care with my horse." He exhaled. "And he will do about anything for a turnip."

"You have my promise."

Joshua watched him walk toward the barn and turned to the men hurrying about with swords and buckets to gather pitch. On the other side, down the hill where the doors to their homes sat, a group of children were being directed by Brenna, her bairn strapped to her chest. They'd found a boulder and had started the work of rolling it toward the doors.

"Bloody hell," Joshua whispered, his gaze once again finding Kára where she directed the men along with Torben. Determination kept her arms and lips moving, hurrying the men to prepare, the thought of her son being frightened and tortured spurring her as fast as she could go.

He inhaled and walked down the hill toward her,

ready to do something he'd sworn never to do—lead unprepared people into battle where they may all die.

• • •

Robert has Geir.

Every time the thought surfaced in Kára's mind, her body clenched and her heart picked up its frantic race again. It was her worst nightmare come to life. "I am coming," she whispered as she tightened the girth belt around Broch. "God, please," she said, leaning her head into the side of her horse.

She heard Joshua walk up behind her, and the warmth of his palm over her shoulder nearly pushed the tears from her eyes. "We will get him back," he said, and she pulled in a ragged breath, trying to stamp the dread down into her stomach where it could stew without interfering with the upcoming battle.

Kára turned to Joshua in the darkness of the barn, a single torch the only light cutting through the shadows of the night that had come on. "Alive. I need him back alive. If the sacrifice must be me or Geir, get him to safety. Do you understand?"

Joshua's face was taut, so fierce she thought he might deny her request. Finally, he nodded. "And I need ye to trust me," he said, "even when ye do not agree with me."

"He needs to come back alive," she repeated.

"Aye, and so do ye, even if ye do not see my strategy."

Her brows pinched together as she stared hard

into his eyes. They were dark in the shadows of the barn even though she knew them to be a light blue. "What is your strategy?"

"It is forming in my mind," he said, frowning.

"Things you have learned from your little book," she said, referring to the small book translated into French that Osk said was called *The Art of War*.

"Aye, and from my experience."

"But you do not have five hundred horses this time," she said.

"That is something of which I am *well* aware," he said and caught her arms in his hands. He bent his head to level his gaze with hers. "Kára, we will save your son and ourselves."

She nodded, her stomach still feeling too low in her body. "Or I will die trying, because I cannot live with the failure to save him," she said, shaking her head. How could she make him understand the twisting emptiness of shame that plagued her? "I...I rode with my father to punish Robert last spring when Robert's men attacked the village at Birsay. We rode out before making sure everyone was safe, and... We were not there to save my sister and mother," she said, her voice weak at the memory of finding them on the floor of a house that had been blocked and burned. "And then my father and our horses were taken. They kept Broch but returned my father's body as a warning."

Joshua slid his thumb across her cheek, and her eyes closed for a moment as she absorbed the feel. Memorizing it as if this might be a goodbye. "I cannot fail again," she whispered.

He pulled her into him, and for a moment she

took the comfort he gave, building strength back from it. She opened her eyes at the deep timbre of his voice.

"Despite my calling, I do not relish war," he said. "But I have studied it my entire life, and I am very good at it." He pulled back to brush her lips with his. "I rage war against anyone who would harm ye and your son, Kára Flett. If that brings treason on my head, I will take ye to Caithness to my brother, and I will head south."

The thought of him leaving her to travel on alone… It tumbled like stones in her head, making it even harder to swallow. "I will go with you," she said without thought. It was an emotional reaction without concern for her family, her son. But at that moment in the darkness of the barn, with the feel of his touch still on her, she would not let him walk away from her.

He kissed her lips once more, sliding his hand down the side of her face. He said nothing, just stared down into her face. Was there no sense in planning a future that would not happen? He took her hand, and they walked together out into the firelit night to prepare her people to fight.

CHAPTER EIGHTEEN

*"Birds rising in flight is a sign that the enemy is lying
in ambush; when the wild animals are startled and
flee he is trying to take you unaware."*
Sun Tzu – The Art of War

"Do ye understand?" Joshua asked Erik Flett. As
the chief of Kára's people, his acceptance of Joshua's
leadership in this was crucial. "Ye must stay in the
dark with your men. Let Robert think Kára, Torben,
Calder, and I come alone." The man frowned but
nodded.

Joshua turned to the gathering of men and some
trousers-clad women standing with torches in a
semicircle around Erik and him. They'd gathered
sharpened swords, daggers, and pitchforks, as well as
spears, poles, and bags stuffed with hay. "Ye will all
wait crouched in the tall grass, each of ye and your
extra warrior," he said, holding up a stuffed head of
straw.

"Stay hidden by darkness and grass until ye see
my signal." Joshua raised his torch high into the air.
"That is when ye will rise and Chief Erik will pass
the fire among the ranks. Ye will set up your false
warrior and keep the light away from them. Robert
will but see a shadow of what he thinks is another
warrior."

"He will think we outnumber him?" Osk asked.
For once the boy's tone did not hold contempt.

"Even doubled, we would not outnumber his hundred warriors, but twice the number will at least stall him from attacking immediately. Hopefully, half his men will be off duty in the village north of the Palace." He held up the false warrior's head, setting it on the end of a broom handle. "Be sure to keep the fire away from them or Robert and his men will see through the trick."

Corey held his stick with a stuffed head on it up high. "And if they catch on fire, that will alert Robert that they are not real."

"Aye," Joshua agreed, rubbing a hand up the back of his head. "No catching them on fire." He waited for them to nod, several of them securing the string they'd tied around the neck of their poppet.

Kára walked up to stand beside him, but he kept his gaze on the group of forty. His voice filled the night around them. "We march tonight to bring back a lad, one who was taken from his mother and ye. We will avoid battle," he said, looking directly at Osk, who frowned. "Because Robert's men have trained longer, have more weapons, have a nearly fortified structure in which to hide, and outnumber us. And they are being paid by Robert to do whatever he asks, paid so they can feed their own families. They are men like ourselves."

Torben scoffed but didn't say anything.

"They have wives and children, too. Some are vicious like Robert, but some are in his employ only so they can feed their families and better themselves like any other man. I will use that knowledge in this." He nodded to the Hillside warriors.

Knowing the thoughts of one's enemies was

essential to winning any conflict. Robert's men were Scotsmen like himself. Joshua even liked some of them, but tonight they were the enemy. "Who here has been to Robert's palace within the last month?"

A few, who had been forced to work on the new wall, raised their hands. "Those of ye who have not, be sure to be near someone who has in case we must advance. They will have better knowledge of the layout of the palace grounds."

He looked out at the grim faces. "We have the advantage of surprise, and under this moonless, cloudy sky, we will be virtually unseen spread across the hill leading down toward the palace." A ridiculous location for a fortress; it should have been built on the highest ground. "Robert expects us to be in small numbers, so that is what he will be shown." Joshua pointed to Osk, Calder, and Torben. "Ye three will accompany Kára and me to the front gate." It was best to keep the disgruntled Torben close so Joshua could keep an eye on him. Calder nodded. Osk stood straighter. Torben frowned and crossed his arms.

"We are outnumbered, but we will use stealth and divide them to different sides of the fortress. That weakens their defense. When we arrive, I want four men, plus their poppets, to go to each of the other sides of the palace: coast, back, right flank. Have a fire source with ye, but keep it hidden until ye see my signal." He had already checked the tide, and it would be low enough to allow one group to follow the shoreline.

Corey started choosing and dividing up men and the few women.

Joshua nodded. "My first signal"—he raised his unlit torch in the air—"will be for the three small groups to light their torches and draw Robert's soldiers into four smaller groups within the palace. When I raise it twice"—he jabbed it high in the air two times—"then everyone else will light their torches on the hill behind us." He lowered his arm. "But wait for my signal. There is a chance I will not raise my torch at all."

"What is the signal to attack?" Torben asked.

Joshua turned his focus on the man. "The goal is to retrieve Geir without attacking." Joshua's gaze slid out to the warriors before him. "But if I jab my torch in the air three times, those armed with the pitch-soaked arrows will fire them over the wall and at the gatehouse." He took a deep breath. "And if I wave my torch over my head back and forth, we move forward." Attacking Robert's men meant most of these people would die. He would try to remedy this mess without the need.

"The best outcome will be winning back the lad without bloodshed." His gaze stopped on Erik Flett. "On both sides." He paused, but the man did not nod, and Joshua scanned the rest of the crowd. "A forward, all-out attack would see many casualties and deaths, mostly on the side of Hillside. I will avoid it, but if it comes to that, set fire to the fields around the palace." He looked to three men who held bows. "There are hay piles inside the gate to the left when entering. Fire up your arrows and shoot them high over the wall. Hopefully, they will hit and catch. Either way, the fire will disrupt."

He had taught Robert's soldiers to remain calm

in attack, but would they adhere to his teachings under John Dishington's brutal leadership? When Joshua had been there, none showed loyalty to the mercenary.

Damn. Would he be up against young Mathias or lovesick Angus? Civil war was the worst kind, pitting friend against friend and brother against brother.

He glanced at Kára. Her love for her son and determination to get him back added to the strength in her stance. She would march against Robert Stuart, even if she knew she would die in the effort. And bloody hell, he wouldn't let that happen.

Joshua turned back to the Hillside warriors. "I will ask for Robert to bring Geir forth, so we can see that he is alive. We will also know exactly where he is."

"Why is Chief Erik not leading us?" Torben asked, his voice loud, cutting through the breeze off the sea. "Let Robert see he hasn't conquered his or our spirit."

The Hillside warriors knew very little about battle, the mental game that, if played right, would lead to victory. "First," Joshua said, "Robert thinks he has broken your chief's spirit by taking his arm, or his life if he did not heal. By giving Robert something he expects, the absence of your chief, he will be more lulled into thinking he knows what is going on and will act in a predictable manner. There is time for surprise, but there is more success by making the enemy feel they have the upper hand." Which they bloody hell did.

Joshua looked to the man standing tall, his stump wrapped tightly with a poultice and linen strips.

"And, secondly, I am your general. Chief Flett is your sovereign and leader. He orders the recovery of Geir Flett, and I devise the best chance of doing so successfully."

Erik stood stoically, staring out at the men. Was he expecting Joshua to say he was not strong enough to lead without his arm? Hardly. The fact the man had survived the torture, mistreatment, and dismemberment at the sadistic hands of Robert Stuart showed just how strong he was. But Joshua needed him to confirm his appointment as general or the Hillside warriors would have doubts about whether they should follow all his orders, which would seal their doom.

Joshua waited. Slowly, Erik shifted his stance, his lips parting. "The Highlander's plans are sound. He is my general in this crucial bid to save young Geir. Follow him to confront Lord Robert."

When Erik looked back to him, Joshua nodded and turned his gaze to the soldiers standing in the deep night, their torches cutting firelight across their serious faces. "With your chief's order, make sure to do exactly what I say and signal. If ye do not…" His gaze moved to Kára. "We will lose this clash with much loss of life."

• • •

Be alive. Be whole. Be brave.

Kára continued her silent litany as she thought about her son. She saddled Broch, imagining him alive and smiling to keep her breath from galloping too fast and bringing on stars in her sight. He was only nine years old, too young to have learned enough to outmaneuver a sadistic tyrant and his sons and mercenary.

Why had he also gone to the chapel alone? To see the graves on Samhain, of course. They should have all gone together. Then Patrick wouldn't have found him alone there when he dropped Erik in the middle of town. What better way to cow the local people than to steal and threaten their children?

She stopped, her fingers clenched around the leather strap, and leaned her forehead to rest on her horse's neck. *Lord, keep Geir alive.*

"Kára." Joshua's voice came from the doorway. "We will march soon."

She didn't move and listened to his steps drawing closer. His touch on her shoulder made her lift her head, and she turned to him. He held a torch, the light bright, and she squinted against it. "Broch is ready."

He bent his face to level his gaze with hers. "We will get Geir back, and then I will take ye and your family away from here. Somewhere ye can be free of all this."

She was ready to leave Orkney. Before, it was an idea to be considered and weighed. But now, faced with the reality of Robert picking off her family one by one, and his cruel sons abusing their position as they grew into the image of their father, the need to leave was obvious.

Kára nodded. "I will go with you to Caithness. Only death will stop me."

He caught her chin, his face firm. "Ye are not permitted to die, Kára Flett. I will not allow it, and I am your general."

The side of her mouth twitched upward. "God rules how a battle turns."

Joshua leaned forward. "And I am a Horseman from God." He dropped her chin but kept her gaze. "I have studied war my whole life. I know how to run a battle."

She watched him closely, his back straightening, his fists clenching. "What happened in South Ronaldsay?" she whispered.

"I did not watch the birds," he said without hesitation. His hands went behind his head, cradling it, his massive biceps framing his face as he lifted his gaze to the rafters.

"Birds?"

"Aye." He dropped his arms. "I was too caught up in the challenge of helping the one side of the conflict there to remember to watch the terrain when approaching an enemy." He shook his head. "There was a boy there, Adam. A few years senior to Geir. He followed me around for days, mimicking my moves and asking me to tell him everything about battles. Smart lad. Starting to grow his strength, too."

Joshua leaned against the stall, the firelight casting an orange hue across his skin. "I knew they should not war with their neighbors and tried to convince the elders, but they wanted to win back their territory, something I could understand. I learned what I could about the enemy but failed to learn they had hired a mercenary to help them."

"Like you," she said simply.

He nodded slowly. "Although I did not fight for

them for gold. I fought for them…because Adam asked me."

"The boy convinced you?" And yet she could not by sleeping with him, using the children to ask him; even the maiming of Erik had not changed Joshua's mind to help them fight. Not until Geir was taken.

"Aye." He rubbed a hand down his face. "He took in all my teachings about splitting the enemy, surprising them…everything."

"Where do the birds figure into this?" she asked.

"We headed out in late afternoon, because I wanted the enemy to see me. I can be intimidating."

Completely. Her heart sped up thinking about how easily he had sliced through Henry at the chapel. No remorse, no chance for Henry to explain or beg or fight back. Joshua Sinclair, when bent on blood, was death as surely as if he did ride down from God to slaughter at his bidding.

"I hoped my appearance would stop them from fighting. That there could be a truce," he continued. "We walked quickly toward a hill. I saw a group of seabirds flying low along the hill, up and over. Instead of disappearing, continuing their flight, they rose up abruptly into the sky."

"It could have been the wind pushing them higher," she said. Would she have paid attention to the flight of birds?

He shook his head. "It shows my conceit, my feeling I was enough to win the day, that I did not pay but a small part of attention to a signal written out in the book I study."

"*The Art of War*," she said.

"Aye. 'Tis very plainly stated. Birds that change

course to fly upward is a signal that there are men hiding beneath."

"There was an ambush?"

He nodded. "Led by John Dishington. He is a mercenary and will fight for anyone who can pay him." Joshua crossed his arms before him. "With the chaos of the ambush, the men I led did not follow my signals, and there was great loss of life, on both sides."

"Who was the victor?"

"My side lost fewer men and called victory," he said, his tone flat.

"What do you call it?"

"No one was the winner. It was a battle that should not have been fought."

"The boy?"

Joshua's gaze slid to the ceiling of the barn. "Dead."

She exhaled long. Finally. She had the reason the Horseman of War did not want to war.

Kára touched his arm, the muscles taut and ready. "Thank you for helping me save my son." She stepped into him so that she had to tip her head back to reach his gaze. "Joshua Sinclair, Horseman of War, who wishes not to war." Her hands lifted behind his neck to pull his head down for a kiss.

Someone cleared his throat at the barn door. "The men are ready." It was Calder.

Kára stepped back, dropping her arms. "And the women and children?"

"Packed and ready to run to Lamont if need be. He and Langston have two rowboats docked in town to get as many as possible out to Lamont's ship if

Robert's men run against us."

"Start rowing them out there now," Joshua said. "The worst that will happen is they spend the night on a ship. The best is that they are not at Hillside if Robert's men storm it."

"There are some who will not leave," Kára said and looked at Calder. "Send those who are willing to go. Those who wish to stay on Orkney must barricade themselves with food and water in one of the earthen cottages."

Calder nodded and strode off.

"I have already packed a bag for me and Geir," she said softly. "I will ask Brenna to take it for us to the ship."

He raised their joined hands between them. "If anything happens to me," he said, "I want ye on that ship. Cain will take ye and your people in. Pastor John is, right now, riding to Girnigoe to tell him of all this." He slid their palms together and curled his fingers inward so that they intertwined, locking their hands together.

"If anything happens to me," she said, "take Geir and my people to Scotia. Help them settle and be free."

He frowned deeply. "Nothing will happen to ye."

She glanced away, not able to look him in the eye.

"Kára, swear to me ye will not go into that fortress, behind the walls, or within arm's length of a Stuart."

She returned his stare, mutiny in the hardness of her face. "If I do not swear, will you lock me below the hill with a boulder before the door?"

"I already considered that," he said, huffing.

"Swear to me, Kára Flett, that ye will not put yourself at more risk than the rest of your people."

He would not release her stare, his eyes penetrating with the glint of firelight in them. If she did not reassure him, he might have Erik order her to stay behind, something she could not do, not with Geir in the hands of those monsters. She frowned fiercely. "I swear."

CHAPTER NINETEEN

"Thus we may know that there are five essentials for victory: He will win who knows when to fight and when not to fight. He will win who knows how to handle both superior and inferior forces. He will win whose army is animated by the same spirit throughout all its ranks. He will win who, prepared himself, waits to take the enemy unprepared. He will win who has military capacity and is not interfered with by the sovereign."
Sun Tzu – The Art of War

"No battering ram," Joshua murmured, as he stood looking down the hill at the preparations. But they didn't need one, since Robert's wall was not complete. Joshua hoped not to get to the point of trying to breach the palace. Robert must know they would attempt to rescue the child. But intimidation and surprise at their numbers would hopefully stop Robert long enough for Joshua to convince him that harming a child was not the answer. Negotiation was truly the only way for the Hillside people to win the day.

Joshua's mind ticked through his mental list of resources as he watched the men light the covered lanterns, which would remain hidden until his signal. Thirty-four partially trained warriors with various weapons and iron shields, three warrior women with daggers, eight gangly lads who were set to guard their das' backs, two hundred five arrows, twenty with pitch, forty poppet heads that would help only if none caught on fire…

His gaze stopped on Kára where she spoke with Brenna down the hill. *One warrior queen willing to die.* "Bloody hell, but she will not," he whispered. "She swore." Would she break an oath? For her child? *Absolutely.*

The two women hugged around the bairn strapped to the front of Brenna, wee Joshua. Brenna pulled back, wagging a finger at Kára as if scolding her. But then she hugged her quickly again, wiping tears from her cheeks, and hurried to join the cluster of Hillside women, elderly, and children hurrying toward the rowboats on the shore below the village. They should have time to evacuate before Robert's men could ride back to retaliate against any of the families of the men raising arms against them. Robert would see this as treason, and his anger would lead to slaughter.

Joshua ran a hand down his face, his gut tight. Lord, he needed to play this conflict perfectly. Could Kára keep to her roles? Or would desperation to save her son make her act unwisely?

His hand cupped the back of his head, his exhale coming out long. He had seriously considered trapping her in one of the underground cottages with a boulder rolled before it. *She would skewer me when I let her out.* And worse, he would sever whatever bond had formed between them.

As if feeling his gaze, she turned to look up the hill and began to trudge toward him. She wore her leather trousers and tunic with fur-lined wool cape.

Fur boots wrapped around her calves, and a woolen cap sat on her head, a long braid over one shoulder.

"Torben and Calder are helping Corey go over your signals again with each warrior," she said when reaching him. "They all have their stuffed heads and unlit torches. Erik has distributed his flame to four other lanterns that will all stay hidden until you signal, and they will light those warriors' torches around them."

He nodded, watching her face in the splash of light from her own torch. The panic he had seen before, which would have pushed her right into a doomed fight, was gone. It was replaced by calm determination. Determination and…trust, something every general must foster within their troops for their plans to succeed. But trust from Kára… It was something deeper, and it honored him. He hoped he lived up to deserving it.

Breaking from the role of general for a moment, Joshua pulled Kára toward him, tipping his face down to brush her lips with his. "This will be difficult, lass. Do not lose focus if ye see Geir frightened or harmed. Where there is life there is still victory."

She nodded, meeting his gaze steadily. "Get him back, Joshua," she whispered. "No matter what must be sacrificed."

"Except for ye," he said. Joshua's mouth clamped tightly together, waiting for her nod, a nod that she would not give.

Calder ran up the hill. "The men are ready," he said, breathing heavily. "We can march when you command."

Joshua tipped his face to the night sky. It was

near midnight, the sliver of moon hidden in the thick clouds. The wind blew the cold about in casual gusts. Robert would be abed, with or without a mistress. Most of the soldiers guarding the palace would be lulled with the quiet night so far, some having gone home to the village north of Robert's.

"We will march soon," Joshua said, and Calder ran back down the hill, yelling orders. Joshua turned back to Kára. "I would send Broch to Asmund to hide in your barn near your den. If we ride her there, she could be injured or taken."

"I asked Osk to take her already," she said.

Aye, she would have already thought that through. His gut unknotted a bit. Calm, thorough consideration of moves and consequences was imperative. He grabbed her hand, and they walked down the hill together. It felt right having her by his side, both of them dressed for war. Even though he'd rather lock her underground, having her next to him made him feel even stronger. He did not need to worry about where she was and if she were being harmed when she was right beside him.

"Stay near me," he said, glancing at her as they walked. She narrowed her eyes as if suspicious of his motives. Could she guess he was determined to keep her alive? He'd never hidden that fact, but he wanted her to trust him to save Geir. He cleared his throat, looking forward. "Your role is one of leader for your people. Ye must be at the front when we speak with Robert and his men."

"I will not run off," she said.

"And ye will not run inside," he said, reminding her. He knew what the dungeons looked like, and as unpleasant as they were, he feared she would be shackled in Robert's or Patrick's bedchambers instead.

"Kára? Swear to me."

She glanced away. "I will not go inside," she said, her words stilted.

He breathed in the chilled air, thankful for the fur-lined wrap he wore over his bare arms and chest. The march would take an hour on foot, for he would not push them to go quickly. Advancing an army gave the enemy the advantage of having rested. But to get Geir back, they must strike at the palace.

They stopped before the organizing warriors, and silence fell over the group as they stood in the pre-winter night. All eyes turned toward Joshua, and blood thrummed through him. This lightning of energy was familiar. He'd been in dozens of battles since his father suited him up and brought him to his first at the age of fourteen.

This, however, was the first battle he'd led since South Ronaldsay. Without five hundred perfectly trained warriors on horseback behind him, a daunting enemy before him, and the ghosts of Adam and his family haunting his thoughts, Joshua should feel uneasy. But it was not any of that which made him start his talk to the troops with a prayer.

"Holy Lord, bless this people and the heroics they are about to enact to save a boy's innocent life…" His words continued, caught and distributed to the masses on the wind. But it was the prayer in his heart that tightened his chest, making the familiar readiness for war twist into the unfamiliar ache of worry. *Lord, keep her safe.*

• • •

They moved in silence across the hills with only
Joshua's lantern showing. Kára walked beside him
with Calder on her other side and Torben next to
Joshua. The men and few women who followed
behind did not falter. They were used to traveling
over the spongy moors and uneven boulder-studded
ground of Orkney, the tall grasses whipping their
legs.

Kára breathed in the sea air. Even though it was
near midnight, the need to find Geir safe and alive
pushed away any tiredness that tried to slow her
pace. Whenever she glanced behind, she saw the
shadows of her people walking just as quickly. Some
of them must thirst for revenge like she, having lost
people to Robert's abuse and neglect. Others
marched to keep Robert's soldiers from running to
harm their families. Still others kept true to their
oaths to follow where the chief of the Hillside
people led, whether they saw that as Erik or her, or
Joshua the general and Horseman of War.

Ahead, the bulk of the Earl's Palace sat at the
base of a hill, perched on the edge of the sea. It was
a structure of rocks and thatching, and yet it looked
to Kára to be as grim as a monster-tale dragon.
Flickering torches sat at intervals along the half-
built wall and under the roof covering the guard
tower at the gate. Another month would see the
fortress fortified with a functioning portcullis and
complete twelve-foot wall of stone.

"There will be four guards on the ground outside

the keep, two in the guard tower, and two rotating inside the fortress on the first floor," Joshua said, his voice low. "They are equipped with swords, pikes, and shields. The ones inside also have bows and guns ready to shoot from slots."

"Damn," Calder said.

"Which is why success will lie in avoiding all-out battle," Joshua said. "Because once it starts, like a stone down a hill, we will continue to the ultimate outcome." He met Calder's eyes. "Let us not start this, because I do not retreat. Ever."

He kept Calder's stare until the man nodded. Joshua glanced at Torben, who kept a scowl on his face. Torben was as stubborn as his mother. He would never nod an approval about anything Joshua said.

I will never retreat either, she thought, not without Geir. As a leader to her people, was she supposed to sacrifice her son to save them? She would never be an adequate leader if that were the cost.

Joshua stopped at a point where the gatekeeper should see his small lantern, like a beacon lost on the ocean of darkness before the palace. He kept it level, knowing the Hillside troops were quietly spreading out, crouched in the tall grasses, waiting for further signals.

"Kára and I will go forward," Joshua said. "With ye two behind us. If they attack," he said, looking at Calder, "wait for my signal and then repeat it with your own torch. One thrust of my arm into the air. The other torch holders will mimic the signal so the troops waiting on the shoreside and the east side of the palace will know. Two thrusts to reveal our false numbers."

Calder nodded and Joshua glanced at Torben. "Ye are to assist Calder if he needs it," Joshua said. "Otherwise, follow my signals."

He and Kára began striding toward the gate tower. "I will speak," Joshua said. "Keep your shield ready and your oath not to enter."

"Do not worry, Highlander. I have no plans to rush into the devil's den."

His gaze moved to the fortress where several men stood with torches, watching them approach. Joshua yanked the ties at his neck, shucking his wrap. He did not wear a tunic, only the end sash from his kilt. The muscles of his shoulders and arms contracted, mounding to show his obvious strength. The tattoo of the horse head on his arm and the sword across his upper back marked him as the Horseman of War. The fierce bend of his brows, flaring nostrils, and clamped teeth behind rolled-back lips marked him as the harbinger of death.

If he were marching *against* her instead of *for* her, they'd be doomed. The realization that Joshua had spoken truthfully about not trying to hurt her people struck inside her like lightning illuminating the landscape. If he'd wanted to harm her people under Robert's orders, they would all be dead.

"Joshua Sinclair?" a man yelled down.

Joshua stopped, Kára next to him. "We have come to negotiate for the release of Geir Flett, an innocent boy of only nine years."

Two of Robert's warriors rounded the unfinished gate and approached. Joshua let them get within six feet before stopping them with his palm out. He nodded. "Angus. Mathias."

"What are ye doing here, Joshua?" the older man asked, glancing up at the tower. He lowered his voice. "Robert counts ye as an outlaw against him and the crown for taking his healer and horse."

"And there are some who think ye had a hand in the disappearance of Henry Stuart," the younger soldier added, looking at her and then back at Joshua. "We have orders to kill ye."

"Do ye think it wise to attack me, Mathias?" Joshua asked, his voice even.

"Bloody hell, no," Mathias answered. "But Robert will dismiss us if we do not follow orders. Or count us as traitors, too, and arrest us."

"Then let the boy free without anyone seeing," Kára said.

Both soldiers looked at her as if she'd asked them to murder Robert themselves. "There are five men guarding the lad," Angus said, shaking his head. "There'd be no way to do so."

Mathias looked back at the gate over his shoulder. "As soon as Liam knew it was ye, he sent someone to rouse Lord Robert and Dishington. Soon the whole palace will know ye are here."

"And we will be ordered to attack," Angus whispered.

"If ye survive," Joshua said, his voice low and even, "what do ye think Robert will order ye to do next? Kill a nine-year-old lad? Deliver his head to his mother? Turn against your own family if they are caught being kind to the native people?" Joshua looked up at the tower. "Ask Liam what Lord Patrick will do when he discovers his sister there in the village. I know he keeps her hidden away from the lustful bugger. And ask Tuck how he feels about flogging old men when they refuse to build another palace for Robert's son."

"Bloody hell," Mathias cursed, rubbing his face. "We do not have time to go around talking to them. Robert will be out any moment. We but came to warn ye."

Joshua let something of a smile touch his lips, but with the dark promise of death there, the leer made a shiver erupt within Kára. Did the two men feel the same?

"A warning?" Joshua said.

"Aye," Angus said, glancing behind him. "There is but four of ye against fifty of us here and fifty more in the village who will run here if the beacon be lit." He pointed to the gate tower, above which a large torch was held, likely soaked in pitch.

"Then the beacon should *not* be lit," Joshua said, staring hard at Angus. The man blinked several times, his face pinched in unease as he gave the smallest tilt of a nod.

A flicker of hope caught inside Kára. There were only fifty soldiers at the palace right then. They would be almost evenly matched in number even if not in training and experience.

"Ye may join us if ye wish to win this conflict," Joshua said.

For a moment, Kára thought that they might, but then the younger one shook his head. "Lord, I truly want to go back to Edinburgh."

"If ye walk off into the night," Joshua said. "I will tell Robert I slaughtered ye and ye can find a ship to cross with me."

"Bloody hell, Joshua," Angus said, his voice low. "Ye and Dishington trained us to battle well. Ye must retreat before Lord Robert orders us to slaughter ye."

"I have never retreated a day in my life," Joshua said, his words even and rough. "I do not intend to do so now."

Before either of them could respond, a voice boomed down from the watchtower.

"Joshua Sinclair, mercenary Horseman of War." Robert Stuart's voice made Kára's stomach tense.

Joshua turned away from the two men who ran back behind the wall into the bailey before the keep. Kára stepped along beside him as he approached the tower. "Return the Flett boy," Joshua said, "and we will leave ye unharmed this night."

Robert's face pinched in anger. "I am already harassed with the disappearance of my son Henry, and Jean's horse, and wise Hilda, all of which has happened since you left my palace." His gaze slid to Kára. "If they are paying you to fight for them, it is with stolen money, my gold."

"I fight for what is right, Lord Robert," Joshua said. "Not for gold."

"What is right is respecting the Scottish crown and those who serve it, which these people of Orkney do not understand. And, it seems, neither do you."

"Respect for a man who steals away a child?" Joshua asked.

"A child for a child," Robert said. "When Henry is returned to me unharmed, then their child will be returned unharmed as well."

Kára's mouth opened, but she clenched it shut again. How could Robert compare his raping, terrorizing, malicious son to a nine-year-old boy who still picked wildflowers for his mother?

"We would see that the child is alive and unharmed," Joshua said.

Kára held her breath as Robert signaled someone below the tower and turned back to them. He squinted out into the night as if he saw something. "Get that bloody torch away from me. I cannot see a damn thing with it blinding me," he said to the man whom Joshua had called Angus. The soldier had climbed up quickly into the tower. Had Joshua truly won his loyalty while he worked there?

Kára sucked in a rapid breath as The Brute walked to the open gate, his hand clutched around Geir's arm as if lifting him to walk. Was he injured?

"See with your own eyes," Robert yelled down. "The boy is safe. Can you say the same for Henry?"

"I have no idea where Henry is," Joshua said, which was the truth, since Lamont had dumped him and his guards somewhere off the coast.

Patrick Stuart came to stand on the ground next to The Brute and Geir. "There was blood on your tunic at the tavern," Patrick yelled. "And we discovered some on the grass beside the chapel of Birsay."

"I am the Horseman of War," Joshua said, his stance as solid as his tone. "I wear blood like maidens wear perfume."

"Dammit," Patrick said. "Whose blood was it?"

"Mine," Kára said, her gaze focused on Geir. He stood, looking out at her, his face fighting for bravery, but she could see the fear in the wideness of his eyes. "'Twas my blood on his shirt and beside the chapel. I hit my head there, and he helped me."

Patrick leered, his smile wry and his eyes predatory. "*Tsk*. Tupping with the Horseman of War against God's chapel. You could have been hit by God's lightning bolt while being slammed against the wall and impaled by—"

"We do not have Henry Stuart," Kára said, her statement loud to cover Patrick's crude words. "Release Geir Flett, a nine-year-old boy who is innocent in any wrongdoing."

"The son of a rebellious woman," Robert said from his perch. "If he is not already guilty of something against the crown, he will be as he grows."

Kára stared defiantly up at the man who represented the oppression of her family and people on Orkney. "Is that how you judge people, Lord Robert? Not by what they have done but by what they may do?"

"Release the boy," Joshua called out, the force of his voice like thunder.

"Not without someone else to hold in his place until Henry is restored to me," Robert replied.

"We are not here to trade. We are here to take back what is ours," Joshua said.

"You and three others?" Patrick asked. "Against our full regiment."

"Half your regiment," Kára said, making the bastard lord's son frown at her.

"And we are not alone," Joshua said, his arm lifting the torch high into the air. Within heartbeats, torches were lit on all sides of the castle as the twelve showed that they surrounded the palace.

With their false warriors in the shadows near them, they looked twice the number. Several guards scattered away from the front to see the other Hillside soldiers.

Joshua jabbed his torch up in the air twice. Without a sound over the wind, light popped up in the field beyond and on the two sides of the castle that she could see. It moved from man to man across the moor and up the hill as the Orkney warriors stood up out of the tall, dark grasses and lit their torches. Looking out at them, she was amazed to see how the poppets, set away from the light, looked like extra people ready to surround and fight.

"Bloody hell," Patrick said, his hand going to his sword. "You raise an army against my father and the crown of Scotland."

"King James would find it quite interesting that Robert Stuart actually considers himself the crown of Scotland," Joshua said, referring to the Latin inscription over the arched doorway into the palace.

Joshua slammed the pointed end of the torch into the ground next to him with such force that it stood up, and he slid his massive sword free of its scabbard. "And we merely want the boy returned to his mother. No blood need soak the ground at the Earl's Palace if ye let Geir Flett walk away. Right. Now." The last two words came like a growl. The promise of pain and death in them made Kára's middle tighten. Thank heavens they had not had to fight against Joshua.

"Take him inside," Robert yelled, and The Brute dragged Geir back. Geir's gaze sought Kára's, desperate as if he held onto it to save himself. Would it be the last time she saw him alive?

"I will take his place!" she yelled. "Stop! I will take his place."

"Kára, nay," Joshua said, his voice low, but his words meant nothing to her. Not when she must save Geir from his father's fate at the hands of another Stuart.

"Stripped bare," Patrick yelled. "Like all our prisoners."

Without any thought except that The Brute had stopped dragging Geir away, Kára dropped her short sword, letting her daggers follow to the frozen ground. Within seconds, she had her cloak and boots off.

"Nay, Kára," Joshua said, catching her arm, but she yanked it free, turning her gaze on him.

"I told you," she said, her eyes running along the contours of his hard face, memorizing the lines and small scars there, the fullness of his mouth, the depth of his eyes. "If it came down to one of us, Geir would live. Take him to your Scotia, Highlander. Take all my people," she whispered.

"Ye swore," he said through clenched teeth.

"I will not let them take him back inside," she whispered.

Turning around, she began to walk toward Patrick. "Let Geir Flett go or I stop," she yelled, her hands halfway lifting the edge of her tunic.

Patrick signaled The Brute to halt.

"I will move for every step the boy takes back to the Horseman of War," Kára said, knowing all eyes were on her. She looked directly at Patrick, waiting, pitting his lust for her against his father's desire to keep Geir.

She drew in a breath when Patrick motioned to Dishington to send Geir forward.

"Do not release him until we have her," Robert yelled down.

If her heart wasn't thumping so fast and the cold not so painful as she yanked her tunic over her head to reveal her stays, she would have smiled. Oh, they would have her. And she would kill and maim as many as she could before they were forced to kill her to stop the rampage of vengeance she planned to inflict.

Geir took another two steps forward, and she untied the wrapping around her breasts. His gaze moved away from her when she had to slip it off, baring her breasts to all the eyes along the wall and in the tower. Patrick flicked his fingers at Dishington, who let go of Geir. Her son ran back toward Joshua. Behind her, she heard Joshua curse and his sword clang on the ground, but she could not turn away from Patrick's predatory gaze. His hand shot out to grab her wrist, and she knew she was lost.

Goodbye, Joshua Sinclair.

CHAPTER TWENTY

"To secure ourselves against defeat lies in our own hands, but the opportunity of defeating the enemy is provided by the enemy himself."
Sun Tzu – The Art of War

"Foking hell, I hate the cold," Joshua murmured as he yanked his belt open, letting his woolen wrap follow his sword to the ground. If he ran to Kára fully clothed and armed, the battle would begin. There would be no chance to save Kára's people from the slaughter that would ensue. Naked and unarmed would allow him to get to her, because nothing would stop him from that.

"Geir," Torben called, and the boy ran past Joshua to the two men.

Calder came up behind Joshua. "What are you doing?"

"Getting her back," he said, his words snapping out as if each one were a curse at the blasted cold.

"We cannot battle without you," Calder said, anger lacing his words.

Joshua's gaze met his narrowed eyes. "Watch for my signal. I still hope we will not battle. If we are taken, retreat to Hillside. If Corey sees Robert, he will order the ship to sail to the mainland. Ye will have to find passage farther south. If I am successful, I will switch places with Kára. Do not wait for me." He looked again at the young warrior who had so much to live for: a new wife, a new son, a people to protect. "Understood?"

Calder nodded, and Joshua looked forward to where Kára stood, her bared back straight and perfect. Shucking his boots, Joshua strode forward, completely nude, like Erik Flett the day Joshua rode away from the palace with plans to be at Girnigoe by Samhain. But then he'd met Kára.

"Bloody damn hell," he murmured through gritted teeth as gooseflesh rose over his skin and his ballocks tried to crawl back inside him. Stones pressed into his quickly freezing feet, but he ignored the bruising and cut of the wind.

In four long strides, he reached Kára and grasped her other wrist, halting her. His empty hand swooped down to grab her cape, and he tossed it around as much of her as he could. John Dishington came up alongside Patrick, both of them armed and furious. Before they could say anything, Joshua stepped between Kára and Patrick. "Let her go," he said. "I take her place."

"No!" Patrick said.

Without taking his eyes off him, Joshua spoke, his voice cutting through the cold. "Robert Stuart, would ye rather have a village girl doing your bidding or the Horseman of War?"

Patrick started to argue. "Hold your tongue," Robert called down. Joshua glanced above to where the torchlight showed Robert's pensive face. He weighed Joshua's words.

Joshua saw Angus up at the watchtower where the other soldiers tried to light the beacon that would call Robert's army from the village. The man's arms flew up in the air as if he were panicked, but the beacon was still dark. Angus had apparently chosen to keep his oath to Joshua. He had done something to wet the beacon. Having a loyal man in the nest of an enemy was more valuable than gold.

"Think about it, Lord Robert," Joshua called out as Kára still stood caught by Patrick. "The Horseman of War to do your bidding, to frighten and cow the native peasants so they work for ye, thankful for being alive at all."

"He has The Brute of Scotland and Orkney for that," Dishington called out.

Joshua raised his muscled arms and turned partway around without releasing Kára. His arm raked out toward the lit moors around Robert's palace. The poppets did look like shadows of more men ready to attack, outnumbering them now that Angus had told him only fifty were quartered there. Joshua turned back to Robert. "That does not seem to be working for ye." He heard Dishington's sword slide free.

"Hold her, Patrick," Robert yelled down. "And let us see if the Horseman of War is really protected by God as he fights my Brute with nothing but his frozen jack. If you are slain, Joshua Sinclair, we will take Kára Flett in your stead." Robert crossed his arms. "Can you conquer my sheriff?"

John Dishington was fully clothed and armed with a sword and likely a *sgian dubh* or two hidden on his clad body. It was most certainly not a fair contest, but war was never fair. Joshua forced his fingers to release Kára's wrist, and she was able to pull her cloak up around her nakedness.

Dishington did not even wait for Joshua to accept the challenge. With a roar, he plunged forward as Patrick grabbed Kára out of the way. The weight of his muscle and clothing added to the power behind his rush. Joshua sidestepped, ducking down to avoid his sword strike.

Toes and fingers growing numb, Joshua knew he would need to finish this quickly if he was to save Kára. And he would never allow her to be taken into Robert's Palace. Even death would not stop him. He would rise up and kill anyone who dared harm her.

What weapons did he have to pit against Dishington? Only his strength and his training in hand-to-hand combat. Both were in jeopardy with the cold making his muscles stiff. Joshua breathed in large inhales through his nose to feed both muscles and brain.

He also knew Dishington's fighting tactics. The mercenary's style was brutal, without elegance, and easily guessed. His entire stance hinted at his next move, and he obviously depended on his weapons.

Step one: remove his weapon. Instead of avoiding Dishington's next lunge, Joshua lowered at the last second, hands clenched together. Slanting his weight, the force of his strike hit Dishington's grip on his sword, right at the man's wrist. The immediate reaction was for the grip to open, and Joshua continued the thrust of his shoulder to hit Dishington's arm. The sword thudded against the packed dirt, skidding to be caught in the tall grass along the path.

Dishington unleashed a dagger from his vest, but Joshua dove, rolling along the pebble-strewn ground. The sharp stones had surely carved scratches into his back, but the cold had numbed his skin, and it hardly mattered. He rose quickly, his thigh muscles still warm enough to lift him, and turned in a battle stance toward his adversary.

"No other blade, Dishington?" Joshua asked, his voice low and goading. Step two: antagonize the enemy to get him to reveal his weakness.

"Once you are dead, Horseman, I will cut your ballocks off and feed them to your woman once I can get Patrick off her."

Joshua allowed a smirk to grow on his mouth, as he remembered another weapon he possessed. Dishington frowned deeper at failing to win Joshua's disgust. Joshua stood tall, his arms raised together as if he held his sword high in the air.

With a large inhale, he spoke. "When the Lamb opened the second seal, I heard the second living creature say, 'Come!' Then another horse came out, a fiery red one. Its rider was given power to take peace from the earth and to make people *kill* one another. To him was given a *large sword*."

With the emphasis on the last two words, his muscles mounded and bulged. The way he held his arms gave the impression that he did, in fact, have a sword in his hands, a sword wrought by God himself.

Joshua did not need to look along the wall to know his words stirred something primal in those men who heard him, God-fearing men who were raised on legend and biblical warnings. His gaze centered on Dishington. "And when I kill ye, I will walk away and forget all about ye, as will everyone else. And your name will fade into nothingness."

The tightness in Dishington's face told Joshua

he'd chosen the right threat. The man had named himself The Brute, a name he felt would haunt the world well after he was gone. The biggest insult to the mercenary was to promise him that he would be forgotten.

Step three of combat without his sword: use the environment at hand. Joshua did not have time to rummage around on the side of the road for the lost sword or dagger, and he really did not need them at this point. With a scrape of his nails and numb fingers, he grabbed a handful of dirt and stone. Before Dishington had a chance to rethink a strategy, Joshua ran at him, whipping his arm around with the force of his entire body. The fragments hit the seething man in his face and eyes. The man yelled. Temporarily blind, he swung wildly with his meaty fists.

"Son of a whore," Dishington roared.

Step four: hit where unprotected. Joshua ducked and kicked the man's shin with the side of his foot. Leaning the other way, he swung around his other foot to hit the other in rapid fire. Dishington lost his balance, grunting as he fell hard onto the ground.

Joshua stepped his one bare foot on the man's leather-clad chest, placing the majority of his two hundred pounds square over his lungs so that Dishington gasped. As he managed to clear the gravel from his eyes, he stared up to the sight of Joshua's ballocks and jack hanging over him in utter disrespect.

"Fok," Dishington spit out, gasping for air as Joshua pushed down harder.

"Ye have lost, Dishington."

"I am not dead," he said, swiping at Joshua's leg.

Joshua lifted it, setting his heel back down, but this time on Dishington's jaw, making his head turn to the side so far that if he continued, the pressure would break his neck. "Not yet, but it can be remedied if ye wish."

Dishington struggled to lift his legs but could not reach Joshua, who continued to twist his head to the side. Joshua glanced over to Patrick. "Release her now."

"I will not," he said. He had dragged Kára before him, a dagger at her throat to prevent her from pulling away. "He is not dead."

"That was not the contest," Joshua said. Step five: make the enemy think they had won. War was built on deception. He raised his voice. "I have won, Lord Robert. Order her release, and I would talk with ye about my services."

He felt the movement before he looked, knowing Dishington had decided it was better to die than lose and live. Before Robert could answer, Dishington kicked his legs over, rolling toward where Joshua smashed his face into the ground. Joshua let him rise, but before he could run at him, Joshua punched him directly in the nose with a jab and then swung his other fist around to hit his jaw, making his head swivel the other way. Dishington hit the ground and did not move.

Joshua turned back to Patrick. "One step and she is dead," Patrick yelled.

"I have won," Joshua said evenly. "Let her go, and I will go inside as your father's servant." He would, giving Kára and her people time to escape.

Then he would find his way back to Caithness eventually. Nothing but death would stop him from finding Kára again.

He did not move his gaze from the blade at her throat, but his voice rose for Robert's ears. "They will attack, Robert Stuart, if harm comes to her. Brutality against a child and a woman will not be tolerated by the people of Orkney."

"A hundred weak peasants against a fortified castle means nothing," Robert yelled back.

Joshua raised his fist in the air, jabbing thrice. Calder mimicked it with the torch Joshua had left with his clothes so the Hillside warriors could see. The leaders of the small groups set up to attack from each of the sides of the fortress passed along the order with their own torches. Arrows were lit by lads running between the groups. Before another insult could form on Robert's tongue, arrows shot through the dark night air, balls of fire flaming with their pitch-soaked ends in a high arch from all sides.

Bloody good hell. The Hillside warriors had followed orders and followed them well. Pride pushed Joshua's numb lips into a smile. Maybe if they set the whole place on fire, he could feel some of its warmth.

Shouts came from within as the arrows hit areas where Robert's men kept their dry peat and hay-stacks. Apparently, they hadn't built covers over them like he'd suggested. Several fireballs fell upon the thatched roofs of some of the smaller buildings inside the wall.

"They are trained, Lord Robert," Joshua said, his voice booming. "Trained by the Horseman of War!"

Even as he spoke, he kept his gaze centered on Kára and the soon-to-be dead man who held her. "And if one drop of her blood is spilled, you and your family will perish tonight."

"Traitors to King James!" Robert yelled, his eyes wild as the fire leaped up behind the walls. "He will send troops."

"To pay their respects at your mass grave?" Joshua yelled back. "Or will ye release the woman and let me walk into your fortress alone, sending these hundred trained Orkney warriors away?"

Joshua forced himself to breathe, ignoring the slicing wind. Behind him, he heard Torben swear. What did he have to damn? He wasn't standing naked in freezing temperatures. Joshua shifted his weight, wishing for action to warm his muscles. Perhaps he would rush Patrick and kill him in an effort to stay warm.

"You will pay for your treachery," Robert said, pointing down at him. Then he looked to Patrick. "Release her."

"No," his son answered, his lips in a snarl. He still held Kára before him, her wool cloak barely covering down to her knees.

Robert disappeared from the top of the gatehouse to leap down the ladder. He strode out the gate yelling, "I said release her and take the Horseman!"

"And ye will let her go with her people," Joshua said.

"No!" called Torben behind him, but Joshua did not take his eyes off the situation before him. Kára in the arms of a man bent on raping her and Robert

Stuart, a sadistic strategist who had no respect for the Orkney people.

"What are you doing?" Calder yelled.

"Ending the rule of Robert Stuart, my bastard father," Torben called, making Robert momentarily shift his gaze away from Joshua.

His father? Torben was a Stuart bastard? No wonder his mother wanted Robert dead with such vehemence. Had she been his mistress or raped?

"No," Calder yelled. Joshua waited until Patrick also looked past him to glance over his shoulder. What he saw made his stomach clench. Torben swinging the torch wildly, the signal for complete attack on Robert's palace.

A roar rose behind them as the Hillside warriors rushed forward. More lit arrows flew high overhead like large shooting stars falling to earth. Horns blown by the boys in the back blared angry notes to send a chill through the earl's soldiers. Loud and long, the notes rose with the war cries, heralding death and destruction. Those without blades swung long, leather straps that hurled stones with such force that they could cut through any unprotected flesh. The small holes drilled into the stones made them shriek as they flew, adding to the noise.

"Bloody hell," Joshua cursed, but things were in motion. There was no going back. From the back fields, the waiting Hillside warriors could not see that it was Torben and not Joshua who waved the signal torch.

Torben dropped the torch and leaped forward to attack Robert, but the wiry man had his own sword. Joshua took a step closer to Patrick and Kára, noting that Erik Flett ran forward to come even with Torben, the two attacking Robert.

"I will kill her," Patrick called, dragging her backward with him. "Leave her with me, and she will live. Unless one of her own people kills her. The fools!" he yelled, using her as a human shield.

Robert's men ran out from the open gate, armed with shields and swords. Liam and Tuck clashed with Calder and another Hillside man. But Joshua focused solely on Kára. Where was Patrick taking her? Wild eyes and clenched teeth told Joshua that the man probably did not have a plan and was spurred by panic. In his haste and insanity, he could easily slit her throat.

Around Joshua, the chaos and noise of battle splintered the night. More flaming arrows shot overhead, lighting the space before the wall. Clanging of iron pitchforks and yells filled the air with the shrieks of the flying stones as the horns continued to blow a call to arms across the moor. He could try to run back and order a retreat, but experience told Joshua that, like a boulder building speed racing down a hill, a battle, once started, would not stop until it had played out. *Bloody foking hell.* Both Hillside men and Scotsmen that he'd trained at Robert's palace were hammering away at one another, and there was nothing he could do but throw his powerful weight into one side or the other if he were to join in.

Torben swung at Robert wildly with obvious fury, almost hitting Erik in the process. Robert, a swordsman of experience, sidestepped the man in one turn, and ran Torben through with his sword.

Torben Spence crumpled to the ground on the end of his father's own blade. Erik held his short sword in his left hand. Robert laughed, saying something to him, and walked away. Erik threw his blade, but it fell without power.

Without his sword or blades or even his clothes, Joshua ran toward the palace, dodging the lowering portcullis to follow Kára into the smoke-filled bailey. He stopped, his head snapping right to left as he tried to see where Patrick had taken her.

"Joshua!" A man's voice caught his glance. Angus, up in the watchtower where he continued to keep anyone from lighting the beacon that would bring more soldiers, jabbed his sword around the left-side corner of the keep.

Joshua ran, the cold forgotten as the heat from his run and the fires building around him radiated warmth. Avoiding the flaming arrows on the ground, he dashed around the side of the keep, being sure to avoid the slits from where at least two guards would be firing. Coming to the base of the wall, he saw no one.

With a quick glance around, he ran to the wood-plank door at the edge of the sea. Four Hillside men held torches there, two with swords and two with more flaming arrows to send. The soldier guarding the back doorway lay facedown in the tide.

"The boy is retrieved," Joshua yelled to them. "Return to Hillside."

"But Kára was dragged inside," one man yelled.

Joshua didn't have time to argue with him, turning away to push into the darkness of the narrow, damp stairwell. A distant illumination at the top pulled his focus.

"Let me go, you swine." Kára's voice from above made him surge upward, keeping one hand on the wall to guide him blind, his bare feet slapping the granite as he climbed. Where was the whoreson taking Kára? He did not call out to her, not wanting to alert Patrick that he was chasing. Patrick should expect as much, but forethought was not ruling his mind. If it were, he would have left Kára outdoors. Taking her by force had completely sealed his fate.

I will kill him. Vengeance whispered in Joshua's mind as he continued to pound up the steps. His bare toes dug into the damp stone, and his hand gripped the wall to keep him from falling. Patrick had held a knife to Kára's throat and had dragged her, nearly naked, away. He would die painfully.

"Let me go." Kára's voice funneled down the stairwell. She was struggling, slowing him down, and Joshua was gaining on them rapidly.

"Hold your tongue, woman," Patrick yelled back, probably realizing she was trying to alert Joshua to her location.

He heard an intake of breath as if Kára struggled, and he let go of the wall, using both his fisted hands to propel him in leaps up the steps. When he reached the top, it was empty, and he threw open the door into what must be Lord Robert's bedchamber. The door leading from the room into the castle was partway open, showing their route, and he followed out into the corridor.

"Joshua?" Jean gasped, standing outside her room. Her gaze dropped immediately to his nakedness.

"Get back inside your room and bar the door," he yelled. "The palace is under siege."

"What are you doing here? Why are you naked?" she asked.

Down below, men yelled, and a door slammed at the end of the hall. "Bar your door, Jean," he yelled and ran down the corridor. He must reach the door before Patrick could put a bar over it. Joshua's hand hit the latch on the outside, pressing down as he threw his weight against the door, and it thankfully flew open.

"I will slice her open!" Patrick yelled, holding Kára up against him, the blade at her throat.

Her gaze connected with Joshua's. He saw so much in her eyes—relief, courage, and something he wasn't sure he deserved. Trust. She'd given him her trust that he would save her people. Did she also trust him to save her?

A lifetime of worshipping everything to do with war, and all Joshua wanted to do now was stop it. "If ye kill her, Patrick, her people will see ye as a murderer of a woman, a mother."

"I do not care what her people see," he said, spittle coming from his mouth.

"And that is the problem," Joshua said, speaking in a calm voice. "Ye do not care about these people. Ye do not take a moment to think about what it is like to have hunger gnaw at your belly or your bones ache with cold from inadequate shelter. Or have your few possessions stolen away because ye are part of the common people. Ye see them as criminals when ye are the one to break laws against them. Ye convince yourself they are less than ye, that they deserve whatever befalls them, that somehow God does not see them the same as ye."

Patrick snorted. "God? Where is He in all this? I see nothing of Him in this world. You should know, Horseman of War. It is the strong and powerful who rule the world."

How had something that Joshua had been raised to believe seem suddenly so very wrong? But it hadn't been sudden. It had started with the disaster in South Ronaldsay, where he watched good people die because of his self-conceit and inexperience with weakness. The conflict grew within him as he trained Robert's soldiers and even more as he tried to talk the Hillside people out of fighting a war they could not win, finally giving voice to what he'd learned. And now, as he saw Kára, so beautiful and strong but so damn vulnerable with a blade against her, he realized the foundation on which he'd always stood was sharp, crumbling sand—unstable, vicious, and wrong.

What mattered right now, above victory or revenge, was getting Kára safely away from the madman who stood with full conviction on the very foundation in which Joshua had built his life.

"Let her walk away," Joshua said, his voice low and even, as if he spoke to a spooked horse. "There is no war between her and ye."

"She killed my brother," Patrick said.

"I killed your brother," Joshua said. "Your revenge should be on me, not her."

Patrick's lips rolled back, showing his clenched teeth. "You bring destruction to your whole clan by killing a royal."

Joshua held his arms out wide. "I am naked and obviously unarmed. Take out your revenge on my body."

Patrick's eyes narrowed as if he knew Joshua's words were a ploy.

"Joshua!" Jean's voice came from behind, followed by a gasp.

Kára's hand pushed against her captor's arm. She dropped down to twist away under the blade. Joshua lunged forward to grab her, but she was too far away.

Eyes wild and snarl in place, Patrick yanked his arm and sliced in a sweeping downward swing into Kára's side. She screamed, and Joshua's heart fell inside his chest, leaving him hollow as Patrick threw her to the stone floor.

CHAPTER TWENTY-ONE

*"Therefore, just as water retains no constant shape,
so in warfare there are no constant conditions."*
Sun Tzu – The Art of War

"Nay!" Joshua yelled, his gaze tethered to Kára where she fell on the floor, crumpled and unmoving.

Joshua reached Patrick, his fist hitting the blade from the bastard's hand. He could easily swoop down to grab it, thrusting it into the man's belly. Even without a blade, Joshua could kill him viciously with his two hands alone. But the usual fury within Joshua had changed to desperation to reach Kára. The cape had fallen open to show a red line swelling with blood, skin flayed open. Eyes closed, she lay unmoving.

Nay! Bloody hell, nay!

Patrick dodged past Joshua as he fell to his knees beside Kára.

"Get out of my way, Jean!" Patrick yelled as he shoved her out of the doorway.

"Kára," Joshua murmured and glanced around for anything to staunch the blood.

Jean stood in the doorway, holding what looked like a length of plaid. But his gaze fastened on her linen smock. Jumping up to face her, the woman's eyes went wide.

"Joshua?" she breathed, fear in the tightness of her face as if she thought he would tear her in two.

He dropped before her, yanking the edge of her smock. She gasped as the fabric tore in his frantic hands, ripping the stitched seam that encircled her. Without pause he twisted around to return to Kára.

How deep was her gash? He could not tell, but the wet crimson that dripped down from it showed it had not remained merely on the surface. Taking the white linen, he gingerly but firmly wrapped it around her middle to hold the flesh together. "Lord in Heaven," he whispered over her, his hands moving swiftly as he'd been taught to do when staunching blood on the battlefield. Her face seemed to grow pale under his stare, the darkness of her lashes stark against her skin.

Joshua's lips moved as his fingers worked. "If ever there was a time for me to ask for miracles, Horseman or not, please…take me over her." His whisper was hardly heard over the deep thudding of his heart.

"Joshua," Jean said from beside him, some of her normal arrogance returning to her voice. "I brought you this." She dropped a length of wool plaid. "Whatever happened to your clothes?"

Joshua moved to Kára's head, feeling the side that hit the stone with enough force to steal her consciousness. A large bump formed under her golden hair, but no blood.

"I said," Jean continued, "what happened to your clothes? And why are you with this…woman?" He stood slowly as she continued to speak. "Father said you had turned traitor, working with the enemy. That you stole away Hilda and my horse that night you did not return to me." Her voice held anger and pain.

Joshua picked up the length of wool, shaking it out. Jean grabbed his arm, making him turn to her. She was pampered and perfumed and perfectly ignorant. How could he have ever felt her enticing?

"The horse and the woman, Hilda, were not yours to keep, or your father's to keep, Jean." He shook his head. "Ye either know little or care little about the atrocities done to the people of Orkney. And I have no time to explain them to ye."

He turned away, squatting. Checking the wrapping around Kára's middle first, to make certain it was secure, he took the plaid wrap meant for his hips and laid it over her body, covering her. He tucked the edge under her chin and rolled her enough to get the wool wrapped under her. The heaviness of her sleep felt like death to him, making his heart hammer in his tight chest. He had to get her out of there, out of the battle, somewhere she could be stitched and heal.

"That was supposed to be for you," Jean said as he continued to wrap Kára up in it.

"She has more need of it at present," he mumbled, even covering her head, her pale face the only thing showing. He finished by wrapping her cloak around her and stood slowly, Kára draped over his arms, her face against his chest.

Jean stood before the doorway, her arms wide as if to stop him from leaving. The idea was laughable, but nothing was humorous about a night such as this. "Step aside."

"Joshua, be reasonable. If you continue this way, you will forfeit your life on the gallows."

"And if ye continue this way, Jean Stuart, ye will

forfeit your soul to Hell. Now get out of my way."
His words were low and lethal, making her eyes
widen in the presence of his full battle expression.
She slid aside, flattening herself against the wall.

There was no time to stop to try to wake Kára or
check on the gash in her side. He knew only that he
must get her out of there and to safety no matter
which way the battle turned. Hopefully, Osk got
Geir away and to safety before Torben's vengeful
attack sent everything spiraling toward a bloody
end. To die in vain, Torben's soul would likely haunt
the Earl's Palace forever.

Joshua stepped down the stairwell as quickly as
he could while maintaining his balance and
clearance for Kára in his arms. With the pitch
darkness, he chose to step out on the bottom floor of
the keep instead of continuing on to the back door
where he'd entered. He swung around the arch into
the gallery lined with proudly displayed weapons
flanking the walls and strode forward with Kára.

Liam and another soldier Joshua had trained
fired their arrows from slits cut into the stone walls
for just such a purpose. They turned to him, arrows
nocked, eyes going wide.

Joshua shook his head. "Stand down, men," he
said. "This is a battle started by one vengeful man."

"Ye broke The Brute," Liam said, not lowering
his bow. Made for distance, it would pierce both
Kára and him with one thick arrow.

"With your bare hands," said the other man.

"A fair fight, to retrieve a child and save this
woman," he answered, shifting her harder against
him. "Now let us pass. I mean ye no harm." He

would rather slice through anyone in his way of getting Kára to safety, but words would have to be his shield over her.

"Liam, ye know the tyranny here at the palace, the unjust treatment of the weak." He met the man's gaze, a good man with whom he'd joked on many occasions after a day of training.

"Since when does the Horseman of War care about the weak?" the other man, a soldier named Iain, asked.

In some ways, he had cared his whole life. Joshua had intimidated most people to stop them from attacking and surrendering their lives. When that didn't work, a quick strike against the aggressors saved hundreds of weaker villagers.

"Since ye started bedding them?" Iain asked, nodding toward Kára.

"Shut your mouth, Iain," Liam said and nodded toward the door. "Go on," he said to Joshua.

Rage at Iain's slander battled against his need to get Kára away. The raw, hateful emotion roared within him, his face transforming into the pointed stare of an executioner. Iain took a slight step backward, his arrow held before him like a shield. He would have one shot. If he missed, Joshua would tear him apart.

"Iain," Liam yelled. "Put it down." A glance at Liam showed him aiming his arrow now at his fellow soldier.

"What the bloody hell?" Iain yelled, dropping the point of his arrow to the floor. "'Tis treason."

"I will foking tear your limbs off if ye miss," Joshua said, letting out in his low tone all the pent-up rage he'd felt.

Iain's face turned pale as Joshua strode toward him. The man seemed to shrink, and Joshua dodged at the last moment to move past him and out the door of the keep, leaving Liam to deal with him.

Outside, fires burned high in the wind. Smoke flooded the bailey, and the familiar clash of men and weapons broke any peace the night might bring. Robert stood inside the gates, his shirt blackened with smoke and dirt. He yelled orders to his younger sons and his soldiers. Without other orders, the trained soldiers followed his. Joshua had seeded the idea of turning against Robert in the men he trained before he left, just in case. In some instances, it worked, like with Liam, Angus, and Mathias, but some remained loyal to the crown, which was Robert here on Orkney.

"Johnathan, Edward, stand down," Joshua yelled as he walked across.

Robert charged up to him, making Joshua shift Kára to his shoulder where she moaned at the pain the movement inflicted. "How dare you!" Robert yelled, throwing his hand wide. "To bring these people to storm my palace after I housed you for months."

Joshua had no time for arguing with the tyrant. "Get out of my way, Robert Stuart, or ye will meet the same fate as your Brute."

"That is right! I am Robert Stuart," he yelled in full tantrum. "I am a royal Stuart, and you are a traitor, you and all the Sinclairs."

Joshua came up close to him, looming down while keeping track of the man's blade. But the look on Joshua's face seemed to freeze Robert as he stared up at him. "I am independent of the Sinclairs, rescinded my oaths, and have no ties to them."

"Does not matter! Someone must die for your insolence and treason." Robert lifted his short sword.

Naked and with one hand holding Kára over his shoulder, Joshua twisted as Robert thrust. The palm of Joshua's hand hit the blade at the hilt, knocking it from Robert. He was like a spoiled lad, sitting in his palace, eating and sending soldiers to steal away Kára's people and their possessions and peace. Torben's fury and impatience must have been the only things that made him fail against the pompous man.

"Perhaps ye should be the one to die," Joshua said, taking a step toward the man. Robert raised both hands as if ready to defend himself. That he did not draw another blade meant he had none.

Joshua shifted Kára to lie across his arms and turned his back on the bastard. He strode away toward the half-finished wall. He stepped past men he had trained, who paused to watch his march. None of them tried to stop him. Some of them halted their friends from firing out into the night when Joshua shook his head at them. There was no time to do more. He must get Kára somewhere safe.

Stepping around an incomplete wall, he traipsed away with large, ground-eating steps. Calder battled a man known as Bull. Erik Flett stood apart, his sword in his one remaining hand. Fire raging behind him, Joshua strode forward carrying Kára, completely unarmed, completely naked. She lay bundled in her cloak and yards of wool that he refused to believe would be her death shroud. On his way out into the night, men stopped fighting to watch him.

"You abandon us," Chief Erik called, sweat and ash on his face.

Joshua paused, turning his face to the man. "'Twas Torben who signaled to start the battle, so 'tis not my fight. I strongly suggest that ye cease it."

Without wasting another moment, Joshua took off in a run as smoothly as he could. Even so, Kára whimpered at the jarring. But the noise meant that she was alive. "Hold on, lass," he said as he ran her out of the fray. Men of both sides paused to watch him. Did they think that he retreated in fear?

Death before retreat. His father's words shot through his head, almost making him stumble with the rocks digging into the arches of his feet. Damn. George Sinclair could still haunt him from the grave. Never in his seven and twenty years had Joshua ever run away from an active fight. Even in South Ronaldsay, when people died around him, he did not give an inch of ground. Maybe if he had, more of Adam's people would have lived to see the next day.

As he neared the top of the hill, he saw the shadow of two people. "Holy God! Kára!" Osk ran over, Geir with him. "Is she…?"

Joshua slowed but continued to walk. "She lives, but she has a gash in her side and hit her head hard when Patrick threw her to the ground."

"Did you kill him for it?" Geir asked.

Joshua did not answer him. He would not defend his choice to go to Kára instead of giving in to the need for vengeance. "I am taking her to her den."

He glanced at Geir. "She would want ye two to leave this scene. Come with me."

"No," Geir said, anger on his face.

"Aye," Osk said at the same time. He grabbed Geir's hand. "As your uncle, I am getting you out of this mess or Kára will have my head." He started to pull the boy along. "And my liver and bowels and heart." Two steps farther and Osk seemed to remember what he was carrying. "Joshua," he said and threw Joshua's discarded boots at him. "It will be faster if you are wearing those."

"I'm not putting her down," Joshua said and began to walk.

"Bloody hell," Osk yelled, dropped Geir's hand, and ran to get the boots. He caught Geir's hand again as he ran by, dragging the boy to get in front of Joshua. "We will put them on you. Blast it! Stop for a moment."

Osk dropped down to the ground with one boot, and reluctantly Geir followed. "I still think we should stay to fight," the boy said.

Joshua glanced over Kára's head at her son. For him to grow into a man someday, he must learn when not to fight. "I will teach ye from my book starting on the morrow. Right now, we leave to save your mother." His tone allowed for no refusal, and Geir nodded.

Behind them, the night was lit with the red glow of burning thatch and hay, but Joshua noticed that shadows of men were fleeing the scene. Had Erik called for them to retreat?

Boots tied and the cloak that Osk had also retrieved thrown over his shoulders, Joshua ran across the rocky ground and through tall grasses hiding ruts. The pounding of his legs and the huffing of the two lads keeping up with him as he ran with Kára in his arms were the only sounds he heard over the wind rushing past his ears. How long had it been since he'd bound her wound? It seemed like hours when it was likely less than half of one. How deep was the gash? Kára's survival depended on the answer.

He held her close into him, so he could run faster without faltering. If it were up to him, he'd have pulled her inside his body, but the best he could do was wrap her completely in the wool length. *Please live.*

Bloody hell, live. Live. Live. Live. The word became a mantra in his head, beating with the quickness of his steps. Because the alternative would tear him apart.

• • •

Voices. Low, rough, continuing voices, their ups and downs were like waves on the ocean. She tried to focus on them but slipped away again into the nothingness, the fire of pain ebbing into an ache in the darkness.

"Come back to me, Kára." The voice pulled her, but darkness won.

• • •

Voices drew her again, words that at first hovered without reason.

"Hunting us."

"Burned."

"Hilda will not leave."

"Fever."

"Will not stop."

"Treason."

Slowly, the random words threaded together into sentences that wavered in and out in volume.

"Robert will not stop until he finds you." The strong voice came from her amma.

"Until he kills you," said another, Osk perhaps.

"Or you kill him." That was Geir. She exhaled, her body relaxing into whatever bed held her. Her son had survived.

"And then Patrick will hunt you. I am sure he's already sent word to King James about the uprising," said another man. Calder?

"I have seen no rider."

"There will be one eventually."

The voices moved back and forth with more words, always more words. She almost succumbed to the darkness again, but she stayed afloat, listening, waiting. None of the voices was the one she needed to hear, the one that had talked to her through the darkness and pain slicing through her skull and side. *Joshua.*

"Take this with ye. Give it to my brother. Tell him I am dead." It was Joshua's voice. Like the sun wavering through layers of water above the surface of the sea, Kára tried hard to swim up through the murky depths toward it.

"Two scraps of material with a knot holding them together?" someone asked. "What does it mean?"

"Cain will know."

Kára fought harder to focus on his voice. *Joshua. Joshua.* "Joshua," she whispered on a breath. The words around her stopped. Silence surrounded her. *I have fallen back asleep.*

"Lass?" The vibration of the voice tickled her awareness. She held on to it, following it like a fishing line up from the depths. "Kára?" Her name rolled from his mouth. He was there. She fought to answer him, her eyelids so heavy.

"I heard her say my name," he said, as if talking to the room. She felt someone cradle her hand. Fingers slid along her face, brushing her hair from her cheek.

"I am here, lass," Joshua said. She clung to the words as she fought to open her eyes.

"Give her some drink," her amma said.

Kára felt her head and shoulders lifted and a cool cup pressed against her lips. The coolness of honey mead slipped into her mouth and down her throat. She swallowed, and her eyes flickered open.

Dim firelight filled the space, and faces peered down at her. She couldn't tell where she was, but her gaze fastened onto Joshua's eyes. Light blue in the sun, they were dark as he stared back, his brows furrowed and hair mussed. His strong jaw was bristled, and she raised her hand to lay against it. "I have been asleep," she said softly.

"Aye," he answered, taking her hand in both of his. "For four days, lass. Ye had a fever from the dirty blade Patrick sliced ye with. It set in right away and would not let go."

"What has happened?" she asked. She blinked,

trying to shift, and felt the pain in her side. At least her head did not throb, but it felt heavy like the rest of her.

"I am well," Geir said, coming to sit by her. She smiled at him, and he kissed her forehead like he was a little man already. "You and Joshua saved me."

Memories flooded back like a nightmarish wave. "Torben signaled an attack," she said, feeling her chest tighten.

"'Twas my fault," Calder said from behind Geir. "He snatched the torch away from me. I should have been prepared."

"He has died for his crimes," Amma said, shooing Geir back so she could get in, giving Kára more to drink. Her stomach rumbled. "You need to sip some broth," Amma said, motioning Geir to bring her some from the fire. He hurried over with a cup.

Kára sipped at it; the rabbit broth was seasoned with herbs, and her stomach unknotted more with each swallow. Joshua helped her sit, and she realized that they were all underground in her den. How had Amma gotten down there? "Are we hiding?" Kára asked.

"Ye needed a safe place to heal undisturbed," Joshua said.

"Because Robert is scouring Orkney for us and anyone he thinks raised a sword against him," Osk said. "So aye, we are hiding, but the ship sailed."

"Those who survived?" she asked, afraid to hear that none had.

"I gave word to retreat as I ran ye out of there," Joshua said. "Many of Hillside's warriors listened. They are hiding underground."

"Retreat?" she asked, searching his strong face. "You said you never would. Once the stone rolls down the hill, it must finish."

His mouth quirked to the side, reminding her of the teasing times they had before. "And ye swore ye would not surrender yourself to the Stuarts."

She gave a small nod. "So Robert is not dead?"

"No," Osk said, standing behind Joshua. "He has been busy burning the village of Birsay."

"Asmund?" she asked. Would he have tried to keep the soldiers away from his tavern, his home?

"Lamont got him out to the ship," Calder said. He looked at Joshua. "'Twas a blessing that those not fighting ferried out there before we marched. There would not have been time to send them off safely once we returned from the palace."

Osk snorted. "Robert and Patrick are having fits that they cannot find anyone to kill. And The Brute—"

"He is alive, too?" Kára asked, looking to Joshua.

Calder shifted. "He was unconscious for most of the battle."

"Who did we lose?" Kára asked, softly. What lives had been lost to regain Geir?

"Torben," Calder said. "Slashed down by Robert." He shook his head. "He let vengeance rule his rage against a father who never acknowledged him."

"Fiona built his hate," Amma said. "Robert got her with child and sent her away. She hated him and spurred her son to kill him." Amma's lips pinched tight. "She sailed with the rest and will mourn when she finds out."

Silence settled briefly. "Who else?" Kára asked.

"There were some injuries, cuts, a few twisted ankles, but no more deaths," Calder said. "It seems that Joshua was respected quite a bit by Robert's soldiers. When he told them to step down, most of them did."

Kára glanced at Joshua as Calder continued. "They defended themselves, but from what I could see, they were not attacking except the bastard who I felled." Pride filled his voice, and Kára noticed the bandage across his head, his arm in a sling.

"With no more deaths?" Kára whispered, searching Joshua's handsome face.

"No more deaths," he repeated. His hand came up to cup her cheek. "I told ye that I would save your people. Not through war but through peace."

The ache of tears pressed against the backs of Kára's eyes. "Thank you," she whispered.

Joshua lowered his face to hers, kissing her lips gently. Backing up, he nodded to her, a smile tugging at his lips.

"But now Robert wants Joshua dead," Osk said. "He says your life is forfeit, too, Kára, for not trading places with Geir. Joshua is to die for killing Henry and turning traitor against the crown of Scotland."

"Would he follow us to your home?" she asked, looking to Joshua.

"His fury is great," Joshua said. "It will likely push him to journey there or Edinburgh to demand retribution against my clan and any of your people settling there."

Her eyes widened as the weight of Joshua's

sacrifice descended upon her. "You sent a letter to your brother saying that you broke your oath to him. We could go farther west, maybe to the isles there."

Joshua met her gaze. "I want ye to meet my family, Kára. Next to me."

"And Robert is out for blood," Amma said. "He will cause a big enough complaint with King James that Joshua's brother will be forced to give him up if he stays in Caithness. Unless…"

Amma looked up to meet Joshua's gaze. "Unless…" she repeated.

Joshua's eyes turned back to Kára. "Unless Robert kills me and sees us both buried."

CHAPTER TWENTY-TWO

"It is only one who is thoroughly acquainted with the evils of war that can thoroughly understand the profitable way of carrying it on."
Sun Tzu – The Art of War

Joshua's head rested on his arm that stretched over his head. He lay next to Kára under layers of quilts and furs, listening to her easy breaths.

Only days ago, her breathing had been shallow with fever, a sound he never wanted to hear again. When he'd seen that the slice in her side was not too deep, he'd been hopeful, but then the fever had sunk its talons into her. She had roused from the bump to her head just to go under again with fever. He'd run to Hillside and fallen to his knees in thanks that Hilda and Harriett Flett had stayed behind to tend the wounded. With Hilda's tinctures, poultices, and stitching and Harriett's constant tending, Kára's fever had broken, soaking her and flooding him with relief. Praise God! If Joshua hadn't been raised to slay, and planned to tup throughout his life, he'd have taken up the cross as a priest.

With the sun giving way to the security of night and the others gone back to their own hiding holes, Joshua had helped her wash with warm water and her sweet spicy soap. Alone, they'd eaten, speaking about Joshua's plan in quiet tones.

The night was cold, and they'd opted to put out

the fire in case Robert's men searched nearby. The smell of smoke and the glow of fire up the old well that led to her den might bring them. Tomorrow would be soon enough to die. If anything went wrong, this might be the last time he got to hold her. "You are not sleeping," she whispered where she lay, spooned against him.

"Neither are ye."

Gingerly, she pressed back so she could lie flat, looking up at him. Without the fire, she was a shadow in the sea of darkness. His other senses took over. The feel of her warmth against him under the heavy throws, the sound of her breath and soft words. The smell of the dandelion poultice tied around her waist and the sweet essence from her soap.

Joshua's fingers brushed the hair framing her face back as if she were as fragile as the flowers of which she smelled. He leaned into her, meeting her lips. They were already open as if she'd been waiting for him to kiss her. They breathed against each other, the press together deepening, and he felt her fingers tangle in his hair. He held her face in his hands, kissing her, breathing her in, long draughts of Kára. She was everything good, even with her stubbornness and risk taking. Aye. Everything.

The lass in his arms there in the dark was more than a mere woman. Kára was brave and clever and so deliciously sensual that he could not imagine thinking of another woman to bed ever again.

She could shatter his plans and hold her head high in doing so. She could sway his mind even when he'd sworn not to bend. She was all-powerful, and

his bloody life seemed to hang on her well-being
and happiness. He'd realized that when he'd watched
her crumple to the stone floor.

Pulling back, Joshua wrapped her in his arms,
burying his face in her still-damp hair. He lifted the
quilt over their heads to keep her from getting a
chill. For a long pause, he held her against him,
wishing he could pull her fragile body inside his
large one. The slice of a blade, a thrown rock or shot
arrow, even a fall from a horse could steal the life
from her.

"You're holding me rather tight," she said,
against his shoulder.

He loosened quickly. "Did I hurt ye?"

"I am not so breakable, Highlander."

"Aye, ye are, Kára," he said. Under the blanket he
could not see even a shadow of her, but he knew
exactly where she was and probably what frown she
was giving him. "I will protect ye more. Keep ye
close. No more battles."

He felt her stiffen. "Joshua, I have been taking
care of myself for the last nine years. Well, except for
the Henry attack. And I suppose Patrick, but
otherwise I am perfectly able to stay whole and
well."

"I do not want ye anywhere near the palace on
the morrow," he said, using his fingers to stroke
through her unbound tresses.

"I do not think Hilda would let me. Plus, I am
already supposed to be dead."

Her words chilled him. He kissed her forehead. "I
would rather put ye on your horse and send ye to
Skaill to find passage across."

"I will be well, Joshua. I survived too much to die from acting dead." She laughed lightly.

She did not understand. Joshua barely did. This turmoil within him, this simmering rage that her presence calmed. Never before had he felt…peace. But when he held Kára, his warring heart calmed.

There was a long pause between them. "Joshua?"

He ran a hand over his face. "My mother died birthing my youngest brother," he said.

"The one named Bás or Death?"

"Aye." He laid his head back down on the pillow level with her face. He knew she was directly before him even if they could not see each other. Perhaps the darkness made it easier to talk.

"My father was a warlord. He loved strength and victory, and he also loved my mother. I remember him laughing with her, deep bellowing laughter. I was young, but I remember it clearly. Because when she died…"

He felt Kára's hand find his along his naked hip under the covers. Her fingers intertwined with his. "When she died…?" she prompted in a whisper.

"He… His laughter turned to roars, his smiles to gnashing teeth, his tolerance to bloody fury. It was then that he began weaving the legend of my brothers and me being the Four Horsemen."

"He grieved for her," she whispered.

"It was as if the shackles that he kept on the frenzy within him shattered with his sorrow, letting out a beast that raged against anyone he saw as an enemy. I never understood how someone as small and gentle as my mother could have tamed him while she was alive. But in the palace, when I saw ye thrown to the floor, blood wetting your tunic…"

She squeezed his hand. "You worry overmuch about me," she said.

"I do, but I also worry…" He pushed up on his elbow to touch her hair with his free hand. "Ye bring me peace, Kára. I have never felt calm in here before," he said, raising their intertwined fingers so that her hand rested over his beating heart. "Ye have altered me, helped me quell my want to battle, even as ye did everything to get me to lead your people in war."

"I thought that was South Ronaldsay," she whispered.

His chest squeezed. "That altered me, too, but not enough to stop me from journeying on to Lord Robert's to train his men to fight."

"But you trained them to defend, not attack."

"'Tis a thin line between the two."

"Well, you did something," she said, "because my people survived the other night."

He exhaled long. She did not understand. Something had changed in him, something that could prove his complete unraveling. "I worry that if ye die," he said, "I will…" His lips curled in as if they were unwilling to speak. "I will truly become the harbinger of death, a warrior full of unchecked rage. A perfect version of my father." Bloody hell. He had said it. "Do ye understand?"

She was quiet for a long moment. Could she hear the thumping of his heart that echoed in his ears? Wrapped together under pounds of bedding in total darkness, he'd opened enough to expose his darkest secret, the thing that made him the most vulnerable.

"Kára—"

"Shhhh…" She unlaced her fingers from his, her finger rising to his lips to gently lie across them.

But he would not keep quiet. "Do ye understand what I am saying?" Did he? Maybe she could put this worry, this frenzy to protect her into perspective.

She leaned into him until he could feel the slightest brush of her breath upon his lips. "Love me tonight, Joshua Sinclair."

• • •

Kára's heart pounded inside her. Did she understand what he was saying? That he would go insane if she died? That her life meant so much to him, that her death could threaten the world in which they lived? That he possessed such deep feelings about her?

Pressing forward, her lips found his directly before her. Her questions melded into a growing heat inside her, a heat that teased her, giving her hope. Joshua Sinclair, mighty Highlander, was rugged, kind, and clever. Full of courage and honor. And he felt something for her: maybe something powerful and maddening, something she was feeling, too.

But she dared not speak. If she were wrong, the pain would hurt her more than Patrick's blade.

What had at first been built on carnal satisfaction had grown into much more. She had pushed thoughts of him away to protect herself, allowing it to grow only when she realized that they may not part ways. And now he was asking her if she understood him. She was not certain, and she was too anxious of the pain of being wrong to answer.

Joshua met her kiss with immediate intensity when she slanted her mouth against his. For long minutes they tasted and touched, inhaled and exhaled within their small circle. Her hand slipped down to his hard jack that sat between them.

"Ye are healing," he murmured against her lips.

"I feel no pain," she whispered, hooking her knee up and over his hip, bringing their bodies into contact. It was ever so obvious that Joshua's body had no reservations about her request, and losing herself in the feel of him would push away her worry that she'd said too much. "Love me tonight, Joshua Sinclair," she whispered as she took ahold of him.

He groaned into her mouth and pressed her back into the bed. She could feel his arm against the side of her head as the other hand slid along her arm to cup her breast. The strumming pulled a cord inside her that resonated all the way down to the crux of her legs.

Keeping his weight off her, his hand continued down her body, riding the hills and valleys of her curves, teasing out all the deliciously sensitive spots. Kára moaned low, his mouth sliding to kiss a path along her neck, sending shivers of building heat up and down her.

As his fingers skimmed the tightly bound bandage around her middle, he paused. "Do not stop," she said with as much authority as she could muster under the urge to surrender.

He pushed her gently away from him. "Trust me." The deep resonation of his voice stopped her cry of

unjust treatment long enough to feel him pull her
back against his chest. With her injured side facing
upward, the pressure that made it hurt was gone.
Joshua's top arm wrapped around her, his hand
beginning its leisurely strokes along the front of her
body. As he reached her crux, his fingers expertly
found her, playing a rhythm that made her pant.

Body on fire, Kára kicked at the heavy blankets
until some of them slid off to the floor. She arched
her back, rubbing her backside against his raging
jack. "Do not make me beg, Highlander," she rasped,
raising her knee to give him access. "Or I will make
you beg."

He chuckled softly behind her, his teeth nibbling
along her nape to send shivers and chill bumps
along her skin. "Threats from my warrior queen," he
whispered at her ear as his fingers plunged into her
flesh.

Her gasp turned quickly to a groan as he touched
every aching part of her inside. She felt his jack from
behind, seeking her, and arched backward. Holding
her open, he teased her, the tip poised for entry.

"Joshua," she said between pants.

His mouth came up to her ear. "Kára Flett, I give
myself to ye." He thrust into her open body. "Bloody
hell," he roared, passion changing the curse into one
of sheer pleasure.

"Yesssss…." Her moan drew out as his fingers
found her most sensitive spot while he started a
deep, plunging rhythm in and out of her open, wet
body.

She could not reach him with her arm. Twisting
would hurt her side, so she clutched the pillow

before her, pressing back against him with each thrust into her. His lips pressed against the back of her neck as he groaned, and she lifted her top leg to curl back, tangling with his. The vibration of his passion against her nape shot more lines of passion through her body. It was as if she were being pulled apart but building into a tight ball at the same time. Chills and heat, the pleasure built higher and higher, until the tight ball inside her exploded.

"Joshua!" she screamed as the passion overtook her, her breathing so fast she saw stars in the darkness.

His own roar filled the underground den as he flooded her, rubbing to squeeze out every drop of passion in her as he pumped into her from behind. The two of them rode the waves together until they ebbed, leaving Kára with a languid feeling. Silence wrapped around them as their breaths slowed.

Neither of them spoke after saying so much. His little words to her, just a few, but strung together, "I give myself to ye" meant more than breath to Kára. Was it love he proclaimed? That she herself felt? She had never experienced the mix of heaviness and light within her before, the heaviness when Joshua battled, the light when he smiled at her or held her. Not only did he cherish her body, making her cry out in shameless rapture, he respected her and her people.

She hugged his arm where it rested over her. Joshua pulled her into the curve of his body, holding her close in the darkness until they both fell into a gentle sleep, wrapped up in warmth and revelations.

• • •

Kára's eyes opened slowly, her hand sweeping under the blankets. She was alone. Twisting and then grimacing at the pinch and pull in her side, she gasped softly, remembering the wound. "Joshua?" she called out.

"I sent him away." Amma walked over, holding out a cup to her.

"What? Why? Where did he go?" Kára threw back some of the blankets, wrapping the sheet around her nakedness as she sat up and set her feet on the freezing stone floor. Someone had started a fire, so it was not as cold as the night before.

Amma frowned at her. "To Hillside underneath, to ready for the ordeal today. He did not want to leave, but I sent him on his way." She held the cup out again for Kára to take. "Drink. Eat, and then we will make you into a corpse."

Kára's shoulders relaxed, and she took the cup, drinking of the broth. "Is Calder with him?"

"Yes, and Osk. They will help him get ready and will accompany him to the Earl's Palace."

"Where is Geir?"

"He is with Erik and keeping an eye on your horse. Broch will carry you and the Highlander quickly away."

"You can come with us," she said. Her amma should have gone on the ship, but she and her sister, Hilda, had remained. Together, they'd stitched Kára up and saved her from fever. "You and Aunt Hilda."

Amma shook her head. "We are too old to start

over in another land."

"Ridiculous. You are obviously young enough to climb down a rope into a well," she said, indicating the way into her den. "You can surely travel to Scotia."

Amma smiled at her, pausing over a long moment. "Well, perhaps, but Hilda is staying."

"Robert will steal her back."

"That might be what she has in mind," Amma said and then waved off the comment.

"What will she do?"

"I will speak no further on it," Amma said with tight lips and a tilt to her chin that told Kára there was no use in arguing with her. "Eat up, child. I have white paste to wipe you with, and we must collect things to lie with you in the grave."

Kára exhaled. "Will this work, Amma?"

Her grandmother sat down next to her on the bed and patted her knee. "'Tis an unexpected plan, wild in fact. And Joshua has made contact with the men in Robert's holding who are loyal to him. They will help with the act."

Kára shook her head. "I still cannot believe the Horseman of War is sacrificing himself for our people. You know, Joshua has never lost a battle in his entire life. And he is now planning to do so to keep our people safe."

Amma smiled, the wrinkles around her eyes turning into deep grooves. "Our people?" She huffed a small chuckle. "Child, the man, warrior from God or human made, is sacrificing for you. We but reap the benefit." Her weathered hand came to Kára's cheek. "He wants to bring you to his home, to meet his brothers and sister, his aunt. He wants you to live with him there, surrounded by his clan. Otherwise, he would merely escort you there and leave you, set out on his own as the powerful Horseman of War he has always been." She shook her head. "Nay, he surrenders himself today so he can give you a life with him, and the Hillside people benefit." She leveled her eyes with Kára's. "You have succeeded in saving your people, Kára Flett, daughter of King Zaire, by winning over the heart of the fiercest warrior on earth."

I give myself to ye. His words in the darkness resonated through her body, making her heart pick up a rapid dance. Without sight, last night seemed like a dream, a dream full of every other detail. Their entire beings mingling with a mix of scents, sensations, and sounds. But now she wanted to see him, to stare into his eyes. Was there commitment in his eyes, an everlasting loyalty? Love?

Amma stood, pulling her gingerly from the bed. "Now sit, eat, and I will whiten your skin. After all, you will be several days dead. Geir found a half-eaten seal washed up on the beach. He will hide it under you in case anyone comes close enough to smell death."

"Is the ground frozen?" she asked.

"Calder built a fire with peat to burn through the day and night up at the chapel over your gravesite next to Zaire, Astrid, and Eydis. It will be thawed enough for a shallow grave, which is what we want anyway."

Kára nodded and took a bite of the barley bread with butter, her mind a tangle of the wild staging they were going to enact. "I thought the Horseman was invincible," she murmured, thinking of the sacrifice Joshua was about to make. "That he would never show weakness or crumble."

Amma sat down opposite her, propping her elbows there. She leaned forward as if to impart a great secret. "No one is invincible to love. It is what makes us vulnerable and strong at the same time, doing things we never thought possible."

Kára's gaze snapped up to Amma's. "Do you...?" Kára wet her lips between shallow breaths. "Do you think he could love me?"

Amma smiled softly. "The Horseman of War? No. Joshua Sinclair? Aye." She clasped Kára's hand. "What he does today, he does for you."

Kára shook her head. "He plays out this trick to protect his clan from King James."

Amma leaned forward. "He has already broken his oath to them in writing. He could leave Orkney and strike out alone in Scotland, yet he wants you and your people to live in safety and the protection of his clan."

"He could just be an honorable man," Kára whispered.

"He wants to bring you home," she said, sitting straight. "You both must survive this day."

Kára's chest squeezed as she thought about the risky details of their deception. Aye, they would live or die together—today.

CHAPTER TWENTY-THREE

"All warfare is based on deception."
Sun Tzu – The Art of War

"It is an inch at most," Calder said, shaking his head.

Joshua looked out across the moor that stretched down toward the Earl's Palace. "An extra inch of flesh can save a man," he said, glancing down to his tunic where the inch-thick bladder of chicken blood was strapped underneath around his ribs.

"It better save you," Osk said behind them. "Or Kára will chop us up for letting you die, for real."

"If Patrick Stuart cuts deeper and draws my own blood, too, so be it," Joshua said, ignoring Osk. He could not think of Kára right now, or he might lose his concentration. Everything about the next steps in this farce must be concise. He looked to Calder. "Make sure ye carry me out of there before a Stuart can check my pulse." He could hold his breath for long minutes, having built up his lung capacity with constant training, but there would be no stopping his heart from feeding his body with blood.

"I doubt they will go anywhere near you," Calder said, pointing to the blackened tips of Joshua's fingers and the realistic shading and lightening that Hilda had painted on Joshua's neck to make part of it look swollen. "Remember to cough and act like you are getting tired when fighting."

"Will those loyal to you in the palace really

help?" Osk asked, his lip curling so his upper teeth sat exposed.

A lot could have happened since Joshua had woken Angus in the night at his cottage in the village beyond the palace where the soldiers and their families lived. Angus had asked his lady to journey back to mainland Scotland with him and Mathias after the battle, but she may have given him away to Lord Robert. Joshua had never met the lass, so he could not judge her heart.

"We will know if they are absent this morn," Joshua said. "Then your small band must get my corpse out of there."

"What if he wants your body to be hung, drawn, and quartered?" Osk asked. "He is calling you a traitor."

"If the false symptoms and pretend gangrene do not deter them, Hilda took care of adding a definite symptom," Calder said, flapping his hand toward Joshua's kilt.

"What?" Osk asked, staring at the wrapped wool.

Joshua yanked up the edge of his kilt to expose his jack and ballocks. Nestled into the groin was a blackened ball that Kára's grandmother had glued on.

Osk's mouth dropped open. "My grandmother really did give you the plague."

Joshua dropped his kilt. "Aye," he said, his lips tight.

"You let Amma down near your ballocks?" Osk asked, incredulously.

The old woman had seemed to take great delight in pasting on the blackened nut while Joshua cupped himself. "One of ye will notice it when I am... defeated. Yell a warning." *Bloody hell, defeated.* He had never been defeated in his life.

His father was surely turning in his grave. George Sinclair did not stand for defeat or weakness in any of his sons. And he had outlawed illness, saying God would never let one of his Horsemen die from disease. Yet here Joshua stood, feigning illness and defeat.

"You have brought the plague to Orkney," Osk said, glancing back down the hill where the men who remained on Orkney waited. Half of those who'd battled for Geir had already journeyed on to Caithness.

Joshua looked over them, their weapons and attention ready. "Hilda visited several ladies in the village three days ago, asking if anyone was ill with it. That she'd heard it was moving up from the south and Pastor John had brought it with him from Edinburgh. Three days should be enough time for the rumor to have reached the palace."

"Can you battle with that on you?" Osk asked, dropping his gaze to the front of Joshua's kilt.

Joshua met his round eyes that were the same gray-blue as his sister's. "I have battled with broken bones before. A nut is not likely to slow me down."

"It better slow you down enough for Patrick to get in a strike," Calder said as if reminding him. "Do not kill the bastard or you will have more problems."

Merely thinking of the smug man made Joshua's fists clench. Feigning weakness. *Lord, help me do it.* He was the Horseman of War, a warrior from the cradle, vengeance made flesh. Patrick deserved to die, along with his father, for the atrocities they'd brought down upon the people of Orkney. Like the rapist, Henry. Fury welled up inside Joshua as he remembered Henry slamming Kára against the chapel wall. He inhaled to rid himself of the image only to have it replaced with the vision of Patrick throwing her to the floor. And yet, Joshua must fall under his sword. For Kára and for Clan Sinclair.

• • •

"Here," Amma said, nodding at Kára. "This will make you pale as death," she said, mixing the paste in the carved bowl. "We will add subtle touches of gray where your flesh has begun to loosen."

"And I will be lying on a dead, stinking seal?" Kára asked. Amma nodded. "And I will be buried alive?" Amma nodded again. "And this is the only way to stop Patrick Stuart from coming after me?"

"Death is the final escape from a determined madman," Amma said.

Kára looked at the wavy reflection in the polished glass. "For both Joshua and me."

"Aye."

"The Horseman of War." Kára shook her head.

"Will die for you this day," Amma said and kissed her on the top of her head, taking up the paste-smeared rag.

• • •

"Patrick Stuart, come meet the Horseman of War." Joshua's voice boomed up at the men in the gate tower. "Pay for your crimes against Kára Flett, you murdering bastard."

"Did your woman die from her wounds?" Angus yelled down, signaling that his betrothed had not given him away or he'd be in Robert's dungeon. Hopefully, Mathias was also about the grounds.

"Aye, from the cruelty of Patrick Stuart against a woman. Tell him to come answer for his crimes," Joshua yelled. He stood in a battle stance, sword in hand, feet braced, death etched into the lines of his face. At least this part he did not have to act. His hatred for Patrick Stuart and Lord Robert practically shot outward from him, making him intimidating enough that the five soldiers who came forward remained way back near the portcullis that was partway open.

In the week since the attack, Robert had ordered the men to work from sunup into the night to finish the defensive wall around his palace. Angus had told Joshua that Robert and The Brute had railed at them for not lighting the beacon that would have called warriors from the village to help. That they believed the Orkney warriors had numbered over a hundred strong, conjecturing that men must've marched up from the southern isle of Hoy and the East Mainland of Orkney to join the Birsay peasants in revolt. The farce had kept Robert from immediately ordering his men to give chase when the Hillside men retreated.

And now another farce must play out expertly, a farce on which *The Art of War* had no advice. Staging his own death.

Joshua stood strong facing the raised portcullis.

"Cough or something," Osk whispered from behind and backed up as if afraid to get too close to Joshua.

Joshua coughed from deep in his chest, not bothering to cover his mouth. He wiped his arm across his forehead as if he might be hot despite the near-freezing temperature. Hopefully, they saw the black on his fingers as if gangrene were setting in. "Ye have taken Kára Flett from this world, and I will take all of ye." He coughed again. "Send out Patrick Stuart and Lord Robert if he wishes."

"Lord Patrick is no coward," Angus yelled. "He will meet ye."

Mathias was one of the men on the ground, along with Liam and Tuck. "He will split your brain, Horseman," Mathias yelled, making Liam and Tuck look at him like he was insane.

"Send the bastard out," Joshua called, holding his sword pointed upward.

Robert, Patrick, and John Dishington walked through the gate. "You are a traitor to the crown," Robert said with a sneer. "You will be hung and disemboweled for your dishonor."

"I very much hope ye are the one to do it," Joshua said and laughed darkly. "But first I will seek revenge for my love's life on your son's worthless body."

"The little Flett girl?" Patrick said, his voice goading. "Your love?" He smirked. "Her death is even more warranted."

"Bastard!" Joshua yelled and then forced a cough up out of his lungs. Hilda had wanted him to drink something that would encourage phlegm, but he refused. A third ballock, blackened and pasted on, was enough. "Come forward and meet your fate."

Patrick unsheathed his sword, The Brute walking with him.

"Ye are frightened enough to bring Dishington to play nursemaid?" Joshua gave him a look that called him a coward. "What a poor Stuart ye are. Are ye shamed, Lord Robert, for raising a quaking lad?"

Patrick held his hand out to Dishington, speaking to him over his shoulder, and he stopped. Och, but it was so easy to manipulate them. Dishington seemed like he would argue but halted. The look of eager violence told Joshua that if he didn't fall to Patrick, Dishington was obviously continuing the attack.

Joshua kept his stance ready. The man would likely strike low, but Joshua would be ready. He must give him a challenge to make the farce look credible.

"You foking Highlander," Patrick said, striding toward him. "I will kill you, and you will be cut up and fed to the fish."

"Or…" Joshua dragged out, giving him a fierce grin, "I will run my blade from your black heart down to your wee jack so ye trip over your shite-filled bowels when they fall out." He could imagine his brother, Cain, rolling his eyes over Joshua's colorful threats. Aye, he missed home.

Patrick's grin dropped away only to be replaced by a snarling scowl, lips pulled back, yellow teeth showing. Surging forward, Patrick ducked, swinging low for Joshua's legs. He stopped him soundly without budging, his muscles superior. *Deflect and stagger. Bloody hell.* Joshua shoved Patrick back, the man almost losing his balance. Instead of following him to swiftly end the contest, Joshua staggered as if the effort had cost him much.

How easy it would be to kill the man now that Kára was safely away. Joshua could lop Patrick's head off, and then Dishington's, and then Robert's. Would the next eldest brother come running out to meet his fate next? *Mo chreach!* He was the Horseman of War, not the executioner. And when word reached King James, the Sinclairs would suffer whether or not he withdrew his allegiance to his clan. Damn! There were too many factors to deviate from the plan he'd made. *Bloody hell.*

Strike. Withdraw. Stagger. Cough. Deflect. Swipe downward.

• • •

Swipe.

"A thin coat will give you the pallor of death," Amma murmured as she wiped the cloth down Kára's cheek. "Three days dead."

• • •

Swipe. The blade whistled in the growing wind as Patrick sliced downward, and Joshua stopped it with his own sword. "You are dead," Patrick said as he stood pressing into the crossed swords that separated him from Joshua.

A slow grin crossed Joshua's mouth. "I may be, but ye, too, will be soon enough. Where will your soul be going when ye are in the grave?" Joshua finished his question with a cough right into Patrick's face.

Joshua shoved him back and slashed his sword downward.

• • •

Amma swiped downward from the outside corner of Kára's eye to her jawline. "There now, pale as death. On to making your skin look sunken in with the blackening."

• • •

Joshua made certain to cough again and lowered his arm as if his sword grew heavy. Now he must stagger. Lord, he was hardly breathing hard, and he certainly was no actor. He was a warrior, the Horseman of War, a fierce, hardened swordsman. How did a stagger even look real? He let his knee bend deeply, making him look like he'd lost his balance.

"Do not touch his blackened fingers," Mathias called out to Patrick.

Patrick's gaze dropped to the black coating on Joshua's two fingers. "What are you about?"

When the enemy played their part exactly as prompted, Joshua almost felt redeemed for not noticing the soaring birds in South Ronaldsay. He let a slow smile spread across his mouth that did not match the contempt in his eyes. "We all go at different times and in various ways, but death comes for each of us."

• • •

"Death has come for you," Hilda said as Kára and her amma walked up to the three cottages aboveground at Hillside. Hilda smiled, but a shiver still tickled up Kára's spine.

She looked over the moor that led to the Earl's Palace where Joshua was right now playing his part in this outrageous farce. Would it work? Could she possibly be free of the Stuarts? They had threatened her and her family her whole life. Death was the only way to freedom.

• • •

"To freedom!" Joshua yelled as Patrick struck downward. Joshua twisted the scant amount for the edge of Patrick's blade to slice into his side. He felt the bite of it into his flesh and knew the sack of chicken blood had been broken. He grunted as he ordered his muscles to give way, and he hit the hard ground, flipping his kilt up at the last second.

The rest of the act was up to his Hillside warriors and his faithful men under Lord Robert. Would he feel Dishington's blade stab into him? He'd never put his trust in anyone other than his brothers, but he concentrated on making all his muscles go limp, his breath growing shallower.

"Drag him inside," Robert ordered.

"Nay!" Mathias yelled. "Look. He has black death on him!" Had he spotted Hilda's handiwork or was he saying what Joshua had told him to say when he'd snuck into his home to tell him about the insane plan?

"We will all perish if ye bring the traitor inside," Angus yelled from above in the tower. "Keep back."

Joshua heard the scrapes of boots moving toward him, the crunch of pebbles near his ear. "He seemed weakened," Patrick said, breathing heavy. "And was coughing."

"'Tis the black death," another soldier called. "Send him back or burn him there where he lies."

"The tainted smoke will be in the air," Mathias said. "Take your diseased dead!"

Joshua could tell someone bent closer to him. He tried not to move even to exchange air. "If ye are dead, I will cut my own ballocks off." The harsh whisper came from John Dishington. Joshua kept his eyes closed and did not breathe.

"Get back," Calder said, throwing a blanket over him. "We bury Kára Flett today at the chapel in Birsay and will lay him with her. You, Patrick Stuart, could even now be struck with the plague."

Dishington chuckled, and a brief scuff of the pebbles preceded pain. Bruising pain tore through the cut in Joshua's side as Dishington kicked him twice.

"What the fok!" yelled Osk, but Joshua kept a tight hold on his breath and movement. If he hadn't been covered by the blanket, he'd have likely jumped up and taken Dishington's foul head.

"If he is dead, he will feel naught," Dishington said. "If he is alive, he deserves worse for acting the *coward*."

His words were meant to goad Joshua into

revealing himself, and if Calder and Osk did not get
him out of there soon, the bastard might get his
foking wish. But the ruse would be up, and Kára
would not be free of the Stuart family. If he were not
actually dead, they might demand to check her
thoroughly.

"You are risking the black death," Mathias called.
"I saw a black knot under his kilt. 'Tis a very usual
place to spot it. My uncle had it down in the
Lowlands. Died within days of getting the black
knots. Took my aunt with him, he did."

More boots scratched at the pebbles, and Joshua
tightened his stomach for another kick. But instead,
someone grabbed him by the arms while someone
else grunted, lifting his legs. "Bloody hell, he is
heavy," Osk said.

They paused. "Out of the way," Calder said.

Dishington's voice came from beside Joshua's
covered face. "I will be sure to pay my respects when
you put the Horseman of War into the grave." The
man's laughter faded on the wind as they carried
Joshua across the uphill moor.

• • •

"You look diseased," Kára said, as she held his
blackened fingers up in the dim light of the Hillside
cottage.

"Ye look dead," Joshua replied, his fingers sliding
in between her own.

"You will smear off the black," Hilda said, scolding as she tied a fresh bandage around Joshua's
middle.

Kára's stomach had turned in on itself when Joshua had removed the blood-soaked tunic. Much of the blood was not his, but a gash across his side showed some definitely was. Now cleaned, sewn, and wrapped, it was protected from the dirt that would soon cover them.

Osk popped inside, breathing hard. "The grave is dug. We widened it for you both. Douglas has chiseled a marker with both your names on it." He shook his head, looking at his sister. "The sight of it propped next to Da, Ma, and Eydis leaves me cold. Geir, too."

"I want Geir gone," Kára said. "He is not to be anywhere near Robert, or his men might take him again."

"Aye," Calder said.

"I will take him to your den now," Hilda said. "Only Osk and Harriett will be there to mourn with Calder and the half dozen men who have not yet set out on foot to find passage to Scotia at the bay of Skaill."

"Ye should have only one lantern," Joshua said, turning. "The less anyone can see, the better."

"And you have something to cover our faces?" Kára asked.

"All set up at the chapel," Osk said. Kára tried not to notice that he looked worried over the plan.

She squeezed Joshua's hand. "Will this work?"

In the lowering light that cast through the window, his features were dark. "Patrick and Robert think I am dead with the scene we acted out before the palace. They have only to hear that we were actually buried to believe the whole thing."

"But what of The Brute?" she asked. Osk had told her how the monster had viciously kicked Joshua in his wound, opening it up even deeper with the toe of his boot. "He will have told them his suspicions."

Joshua's gaze slid over the hollow shading Amma had given to the pale paste, making Kára's face look sunken, on the edge of decay. She had darkened the bruises that were still on her neck from Henry's attack. "My men," he said, "Angus and Mathias will have encouraged rumors that people in the village are showing up with blackish buboes in their groins and armpits, saying that the cleric who had visited here was dead on Hoy with the same disease. By the time they realize it is merely a rumor, if they ever do, we will be buried and gone."

Kára shivered, wrapping her arms around herself. "Buried and gone. I believe I will have nightmares for the rest of my life about this night."

Joshua pulled her closer into him, his arms circling to her back. There in the fortification of his strength, her worries seemed nonsensical. *I give myself to ye.* His words from the night before seemed like an oath. Whatever it meant, she knew he had not given it lightly. His mouth moved to her ear where his whisper tickled a path of warmth into her. "I will chase the nightmares away for the rest of your life, lass."

He pulled back, looking into her eyes, which widened. The rest of her life? She opened her mouth to ask what that meant.

"Time to wrap you two in your shrouds," another Hillside warrior named Aiden said, ducking into the cottage. He looked to Joshua. "The scout you left watching the palace returned. He says there is activity in the bailey. Robert and Patrick and The Brute are out with their horses."

Hilda gave Kára a fierce hug and hurried out the door, calling for Geir. Geir had already said his goodbyes, but he ran back inside right into her arms once more. She wrapped her arms around her strong, brave boy. "Whatever happens," she said, "you will come out of this stronger. Calder and Osk will get you to safety with the Sinclairs."

"I would rather have you alive than be safe," he murmured against her, and she squeezed him harder. He did not yet know how hard life could be if they stayed on Orkney under Robert's brutal rule. She did. She'd been living it for twenty-six years.

"Joshua will keep me alive," she said and pulled back.

Geir looked from her to Joshua, his young face looking much too hard. "If it comes down to you or her," Geir said, "save her."

Joshua nodded, his fisted hand going over his heart. "I swear it."

It was enough to loosen Geir's hold on Kára's hand, and Aiden dragged him out to take Broch on a mad dash with Hilda to Kára's hideaway den. Kára stared at the empty doorway and blinked back the unbidden tears. Would it be the last time she ever saw her baby boy?

Calder threw one of the woolen wraps at Osk, and they both shook them out. Joshua bent down to brush a kiss across Kára's lips. "We will be well," he said.

"Are you certain?" she whispered.

Calder cleared his throat. "We really need to get you up there. Corpses do not walk to their graves."

Joshua touched his forehead to hers. "We will be better than well on the morrow," he murmured.

She nodded against him. "We just need to get through this night."

CHAPTER TWENTY-FOUR

"Let your plans be dark and impenetrable as the night, and when you move, fall like a thunderbolt."
Sun Tzu – The Art of War

The wind whipped at the cloaks of those family members standing above them in the churchyard. Joshua stared up at the slip of dark blue sky that peeked past gray clouds. Darkness was descending, but not fast enough. "Do not let them get too close," he said, "Only enough to see it is us before ye cover us."

It was the oddest view to have people gathered around, looking down at him as he lay in his grave. Dirt fenced Kára and him in on all sides as they lay together two feet down in the cold earth.

"Amma will warn them back because of the plague as she sprinkles us with fresh herbs," Kára said, wrinkling her nose over the smell of the decaying seal hidden beneath a ragged blanket under her. They smelled like a combination of low tide and a three-day-old battlefield.

Wrapped in white linen, he and Kára rested next to each other. Under the cover of another blanket, their hands were free, interlaced together as if in eternal slumber as one. It felt natural, as if there would be no other way to lie next to each other. The warmth in her hand was a testament to their continued living even as cold pressed upward from the frozen ground under them.

"Close your eyes," Osk whispered. "No breathing or twitching."

"Stop," Calder called out, his head turned away. "This is a family burial. You are not welcome here."

"Welcome or not, I am the Earl of Orkney and have come to see the traitor buried," Robert intoned from not too far off.

"Both of them," added Patrick.

"Stay back," Kára's grandmother warned, and Joshua felt the pelting of dried herbs on his face. Caught on his lip, he held still, stopping himself from blowing it off. "They are both touched with plague," she called, and Joshua could hear the tears in her voice.

"We must verify they are dead, plague or not." *Bloody hell.* Of course John Dishington was with them.

"You have been warned," Harriett said. "See what horror you have wrought on my granddaughter."

"You bury them together?" Patrick asked.

There was a pause. "They wed before you killed my sister," Osk said, a sneer in his voice that Joshua could plainly hear over the sea breeze. Hopefully, Patrick was getting a nose full of the dead seal.

"You mean," Robert said, "before she and her rebel people marched against me and my family."

Keep quiet, Osk. Kára's brother was always smoldering, ready to explode, but right now nothing good could come from it. *Mo chreach.* Would he have to act like a ghost and break back into the Earl's Palace the next eve to rescue Kára's brother?

"Leave us in our grief," Calder said, and Joshua could hear Kára's grandmother crying above the wind.

"The grave is shallow," Dishington said, his voice closer as if he braved the plague or did not believe any of it.

The blanket, linens, and the heavy targe that lay across Joshua hid the slight rise and fall of their chests. He concentrated on not moving by relaxing his facial muscles. Lord, let the darkness hide any signs of life.

"We baked the earth with a mound of burning peat," Calder said, "but this was as deep as we could dig before hitting ice."

"Look, Lord Robert," Dishington said. "A marker for them. And it says nothing of Joshua Sinclair being the Horseman of War. I believe he has much to answer for before God, how he failed so terribly. Dying not only from a sword strike but also from disease. God has surely forsaken him. Joshua Sinclair, a weak failure of a man."

The bastard was goading Joshua, daring him to leap up from the grave in vengeful outrage. Kára's hand tightened in his as if she were afraid that was exactly what he would do, but Joshua lay still, imagining Dishington's gaze waiting on his face for any twitch of life.

"He even lost at South Ronaldsay," Dishington continued. "Practically killed that lad who trusted him."

Joshua summoned his strength to stay still, unmoving as the man slandered him. In times past, Joshua never would have been able to rein in his temper. But the warmth of Kára's hand rooted him, shielding him from the effects of the man's insults.

"Now leave us to our goodbyes and prayers," Calder said.

"The marker does not say she took his name," Patrick said from above their heads.

"There…there was no time to consummate it," Osk said, sounding like he was at the end of his patience.

Dishington snorted. "If it had been me, I would have leaped upon the woman before the cleric could make the sign of the cross. Joshua Sinclair, a failure of a man, too."

"Blasphemy," one of Hillside's men muttered. As planned, a number of them had moved out of the shadows to encircle the chapel and graveyard, outnumbering Robert and his small band. Would it be enough to deter them from meddling more with the burial?

Harriett began to cry harder, her breathing becoming labored as she crooned in their ancient Norn language.

"Hold your tongue, old woman," Robert called from a distance.

"I want to see you cover them," Dishington said. "Completely buried."

"Stay away from my girl," Harriett wailed.

"Lord Robert, beware the plague," a voice called from farther off. It sounded like Mathias. "Your son, and certainly Sheriff Dishington, are too close to the bodies."

"Back away," Calder called, "so we can lay them to rest."

Dishington's voice came close to Joshua's face. "I am no fool, Highlander," he whispered and stood. The sound of his boots crunching pebbles as he spun and strode away allowed Joshua to draw in air once more. The man did not believe he was dead, despite the blood and marks of disease, despite the burial and goading without winning a reaction. John Dishington was not ready to let him go. The realization that he never would stop hunting him hardened inside Joshua's chest.

As Harriett lowered small treasures into the grave around Kára and him, she whispered, "He watches but cannot see inside the grave. Breathe before we cover you."

The large jug that they had carefully cracked in half was lowered inside. Under the edge of the grass, Harriett split it open. Joshua smelled the rank seal beneath them, the soil, and the herbs scattered over them. Harriett lowered one half of the clay vessel over his face, blocking out the sound of the sea birds overhead. The wind was muted, as were the voices around them. The first toss of dirt onto his targe sounded loud, a hollow *thud* that almost made him jerk upright in defense. Kára squeezed his hand hard at the macabre sound of them being buried alive. He might have nightmares, too.

Joshua turned his thoughts from the dirt piling up over his legs and chest to the fact that Dishington would try to make certain he was dead. He had his arms left unwrapped under the outer blanket and targe in case he had to punch his way up out of the soil to save them. Kára had opted for the same. Did Dishington believe her to be dead? Or would he try to make certain she was truly a corpse, too?

Bloody hell. This ridiculous plan had too many parts that could go foking wrong. He had anticipated Robert and Patrick would believe the farce because they wanted to. Patrick could brag that he had killed the Horseman of War and Robert would not risk infection to verify it. The killing would feed Patrick's conceit, and the disease would feed Robert's fear. But John Dishington wanted Joshua to be alive and cared little about disease, living his life by walking the thin line of victory and death as a mercenary. Of course, he was not fooled. But what would he do about it?

. . .

Kára concentrated on breathing evenly as the weight of the dirt pressed in on her. Osk had pulled out all the heavy rocks, but the soil itself was heavy after several inches. Their faces, under the pottery jug, would be last to be covered, giving them as much air as possible.

Slow breaths. Birds flying in a blue sky. Wide open moors covered with purple thistle and bluebells. The scenes were to keep her calm, but with each drop of dirt, her breath stuttered, threatening to make her gasp. Instead, she squeezed Joshua's hand, and he squeezed back, his thumb rubbing against her own the smallest amount that the encasing dirt would allow. Could the dirt grow heavy enough to crush her chest? Of course it could, but they would fight their way out before that happened if Osk didn't shovel it off fast enough. The thought made her heart thump faster, which made her pull in a fast couple of breaths before she caught herself.

Tears leaked out of her eyes, sliding down the sides of her face. Amma would be angry if she smeared the white paste with them. The thought made her smile there under the pottery in the dark, cold grave.

Joshua squeezed her fingers again, and she returned it gently. One squeeze only. They had worked out the signals beforehand. Three squeezes in rapid succession meant that they needed to get out fast. It was her key to unlock this hell if she felt like she couldn't breathe or bear the press of death anymore.

"I promise I will uncover you soon." Kára heard Osk's voice outside the pottery covering her face right before the sound of dirt falling on it startled her. Soil, cold and grainy, filled the narrow space between the pot and the blanket covering her body. Chills raced up and down Kára, and she fought to keep calm. She squeezed Joshua's hand. Once, just once, although she nearly panicked and squeezed many times rapidly.

Summer breezes. Beams of sun sparkling on the white caps in the ocean. She remembered Geir's smile and how it made him look years younger, almost like her unbreeched lad again. *Joshua… Joshua…* The sparkle in his light blue eyes when he teased her. His luscious mouth that gave so generously. How he taught Geir to throw a dagger and slowly won the respect of Osk and even Amma. How he was sacrificing his honor to…save her people? No. Amma was right. He could have helped her people and traveled on, saving his clan by staying away from his brother. To go through this play, this horrible farce, that made him look like the failure that The Brute pronounced over their grave, Joshua was doing more than saving her people and his clan— He was creating a way that he could go home and be with her there.

He squeezed her hand again, and she returned the pressure. At the same time her heart squeezed with the realization that he was willing to be buried alive with her so they could be together in his home. Together. *Joshua. I love you.*

She sucked in air, probably too much, and swallowed past the lump in her throat. More tears leaked out of her closed eyes, sliding down like a river to her temples. *I love you.* Why hadn't she told him before this? What if something went wrong, and they died without her telling him? *I need to tell him.*

The dirt stopped falling, and the weight of the inches over them held her firmly stuck in the ground. Planted in darkness, encased in cold. The need to stretch and move pulsed through her. How much longer? How much longer before she could feel the breeze once more and look into Joshua's face and tell him what she'd discovered? Long minutes continued as she concentrated on even breaths. When would it be safe enough for Osk and Calder to start uncovering them?

A voice above, a deep rumble, and the earth above her pressed down harder. She sucked in the air under the jug as she felt a crushing weight. Next to her, Joshua squeezed her hand. Once. Twice. Thrice.

• • •

Dishington was above him. Joshua knew it, his instincts fully alert. They'd been buried for a slow count of nine hundred, which should be about fifteen minutes. Their air would run out soon, but that was not the current threat.

After giving Kára the signal that they'd be coming out, he pulled his hand through the heavy soil. He would not be able to press the targe up with all that weight on him, not from a supine position. He had calculated that it would weigh about three hundred pounds, and he could not get his legs under him. Nay, he must punch up through the soil first.

A yell came from above. Pressure thrust down across his chest as his targe radiated a strike against it, making him inhale. The tip of a blade pricked the skin of his chest under the layers of wool wrappings. Dishington meant to stab him in his grave.

It was time for the dead to rise!

He moved his hand that lay between Kára and him, but it was his right hand that he'd kept bent, his fist ready as Osk and Calder had finished their burying, leaving only several inches of soil over his fist.

For a second, he felt a tug across his chest, a lessening of pressure, as Dishington fought to yank his sword free of the targe and what he likely hoped was Joshua's bleeding body. With the next tug, Joshua punched his fist up through the soil. The movement of wind touched his knuckles. With all his strength, he moved upward, all his muscles struggling to lift.

He shifted his knees up and down, dislodging the soil. His other hand reached the jug at his face and punched up through the crumbly loose earth.

"Bloody foking hell!" Dishington's voice penetrated the thinning soil as he tried again to yank the tip of his sword free of Joshua's targe and the soil over it. It became a race. The liberation of his sword against Joshua's rising, with deadly force, from the grave. It was a game of survival for both him and Kára, and Joshua would use every weapon he had to win.

Joshua whipped off the broken pottery from his face, using all his abdominal muscles to lift his torso up through the soil that Osk and Calder had left as loose as they could. Where were they?

He sucked in refreshingly cold air. Kára was rising, too, beside him, but Dishington was focused on Joshua. In the flickering glow of a lantern set several grave markers over, Joshua could see the widening of Dishington's eyes as the dirt fell away from him. Dishington yanked once more, and his sword slid free. He stumbled backward.

Ignoring the grime caking his mouth, Joshua's voice rang out with the power of the legend upon which he'd been raised. "Then another horse came out," he said, moving his legs to loosen the earth still entrapping him. "A fiery red one. Its rider was given power to take peace from the earth and to make people kill each other."

"Shite!" Dishington yelled. "Hold your foking tongue!"

Lowering his fist back into the dirt, Joshua grabbed the hilt of his sword, sliding it up and out of the earth. "To him was given a large sword," he bellowed and lifted the sword up into the air as if it, too, rose from the grave by God's hand.

Dishington's eyes opened even wider, and he raised his own sword.

"And with this large sword," Joshua continued, using all his might to break free of the loosened dirt, "I have come back from the grave with vengeance against those who show no honor. I have come for ye, John Dishington."

The ominous words, resounding in the chilled wind, from someone breaking out of a grave in the middle of the night, were enough to make Dishington hesitate. Even if logically he knew the whole spectacle was a farce, the combined elements fed the fears owned by every mortal man. He took another step back, which gave Joshua enough time to pull his legs free of his earthen shackles.

Muscles aching from the pressure and cold, Joshua called on his fury to heat his blood. "Ye dare to strike against God's messenger," Joshua declared, his voice thundering as he leaped from the shallow grave, striding slowly toward his adversary.

Off to the side, he glanced at Calder and Osk tied up against the chapel, Osk bent over unconscious while Calder struggled in his ropes, a gag in his mouth. But no one else was about as Joshua stalked after the grisly man who seemed to have recovered from his unease.

"Lying bastard," Dishington said and surged forward, his sword point out as if he were jousting. Joshua held himself ready to deflect it. At the last second, Dishington tripped, flying forward with the force of his run. Eyes and mouth opening wide, he hurtled directly into Joshua's sword point. Shock and pain molded his face into a death mask, and he crumpled to the trampled grass.

"I hope it is a painful trip to Hell," Joshua said, wiping an arm over his face to rid his eyes of grit. He spit out more grime.

"Joshua."

Joshua spun around to see Kára struggling to free herself completely of the dirt. The glow that the lantern cast across the stone markers, along with her rising from the grave, was indeed a sight to make a grown man hesitate. Joshua hurried over, cupping his hands to shovel off the layers weighting her legs and reached under her arms to slide her out. "Kára. Are ye hurt?"

"I… Joshua… I…" Kára could not seem to catch her breath. "You need to know."

Wiping at her face with his thumbs, she caught his hands, looking up into his face. "Under the ground I realized…" She reached up, catching his face in her hands. He could feel her trembling. "I…I need you to know… If one of us died without you knowing…"

"Aye, lass?" he prompted, catching her hands with his.

Behind him, someone spit. "God's bones, you two, set us free," Calder called, followed by a low moan from Osk.

Kára dropped her hand, her gaze sliding past him. "Oh God," she whispered and hurried past him. "Where is Amma?" She crouched, yanking free her dagger, to saw at their ties. Joshua glanced at the unmoving body of Dishington and followed her, drawing his own *sgian dubh* to help.

"Back at the tavern waiting for us," Calder said. "After Lord Robert, Patrick, and his men rode away, the Hillside men urged her to walk back down with them before taking her to your den to wait with Geir and Hilda. We stayed back here in the dark to help you dig out."

"Then that bastard snuck up on us. Hit us hard," Osk said, rubbing his head, his hair sticking out in all directions. He looked at blood smeared on his fingers and cursed.

Calder gathered the rope. "I woke in time to see him stepping on Kára's grave and then kneeling near where your head was buried," he said, nodding to Joshua.

Kára rubbed her chest. "I felt his weight."

Calder walked over to where the unmoving body lay. "He tripped running at you." He shook his head and crouched down near Dishington's feet. He looked sideways at them over by the chapel, stopping on Kára. "He tripped over your family's grave marker."

Her brows lowered. "'Tis impossible. Their marker is on the other side of me," she said, walking over. The dirt-stained wrappings of her shroud dragged behind her like the sash of a muddy gown.

"See," Calder said from his position. "It has their names."

Kára grabbed the lantern, dodged around Dishington's body, and held the light up to illuminate the slightly sunken area of undisturbed grass on the other side of where minutes ago she'd been buried.

"It is…" She stared up at Joshua, her eyes and mouth wide. "The marker has been moved," she said looking back at the stone where Calder stood.

"Into the perfect place to trip Dishington, sending him flying into your sword," Osk said as he rubbed the rope marks on his wrists. He smiled. "Da was helping you out, Highlander."

He could have finished Dishington himself. "It was my sword," Joshua murmured. "And my words that frightened him back."

"Maybe he saw Da's spirit behind you," Osk said. He was in shadows, but Joshua heard the jest in his voice.

Calder scratched his head. "If you had been awake, Osk, you would not say that." He glanced at Joshua. "I nearly pissed myself when I saw you punch your hand up through the dirt and then sit up, spouting biblical prophecy as if God spoke through you." He shook his head and looked at Osk. "Even if your da had been floating above, watching the Horseman of War lift his sword from his grave was more startling."

Kára took Joshua's hand. She inhaled. "My menacing beast." She pulled closer to him while Osk made a few retching sounds at her words.

Joshua wiped his hand over her dusty hair, pulling her close once again. "It is time to go."

"Where there are trees?" she asked, searching his face.

"Aye, and horses," he said slowly.

"You two could stop gazing at each other and help us get Dishington into your grave," Osk said, and Joshua heard his sword thump on the ground behind him. "It seems fitting for him to lie for eternity with a stinking seal."

Kára continued to gaze at Joshua as she spoke. "We need to get cleaned up so we can travel as soon as you finish."

"But he is heavy, and I was just unconscious," Osk said.

Kára glanced at him. "And we had to dig our way out of our own graves with no help from you." She caught Joshua's hand and tugged him to follow her out from behind the chapel. He stalled her only to pick up his sword.

With the moon hidden in the dense clouds and the lantern light blocked by the stone church, darkness enveloped them. But with the fresh air, it was nothing like being underground in a cemetery. Even the cold that cut through his tunic did not bother him.

As soon as they rounded the second corner to see the dim lights of the village of Birsay below them, Kára pulled Joshua with her around the chapel wall. She pressed him up against the stone like she had done in the barn when they first met and pulled his face down to hers for a kiss. They were dirt-coated and smelling of earth and dead seal, but none of that mattered. Only Kára mattered, Kára…warm and soft and alive.

The kiss was gentle, but she clung to him, and he could feel her tremble slightly. She breathed deeply against him without backing up.

"When I felt you squeeze my hand three times," she started, pausing as she inhaled and exhaled, "I frantically started to try to move, and for a time I could not even pull my hand out. I was trapped." Her trembling increased. "But the whole time I kept thinking I had to get out to tell you…" Her hands slid over his face, and he could see the outline of her staring up at him. "Joshua Sinclair…I love you. I need you to know that." She shook her head. "I could not imagine the pain of dying without being able to tell you what I have only now discovered in my heart."

Inside Joshua's chest, the space he didn't even know was hollow swelled full, and his arms gathered her up against him, his mouth capturing her lips. Never before had he felt such power growing inside him and yet such raw openness at the same time. He was filled with conviction, a new direction, as if coming out of the grave had given him a rebirth. But it was not the earth that had wrought this change in him; it was the woman in his arms, the woman he realized he could not imagine life without.

Her presence in their grave had kept him rooted and strong, patient when the world was erupting around him. Knowing he must live to get her out alive had driven him up out of the earth like a true harbinger of God's end of days. The words he had used to disturb Dishington had come from a place of desperate need, a need to protect, a need to love Kára Flett.

His palms raised to her cheeks, cupping her gingerly. "I would have ye see me in the light of day, to see what is in my soul through my eyes," he whispered. "But aye, Kára, I love ye, too."

Her arms tightened around him, her face reaching up to find his lips again as she stood between his straddled legs, leaning against the chapel. Their kiss was gentle with the promise of passion. The possibilities for a future grew from the kiss, nurtured by her words and the press of her in his arms. A feeling, new and fragile, yet it grew stronger as they clung to each other. The feeling was…hope.

CHAPTER TWENTY-FIVE

*"The general who advances without coveting fame
and retreats without fearing disgrace, whose only
thought is to protect his country and do good service
for his sovereign, is the jewel of the kingdom."*
Sun Tzu – The Art of War

The sway of the ship continued to lull Kára even as
the sun rose until it lit behind her closed eyes.
Nestled in the comfort of Joshua's arms, warm and
content, she let herself enjoy the sensation instead
of pushing fully out of the bliss of sleep. After all,
the night had been long, the distance great to reach
the Bay of Skaill south of Birsay. Her horse, Broch,
had carried Amma and, at times, Geir when he
stumbled in exhaustion.

The ship that Calder and Joshua had secured to
carry them south to the mainland of Scotland was
full beyond capacity. Twenty-five men had remained
in Hillside after the initial battle to gain Geir's freedom from Lord Robert. Even Broch had to stay up
on deck, tethered to the rail, swaying over the swells
of ocean through the last hours of night.

A groan, followed by the unmistakable sound of
retching, made her crack her eyes open. Osk stood
leaning over the side, Geir asleep at his feet. Osk
wiped his mouth, his gaze turning to her. "Bloody
waves," he murmured.

"'Tis best to stare out at the sea from the bow,

face into the wind," Joshua said from behind her.

Osk nodded and turned, walking toward his chance to feel better. Kára tipped her face up to Joshua. The muted dawn light revealed his strong features, his eyes the color of a summer morning. He stared down at her. The harshness that she'd seen in his face when they'd first met had softened into something like contentment.

She smiled. "You are happy to be going home."

"I am happy to be bringing ye home," he said, pulling her up a little higher against him.

She stifled a yawn, enjoying the feel of security against him.

"Ye can sleep longer. There are a couple more hours to go," he said.

Her mind drifted forward, and her smile faded. What type of reception had Brenna and Corey had? What of the ones who had not wanted to leave Orkney? Would they return on the ship to face the disappearance of The Brute, or would they wait until spring? And she still needed to deal with Torben's mother. Had word reached her yet of her son's death? His insolent actions that may have brought death to them all?

"Will your brother be angry that more are coming to your shore? After so many have already shown up?" she asked.

Joshua grinned. "Cain will be…perplexed, I think. He does not anger easily." He glanced up. "I do not think he would expect me to help your people. When I left months ago, I was…full of discontent, untrusting of his leadership and his decision not to war when we were strong enough to win all of Scotland. I thought only of myself and the power of Clan Sinclair."

He looked down into her face, inhaling fully through his nose. "Then I met a boy named Adam in South Ronaldsay." He touched her cheek. "And then I met a lass called *dróttning* and her proud and honorable people."

A gentle smile returned to Kára's face. "Whatever brought you into Asmund's tavern that night…" She shook her head, feeling it brush against him. "I will be forever grateful."

He met her smile with his own. "Grateful enough to give me your name?"

Kára's brows bent with confusion.

"Joshua Sinclair, the Horseman of War, is dead, buried in the graveyard behind a stone chapel near Birsay on Orkney. I was rather hoping ye would ask me to wed so I could become Joshua Flett."

Kára's heart pounded, her lips opening. She sat up straighter in his arms, turning fully toward him. "You want to wed me?"

He slid his palm along her cheek. "Aye, lass. I want to wake up next to ye every morning and kiss your frowns away. I want to build a home for us and Geir and any other strong, bonny bairns that come to us. I want to ride the heather moors with ye and love ye in the shade of a tree on a summer day. I want ye to know peace and contentment by my side and know that no one can harm ye or your family." His fingers slid along her cheek. "I want to love ye all the days of your life, Kára Flett. Will ye wed me and give me your name?" A slight bend furrowed his brows as he waited for her answer.

Kára released the breath she had held during his words. The cavity within her that had been filled with vengeance flooded with joy, pushing out the darkness of worry and hate. She inhaled, the openness of her heart allowing more air than ever before until she felt almost dizzy with it. She nodded, his hand still on her cheek, and blinked as the ache of happy tears filled her eyes. "Aye," she said. "I want nothing other than all you just said." She turned, coming up on her knees so they were level. "I love you, Joshua Sinclair. Will you marry me?"

The furrow along his brow vanished as his smile spread, not only along his mouth but over his entire face. "Aye, lass, absolutely with all my heart." Joshua wrapped his arms around her, pulling her close into his warmth.

She met his kiss, her fingers threading through his hair. Love welled up within her like a flood of warmth, the whole world melting away around them as they sealed their oaths.

• • •

"There is an army along the shore," Calder said, his face pinched with worry. "You said we would be welcome."

Joshua stared out at mainland Scotland as they neared the port most convenient to cross between it and Orkney, north of Girnigoe Castle. A mass of men and horses stood in four regiments on the bank with a line of them riding down toward two ships docked. Joshua's gaze was drawn to the four distinct groups of horses: white, black, bay, and an odd gray that he knew would look green the closer they sailed.

Brow furrowed, he snorted. "Those are Sinclairs, my Sinclairs. Now where the bloody hell are they going?"

"It looks like they go to war," Kára said next to him.

"They are *all* Sinclairs?" Osk asked, his face still greenish to match Bàs's horses that were stained green to represent the fourth horseman, Death.

"Aye," Joshua said, squinting. Three men stood on the docks. As the ship drew closer, he was able to pick out his brothers, Cain, Gideon, and Bàs, where they spoke with people from the ship. Damn, it was good to see them.

Geir ran up to the rail. "You were not jesting about having hundreds of horses." The boy's eyes were round, anticipation in the tilt of his smile. And Joshua hadn't even told him yet that one would be completely his.

"The bays are my army," he said over the shouts of the sailors dropping the sails to slow their approach. "And each warrior cares for his own mount, so they belong to them, but several live in my stable at Girnigoe Castle." Thick lines of twisted rope squeaked with the tension, and the slowing made them pitch forward in unison, although the gentle rolling remained constant.

Joshua watched Cain raise a fisted hand as he stared toward their ship. Joshua returned the gesture. Cain seemed to stare at him and then spoke to Gideon.

There were several deep-water slips at the docks,

but the Orkney captain dropped anchor in Sinclair Bay. Intimidated by the show of force, Joshua could understand why he did not want to draw closer. He pushed off the rail and caught Kára's hand.

He called up to the captain. "They are Sinclairs and not a threat."

"The other ships make docking difficult. I will wait until one of them sails."

"I am rowing across, then," Joshua said, and the captain signaled two of his men to lower the dinghy.

Kára caught his arm, halting him. "Should we go alone first?" She glanced toward her grandmother, who had come up on deck.

"They are not a threat, Kára."

"You have sent word that you broke your allegiance to them. Are you certain?"

"Aye, most certain." He kissed her forehead and tugged her along to the rope being lowered into the bobbing rowboat.

"I want to go across now," Geir said, lining up behind them.

"And nothing is going to keep me on this floating Hell," Osk said, wiping his mouth.

Calder called out as he walked up. "I will not be left behind when Brenna and my babe are on that shore."

Joshua glanced into Kára's anxious face. "Well then, we have an army of our own." He smiled.

Joshua climbed aboard first, glancing up to where Kára spoke to her grandmother before stepping over and onto the slack rungs of the rope ladder. Once the five of them were onboard, he and Calder took up the oars and put their backs into rowing toward a strip of sandy shore along the crescent of Sinclair Bay. Sea spray and wind added to the cold, but all Joshua could do was smile. He was bringing home the woman he loved.

"Ugh!" Osk yelled and leaned his head over the rail.

"The waves are even more tossing in this," Geir said, patting his uncle on his leg. "We are almost there."

As they came level with the piers off to his left, Joshua peered over his shoulder. Waiting on the beach were his three brothers, Cain and Gideon scowling, Bàs wearing his skull mask that hid most of his face. Joshua turned back, a grin growing. Even though it looked like he might be going to war right away, it would be good to be with his family again. His smile fell as he looked to Kára. *I will ask Kára to come with me.* The thought eased the tightness in his chest.

The rowboat ran aground on the sand. The splashing behind him made him twist to see Gideon and Bàs grabbing the bow of the dinghy to pull it in. "Appreciated," Joshua said, smiling broadly. He leaped out and reached back for Kára, but she had already jumped onto the sand. Osk was out and on the beach, plopping down and sucking in large gulps of air. Geir and Calder also leaped up onto the beach, their eyes wide as they stared at Bàs in his skull mask. Joshua helped his brothers haul the boat up high onto the beach.

Bàs stripped away his helmet and stepped forward to hug Joshua, slapping his back. "Good to see ye alive, brother."

Joshua pulled back to match his brother's smile with his own. "Ye, too, brother."

"First Pastor John brings me this ridiculous letter," Cain yelled as he stalked closer, his Horseman of Conquest crown on his head and his nostrils flaring. He waved a folded parchment in the air. "Saying my brother breaks all ties with his clan."

Joshua walked toward him. "I have an expla—"

"And then…" Cain yanked out the two scraps of fabric that Joshua had knotted together. "I am delivered this by a hundred people from Orkney who say ye have gone to war against the Earl of Orkney, Robert Sinclair, uncle to King James."

"A definite treasonous act," Gideon added, his deadly sword strapped to his broad back, bare arms crossed. He frowned fiercely, giving him the appearance of a condemning judge. He possessed the natural ability to look condescending, irritated, and damning all at the same time.

"Are my people safe?" Kára asked, coming to stand in front of Joshua, her hands fisted and legs set as if to battle. She seemed to be protecting him. Gideon's eyebrow rose in surprise. Joshua could not stop the grin that spread across his face as he stared out at his brothers over her head.

Gideon and Bàs both studied her, but Cain kept frowning. "Aye, they are well," Cain said. "Odd, but well."

"Odd?" Calder asked, his gaze lifting to the bank where the armies stood ready for war.

"Are those…green horses?" Geir asked, squinting.

Gideon looked at Calder. "One woman, with a new bairn strapped to her, wanted to know if the fae or trolls lived in trees here and stole bairns away in the night."

Calder met his gaze. "And what was your answer?"

Cain blinked once, and Joshua swore he saw his eye twitching. "Nay, of course," Cain roared.

"Hannah took her into Girnigoe," Bàs said, recognizing the concern in Calder's face. "They are both well, although she will not put the bairn in a cradle unless it has a dagger beneath it."

"Really," Geir said, still staring up to the bank. "You have a herd of green horses?"

"Aye," Gideon said quickly.

"They just look green," Bàs said.

"Are they ill?" Geir asked.

Cain waved the tied scraps again, his voice carrying over everything. "Red for ye and black for dead, and the ties mean I am to do nothing about it. Did ye really think I would do nothing about this?" He shook the tied scraps violently.

Joshua's smile faded as he looked above at the standing armies. "Ye were planning to bring war to Orkney?"

"Bloody hell," Geir said. "You could wipe out Robert and all his damn sons."

Anger sparked inside Joshua. "And make all of Clan Sinclair traitors to the crown? What the fok were ye thinking?"

"We are strong enough to take on the crown," Gideon said, his jaw firm as if he'd studied all the outcomes.

"And put all these people at risk?" Joshua threw his hand out to the armies above. "Whose stupid idea was that?"

Cain walked up to him but couldn't get right up in his face with Kára standing between them. He looked over her head to stare Joshua in his eyes. "Mine," he said and clenched his teeth. He held up the tied scraps. "Did ye really believe I would think ye were dead from this? Dead and gone, so we should do nothing?"

"Nay," Joshua said. "Ye are smarter than that."

Gideon stood beside them. "We questioned every person coming from Orkney as to what the scraps meant, and not one of them could explain the signal. Therefore, ye must have tied and sent it *before* ye were dead."

Joshua kept his fierce expression. "I gave the scraps to the group fleeing so ye would know I sent them to Caithness. If I had sent my sword, ye might think they stole it from me."

Gideon snorted. "Who could steal the sword of the Horseman of War?"

"I did," Kára said, and Joshua wrapped his arm around her upper chest, pulling her close before him.

"Ye stole Joshua's sword?" Bàs asked, his mouth turning up on the side in a teasing smile.

"And I needed it," Joshua said. "So the scraps were the better signal to ye that these people have my support against Robert Stuart, tyrant of Orkney."

Cain fisted the cloth in his hand. "We learned a great deal about Earl Robert Stuart and his sons from your people." His gaze dropped to Kára. "And those who stayed alive hiding underground, surviving in constant oppression." His eyes lifted back to Joshua. "I decided we would go to find ye and discover what type of trouble ye were in. Trouble that would make ye foolish enough to break your oath to me and our clan."

"'Twas to protect ye," Joshua said.

"Pastor John said that," Bàs added, more to Cain than to Joshua.

"We do not need protecting." Cain ran a hand up through his hair. "And then to send the lie that ye died…"

"He did die," Kára said. "We both did. Our gravestone says as much back on Orkney. Robert Stuart watched us be buried."

All three of his brothers stared at her. Joshua rested his other palm upon her shoulder. "This is Kára Flett, queen of her people, and my very-soon-to-be wife."

"Ye died and were buried?" Bàs asked.

"Queen?" Gideon asked.

"Ye want to marry?" Cain asked. "One woman?"

Joshua chuckled. "One very special woman. And aye, to all three."

His brothers looked bewildered, making the anger within Joshua abate. He wrapped both arms around Kára. "Kára is quite the warrior."

"And she puts up with ye?" Gideon asked.

"Barely," Kára said, making Bàs laugh, his deep chuckle so rare that his brothers glanced his way.

"And I wish to thank you, Chief Sinclair," she said, bowing her head to Cain, "for allowing my people to land here in Caithness."

"More people to strengthen the Sinclairs are always welcome," Cain said, returning her bow.

Joshua glanced at the armies above. "And I suppose... Well, bloody..." He rubbed the back of his neck, realizing what his family had been about to do for him. "Thank ye for thinking to come after me. That was not something I had even considered."

Cain grabbed Joshua's other shoulder, squeezing it. "Ye are my brother. Oath or not, my blood would run for ye if needed."

Joshua smiled. "Like I said, I did it to protect ye and the clan."

Geir stood off to the side, staring up at the legions of horses and men who had paused in their preparations to sail. "You could still all go," he said, looking to Joshua. "We could take over Orkney. Robert would be trampled."

"Nay," Joshua said. They had gone to great lengths to leave with little loss of life.

"No," Kára said at the same time, and he felt himself relax at her word.

"War should be avoided when possible," Joshua said, garnering shocked faces from his brothers. "It weakens both sides and should only be a last resort."

Gideon's brows rode high on his forehead. "So, the real Joshua Sinclair died on Orkney. Who exactly are *ye*?"

Joshua chuckled. "Joshua, a warrior loyal to Clan Sinclair. A man soon to be Joshua Flett."

Bàs's smile faded. "The Horseman of War is... dead?"

Joshua took Kára's hand and walked toward his youngest brother, looking him straight in the eyes. "We *can* choose not to be what Da told us we are. Something to consider, brother," he said and slapped a hand down on Bàs's shoulder.

He interlaced his fingers with Kára's. "Let us disperse our warriors and open up a slip for the last group from Orkney to dock. And then we can go about getting these odd Orkney people settled."

"More?" Cain asked. "How many people are ye bringing over exactly?"

"Two dozen more," Kára said. "And the ship can take back any of my people who wish to join Erik Flett and my aunt Hilda, who remained on Orkney."

"There is only one woman who has demanded to return from the moment she set foot," Gideon said, his face pinching as if the memory was painful.

"Fiona Spence?" Kára asked.

"Aye," Gideon said. "She is an angry sort of woman."

"She and her son tried to start a war," Joshua said. "We do not need her here. Chief Erik stayed behind. He can deal with her." They still needed to tell her about Torben dying. Losing her son would be punishment enough for the woman.

As they walked up the path, sandy pebbles crunching under their boots, Geir ran ahead, anxious to see all the horses. Osk followed after him, the greenish tinge having faded from his face.

Kára squeezed Joshua's hand, and he looked down at her. "I did not know your family was so large."

He smiled. "In size or number?"

She laughed softly. "Both." She glanced back over her shoulder where Calder asked Gideon tactical questions about their cavalry units. "It seems crowded, this new home of ours," she said, keeping her smile. "We may never find a quiet, peaceful place again."

Before he could respond that he planned to carry her to a most private place as soon as possible, they rose to the level of the four armies on the bank. A great cheer erupted through the ranks as the men saw him. They roared, their fists high in the air, in welcome. He looked behind him to see his brothers doing the same; even Cain roared in celebration that Joshua was home and very much alive. Kára smiled up at him, laughing at the surprise lighting his face. It grew into a joyful smile.

In answer, he raised his own arm with Kára's, their fingers linked. "To Clan Sinclair!" he yelled.

"To Clan Sinclair!" the men responded, their voices sending a deafening wave of force. These were his people. And now Kára and her family would join them in peace and continued prosperity. Happiness welled up within him until it felt like a tangible flood to pour out, and he laughed. He pulled Kára into his arms, kissing her before the clan.

Another wave of cheers erupted, but he was lost as soon as the warmth of Kára's lips pressed against his own. Power roared around him, but it was small in comparison to the power of the love that joined them together. As she pulled back, a dazed smile curling her lips, she mouthed *I love you* to him.

He leaned in, his lips to her ear. "I love ye, too, in

war and in peace, forever." He raised his fist to his heart, giving her his oath. She blinked, her eyes filling with tears in contrast to the huge smile she displayed.

"In war and in peace," she said, and he could hear her as the cheers subsided. "I love you forever."

Summer 1590

EPILOGUE

"Kára is with child," Hilda said to Erik as she squinted over the letter. Smiling, she held it closer to the peat fire spreading light throughout the earthen house. The flames crackled to punctuate the sea breeze that whistled across the hole leading outside above them.

"Mayhap she will have a girl this time after Geir," she said. Her sister, Harriett, would probably be the one to help with the birthing.

Erik held the soles of his feet to the fire. "So the Sinclairs have truly taken them into Caithness." He picked up an iron stick and poked the hot embers with his one hand.

Hilda exhaled. "I stayed here to help those who remained behind or returned, but only a couple returned to Orkney. And they moved away from Lord Robert's immediate reach. It is only you, Fiona, and me here at Hillside now." She folded the letter, tucking it into her shawl. "I will journey there before winter sets in," Hilda said. "I wish to see my sister again and Kára and all the others."

Erik looked at her, his eyebrow cocked. "Then who will lay flowers on their graves?"

"You should come with me," she said, ignoring his bait for another argument about her keeping up the appearance of Kára's death. The disappearance of John Dishington had been easily explained with a forged letter saying he had journeyed back to mainland Scotland. No one knew that as Hilda placed flowers on the graves of her nephew, his wife, and their two daughters, she spit on the grave where the bones of The Brute rested under the headstone of Joshua Sinclair.

Erik rubbed the stump where he had been thieved of his right arm. "What would they want with an old chief who cannot even raise a sword?"

"The great Sinclair warriors could train you to swing with your left arm."

He grumbled something and stared into the fire. The flames bent as the door opened. "I am off to the palace," Fiona said as she ducked inside. Even bent with age and regret, she whisked over to the jars along the back shelf. Since her son, Torben, had died, her vengeance had grown until she was nearly unbearable to live with. All she talked about was the need for Robert's death.

She sniffed into a few jars, selecting two of them that held the sleeping herbs Hilda used occasionally. "I hear Lord Robert is ailing, and I have something to help."

"Help?" Erik snorted. "Likely you will be giving him poison."

Fiona spun around on her heel to stare at him, a slow smile spreading over her features. "Tut," she scolded. "Do not let the fae folk hear such talk or they may poison him." She cackled at her own jest and darted out the door.

Hilda looked to Erik and shook her head. "That man will likely not live out the year."

• • •

The door flew open. "Kára!" Joshua called, dodging past Harriett, his aunt Merida, and Brenna to where Kára kneeled on the bed, Brenna's hand supporting her back as best she could.

Kára panted. "'Tis about time you got your arse here, Highlander," she yelled. She called him that when she was angry at him or ready for a night of raucous lovemaking. And, since she was in labor with their first child, it was definitely anger.

"I was at the MacKay castle, helping Gideon move his belongings there," he said, but knew that no one was listening to him. "Angus and Mathias rode to tell me, and I jumped on Fuil to race home."

"I need to take a look, Kára," Harriett said.

Kára let out a low moan and then seemed to hold her breath.

"Remember to breathe," Aunt Merida said and sucked breath loudly in and out through her teeth. She lifted and lowered her aged hands with her breaths.

"She must lie back on the bed or hang from the rope," Harriett said, indicating the loop hanging above.

"I will hold her up," Joshua said, kicking off his boots as he climbed onto the large bed that they shared at Girnigoe Castle. They were almost done building a secluded cottage in the woods, but Kára had become such great friends with his sister, Hannah, and Cain's wife, Ella, that they would continue to live mostly in the castle with the growing

Sinclair family.

"He is very good at that," Brenna said, nodding vigorously. She fetched the stack of clean linen and then glanced about. "I will find a knife for the cradle."

Joshua lifted Kára under her arms, helping her into the rope that hung from the rafters and through a cut in the canopy draped over the four corner posts of the bed. He braced his feet, holding her fully against him, his arms wrapped under her breasts. His mouth dipped to her ear. "Geir will be pleased to have a wee brother or sister," he said, trying to distract her as he felt her body tense again. "He helped me build the cradle," he said, glancing at the smoothed wooden bed for their bairn.

"I found it," Brenna said, holding up a long *sgian dubh*. She set it in the cradle.

Harriett sat back, and Joshua released his breath at the sight of her smile. "I see a wee head. Just a bit more, Kára."

"Ye are doing fine, lass," Aunt Merida said, patting her hand.

"Joshua," Kára said.

"Aye?"

"Next time we have a child, you should be the one to bring it forth. Speak to God and have him send down another horseman on a cloud from Heaven instead of a babe from between my thighs."

He chuckled, hugging her close. "I would take this pain from ye if I could, my brave warrior queen."

"'Tis time. Push," Harriett called.

Kára's lips pulled back to show her teeth as her

groan turned into what Joshua could only call a war cry. As the sound faded, the sweet sound of a bairn's first lusty cry came from the bed where Merida and Harriett worked. Brenna had tears in her eyes as she smiled up at Kára. "'Tis a boy, Kára, a sweet wee lad."

Joshua held her tight, slowly lowering her down to the thick tick where the two experienced women worked to cut the bairn free of Kára, wiping him clean. Joshua kissed Kára's head as they watched. "Ye did it, love." He moved to sit beside her on the bed and wiped her hair back from her face.

"Look at you," Harriett said, smiling at the bairn. She lifted him up for them to see.

"Bloody beautiful," he said, and she set him in blankets that Merida had ready, wrapping him deftly.

She placed the swaddled lad in Kára's outstretched arms, and Joshua realized she had tears running down her face. "He is perfect," she whispered and smiled up at him. *Lord!* He was certain he had never seen anything so beautiful before in his life. He would battle a million wars to keep them safe, or sail a thousand seas to take them to safety, or build a hundred castles to protect them.

"Thank ye, Kára Flett. I love ye and our wee bairn," he said.

"Adam," she said, touching the blinking bairn's cheek with her thumb. She looked into Joshua's eyes. "I would call him Adam," she said. "To honor the boy in South Ronaldsay."

Joshua inhaled deeply, feeling the sting of tears in his eyes, as his chest filled with even more love. He nodded. "I would like to bring another Adam into the world," he said. "'Tis a strong name for a strong lad."

"Like his da," Kára said, smiling brightly up at him. "I love you, Joshua Sinclair Flett."

Joshua leaned in to kiss her lips, and they both turned to the bairn whose blue eyes seemed to focus on their near faces. Gently, Kára handed the bairn over to Joshua. He took him into his arms. "This babe you can hold as much as you want," she said.

"Aye." He smiled down at wee Adam, his gaze sliding to meet Kára's.

How much his life had changed once he let love into it. A year ago, he was a cold warrior, discontented with life and the world. Unsure about his purpose. But now… As he sat next to his warrior queen wife, holding his newborn bairn, he had never felt so content in his life.

Love was risky. It could tear one apart, but it could also build one into a mountain of strength. It made life sweeter, brighter, and so worth living. Love had conquered the constant simmering anger within him. Aye, his brother might call upon him to be the Horseman of War, and he would go to defend his people. But in his heart Joshua was now truly a man of peace.

Join me back in Caithness, Scotland to continue the adventure in the third book of my Sons of Sinclair series! Gideon Sinclair, the Horseman of Justice, is tasked to bring Clan MacKay to heel at Varrich Castle. Weighing the scales of justice, everything is good or evil in Gideon's world, until he meets a lovely MacKay lass who excels at breaking his laws.

HISTORICAL NOTE

Lord Robert Stewart, Earl of Orkney, was considered a tyrant by the people of Orkney. He had nine legitimate children and several illegitimate children from several mistresses. His first son, Henry, died "mysteriously" when he was twenty-five, leaving the second son, Patrick, in line to gain the earldom. Even though Robert was imprisoned during his lifetime on suspicion of treason, he was released to the Earl's Palace and died on Orkney, in his bed, in 1593. Of natural causes? Or from the handiwork of a vengeful mistress? The history books do not say.

In 1594, Patrick Stewart, Second Earl of Orkney, accused three of his brothers of trying to kill him when poison was found on one of his brothers' servants. The servant and "a witch," who was thought to be an accomplice, were tortured and executed even though the brothers were later acquitted.

Using mostly forced labor, Patrick built his own Earl's Palace at Kirkwall on Orkney, southeast of Birsay. He is considered one of the most tyrannical noblemen in Scotland's history. Patrick ran up such high debts and was so brutal to his subjects on Orkney that he was called before the Privy Council of Scotland in 1609 and imprisoned at Edinburgh Castle and then Dumbarton Castle. When imprisoned, Patrick had his illegitimate son, named Robert, rally a rebellion back on Orkney to take back both Earl's Palaces. Robert succeeded, but then the Earl of Caithness, George Sinclair (named Cain Sinclair in my series), besieged the palace with the backing of the crown.

The Sinclairs won, and Robert was arrested. Robert was hung and Patrick was taken to Market Cross in Edinburgh and beheaded. After Patrick's death, the palace at Birsay was rarely occupied, and the palace at Kirkwall was inhabited by the bishops of Orkney until 1688 when it became the property of the crown of Scotland.

. . .

The Art of War was written around fifth century BCE by a Chinese strategist noted most frequently to be Sun Tzu (although some feel the manuscript is a compilation of warring advice through the ages). There were several translations and interpretations created throughout the centuries. By the eighth century AD, the work was translated into Korean and Japanese. It was translated into French by a Jesuit missionary in the 1770s, which is where I deviated from the historical timeline, giving Joshua's father the ability to find a French copy much earlier. It wasn't translated into English until 1905. The teachings, captured in thirteen chapters, are still studied today by people from CEOs of successful companies to military commanders.

ACKNOWLEDGMENTS

Thank you so much for reading the second book in my Sons of Sinclair series! The more I write about this family, the more I fall in love with them and want to share their stories with all you wonderful readers. Every note or comment you send, or review you give, brings me such joy. Sharing my stories with you is a dream come true.

Thank you to my fabulous Highlander husband, Braden, for being my inspiration (especially for the love scenes) <wink>. We will get to Orkney someday!

Thank you to my fabulous agent, Kevan Lyon, for always being in my corner and "talking me down" when the business gets daunting. To my publisher, the fabulous Liz Pelletier at Entangled Publishing, thank you for helping me create my dream career! To Alethea Spiridon, my talented editor, thank you so much for coming back and working with me again! You are smart and funny and so kind when you tell me all the things I need to fix. And a huge shout-out goes to my publishing team at Entangled, book reviewers, and book bloggers. Without you, no one would be able to find my books!

Also…

At the end of each of my books, I ask that you, my awesome readers, please remind yourselves of the whispered symptoms of ovarian cancer. I am now a nine-year survivor, one of the lucky ones.

Please don't rely on luck. If you experience any of these symptoms consistently for three weeks or more, go see your GYN.

Bloating

Eating less and feeling full faster

Abdominal pain

Trouble with your bladder

Other symptoms may include: indigestion, back pain, pain with intercourse, constipation, fatigue, and menstrual irregularities.

Get swept away with Heather McCollum's
bestselling Highland Isles series.

THE BEAST OF AROS CASTLE

On the run from a dangerous man, Ava Sutton flees to the Isle of Mull off the coast of Scotland. Ava must convince the cynical and darkly handsome chief of the Macleans of Aros to wed her before the devil tracks her down.

THE ROGUE OF ISLAY ISLE

Waking up not knowing who she is or where she comes from, Rose is at the mercy of the man who found her, but the more she recalls, the more she realizes the jeopardy she brings to the Highlander who has captured her heart.

THE WOLF OF KISIMUL CASTLE

Mairi Maclean is kidnapped on her wedding day and taken to Kisimul Castle where she is held captive. Alec MacNeil, The Wolf of Kisimul Castle, soon learns Mairi is not a docile pawn in the game of war between neighboring Scots.

THE DEVIL OF DUNAKIN CASTLE

Is Keir MacKinnon the passionate, kind man Grace Ellington saved in a Highland blizzard, or is he truly the cruel executioner who seeks to solve all issues by the sword?

The marriage game is afoot in this clever blend of My Fair Lady *meets* Pride and Prejudice *with a twist!*

THE
SPINSTER
AND THE
RAKE

NEVER A
WALLFLOWER SERIES

USA TODAY BESTSELLING AUTHOR
EVA DEVON

Edward Stanhope, the icy Duke of Thornfield, likes his life in a certain order. Give him a strong drink, a good book, and his dog for company, and he's content. But when he goes to his library and finds a woman sitting in his chair, petting his dog, what starts as a request for her to leave quickly turns to a fiery battle of wits, leading to a steamy kiss that could ruin them both if they were caught.

So of course, damn it all, that's when Edward's aunt walks in, and thereafter announces Miss Georgiana Bly is the future Duchess of Thornfield.

Georgiana was content to be a spinster, spending her days reading and working to keep her family out of debt. But now her days are spent locked away with a growly duke, learning how to be the perfect duchess, and her nights spent fighting the undeniable attraction to a man who was never meant for her.

As their wedding day approaches, the attraction between them burns hot and fierce, but is it enough to melt the duke's chilly facade?

Sleeping Beauty meets *As You Like It in this continuation of award-winning author Amalie Howard's Regency series that is sure to keep you up way past your bedtime.*

The
RAKEHELL
OF
ROTH

AMALIE HOWARD

As owner of the most scandalous club in London, the last thing the notorious Marquess of Roth wants is a wife. Keeping up his false reputation as a rake brings in the clients with the deepest pockets—money he needs to fund a noble cause. Even though everything inside tells him not to leave his beautiful, innocent wife behind at his country estate...he must.

But three years later, tired of her scoundrel of a husband headlining the gossip rags, Lady Isobel Vance decides enough is enough. She is no longer a fragile kitten, but as the anonymous author of a women's sexual advice column, she's now a roaring tigress...and she can use her claws.

Isobel decides to go to him in London, channeling her powers of seduction to make him beg to take her back. But she didn't expect her marauding marquess to be equally hard to resist. Now the game is on to see who will give in to the other first, with both sides determined like hell to win.

*The Wild West was never quite this funny—
or this steamy!—in this laugh-out-loud new
romance from bestselling author
Michelle McLean.*

HITCHED TO THE
GUNSLINGER

MICHELLE
USA TODAY BESTSELLING AUTHOR
McLEAN

Gray "Quick Shot" Woodson is the fastest gun in the
West. And he's had it. Sure, notoriety has its perks,
but the nomadic lifestyle and people always gunnin'
for him sucks.

He just wants to spend his retirement quietly
staring at the damn sunset. And sleeping. He could
use a nap.

So when his stubborn nag of a horse drags him
into a boondocks locale called Desolation, the last
thing he wants is to get embroiled in a town ven-
detta…and in a fake marriage with a woman named
Mercy. She's relentless. Insufferable. And alluring in
ways he never knew existed… With an unfortunate
proclivity for life-threatening altercations.

Damn it all. So much for peace and quiet.

*Eloisa James meets Sarah MacLean in this
fresh, fun take on women rising up
and taking what's theirs.*

HER
WICKED
MARQUESS

USA TODAY BESTSELLING AUTHOR
STACY REID

Miss Maryann Fitzwilliam is too witty and bookish for her own good. No gentleman of the ton will marry her, so her parents arrange for her to wed a man old enough to be her father. But Maryann is ready to use those wits to turn herself into a sinful wallflower.

When the scandal sheet reports a sighting of Nicolas St. Ives, the Marquess of Rothbury, climbing out the chamber windows of a house party, Maryann does the unthinkable. She anonymously claims that the bedchamber belonged to none other than Miss Fitzwilliam, tarnishing her own reputation—and chances of the dastardly union her family secured for her. Now she just needs to convince the marquess to keep his silence.

Turns out Nicolas allows for the scandal to perpetuate for his own reasons… But when Maryann's parents hold fast to their arranged marriage plan, it'll take a scandal of epic proportions for these two to get out of this together.

AMARA
an imprint of Entangled Publishing LLC